March Hares

Aidan Higgins

MARCH HARES

AN UNCOMMONPLACE BOOK

DALKEY ARCHIVE PRESS

Library of Congress Cataloging-in-Publication Data
Names: Higgins, Aidan, 1927-2015, author.
Title: March hares : an uncommonplace book 1927-2003 / by Aidan
Higgins.
Description: First Dalkey Archive edition. | Victoria, TX : Dalkey
Archive Press, 2017. | Includes bibliographical references and index.
Identifiers: LCCN 2017006167 | ISBN 9781943150069 (pbk. : alk.
paper)
Classification: LCC PR6058.I34 A6 2017 | DDC 828/.91409--dc23
LC record available at https://lccn.loc.gov/2017006167

March Hares has received financial assistance from the Irish Arts
Council.

www.dalkeyarchive.com
Victoria, TX / McLean, IL / Dublin

Dalkey Archive Press publications are, in part, made possible through
the support of the University of Houston-Victoria and its programs in
creative writing, publishing, and translation.

Printed on permanent/durable acid-free paper

For my grandchildren,

Paris Denry Brooke-Higgins, Yamika Brooke-Higgins, Oscar
Santi and Reuben Harvey of Yeovil in Somerset.

A long read for when you have all grown up, supposing
anyone will be reading in the merciless racket and loud and
fierce dingdong of the coming times.

And for my dearest Zinnia, always and ever.

'This time, then once more I think, then perhaps a last time, then I think it will be over, with that world too.'

Molloy (1956) by Samuel Beckett, first published in French (1950) by Editions de Minuit.

CONTENTS

Part One (1993–1999)
Out of Sorts

Part Two (1969–1979)
Of People and Places

Part Three
Mnemonic

March Hares

Part One

Out of Sorts

1993-1999

The Hollow, the Bitter and the Mirthless in Irish Writing

Paper read at Orchard Gallery, Derry Octoberfest, 16 October 1993

1. How James Joyce Frightened W. B. Yeats

JAMES JOYCE'S *ULYSSES* took Yeats by surprise. Not by its scabrousness nor the fetid reek of impoverished Catholicism in Dublin at the turn of the century; but by its cruelty, which he compared to that of a great playful tiger.

One assumes that Senator Yeats had not penetrated much beyond the atmospheric opening section—'Telemachus'—never reached the brothel ('Circe') and the high jinks which include the ritual hanging of the Croppy Boy, with the Dublin society ladies hurrying forward to mop up his final ejaculation with their pocket handkerchiefs.

Not that Joyce had deliberately set out to shock and scandalise; it wasn't his intention to offend. But delicate sensibilities he did upset, brought a touch of colour to the pale cheeks of Virginia Woolf, whom the novel signally failed to amuse.

The pent-up grievances of an underclass that refused to kowtow or act in a decently subservient manner must have seemed alarming to her, like a servant farting; one expected one's own servants to show proper respect. Bloomsbury had never expected to encounter Biddy the Clap and Cunty Kate or all the foul rage and bone shop of the heart in and around Dublin one day in June 1904. None of the characters were house-trained, some

3

seemed to have no homes to go to. Mrs Woolf took Joyce to be an underbred fellow—a voice not permitted to speak. The damnable ambitious and Irishly excessive nature of the undertaking must also have worried her; as never before, sentences as thunderbolts, a shot from above in a jelly of love.

Joyce, who was in his own private life the most prim and proper person alive, who liked to sing when in his cups, preferred white wine to red, had bad teeth but was not malicious or scurrilous as were so many of his fellow citizens, only in intimate love letters to Nora did he reveal the seamier side of his nature, and this only for her eyes. He was himself the most private of men, though the broad mass of Hibernophiles have long regarded him as both dirty and obscure, as set forth in works which they by and large didn't bother to read.

2. Yeats Looked Up At The Sky

Yeats looking up into the blue of the sky, saw or imagined he saw 'stiff figures in procession'. 'How base at moments of excitement are minds without culture,' he observed frostily, thinking of attacks made against him by an underbred Dublin editor.

At half past eleven of a February morning in 1904, Elizabeth Bowen, aged five, the only daughter of upper middle-class Protestant Anglo-Irish parents, was out walking along Upper Baggot Street with her young English governess, Miss Wallis, and looking up saw a 'timeless white sky, a solutions of sunshine in no imminent cloud—a sky for the favoured.' It would not be the same sky that the young Joyce saw over Dublin.

Yeat's love-poetry from Crazy Jane onwards was as steamy as John Donne's and beginning to alarm Lady Dorothy Wellesley. Wombs that sighed for the seed and great-bladdered Emer the Irish Queen, who made the biggest piss-hole in the virgin snow, hardly seemed the proper stuff of serious poetry. Slow to quit the nineteenth century and the Celtic Twilight (what Joyce had maliciously dubbed the Cultic twoilet), Yeats began to discard his old mantle only in the mid-1930s, gallantly proclaiming 'Only the wasteful virtues earn the sun.'

In a prose draft or aide-memoire to his poem 'Coole Park, 1929' he wrote, for his eyes alone: 'Each man more than himself through whom an unknown life speaks.' It could be the rallying cry of Modernism. Divesting himself of all his old airs and graces and the company of the great Celtic dead, King Goll & Co. he amended this to: 'I am a crowd, I am a lonely man, I am nothing.' It was an arrogant sort of humility, hinting at Beckett's reductio ad absurdum, the narrow Anglican pews, those first and last gasps.

Joyce himself had arrived at some such freedom, working with other materials, before the age of forty; history was (wait for it) 'a shout in the street'. *Ulysses*, a mocking gloss on old Homer's *Odyssey*, had a modern relevance for the man in the street, if he cared to read it.

Gone the most secret and inviolate Roses, the Rose of Friday, the Dark Rosaleen, the hymn to intellectual beauty, all that rot; the Pisan Canto man Pound had redefined beauty as 'a gasp between clichés'.

3. Proust & Flaubert

The modern subject matter, Proust's sublime slime of humanity would be internalised, the populace at large given its comeuppance and put firmly in its place; dismissed by Beckett as 'the sniggerin muck'.

Flaubert had already spent hours on his knees one night, studying heads of cabbage by moonlight, in order to tell it once and for all, in French. He thought he was struggling with the intricacies of the French language when in fact he was trying to overcome the densely thick atmosphere of Normandy.

In an acid article commissioned by *The Bookman* in 1934,

the young Beckett had concluded that contemporary Irish poets (still learning their trade) could be counted under two heads: antiquarians and others, the former in the majority, The accepted practitioners (antiquarians to a man) were working along safe, albeit hackneyed, lines hallowed by a tradition which they saw no reason to question. If it was good enough for their fathers, it was good enough for them. To disentangle the tortuous Irish mind from the strangling knots of superstition, the nets Stephen Dedalus hoped to evade, was not easy. The sorry stuff put out by these earnest versifiers could only set Beckett's teeth on edge. (Some of you may just recall that dire organ *Kavanagh's Weekly*, brought out with the help of American money from the Brother and displayed on Dublin newsracks every week like a gruesome family skeleton. John Beckett [cousins?] showed Sam a copy of this. He looked through it and said: 'Wouldn't it make you want to vomit?') He himself, out on his own, and on his own terms, was looking for a light less green and kind of tattered.

The antiquarians, with their lilting and lisping, their blackthorn sticks and the entire Celtic drill of extraversion (rendered manifest), would have to go. Beckett's praise for his peers, Mr Brian Coffey and the elegant Mr Denis Devlin, strikes one now as Beckett just being polite. His own work developing and deepening would leave them standing, frighten them out of their collective wits.

Beckett was as dismissive of the cosy traditionalists of England, with their dependence on wordy William Wordsworth and John Milton, 'the beastly bigot.'

4. Trevor, McGahern, Keane & Co.

Embattled Dublin critics, ever anxious to grind an axe, who refer disingenuously to post-modernist Irish writing, are of course talking through their critical hats, or just singing for their supper; for we never had a modernist movement to begin with. Jack Yeats, of all people, in one or two of his novels, gave a nod in that direction, and then desisted.

Now take a look, if you would, at the old-fashioned and placating nature of that trio of born storytellers, Messrs. William Trevor, John McGarern and the Kerryman John B. Keane leaning over his bar counter down there in Listowel: three famous yarnsters quite content to work away at an old seam.

Their work is pre-modern, a Celtic Classical long set and hardened by habit into a format that has not changed in its essentials since the days of Brinsley MacNamara's *The Valley of the Squinting Widows* and Kickham's *Knocknagow*. Our classics wear thin (hadn't you noticed?); time, that old fornicator, that great leveller, attends to that; corrects and amends, so that even Frank O'Connor seems old hat.

The loners Joyce and Beckett had conducted their experiments in Continental Europe and lived there for most of their lives; both belong to a European tradition of free fall and experiment which goes back to Villon and Rabelais and uproarious, uninhibited guffaws. Their reputations are now secure, even if their books are largely unread by the Irish.

Finnegans Wake (no apostrophe please) and Beckett's *The Unnamable* and *Watt*, curiouser and curiouser, are as cold as refrigerators, chilly books of hypotheses that are difficult to get into , not too rewarding when you do, unfortunately, for many man-hours were spent (wasted?) in their elegant if baffling construction.

5. O'Crohan & The Melodious Gaelic

That freedom of expression has always existed in Gaelic, and still does. It was not the author's idea that part of *The Island-man* should be trimmed, referring to the forbidden subject of sexual relations. In Gaelic you can say anything you damn well please. The thinking and feeling is unsullied and unimpeded by Freudian filth, as it must be for anybody writing in English. That freedom to do as you please, be anything, the flightiness and sheer high spirits that propels *At Swim-Two-Birds* is derived from its Gaelic ancestry; the flaxen Sweenies of Kiltimagh and the good Gaelic of Tyrone.

Beckett had made good his escape into French. Flann O'Brien, Brian Nolan, Myles nagCopaleen might have been better advised to find his freedom through Gaelic. Sufficient intimations are there in *An Beal Bocht*, a parody of Thomas O'Crohan's great book so devastating that if you read it first, you kill the original. The footnotes of the translation suggest that the multiple allusiveness of the original cannot be captured in lean unlovely English, just as the profusion of pseudonyms suggest an uncertainty of stance he didn't know exactly where he stood.) O'Nolan, like Joyce before him, would have to invent his own language, a one-man tongue of buckleppin' Gaelic as frisky as a puck goat.

Joseph Conrad (not his real name), discarding Polish, had the choice of French or English to work with, depending on which gangplank he stepped onto. He chose the English vessel and the lucky throw gave us *The Secret Agent*, as sinister and foggy as anything in Dickens.

6. Blandness

Blandness has always been the hallmark of mainstream Irish fiction writing. The success of a play such as *The Field*, a novel such as *Amongst Women*, or an esteemed critic offering the late Francis MacManus as exemplar of your superior prose stylist, indicates that we are dealing here with a deeply conservative reading public, liking what it knows best and understands best and, what is more, with a very good opinion of itself Nappertan-dywise. I suspect that an Irish reading public as such has been subsumed into Tee-Vee viewers who can feel quite easy and at home with any novel that can be instantly converted into compulsive TV-viewing.

I would not give house room to the abominable contraption and as a natural consequence am behind the times and write novels as arcane as they are incomprehensible and, what is worse, treat of non-Irish subject matter, as far removed as possible from the cozily familiar.

Elsewhere a programmed blandness is set in place from which it is just a short step to theme parks everywhere, a golf links for small obese Japanese businessmen on the Old Head of Kinsale, and Gales in Day-Glo getup and baseball caps work back to front saluting each other ('Have a good day') in fake American accents. Not forgetting barmaids . . . er, bar persons in hot pants serving up gins and tonics with a pert 'There you go!' There we go indeed. Ireland, Southern Ireland, as an annex to Cal-i-forn-ia.

7. Dev running the 880

Know then that my father had been to the same school as Dev and liked to boast of having beaten him in the 880 yards at Blackrock College sports. You can perhaps imagine Eamon's great slow, sinewy ground-covering strides, specs balanced precariously on arched prehensile nose, the loose prudish running drawers and loose singlet on the emaciated frame, the stertorous breathing, the myopic glare straight ahead—a fearsome middle distance runner to compete against. My father would have to get ahead of him and stay there at all costs, if only not to see Dev running.

My dear father always liked to tell my dear mother that

this same Dev had blood on his hands. By an adroit sleight of hand the Long Fellow sent an official message of condolence and sympathy, as from the Irish people to the German Volk, expressing sorrow on the death (by suicide underground, having first dispatched his wife, the late Eva Braun) of the Führer, his passing most deeply regretted.

Here was a two-facedness worthy of the stone heads on Boa Island. The Irish people themselves were not consulted as to the ethics and propriety of this magnanimous gesture of goodwill; for Dev had only to look into his own heart to know the hidden wishes of his people. He had reassured the Dáil that in his veins there ran not a single drop of Jewish blood.

This slippery Fianna Fáilish diplomacy (call it hyperbole or call it hypocrisy) was a slap in the face for the next of kin of all those thousands of brave Irishmen and women who had gone off to fight in Britain's war and never came home to Caherciveen.

8. The James Joyce Papers

The James Joyce papers now brought reluctantly into public view after half a century sealed up in a box in the National Library of Ireland, next to the Dáil, reveal something worse than hypocrisy.

Paul Léon, the Russian Jew and close personal friend of the Joyce family in Paris, had certainly laid down his life when he returned there during the occupation, to recover those very papers; as Joyce was dying in Switzerland, Beckett was appalled to meet Léon in the street and told him he must leave immediately. But it was already too late; the Paris Gestapo wanted him; his number was up. As he was being taken away, the Irish government averted its eye and refused to lift a hand, expressing rather its concern as to whether or not Mr Joyce had died a Catholic in Zurich.

A propos of which I received a letter from Professor James Knowlson of the University of Reading, the biographer of Beckett, which includes some saddening information: 'Your letter has just come through the box with enclosures of the Paul Léon sad saga, very poignant after hearing a few weeks ago from his son, Alexis, the moving account of seeing on the distant platform his father going off to his death. I didn't know about these non-efforts to save him. Beckett had laid his life on the line when he joined the French Resistance; he had said famously that he had made it in the nick of time, preferring France at war to Eire at peace. I once asked him about the background of the trilogy; for Ussy-sur-Marne, down there in the Marne mud, looks not unlike the Wicklow where Beckett's Da, the stout quantity surveyor, had taken him for long rambles in his childhood and youth. Was it France or Ireland? I asked. 'Ireland, all Ireland,' Beckett answered stoutly. He was being a very Irish Prod—'a dirty Low Church Protestant highbrow' in his own inimitable formulation—and maybe more than he knew when he defined art as a contraction rather than an expansion; as if delineating the narrow confines of the Protestant Pale, whereas Joyce, the lapsed Catholic, in more or less permanently straitened circumstances throughout the fifty-nine years of his life, couldn't or wouldn't stop his work expanding. Look at their proof corrections—Joyce forever putting things in ('the limp father of thousands') and Beckett forever striking things out.

9. Protestant Complexions & Gates

When I was but a nipper in shorts knocking about with the poor Catholic sons of my father's tenants, who never appeared to pay any rent, I was stopped dead in my tracks by a wide gate of palest wood which to my craven Catholic eyes looked the very epitome of a Protestant gate, like the striding giants of yore or 'the grim eight-foot high ironbound serving man' mentioned by John Donne the diving, a lapsed Catholic who became of the strangest ornaments of the Church of England.

I am thinking now of a certain gate in the townland of Donycomper opposite the Catholic graveyard in Celbridge where I was brought up. It being the grand front entrance of some hidden Protestant estate; an expansive wooden gate of smooth, hard birchwood with iron-bound cross-pieces and fancy metal scrollwork and many nuts and bolts and latches and locks. It was a formidable gateway that I, as a Catholic surrounded by poor Catholics would not lightly enter, and quite clearly conveyed the message, delivered between clenched teeth in the unmistakable ringing tones of a frightfully superior upper-class accent: 'Look here, you bally Catholics, this is Protestant ground. Clear off now or by God we'll set the dogs on you!'

I've seen the river Liffey starting off as a shallow, narrow, Irish Catholic stream, then flowing through a Protestant demesne and changing colour—as an embarrassed person flushing darkly—becoming a Protestant river for a time; flowing on, but ending up in Dublin as an unclean Catholic river, and so on out into the bay.

10. No Modernist Movement in Ireland

The modernist movement began and ended in Ireland, in full retreat before it had hardly begun, soon sunk out of light, making hardly a ripple. The old lies were merely being perpetuated and no great effort attempted to 'make it new'.

Some exceptions:

Sailing, Sailing Swiftly (1933) by Jack B. Yeats

Murphy (1938) by Samuel Beckett

The Ginger Man (1955) by J.P. Donleavy

Felo de Se (1960) by Aidan Higgins
Night in Tunisia (1976) by Neil Jordan
In Night's City (1982) by Dorothy Nelson
Banished Misfortune (1982) by Dermot Healy
The Engine of Owl-Light (1988) by Sebastian Barry
Cadenza (1984) by Ralph Cusack

In despair of ever being understood by his own race Joyce had
to invent his own language, the nighttime language of baffling
double-talk that was the *Wake*; regressing back to childhood and
infantile word-play, the way we first began to speak.

Beckett had retreated in good order into French. I asked
the late Alexander Trocchi, the author of *Cain's Book* who had
known Beckett in Paris when both were associated with the
magazine *Merlin* (long defunct), what was it about Beckett's
French—what was he up to, what was he at? Trocchi replied:
'Sam is taking the mickey out of the French language.'

Beckett's last throw in English for some time, before he
commenced the trilogy in French, would be *Watt*, a preliminary
study in boredom, employing the comma as caesura, bit and
snaffle, testing the reader's patience to the limit. It was sold in
Nice by the Olympia Press as a dirty book and must have sorely
puzzled maybe horny English tars on shore-leave. He wrote it
while in hiding during the war, to keep his hand in kuskykorked
up tight in his inkbattle house at Roussillon.

But maybe he didn't wish to show his hand, not even to
himself. With only the Irish surnames sticking out of it to reveal
its Irish roots, the Malones and Molloys looking very peculiar.
Something funny is certainly going on there, rather as the
swift exchange of hats between Estragon and Vlaimir in *Godot*;
though behind the bile I suspect stands Swift, the sour Dean,
Beckett's great mentor.

I suspect also that his own translations of the texts failed to
satisfy him. Already frustrated by well-meaning but incompetent

collaborators such as the American, Dick Seaver, and the South African, Patrick Bowles.

Beckett was searching for a language that would be porous. The only other penman to throw a look askance at present and past simultaneously was a man with more than one name, more usually known affectionately as Myles to his many Dublin admirers.

11. *At Swim-Two-Birds* (1939)

At Swim-Two-Birds by Flann O'Brien is notable, among other contradictions, for its cruelty, its tricky misogynistic tone (those same women are kept at bay), some faceless pseudo characters ('offspring of the quasi-illusionary type'), Finn McCool spieling away in his inglenook, Sweeney, who was turned into a bird, errant amobae such as the Good Fairy, participant in a game of poker while making hidden bids in the capacious pocket of the Pooka Fergus MacPhellimey, described as 'a species of human Irish devil endowed with magical powers.'

The Good Fairy, mark you, never to be confused with the Bad Fairy, or the Fair to Middling Fairy, or he whom David Norris has wittily nicknamed 'the Great Irish Fairy', being none other than Sir Roger Caement. The box containing the remains of the Great Irish Fairy was privily removed from Pentonville Prison yard in 1965 and the second-last resting place in a bed of quicklime, for reinterment in Glasnevin. The Tall Fellow (aged eighty-three and already sinking into his decline) rising up from his sickbed to give the funeral oration in the snow—the usual pious cant about the imperishable Irish dead in their everlasting home above in Dev's all-Irish Heaven.

The Unionists above in the North were of course fit to be tied. They wanted no hand, act or private part of an odious traitor to a flag which they recognised as their own. They were fond of walking in procession and beating their great drums.

Eudora Welty thought, 'It is not for nothing that an ominous feeling attaches itself to a procession. The Pied Piper of Hamelin has done more than hint at this.' Processions, be they quasi-religious, political, military, anarchic or merely funereal in character, all have something dire in common.

12. The Big Drums of the Wee Orangemen

'Perhaps all that the masses accept is obsolete,' Yeats had argued in one of his Prefaces. 'The Orangeman beats his drum every twelfth of July—perhaps fringes, wigs, furbelows, hoops, patches, stocks, Wellington boots, start up as armed men; but were a poet sensitive to the best thought of his time to accept that belief, when time is restoring the soul's autonomy, it would be as though he had swallowed a stone kept in his bowels.'

What is Yeats attempting to say? That there is a theatrical element in virtually everything? The lion paces his cage but knows it's in a zoo. The madman acts mad but he is mad too, acting out the role a little. Yeats's Prefaces sometimes make better sense than his poetry, something he shared with Shelley, another poet with a world overview.

13. Stories My Mother Told Me

I never quite believed the stories I was told, touching my own Catholic beginnings, and before my beginnings if it goes to that, in the dark ages before I was born. Nor did I quite believe what my teachers taught me later, treating of an Irish history that had such a punitive ring to it, yet was purporting to be true.

Perhaps one's history could be written in no other way. All history is to some extent man's invention and much of it is untrue; history is famously what we make of it, tit for tat. The bomb going off; the shout in the street.

Nor could I swallow that great anthropomorphic lie about 'Mother Eire', put about so vigorously by O'Flaherty and perpetuated by others after him: the big lie of loving one's land as a mother—Mother Eire who was never young. The ever-contrary Joyce had other ideas and, abandoning the earth, claimed the sea as our universal mother everybody's big yummy mammy, 'our great sweet mother', which must clang a bell for us Pisceans.

14. Pastoral

Nor could I stomach the pastoral scene of the gallant South put out by Messrs. Sheed & Ward. Nothing has changed in those dreary certitudes half a century ago when I began reading *Green Rushes* and *Men Withering* and stories of the Wild West, together with several lives of Eamon de Valera, as if one wasn't enough. 'Cover has damp stains all over,' the wily bookseller warns. Those old dampening prescriptions issued by The Talbot Press when *The Rugged Path* seemed to run forever at the mildewed old Abbey, only to be superseded by a soporific as potent: *The Righteous are Bold*. Don't even trust your own mother down Gloccamaura; she'll only tell you lies.

My dear parents told me endless stories about my own family background, introducing the names of cousins and distant nephews and unknown uncles and aunts living and dead whom I had never seen nor particularly wished to ever meet in this life or the next. My own parents and my three brothers were the family and it was in a constant state of territorial strife, and that was quite enough to keep us occupied and amused—and our own private war and our own private treaties and ceasefires. Whereas Aunt Molly and Aunt Lean and Cousin Sill and

Cousin Pompey, and not forgetting the Aunties Tess and Cissy, were unimaginable revenants living in Longford.

15. Ancestral Voices

But could you trust the Da anymore than the Ma? I ask you. Persons of great power and influence among the West Papuan Islanders, Norman Lewis observed, were not cremated in the usual way but were smoked over a slow fire for several months and thereafter hung from the eaves of their houses. Well what a splendid notion, and thought up for us by primitives. Smoked ancestors.

But to go back a little...when I was growing up in County Kildare amid the nettles and cow parsley, was I not hounded everywhere by the cries of Authority bidding me to be good. 'Now no disrespect!' So that I lived in a perpetual anxiety, if not outright fear; fear of God knows what, mixed up with awe of my elders and betters, making me as anxious as a rat.

Fearful of my teachers (the sisters of Mercy armed with straps followed by the Christian Brothers armed with sticks, followed later by the Jesuit Fathers armed with pandy-bats), fearful of the Civic Guards (for riding a bike without lights, for skiving off school, for climbing over forbidden walls), fearful of the flushed Parish Priest in chasuble and stole in his dark God-box with air holes drilled high up to let the sins out (impure thoughts); fearful not least of my own parents, who rarely lifted a hand against me, but were calling out, forever crying out, 'Pay respect!' In those stagnant times how we fairly trembled before Authority!

The Faceless Creator

Reading at Ireland House, New York University.
11 October 1994

I IMAGINE A number of Americas—as many as there are States in the Union or stars in the sky and then maybe as many more again—one of which is called Texas, one of which is named New York. This is my first visit to the latter place and I can't say I know it yet.

On the other hand I did teach two classes of freshman creative writing—if you can call it teaching, if you can call it creative writing (a trade as recondite as falconry)—for one Fall semester at Austin, where I felt acutely uncomfortable among the squawking grackles.

The desert heat got to me; the air seemed about to ignite; the food tasted of monkey and popcorn, the beer was undrinkable— monkey piss. Wild Bill Hickok himself in his fringed buckskins would have felt quite at home in some of the rougher bars there, where I as sure as hell felt out of place.

To feel out of place is, to be sure, quite a salubrious state for a writer to find himself in: dwelling in a catatonic trance of highest expectations. Both Yeats and Borges had developed this to a high degree.

Brian O'Nolan hid himself behind several pseudonyms, hid himself in another language, Tyrone Gaelic, the very best available, mocked the standard Gaelic classic *an tOileánach* (*The Islandman*). Beckett disappeared into French, as Joyce before him had vanished into obscurities of his own invented language, never spoken by anybody on earth, his very own speakeasy Finneganese.

We tend to forget, because we never knew, how rough was our passage into this world. I was out the other morning on the ferry to Ellis Island to look over the ethnic museum you have there, the chamber of horrors; to see the rites of passage that admitted or didn't admit immigrants into the Land of the Free—a rite of passage as painful as birth pangs that became death pangs for some unfortunates who never made the grade, were refused admission.

A great scroll like the Domesday Book lays down the Law, the severe rules of admittance. The kids look terrified. All the adults resemble heroic extras in an old Eisenstein movie. Since 1600, over sixty million people throughout the world have emigrated to the United States, 'creating a multiethnic nation unparalled in history'. Ireland and our own wretched history seems very small beer by comparison.

'The Irish mind—when there was such a thing—an uncontaminated simple mind, was a far more subtle one than the Anglo-Saxon mind,' said Myles of the Ponies.

I was reared in the country twelve miles from Dublin (I might as well have been in Ballydehob) at a time before TV had blighted the Irish imagination, and all my early loves were non-pictorial—stories in books. The first book that told me that a book can be more than a set of facts, mere fiction, was Joyce's *A Portrait of the Artist*, a gloomy enough account of a Catholic upbringing in those far-off times.

Followed soon after by a very merry book—*At Swim-Two-Birds* by Flann O'Brien, a Dublin civil servant locked in some dull government department, and soon to qualify as a full-time alcoholic—which told me that the imagination can be boundless and the author himself not the first nor the last one to have a hand in that mighty complex undertaking—the writing of a novel.

However, I would not pass James Joyce in the streets of Dublin, whenever I chanced to go there, because he had died in Zurich around the time I was entering my second year at his old college, Clongowes Wood in County Kildare, under the Jesuit fathers. Before I read him I had confused him with William Joyce, the infamous Lord Haw Haw, the Nazi broadcaster, whom the English later handled as a traitor.

I might have passed Flann O'Brien in the purlieus of Neary's pub but nobody knew what he looked like. Didn't I have my hair trimmed by a barber in O'Connell Street who had once trimmed G.K. Chesterton, and had I not once walked behind Frank O'Connor along Wellington Road? And did you once see Shelley plain?

Fifty-two years ago James Joyce's close collaborator, secretary and friend Paul Léon was shot dead by the Nazis. A file of personal papers recently released to scholars by the Department of Foreign Affairs in Dublin reveals that the Irish government had declined to intercede on Léon's behalf, at a time when his life might perhaps have been saved.

A sorry tale of collusion in high places emerges. The Irish envoy in Berne was concerned that Léon might be shot. The Irish envoy in Berlin sent a telegram pointing out that 'interfering on his behalf might be regarded as meddling in internal German matters where no Irish citizen is involved and might even have some effect on our good relations'. The Irish government did not offer to lift a hand. De Valera was Minister for External Affairs as well as being Taoiseach and initialed the note that sealed Léon's fate. The Judas kiss for the Russian of Jewish background.

Paul Léon was taken by the Gestapo, and Nazi and Irish plenipotentiaries de Valera and Count von Ribbentrop, stepping back a pace, washed their hands of the whole unedifying affair. Léon's end was a squalid one. Of the thousand French internees who entered Auschwitz, only seven were to survive the war. Early in April 1942, during a forced march, it is thought that Léon was shot by an SS guard. There is no record of his death, no grave, no headstone.

The Nazis were referred to as 'German' throughout the proceedings, as though the German government—the Nazi dictatorship—and Wehrmacht had law and order on their side. We Irish referred shiftily to our own neutral non-participating country as 'Eire' or the 'Irish Free State'.

Life in the Saorstát carried on as usual. The majority preferred porridge to Corn Flakes or Weetabix—heavy old stirabout guaranteed to stick the guts together and get the bowels moving. As a nation notoriously evasive, we Irish have long made a virtue of not calling a spade a spade, as anyone who cares to listen to Gerry Adams can verify.

The young Beckett was speaking of 'the breakdown of the object,' of 'the rupture of the lines of communication', referring not to matters of high moment in political chicanery, but to how a new kind of Irish letters might one day emerge. Few had heard him or if they had, they didn't know what he was getting at. The Beckett tone was unremittingly lofty, the matter densely obscure, or so it seemed on the other side of the breakfast table.

When writers use up their source material, they come to a pretty pass. It would of course be a merciful relief if some writers were to use up their source material, and I am thinking now, as you yourselves perhaps, of Nin and Jong, the Yin and Yang of the feminist movement and their dreadfully pushy libidos.

Some writers lose their source material, and I think Djuna Barnes was one of those. She lived around the corner in Patchen Place, a European cul-de-sac in the Village, in a time warp that lasted for forty years, during which time she produced nothing in the way of fiction. Her Trappist period she called it.

In *The Green Hills of Africa*, Hemingway spoke prophetically and more so than he knew (because he himself was to be included in the damnation) of how America destroys her great writers. Exposure to the idiot public gaze, a belief in the flattering lies spread about, will in the long run affect the human subject just as it would an ape in the zoo. Beckett, our great Naysayer, was astute enough to recognise this and refused to give interviews.

In the last great widow-making, window-smashing all-out ding-dong war of 1939-45 certain European countries, for their own self-preservation, did not stand up and be counted; and among them was Ireland. Ireland turned its back on Britain, left it to its fate.

Ireland and Spain, Sweden and Switzerland refused to stand up and be counted. The consequences of Irish neutrality on the Irish zeitgeist, and more particularly on the creative numbness this engendered, has never been studied.

A notable exception to the mass of comfortably seated Irish was of course Sam Beckett, who stood up. The man who wouldn't join anything joined the French Resistance and moreover in Paris, practically next door to the Gestapo HQ. When asked to explain this taking of sides—a public demonstration which yet had to be unobtrusive as possible—Beckett said, 'I couldn't just stand by. They were killing my friends.'

About the same time, Seán O'Faoláin (real name John Whelan), editor of the preposterous *Bell* magazine, was complaining to the wife in their bijou suburban home on Killiney Hill that he had no bananas on his breakfast cereal.

Francis Stuart, the man with cloven feet, in an interview published in Naim Atallah's *The Oldie*, has described Beckett as a traitor, but a traitor to what cause, one may ask. In his mountainous retreat in the fastness of County Wicklow, a veritable Irish Berchtesgaten, the patriotic Stuart offered a 'safe house' to Nazi agents who had infiltrated Ireland. This would be during our Emergency, known elsewhere as World War II. One of these Nazi infiltrators taught Stuart's young son Ion the useful trick of how to detonate a hand-grenade. He would be out in the bog at night transmitting messages to Berlin. One night the son followed the infiltrator, found him crouched over the transmitter, pulled the pin from the grenade and lobbed it at the Nazi agent who was busy at his nefarious business. It sank into the bog and failed to explode. The son hadn't particularly objected to messages being transmitted to Goebbels' Ministry of Propaganda building, but had greatly objected to the agent sleeping with his mother. Where the cuckolded patriot was when all these shenanigans took place, we do not know.

I was a friend of Ion's once, a friendship somewhat marred, or should I say terminated, when as a grown man sprawled in the armchair before a great fire, he told me that the Jews had got what they deserved, wholesale extermination; a sentiment that had perhaps percolated insidiously down from the father, a writer who could not think his way from one end of a sentence to the other.

Carlos Fuentes and Maria Callas

THE VAIN MEXICAN diplomat Carlos Fuentes heard Maria Callas sing *La Traviata* in Mexico City in 1951, and was bowled over by that splendid voice.

Twenty–five years later he found himself seated next to her at a dinner party and was taken aback to hear her ordinary speaking voice. 'Her everyday voice was that of a girl from the less fashionable neighborhoods of New York City. Maria Callas had the speaking voice of a girl selling Maria Callas records in Sam Goody's on Sixth Avenue.'

Francis Bacon in Chelsea, London

(Photo of Bacon in London Tube)

SOME YEARS AGO, I was walking down King's road in London's nokshotten Chelsea, when a moon-faced man with a purposeful air passed me by. One stand of dark hair hung down over his brow; he wore a sweater and might have just stepped out of a gym. He had the face of a fighter who has been hit too many times in the ring. In fact, he had probably been gambling and drinking champagne with criminals in some club all night and was not returning home to his studio—a squalid lair.

'Did you see who just passed us?' I asked my wife.

'No,' said she.

'Francis Bacon.'

Francis Bacon had a very selective eye for what interested him and he saw nothing else, moving between the drinking club and his studio, a nocturnal creature by choice; nor did he wish to be seen or recognised by the public. He was free to travel around London by bus or tube and not be recognised.

The Pace-Makers

Sir,

Only the other day in Toronto, I was reading Dr Conor Cruise O'Brien, to the effect that the present IRA ceasefire was a hoax and a sham; and it cannot be said that I disagreed with the good doctor, even opaque in his honesty, which can hardly be said of his detractors.

The squaring of the circle, camel passing through needle-eye or the Mookse getting on with the Gripes would be as nothing when compared to any attempt at parity in the North, as between two feuding rivals who hate each other's guts. The Adamsonian constant reiteration of the catch-phrase 'peace process' makes one uneasy for it always had a phony ring to it, as the man who mouthed it; but no more than Paisley's 'copperfastening' clauses referring to arguments already closed, supportive or irrefutable truths dear to the Unionist heart.

This ersatz lingo of diplomatic intrigue is just humming and hawing which attempt to mask and conceal ancestral suspicions and loathing; and these simply will not go away. All is hoax and sham; all will mince words in their own way—blandman's bluff. Language can be abused like anything else and this factional disparity of opposing terminology reeks of diseased parts. Logic and reason go out the window.

Paisley is merely beating another big drum, Gerry gerrymandering with his sly catchphrases—'peace process' and 'British war-machine.' How creepy this terminology, a flux of untruth, the ticking of a hidden bomb, alarm signals for the Knell of Doom here, if allowed to continue. Orwell already noted these abuses of language and logic.

Thatcher's mouthpiece (mouthpeace?) on the BBC was at great pains during the Falklands debacle to slow down his delivery as if for the benefit of ears unaccustomed to spoken English or those hard of hearing. Come down off the ladder, Ifor, I have taken it away. In former times a man's word was his bond, the handclasp a symbolic token binding as seal on legal document or signature on a will; now it has been debased as 'pressing flesh'. To the closed Unionist mind, as closed as our own, Mary of Phoenix Park must be a cross between the Whore of Babylon and the BVM, another RC icon like the statues of Ballinspittle not far from us, and to shake her hand would be an unthinkable act for Paisley and his kind, for they cannot utter the word Papist or Pope without spitting.

In a circle of fire, your scorpion would prefer to inject himself rather than yield to outside attack and there is a fierce breed of fighting wasp that goes on attacking itself when cut in half, the tail attacking the head, this rage in its genes.

Horses for courses.

En route to the death camps the deportees were just 'pieces' to the SS guards. Inside the Camp the *Haflings* heard the order to get up before dawn for roll call: 'Wstawásh!' Get up, wake up, rise up. The vile bucket aswarm with dysentery and germs was known familiarly as 'Jules'.

Can we speak of a change of heart here? Does a bear shit in the woods? Oh Jeysus fluid! says the poisoned well. Tiers, tiers and tiers. Rounds. Why are we Irish so loath to say what we mean? Is it because we do not mean what we say? – Yours, etc. Aidan Higgins, (Member of Aosdána),

Higher Streeet,

Kinsale.

PS. I recall President Truman's speech, published here in *The Irish Times*, with constant references to 'the free nations of the world,' a confraternity to which Japan did not belong. Informed sources now concede that forty atomic bombs would have been dropped if available, one for good measure on the holy city of Kyoto. In his given name, Harry S Truman, the initial stood for nothing, just a caesura linking the patent honesty of 'Harry' to the surname implying good man and true. Tell that to the Japanese.

Letter to *The Irish Times*, published 07.11.94

Footnotes on Pace-Makers

'Blessed are the pure in heart for they shall see God'
No. 6 of the Eight Beatitudes

Pace, 1883. L. abl. Sing of PAX PEACE as in *pace tua* [by leave of, with all reference to]

Pace. Fig. the third oth' world is yours, which with a shuffle, you may pace aside, but not with such a wife. SHAKS.

The Shorter English Dictionary

THE VOCABULARY OF hatred and deceit, the impossibility of impartiality, the constant presence of skullduggery and chicanery in high places, political oratory as manipulation issuing from the mouths of hardline campaigners such as Hitler, Goebbels, Mussolini, down to Paisley and Adams; political strategy as difficult jigsaw puzzle to work out accents that grate, inter-party intrigue, all are here lightly touched upon.

A pacemaker is a natural or artificial device for stimulating the heart muscle and regulating its contractions.

The pace-maker in athletic track events is the runner or decoy who sets a stiff pace to exhaust the other runners, then falls back to let the more serious contender in the pack burst free and romp home.

'Peace' becomes 'pace' in the mouths of contentious Orangemen and their womenfolk, unable to conceive of any other peace in the sick and troubled sectarian-ridden Province but a one-sided peace involving the amalgamation with priest-ridden Papists of the South whom they loathe with a particular loathing, a lifelong animosity that nothing can change, but must continue until the cows come home.

Their mouthpiece, the bullying Reverend Ian Paisley cannot bring himself to utter the word Pope without insulting the Polish pontiff, dismissing him as 'Old Red Socks."

Some Englishman writing of Belfast in the 1950s was struck by the strangeness of the place and the people, and refers to the 'salt rebuff of speech'.

In no possible way is this hypothetical peace related to the promised peace (equally hypothetical) of Neville Chamberlain's limp policy of appeasement to Herr Hitler's sabre-rattling: 'Peace in our time' sounds hopeful but the rampant, hate-fueled 'Ulster will fight and Ulster will be right' is a scornful battle-cry as offensive to Roman Catholic ears (become very sensitive to insults coming from that quarter) or the lambasting of the big Lambeg drum which is the very heartbeat of Orangemen danders up and on the march. The drone and whine of pipes is indeed music to their ears, celebrating once again King Billy's glorious victory at the Boyne, recurring annually on the 12 July, rubbing salt into the wounds of the defeated, as if the battle had to be fought not once but many times and always with the same result—abject Catholic defeat, triumphant Protestant victory.

The Organisation or Provo High Command makes a public declaration of its sincerest regret for killing the wrong man. This happens over and over again, the wrong (innocent) man is killed, if possible in front of his wife and children, to drive home the message, and again come the sincerest apologies and regrets from those who ordered the murders.

I once had a falling out with a lean, bleak, parsimonious, untrustworthy Northerner who stuttered when over-excited. At a Heaney party he called me out into the yard not to settle matters there and then but to threaten me with rough friends of his in the North, who would be delighted to come south and put manners on me.

This is how it was done in the North, Revenge by stealth, hit and run tactics, the bullet in the back of the head, the bomb in the bush. Rough justice would be done by proxy; this was how the conflict (the 'war') was conducted, dirty work was done by someone else, somewhere else.

An eye for an eye and a tooth for a tooth by all means, but let the hit man do his job, that's what he's paid for, after all.

Dr Kafka has an aphorism that goes like this: Leopards break into the temple and drink the sacrificial chalice dry; this happens over and over again and eventually becomes part of the ceremony.

Paisley's punch-drunk Orange oratory and vile compounds— 'copper-fastening' and 'copper-fastened'—stand for entrenched opinion, an immovable fixed attitude of mind ('mind-cast' in our wretched modern idiom) that goes as far back as self-esteem and self-satisfaction can take the Reverend in relishing yet again (it recurs, I repeat, on ever 12 July) the outcome of that most famous battle.

In bigotry, Northern Protestants are typecast and congenitally incapable of pronouncing the word 'peace', for when it is pronounced, in a sufficiently heavy and one might say militant fashion it invariably comes out (like a belch) as 'pace', hence 'The Pace Process', which holds within itself, as in the most secret recesses of the Orange heart, gone black with bigotry and bile, a ring of tribal hatred with its echo or 'race' as in race-hatred.

The dictator Benito Mussolini was a buffoon who liked to make a show of himself shirtless on a Roman balcony, haranguing the thousands of Fascists assembled in the piazza below. His Army and Navy officers were dressed as fancifully as stage soldiers in a light operetta. His army didn't care much for fighting and could only put up much of a show in Abyssinia fighting warriors armed with spears.

What if the Rev. Ian Paisley were to remove his shirt on a stifling hot still day in Portadown to deliver straight from the shoulder another of his rabble-rousing tirades against Rome and all that it stood for, while exposing is great hairy armpits, cavernous nostrils and that big mouth of his roaring out abuse that fell as veritable manna onto the heads of the true-blue royalists assembled below?

You would not catch *Der Führer* with his shirt off. Never. He dressed to kill. Oratory for him became a spelling binding art that transfixed the *Volk* in adoration, shifting from the placatory manner to promises and flattery ('Mein Deutschland Du bist so schön!') shifting to the menacing manner and finally into pure hatred in hysterical outbursts of rage against Jewry and all that it represented; impurities in the German bloodstream that must be eradicated; expelled for good and all; flushed down the drain, done away with. Squeamishness was out: Jews, after all, were *Untermenschen*.

Spoken German is a threatening language of the cold North, the Baltic Sea, Luther's table talk, different by far to the softer assonances of Italian, better suited to the Mediterranean climate.

The gnome Goebbels was a more persuasive and sinister orator, a stoat upon its hind legs sheltering under an umbrella in a downpour while delivering the funeral oration over the grave of Horst Wessel.

Not to be outdone in crudeness, 'our' Mr Adams has marshalled his own crapulous compounds to annoy his enemies—'The British war-machine, Brits out, peace in' but has at least refined his taste in dress to well-cut expensive suits and unobtrusive neckties. He now prefers fine wines to pints of vulgar Guinness, to match his ambitions and salary in the grim business in which he is involved, and is now pronouncing 'pace' (*sotto voce*) as 'piece" (as in The Piece Process). If only he could bring himself to shave off his bandit's beard he might look as innocuous as his colleague and comrade-in-arms, Martin

McGuinness, the wolf in sheep's clothing, who more resembles a small-time shopkeeper rather than a seasoned political activist; whereas Adams's smile (teeth bared to the gums in a surround of bristling beard after the manner of Che Guevara) looks distinctly wolfish. He is well-trained in political duplicity, taking his place in the House of Commons in order not to take the oath of allegiance to the Queen.

He is attempting to solve a most complex jigsaw puzzle put together with fiendish cunning by experts at false leads and camouflage. This puzzle can only be solved by slow, anxious care in considering and discarding possibilities, picking up and trying out pieces that will or will not fit. The problems set and staring him in the face are taxing in the extreme, requiring superhuman patience to work out and get it right. Will he ever get it right, inserting every piece into its allotted gap, slowly putting it together until the final piece is slotted into place and all problems resolved?

Is it too late already, for he has been long at this self-imposed task, calculated to try the patience of Sisyphus? A less patient many would have given long ago. Of course politicians and party leaders are not like us, for they cannot be described as normal. Is there still time left? Adams has dug in his heels and will not be shifted from the position he has adopted and refuses to relinquish.

It is his *modus vivendi* to orate, and orate he certainly does, though not at the extreme lengths to which Castro was prepared to go. At all costs he must keep the electorate happy and on its toes and this he contrives to do admirably. It is a task as onerous but as necessary at street-cleaning, or sewage maintenance.

Cajoling, cracking feeble jokes, arguing the toss, explaining over and over again what he intends to do and the rightness of his viewpoint, modifying it as he sees fit, when circumstances dictate, this is his *forte*.

The Peace People (sounds like a pop group, charmers about

as useful to the cause as Abba to music) were exposed as shams but accepted the Nobel Prize and then wisely drew away from the vicinity of the quagmire of Northern politics before worse befell, not be heard of again.

A pen-pusher from the south lived for a time in uncomfortable proximity to Paisley's church. And, to compound the offence, lived in sin with his Belfast Protestant Girlfriend, who worked in the Rape Crisis Centre and had a poem written for her by the chain-smoker Nobel prizeman Joseph Brodsky—'Belfast Girl'.

He was careful to stand well clear of the door when a thunderous knocking sounded; for if he threw open the door, he might receive a shotgun blast right in the face. He ventured out into the streets of Belfast as little as possible and to anyone casually enquiring of his name, he was Derek and not Dermot, leaping over the sectarian divide with agility, slippery as an eel.

There is a certain low pub in Newbliss near the border that not even he (Dermot) would venture into and he would venture into most pubs, including a black pub in London where we drank during the 'off' period when it was supposed to be closed. We were the only white drinkers in the place and received nothing but courtesy from the dark-skinned habitués, including the black barman who served us. This semi-moribund pub in Newbliss was part of an Orange enclave of once prosperous Protestant farmers now gone to the dogs. They could sniff out Pauds a mile off.

There is yet another low Irish pub at Cricklewood in north-west London patronized by pro-Provos, pseudo-Provos and real dyed-in-the-wool Provos into which I once stepped with a Norther friend called Rice (Hi, Hal!). He ordered two pints of ale in dumbshow, pointing at the beer-pull and giving the Churchillian V for victory sign ('two of that, Guv.') to mollify the gigantic barman, as though we were a couple of deaf mutes.

When the collection for the Great Cause came around and the box was rattled under his nose, Hal diplomatically dropped some coins into it without comment. 'Up the Republic!' in a heavily inflected Northern accent would be a deadly insult. Up yours.

We swallowed our drinks in silence and left, watched by many pairs of curious Provisional eyes. Were we perchance British intelligence agents up to no good? Consider the sad case of Shergar or of Captain Robert Nairac whom they beat to death with fencing posts and flung his mangled remains into a turnip-shredder.

'You were very quiet in there,' I said.

'Do you take me for a damn fool?' he said. 'My accent would have warranted kneecapping. They were collecting funds to buy arms from Colonel Gaddafi. Let's get the hell out of here.'

So we made our way to Willesden Green where we were to sup with a lady from Omagh (it has since received its baptism of fire) who painted in oils, had a posthumous exhibition that sold out.

'Buy now while the shops last' they say in bombed Belfast. Shops go out of business, change hands (but no Protestant business falls into Catholic hands) to become another business in another city divided and subdivided against itself. The butcher's business is now a betting shop or turf accountant, as we say down here in the South, displaying a true Papist inability or downright unwillingness to call a spade a spade.

Turf is something very old, on its way to becoming coal when dug from the bog and can be used to make fires. Accountants is a statement of moneys received and paid, with calculations of the balance; a reckoning in one's favour; a statement of the administrations of money in trust. One can see in all this palaver the Union Jack flying triumphantly over Stormont.

While on the subject of old forms, 'safe houses' are refuges for those on the run. It must be an ancient form of Irish hospitality for it was used by Synge in *The Playboy of the Western World*. It turned out to have been a botched patricide, as happened to the numerous unlucky ones who in cases of mistaken identity were murdered in cold blood, with fulsome apologies coming from the Provo High Command. They killed the wrong man again and again.

'Grass' and 'Super-grass' have nothing whatever to do with agriculture, but refer to those who betray or finger their accomplices in murder. They are given new identities, moved to another country and lie low.

The harsh Norther accent, with its tough Scots Presbyterian roots and memories of hiring fairs for Celts from over the sea, the Catholic Irish exported like cattle, reveals or betrays more than the speakers themselves realise, for they sound as if perpetually spoiling for a fight.

'He's no friend of mine' is as curtly dismissive as "don't push it,' or 'Off with his head' (her head in the case of the luckless Mary Queen of Scots, beheaded in a century just as sanguinary as our own).

The only Spanish I can utter with any conviction is '¿Requerda me?' (Do you remember me?) or '¡Que lástima!' (What a pity!) Why must lástima be always feminine so close to 'lachrima' (Latin for tears)?

The northern accent grates on Southern ears like a cross-saw cutting down a giant tree. A Kerry or Dublin accent would be as a red rag to a bull to a Loyalist from Craigavon or Derry, and the reverse also hold true.

To pick a right path forward from a multiplicity of wrong paths, seemingly chaotic, is no easy task. Was it the clever Chinese who invented jigsaw puzzles and fireworks; is not the peace-pace-piece process (Der Prozess, Dr Kafka's The Trial) also a sham and a low sham at that? Is there time left before we can hope to solve this diabolically difficult jigsaw puzzle set by the very devils themselves?

Invisibility

WHEN I WAS living quite poorly in Dublin, I developed the useful ability to travel free on public transport, willed myself to be invisible and no bus conductor would approach me for a fare. I could travel all over Dublin for free; it was as good as being an Old-Age Pensioner.

I mentioned this ability to my first wife and she suggested we put it to the test. We sat on the back seat on the lower deck of a No. 12, empty but for the two of us, the conductor and the driver, travelling from Palmerston Park into what is called An Lár in the melodious Gaelic—meaning the Centre, in O'Connell Street, which has no particular center, Nelson's pillar having been blown up by the IRA.

The conductor saw us, or seemed to see us, straightened out his leather satchel, approached halfway down the bus, seemed to remember something or see something or somebody else vaguely familiar passing by, somebody or something that reminded him of something else, which stopped him in his tracks; then he drifted back to continue chatting with the driver.

'You see,' I said to my first wife, 'no fare. Invisible.'

I am thinking now of those painters who stared so hard at the object that they themselves became invisible. In this category were Vermeer, William Blake, Turner, Stanley Spencer, Francis Bacon, Lucien Freud.

There's a famous formulation by Nietzsche, which sounds most thunderous in German, that you might be familiar with:

'Do not gaze too long into the Abyss, lest the Abyss gaze back into thee.' Gide said that Flaubert thought he was struggling with the intricacies of the French language when in fact he was confronting the climate of Normandy.

Two others *sans visage* were Jean-Jacques Rousseau, inventor of the Noble Savage who exposed himself to women, and Henri Beyle, who named himself Stendhal after a small town in Germany.

If we cannot imagine the faces of the created being, not born entirely in vacuum, how less can we imagine the faces of their creators? When Hans Castorp leaves the sanatorium after some years of treatment and a great deal of German metaphysics, we are no wiser as to how he looks. We know how he dresses, what he eats, are privy to his innermost thoughts, his longings, but we do not know how he looks. Nor do we know what Gregor Samsa looked like before he was transformed into a bug.

Malone's stories about imaginary events and possibly real people (only known to Beckett) are as vaporish, or as real, as Malone himself; and, pray tell me, who is inventing whom?

I first met Beckett during the run of the original English version of *Waiting for Godot* in the Arts Theatre in London. Peter Wood-thorpe was playing what the London critics called the senior tramp, and he was accompanying Beckett from Godalming in Surrey to Belsize Park in London where Cousin John and his wife Vera had arranged a supper in their flat, so that I could meet him. Vera served up silverside of beef.

I had read *More Pricks Than Kicks* and *Murphy* and been much taken by these two effusions of bile. Beckett himself, whom I had never seen, was coming from Godalming with a lady he had known in Trinity College. Godalming and Ulm and SingSing penitentiary seemed appropriate Beckett associations; I wondered whom I should meet—Democritus or Heraclitus? The man of flux and hollow laughter or the man of undispellable misery? A penitential association anyway.

In the event I met neither; I met a courteous Anglo-Saxon Protestant gent with piercing blue eye, granny glasses, short cropped hair standing on end like the crest of a cockatoo, who dressed in the fashion of a Teddy Boy, with no discernible trace of a French accent and a manner most self-effacing—a charmer who made no attempt to charm.

The one and only time I ever clapped eyes on V.S. Naipaul, yet to be knighted, was at an André Deutsch party in London for the launch of Updike's *The Coup*. On that occasion suddenly encountering me, the urge was strong in him to be invisible. The sensitive antennae of that dark-visaged reclusive writer had registered "Irish sot!"

The London critics had given a rapturous reception to *The Coup*. I had found it disappointing. *The Coup* was just *Couples* all over again, in black-face. He was the same old panty-sniffer. I had been imbibing in a nearby wine-bar, intending to tell Updike to his face what I thought of his work. I had anticipated encountering a small pasty-faced malcontent, so judge of my surprise to be introduced to a tall man.

'Mr Updike,' I said, 'do you know what I miss in your work?'

He had to lean down to hear me.

'No, sir," said Updike. 'I do not.'

'The poor.'

'Ah,' said Updike with an intent look, the face still wreathed in a smile; and presently he drifted away.

Then out of the press of free-loaders, publishers' marks, nervous agents, bright publicity poppets, blurb-writers and such riffraff, who materialised before but . . . V.S. Naipaul!

But V.S. was having none of this malarkey. He just caused himself to vaporise before me. One minute he was there, a darkly grimacing presence, and the next he was gone, vanished into thin air—which I take to be that natural element of such thin-skinned people.

A correspondent of *The New Yorker* had wittily called Naipaul a 'fastidious sourpuss'. A dark presence menacing as

Lord Vishnu himself had been casting no little chill upon the
jolly Deutsch proceedings.

I thought there is no feeling of the past in Updike's fiction,
which is as modern as formica or plastic, which perhaps
accounts for its popularity. John Cheever, a far better writer,
didn't like Updike, finding him pushy. Sir V. S. Naipaul gleams
with a high-contrast sheen as intractable as ebony. Not a man
to antagonise, any more than you'd antagonise a leopard or a
cheetah.

I am old enough to remember a time when famous citizens were
not even recognised in the streets of Dublin and were as free
as you and me to go about their own business unmolested by
the great common herd whose collective breath is noxious and
whose collective heart is, as you know, shallow and commonplace as a bedpan.

Seamus O'Sullivan (real name James Sullivan Starkey),
looked out of a long window on Dublin's Morehampton Road,
saw a workman passing by, pushing a wheelbarrow piled up
with fresh dung.

'I see Paddy Kavanagh is moving house,' he remarked. 'There
he goes with some of his household effects.'

I am talking of a time before television, that rough beast,
had entered our homes to do great mischief. 'The greatest single
disaster in the history of mankind', in the opinion of the late
lamented movie-man Lindsay Anderson.

I appeared on an early RTE TV black and white one-off arts
programme—an excuse to bring together Ben Kiely, Anthony
Cronin (who later was to become Charlie Haughey's speech
writer), the deathly pale publisher Figgis, your humble, and the
legendary Flann O'Brien, author of *At Swim-Two-Birds*, whom
I was most anxious to meet in the flesh . . . such as it was.

Kiely, himself a cross between Mad Sweeney and Finn
MacCool, a compulsive anecdotalist, and a great man for the

genealogies and Irish family trees, as the Pope O'Mahony before him, had just discovered that he and Flann O'Brien were kinsmen. They were twenty-fifth (or was it forty-second?) cousins, twice removed. They strolled into the Donnybrook studio—I was about to say arena—together, already well-oiled, as soon became apparent.

The plan had been to get Myles into the studio sober and to ensure that he stayed that way by plying him with glasses of water. He seated himself opposite me and a ball of malt appeared as if by magic out of one cuff. He had pudgy hands and a shifty eye and kept moistening his lips, the tongue shooting in and out like a lizard's after prey. As the programme developed, it became clear that a good few balls of malt had preceded this one, because his manner became acerbic, then belligerent, I might say hectoring. He was chain-smoking and seemed to be attempting to remove his dentures, the better to spit venom at 'them'—unidentified parties in government posts or gurriers in high places who were out to get him and who presently would be named.

This now horrendously public crusty manner caused a furor in the control room. A note on yellow paper was swiftly conveyed to the flustered anchorman, and the programme terminated before worse befell and libel writs flew—for it was going out live and unrehearsed.

It was instantly replaced without a by-your-leave by The Dubliners, native sons in raucous session, with Ronnie Drew belting out a rebel song in his own inimitable way.

Meanwhile in the studio, Flann O'Brien turned to me and inquired civilly, 'How did it go?', under the impression that I was one of the studio technicians. I had not uttered a single word (good, bad, or indifferent) on camera. 'It went grand,' I lied.

We all repaired to McDaid's for alcoholic refreshment. I stood the great man a double Scotch and identified myself as another admirer of *At Swim-Two-Birds,* which had been out of print since 1940 when the entire first print-run had gone up in flames in a London warehouse during the Blitz, as had *Murphy,* Beckett's first novel.

What I didn't know at the time was that O'Nolan abhorred his first novel—hated its success, I should say—and was galled by anybody praising it. He refused to accept praise for such 'prentice work, dismissing it as 'a thoroughly bad book.' You should know better,' said he to me, the lizard tongue shooting out again, with the dehydration, 'and you a Christian Brothers' boy.'

Well, you could have knocked me over with a rolled thesaurus. He took me for another! Here we were likely entering another circle of his ceaselessly revolving alcoholic Hells.

The *Cruiskeen Lawn* ran in episodic bursts for twenty-nine years, with gaps while libel actions were settled out of court. The column came out also in Gaelic from time to time, so that neither the editor nor ninety-five percent of the readership could understand a word. A further alarming feature were fingers pointing out like little cannons at adjoining pieces in the paper, and damning judgements were freely dispensed. He also claimed to have written the newspaper's editorials.

No by-line picture identified him, and Brian O'Nolan could walk around Dublin and not be recognised by *Irish Times* readers as the acerb fifth columnist of 'Cruiskeen Lawn'. Interviewed by *Time* magazine, he gave it out that the columnist was the illegitimate offspring of a Cologne basket–weaver, and this whopper was swallowed. Brendan Behan said that you had to look twice at Brian O'Nolan to make sure he was there at all. Flann the Crusher had left instructions with his publisher Timothy O'Keeffe that no photograph and absolutely no O'Keeffe biographical details were to be released. A photograph purporting to be that of the author which appeared in one of the reviews of *At Swim-Two-Birds* second time round in 1960, was not him, O'Brien said. The head seemed unfamiliar.

When Editions de Minuit, the underground resistance publisher in Paris, brought out the first volume of Beckett's trilogy, no photographs of the author were available. He had served in the Resistance and lived in hiding in Roussillon, and no photographs were taken.

I used to play golf in County Wicklow with a friend of mine over the course at Greystones where the young Beckett had played with Dr Gerry Beckett, whom he had nicknamed 'The Plantigrade Shuffler'. My friend Rowe had attended the same school as Jonathan Swift. The boys of Kilkenny School were offered a free day if any boy could find the signature of the famous old boy hidden away somewhere, scratched on a stone, possibly in the latrines. Jonathan Swift had graduated in 1680 and gone on to Trinity College Dublin. A boy claimed to have found the signature and went running to the headmaster to show him where the famous name had been scratched with a penknife so many years before.

Dean Swift

1675-80

in a crabby hand. Dean Swift indeed! The boy was immediately flogged for lying. But why couldn't the young Jonathan have seen himself fit for the Deanery of St. Patrick's one day in the not too distant future, and soon sitting down to write *A Modest Proposal* and *Gulliver's Travels*? And furthermore could tell the year of his death.

My mother, long gone to her reward, used to say that James Joyce had a bad face. Certainly it is not an appealing face, but closed up like a tightened fist. The goggly eyes seem to swim behind the thick lens and will not focus on us; the severe mouth is unfriendly. He overdressed, was fond of rings, went with a cane, wore peculiar hats, struck stiff poses for the camera, looked like a magician.

What I suspect my mother didn't like about Joyce was that he lived with Nora Barnacle in sinful Paris and was the author of a notoriously dirty book called *Ulysses*; so of course he was bound to have a bad face. I would go further: Joyce had no face at all. The death-mask tells you more than the living tissue ever did. None of the great creators have faces. Not Virgil, I dare say not Plato, nor Homer, nor Shakespeare, nor Dante, nor Bosch, nor the Breughels father and son, nor Magritte or Michaux, two eccentric Belgians, nor your Faulkner of Jackson, Mississippi.

Faulkner had his grandfather's face, a soldier's face that belonged to Major de Spain or Sartoris or General Compson or McCaslin or whoever it was, down there in the South, affirming his belief that suffering and grieving are better than nothing.

A friend of mine, a painter now dead, whose ashes were scattered in the Garravogue, compared the face of Kafka to an animal (a fox) caught by the flashbulb at night; the face of a furtive nocturnal creature one is not supposed to see.

Céline (real name Dr Louis-Ferdinand Destouches) had a face worn away by suffering. Beckett's face was a mask, and Baudelaire's before him; as was Antonin Artaud's in Rodez Asylum. Stravinsky said that you'd have to iron out Auden's face to see what he really looked like.

The face of the young Joyce bears no resemblance to the later visages; the fellow playing the mandolin in his Paris flat, the older man paying off a taxi-cab, hat tilted, rose in buttonhole, out visiting his grandson and Ambigums. This was the same chronically impecunious young man (who may have already published *Chamber Music*) photographed in an awkward pose standing before a green house, hands deep in pockets of mismatched suiting, that indicated social ease, gurrier's cloth cap at rakish angle on head, head cocked to one side, studying the photographer. What was he thinking of when the shutter clicked? He was wondering if he could touch the photographer for the loan of half a crown. The exposure would have taken some time, hence the awkward stance. The latter overdressing may have been a form of compensation for indignities suffered in his days of penury, as the compulsive over tipping in expensive Paris restaurants was an attempt to recover lost pride, status; he had always been a free spender of other's money.

Pound had sent a present wrapped in brown paper parcel, tied with Ezra's housewifely knots, conveyed by T.S. Eliot in the company of Wyndham Lewis, which Joyce opened to reveal a pair of Pound's castoff brown boots. Thereafter Joyce was always last out the door—after you, Mr Eliot; after you, Mr Lewis—always first to pick up the tab.

Of the faces not quite belonging to their owners, one that springs to mind is that of Baudelaire as photographed by Nadar. The eyes glare out at you as if belonging to another man standing behind Charles Baudelaire and even more desperate than him. His collar is loosened and disarranged, the thin neck exposed as for the guillotine. *Un condamné.*

John Cheever, the man from Quincy who died in Ossining, had his own reasons for having two faces. Bonnard's is an unformed face, semi-oriental, a self-portrait merely blocked in; the real Bonnard has gone out for a breath of fresh air, or a smoke.

Another face comes to mind—one who supped deep with horror all his life—and I mean Jean Genet. Genet had two faces, and neither belonged to him; the Anima and Animus ever in contention. The author of *Stiller,* the Swiss writer Max Frisch, who knew Montauk, lived for years in a Greenwich Village attic, had no face. With war imminent, Paul Klee's last agonised self-portraits converted his round Swiss face into a blood-red full moon under Saturn. Was it Breughel or Hieronymous Bosch who painted his own face hanging as if decapitated in Hell? Who was it painted God in the Garden like a ghost in a tall hat? Vaguely apprehended, a will-o-the-wisp about to be wiped out, a footstep going out of shape in a puddle.

You see what I mean?

An unknown man with a round face, hidden in a narrow-brim brown velour hat bought in a Talbot Street haberdashery, walks in Dublin with the unmistakable shackled progress or locomotoraxy of a chronic alcoholic, makes his way in McDaid's dingy bar in Harry Street and asks for the usual painkiller. The hat was bought for two quid and seems to be a fixture on his head. You could almost tell the time of day in Dublin, by studying the various slants and tilts of the hat, angled in a more and more truculent way as the day wore on. Sometimes when a storm was brewing, it pressed down over his ears like the lid of a pot simmering on a stove.

His most endearing 'invisible' character is a collective presence, faceless and nameless, the voice of the Plain People of Ireland, who are distant Irish cousins of Faulkner's Snopeses. It is the collective conscience of the race of whom the nameless Dublin Jackeen at the No. 52 bus stop is one, the man who venerates his unnamed clever brother, speaks to a well-spoken gentleman, also faceless and nameless. The Jackeen lives in Drimnagh a nondescript area well suited to a nameless one. These nameless faceless 'invisible' ones speak to us most directly.

The Hidden Narrator

Paper read at Irish Writers' Centre, Dublin, on 2 March 1995

AROUND THIS TIME of year twenty-nine years ago Flann O'Brien, that phantom figure, had taken to his bed, afflicted with all manner of ailments and was sinking into his last decline. On April Fool's Day 1966, appropriately enough, he passed away.

I met Myles once; and here this evening thought I might give you some account of what could hardly be called 'a meeting'—that brief encounter.

It fell to my lot once to read a paper at UCD. After the reading, a lady of surpassing beauty with cornflower-blue eyes sailed up to the podium to say "I loved your line, 'Only ghosts see the wind'."

What I had in fact written was 'Only goats see the wind,' a thought lifted from *The Worm Forgives the Plough*, a title which John Stewart Collis had pinched from William Blake.

When wild goats had the run of the place, we may assume that their perceptions of the surroundings *qua* surroundings were sharper than those of the domesticated variety that came later. Their innate knowledge of upwind and downwind were strategies for survival; at every moment of their existence they knew where they stood, as goats; so they soon learnt to "read" the wind. This useful knowledge has atrophied in us humans; we have no such firm ground to stand on. "Ill half seen" in Beckett's knacky formulation.

And wasn't it Collis who had overheard Yeats humming poetry to himself in a bluebell wood in Coole Park? The thin, nervy edgy voice flitting up and down the emotional scale had reminded him of another voice. But where had he heard it? In Munich? Ja! Herr Hitler captivating the Bavarian ladies in a Munich drawing room.

When the dictator addressed immense crowds, he flew off the handle; it was his way of controlling them. But was the power emanating from the podium or from the people? This spellbinding orator knew how to wind them up, get them on their feet. Goering and Goebbels were bludgeon and rapier, cosh and hypodermic; Dr Goebbels sounded as charged-up as Jim Jones, the madman of Guyana, distraught with power, who in turn was as oily as Bob Guccione, the odious coxcomb of *Penthouse*, purveyor of wet dreams.

Who spoke of the void endlessly generative, of the dark varnish of public moralising? Nietzsche?

Gore Vidal and Paul Bowles (*Sheltering Sky* and *Let It Come Down*) were indifferent novelists who had independently agreed that the novel was on its last legs and would be quite dead at last in spite of all within their separate lifetimes; and possibly extinct by the middle of the coming century, the very noisy oncoming one.

Readers (a quiet breed) would become extinct. The few remaining would know each other by whispering titles, as Freemasons exchange secret hand-signals. Readers of serious literature would have become a hidden confraternity, lending out dog-eared and clandestine copies of Martin Buber and Søren Kierkegaard.

Certainly the rapid onrushing manner in which children are quickly weaned on software and CVs in the nursery, the TV screen (always glowing, forever howling) replacing Nanny and Granny, with hard porn available at adolescence, confirms the worst fears of Huxley and Orwell, neither of whom, in their worst imaginings, could have imagined Desert Storm, with the oil rigs flaming.

The kids of the next century are in for a hammering, a pasting, a Kursk tank battle on the air and ground, miles high, miles deep, for the hearts and minds of innocents. The kids demand their kicks and turn-ons. They'll get it, pressed down and running over. Pictures are too easy. The flickering images on the screen are as idle and arbitrary as the antics of a bored baboon caged in the zoo and idly playing with dung and straw, dying of boredom. It's a discontinued tale that they, the viewers, gape at, an occupation fit for idle baboons and simpletons, which our great-grandchildren will have become with Sky Sport and Murdoch's morons numbed in millions, passive dupes.

But where will the reader's be?

By AD 2045, both Paul Bowles and Gore Vidal will have paid their debt to nature. It is disputable whether either ever wrote a novel, properly speaking. They were just airing prejudices, posturing, stalling, The writing of a novel is a mysterious process, an inspired form of daydreaming. It is not what Saul Bellows call 'cosying up' to the reader, to which Mr Updike (for example) is very prone.

Flann O'Brien certainly wrote two novels, before he began airing prejudices in two other polemical works full of pawky jokes and flatulence, *The Hard Life* and *The Dalkey Archive*.

When I came to be published some thirty-five years ago by John Calder in London, Irish writers were thin on the ground and rarely seen around. They tended to be self-effacing, if not exactly invisible. Nothing was stirring on the home front. *Both More Pricks Than Kicks* and *Murphy* were out of print, as was Flann O'Brien in two languages, and *The Third Policeman* lost. We had to make do with Austin Clarke and Francis McManus's *Men Withering*.

At the old Abbey, the very seat of infection, amid the creaking of ancient corsets and the spent smell of stale porter, *The Rugged Path* ran forever; to be succeeded by fare no less stodgy, *The Righteous Are Bold*. While over the way, at the Metropole, an American tearjerker movie, *The Best Years of Our Lives*, was breaking all records and all hearts.

The Bovril sign still flamed above College Green.

Frank O'Connor, Francis Stuart and Francis MacManus, the doughty penmen of the past, had a faded look about them, sere as withered leaves or the sepia heroes of old celluloid, Gene Autry and Tom Mix forever riding off into the sunset.

The relative obscurity of those poor writers of yore was in striking contrast to the extreme visibility of the pushy pen persons of today, who come into prominence from one Booker or Whitbread prize to the next.

Each new generation of writer loathes the generation immediately before it and the generation immediately behind; and I should know, with seven titles out of print or remaindered, having come through three such baptisms of fire. The self-effacing Señor Borges wrote somewhere that he would like nothing better than, under an assumed name, to publish a merciless tirade against himself, his entire oeuvre.

B. Traven was an elusive fellow with several identities at this disposal; all different none known, all made up, and all fake. Nor was that his 'real' name; he kept it secret and died unknown.

The diplomatic garden gnome, Harold Nicolson, noted in his diary that every family had its secret saying, picked up from reading and set circulating within the closed family circle; a coda or little language known only to initiates. He was of course thinking of privilege, his privilege, the Nicolson and Sackvile-West tenure, the God-given rights of the upper class English to appreciate Earl Grey tea at four in the afternoon, served up in thin china tea-service; as they would appreciate the novels of Jane Austen, each thin and tasteful as well-sliced cucumber sandwiches. Lobster and cutlets in aspic were for the gentry. *Don Giovanni* at Sadler's Wells: 'For as long as Wimpole Street Remains, civilisation is secure,' *qua Flush*. Earl Grey tea served up punctually at four in the afternoon, with muffins, constituted their notion of high art, an art that became them; hence the huffiness and stuffiness of Bloomsbury.

Punctuality begat propriety which begat politeness which in turn begat order which begat good manners which is largely a question of obeying one's best as opposed to one's worst promptings; above all following good sound common sense, for those lovers of the finer amenities. Art for the Woolfs and Nicolsons and the Sackville-Wests was largely an affair of good manners, something to be enjoyed with one's equals (Mrs Dalloway and Lily Briscoe and those twittery debs in *The Waves*, of whom I can only recall Rhoda). Art concerned itself with good breeding and good taste, equals to equals on the croquet lawn and tennis court.

Virginia Woolf mocks Septimus Smith, the suicidal clerk who impales himself on railings, for being unlucky enough to have been born Septimus Smith, thus born to inevitable set-backs (a common clerk—a nothing much), even though it was she herself who had named him thus in the novel *Mrs Dalloway*.

Yeat's own even more hierarchical notion of the common man, your average bloke, the chap in the cloth cap on the top deck of the Clapman omnibus, was 'Jones of Twickenham'. For Yeats the unthinkable would be that Dagenham. No. 7 Eccles street was more than a bad address; it was an unthinkable place. Yet Joyce mocks Bloom by giving us an inventory not only of Bloom's worldly possessions but the sad inventory of his dreams. Dreams of more possessions for the little home which Bloom Dearly loves, Joyce implying that Bloom has poor or no taste.

Now if the unthinkable occurred and the Nicolsons or the Woolfs were cordially invited to tea with the Joyces, they would have been dismayed to find a non-fictional squalor as bad as the fictional squalor they so deplored, with no guarantee that Jim's terrible old man (all too real) would remain reasonably sober.

Virgina Woolf had dismissed Joyce as a low-bred fellow and to this day English critics as sound and level-headed as Sir Victor Pritchett have entertained certain reservations about the unappealing sordidness of *Ulysses*, sordidness being the natural terrain of low-bred fellows.

The sound and stinks of Bloom at stool or the spectacle of Bloom abed, lying upside down in order to ardently kiss Molly's bum, for that close intimacy is foisted upon us readers, must have been deeply offensive to the finer sensibilities of Mrs Woolf.

The idea of the Blooms being invited to tea with Virgina and Leonard in Sussex or with Vita and Harold at Sissinghurst is too ludicrous to contemplate. Like the infamous rubric above the gate of the death-camp, over Sissinghurst flew a banner with the bold device 'C P O J D W T K" which decoded read: Certain People One Just Doesn't Wish To Know. Virgina Woolf was herself smothered in good taste: indeed, she probably died of it. Behind Mr Dalloway one detects the willowy form of Mrs Miniver. During the last widow-maker war which some would wish to aver had nothing to do with us, Miss Elizabeth Bowen was co-opted into British intelligence to act as a sort of unpaid lady spy operating in Dublin and Cork, planted as a mole in Mitchelstown. She was briefed by Harold Nicolson of the Foreign Service, told to keep her ear to the ground and report back to him. She mentions this in a chatty indiscreet letter to her false friend Virginia, so it cannot have been very serious spying.

Writing is in any case a form of spying, and can even be an exalted form or spying and betrayal (step forward Monsieur Genet). Behind any text of value lurks the sub-text. Our family had adopted certain catch-phrases from *At Swim-Two-Birds*.

At Swim has a strong sadistic steak amid deft touches of vernacular lunacy, insouciant as the death wish that runs, or dances, through the work of Synge. The torture scenes in *At Swim* and the cold-blooded account of the murder of old Mathers in the first page of *The Third Policeman* must remind us that our ancient progenitors (Joyce's "horde of jerkined dwarfs'), the daddies of us all, were a rapacious lot and liked to play skittles with human skulls. Philosopher egoarch Arland Ussher used to argue that we Irish are a deeply conservative race; but I wouldn't be so sure. I'm not.

And we had our own spy amongst us.

Nobody knew what he looked like and he operated under a number of pseudonyms, working certain pubs off the fashionable areas processing his information from his office in the Scotch House and then back to HQ at 31 Westmoreland Street; to be published twice or thrice a week in smooth, learned Gaelic in a column in *The Irish Times* which was so much Double Dutch to editor Smyllie, most of the subs, and ninety-nine percent of the readership. The Plain People of Ireland were a match for Joyce's Citizen, when it came to chauvinism and bigotry and poltroonery. Myles surrounded himself with fantasy, for which potent spirits (distilled) added fuel, preservative and afterglow. With five half-ones aboard, the Swords Road began to resemble nothing on earth, and the face he saw observing him in the mirror was no longer his own; he could go anywhere do anything; camouflaged within his pseudonyms, he had become invisible.

He even contrived to make himself *persona non grata* on our freshly established television network. The great hygienic leveler and homogenizing Irish Washing Machine that was to create a living saint from material as saccharine as Gay Byrne could not even begin to digest such an intractable subject as Flann O'Brien.

The revival of *At Swim* by MacGibbon & Kee in 1960 and its progress through ten printings as a Penguin Modern Classic had something in the marvelous about it though its success continued to puzzle and sorely vex the author for as long as he lived. Few knew him by sight. It added a spice of the subversive to the mischievous nature of the columns, 'Cruiskeen Lawn' (The Full Measure? The Brimming Jorum?) appearing now in learned Gaelic, now in lordly English, with woodcuts purporting to be the author's own; one depicting a horse and carriage being driven smartly through an Act of Parliament conveniently suspended across the roadway. No masthead image afforded any clue as to the identity of the author, who claimed to write editorials on the progress of the war now raging in the Soviet Union. He was said to live in high style at Santry Great Hall with a titled da, Sir Myles nagCopaleen. The columns had a secret following, as with the cultured Gaelic-speakers who could follow *An Beal Bocht*. Its true circulation must have greatly exceeded the actual print-run. Odd people read it in out-of-the-way places. Old Martin O'Donnel sniggered over the masterly Gaelic in *An Ingle on Inishere*; I knew two hash-house cooks in Texas who independently devoured *At Swim* for it had made that remote place Dublin circa 1942 close and familiar. I knew a Welshman who landed a job in what was Radio Rhodeia by reciting "A Pint of Plain is Your Only Man" for the audition. And Borges reviewed the novel favourably in Spanish for a women's publication in Bueonos Aires soon after it came out.

When out of print, its fame had spread. Copies were lent around. Undergraduate Philip Larkin discovered it and let it to Kingsley Amis who lent it to John Wain, an improbable trio of admirers. It inspires affection perhaps because you cannot imagine the author; it came out like spontaneous combustion. Dylan Thomas thought it would make a fine present for a dirty boozy sister.

Shabby thought-wracked Stephen Dedalus, with his Italian-sounding name, is an idealised version of the even shabbier young Joyce, as lawyer Gavin Stevens is an idealised version of William Faulkner (formerly Falkner) or as Malcolm Lowry can be vaguely discerned behind the preposterously disguised Sigbjørn Wilderness or William Platagenet, that redoubtable trio of crashing bores in false beards. Lowry was Plantagenet as much as he was Kennish Drumgold Cosnahan, Ethon Llewelynm, the fake Welshman or the equally fake Manxman Roderick McGregor Fairhaven (Lowry was never very good at inventing names). He was all his own heroes rolled into one and was himself his own half-brother, the preposterous 'Hugh' of the deeply absurd novel *Under the Volcano*.

All was posturing, manifestations of an alcohol-induced self-aggrandizement, a puffing up of the old alter ego, the one with pretensions (head-staggers?). But where is the author of *At Swim-Two-Birds*, tell me that? Strangely absented; the fellow who disowned his own book is nowhere to be seen, refined out of all existence.

I was told that a photograph of him did exist, taken at a golf outing of the Dublin Diplomatic Corps, which hung in the bar of Delgany Golf Club, of which I was once a member. The French representative Monsieur Goor was in it as was Bertie Smyllie, the pipe-puffing, monstrously fat editor of *The Irish Times*, with his no less corpulent obituary writer Eamonn Lynch; with some IT staffers lolling on the grass, presumably gold and political correspondents, and Myles.

I found it. The group might have been a Ralph Steadman illustration for one of the unpublished or forgotten novels, a lost novel with himself a character in it. Not the narrator, no; a walk-on character such as Pisser Burke.

I identified Myles in the back row. Just the head and shoulders, chubby face shadowed by the brim of a black homburg; a dark-visaged, a small-sized, portly savant with what appeared to me a *mensur* scar athwart one podgy cheek, lending credence to the

rumour spread about in the famous *Time* magazine interview. I
forget to whom he attributed paternity; his own feelings about
his own da being well disguised. Who is the father of any son
that any son should recognise him or he any son?

If the life of language is in speech, then the O'Nolan family
had two languages at their disposal. Those bilingual Ó Nualláins
of Strabane had smooth Tyrone Gaelic in the home, and they
didn't approve of *At Swim-Two-Birds*, which seemed to hold
the family up to derision. As with Mahatma Gandhi shriveled
up on the pyre, the Gandhi family couldn't make heads or
tail of him. Myles was rather an enigma to his brothers and
sister, one of whom ended in nunnery; the novel was a far cry
from weepy Mother Machree and the cuddly yokels beloved
of Somerville and Ross. I myself could never stomach that
great anthropomorphic lie about Mother-Eire-our-mother-dear
-spreak about like winter's stinking slurry by O'Flaherty.

Even if Joyce himself had praised the novel, Beckett had
refused to open it, from a sense of loyalty to the Master whom the
young whippersnapper aspirant to great things had somewhat
impertinently dismissed (to Sam's face) as 'that refurbisher of
skivvies' stories', a sally that might have gone down well in the
Palace Bar or the Pearl Bar but which failed to amuse Beckett.

The severe features of the great reductionist glares out from
a poster on the cylindrical sides of a *Berliner Litfassaule* hard by
Europa Centre, advertsing NICH ICH . . . Nich Ich . . . Nich
Ich . . . Nich ich . . . Not I Not I Not I Not I Not I.

Sanguivorous Bugaboos

Paper read at L'Imaginaire Irlandais, Centre Georges Pompidou, 2 mai, 1996

COMING TO THESE august premises, already filled to overflowing with what the young Beckett called 'the rare and famous ways of spirit that are the French ways', I was reminded with some horror of all the bad ways, the wrong and embarrassing ways, there are of reading in public.

One can detest doing it, fearful of the awful exposure, and then do it badly, like Marianne Moore. Or love doing it, gloating over it, craving the exposure, like Robert Graves. Or surprise listeners who were anticipating a blustery growl, with an apologetic contralto, that turned out to be that snake in the grass Hemingway. Or frighten them to death with a squeaky doll's foolish voice, neither male nor female, neither fish nor fowl, like a ferret reciting light verse which believe it or not was the authentic voice of Truman Capote, author of *Other Voices, Other Rooms*. Or not do it at all, like Beckett. But then I consoled myself with the thought that even Kafka read his early stuff to Max Brod, and Max Brod in turn read his dire stuff back to Kafka, and both were content.

In recordings, I have heard the voice of Borges theorising about *Hamlet* over breakfast with Professor Kearney in Donnybrook. And heard the voice of Shem the Penman, James Joyce himself, lost in a dream, reading passages from *Finnegans Wake*. I have heard the voices of Nobel Prizeman Bellow, chain-smoking Brodsky, Walcott and Heaney. But who here is not familiar with the voice of Heaney, delightfully surprising us with his mellifluous stuff, gladsome as the cuckoo-bird in springtime.

His sales have vaulted fifteen-fold since the Nobel Prize. Blind Borges, the great Argentinian writer sold only ten or fifteen copies of his first book in the first year of trading. He thought it might be pleasant to meet one of two or those readers. You wouldn't wish to meet twenty-five thousand admirers; unless of course you were as vain as Alain Robbe-Grillet. Faulkner's *The Sound and the Fury* sold 3,000 copes in its first fifteen years.

The Aidan Higgins reader is a *rara avis* indeed. You can recognise him—it's mostly male—by the fact that he carries a sack, like the Bunuel character played by Aldo Rey in *The Obscure Object of Desire*. The sack is crammed with remaindered Higgins titles, which he wants me to sign. I can spot him at the end of the bar counter (I encounter him mostly in bars) throwing significant looks in my direction. The next moment he is at my elbow with the sack open, asking, 'You wouldn't by any chance be Aidan Higgins?' 'A part of him,' I answer. 'That will do,' says he.

So I buy him a drink and sign all his copies.

Some of you sitting here this evening may be familiar with the place once called Ulster and may have had the galling experience of rounding a corner in Belfast, Derry or Omagh to be confronted with a British Army foot-patrol and find yourself staring down the barrel of a high-velocity rifle. I have had this experience; and an equivalent experience in the far west of Ireland on what used to be one of three small islands that were joined to the mainland in Penal times. I wrote a story about it and will read it to you presently.

In 'boulderstrewn Drim' I was in a bar with an English friend, drinking bottled Crusaders. My haughty-tauty accent would immediately suggest to a true patriot that here wasn't the true penny but more likely an Anglican gent from the Home counties—authentic British Army officer material. My friend, oddly enough, was an ex-Tank Corps officer.

Certain remote villages on the Connemara Atlantic seaboard are as rough and lawless as Ballyfermot or a Red Indian reservation. The young lads are taking home unheard-of wages from the Japanese fish-canning factories and are permanently high on poteen. The pubs stay open until all hours and few go home sober if they can help it; some don't even arrive sober. Ancestral grievances simmer there in the very heartland of Republicanism where butcher Cromwell had once threated to confine the entire Irish race. Old grievances weigh heavily as a parasitic growth on trees. I had returned to live again in Ireland, thanks to the American-Irish Foundation grant, to spend six months in the far west drenched in penitential rainfalls that never let up on one of those three former islands that were joined by causeways to Connemara in the Penal days. The modernised cottage that I rented would later be torched by one of the aggrieved lads, denied work pulling pints for Johnny O'Toole, who died last year. Arson must have been in the Irish blood, long before Coole Park went up in flames.

The story is call 'Gas in the Decompression Chamber', from a collection called *Ronda Gorge and Other Precipices*, published by Secker & Warburg in 1989 and since remaindered.

The Maamturks are a range of mountains, 730 metres high ('History's pomps are toylike'). A white marble bust of Roderick O'Connor's head and shoulders is mounted in the lobby of the Great Southern Hotel in Galway. Was he a High King? He was one of the old rulers of Connemara.

In *Finnegans Wake* there is a reference to 'sanguivorous bugaboos'. And Edgar Allan Poe write of 'No bugaboo tales', meaning imaginary terrors, sanguinary horrors. Here's a true bugaboo tale from that time I spent in rain sodden Connemara, in the heartland of the ill-begotten and ever resentful Provos.

Gas in the Decompression Chamber

FEW IN THEIR right minds could doubt that reality is two-thirds illusion in Iar-Connacht, The-Bay-of-the-Ocean called Connemara. The Maamturks loom and recede, appear only to vanish, an unsettling optical illusion. The nights are as still as the grave. Terrain so marine in nature, so embattled in history (defeat for the Irish), is entitled to its grave silence. But foxes are returning over the causeways built in Penal days, into Bealadanganm, Annaghvaughan, Gorumna, Lettermore. The ghost of Sir Roger Casement coughs at night in the Hotel of the Isles, as the Atlantic wind rushes through the palm trees outside, and a miserable turf fire dies in the grate. The turf was truly Irish in its elethumania, it would only burn behind bars.

He dreamed of a free Ireland, a nation once again; confided to his diary: 'A world nation after centuries of slavery. A people lost in the Middle Ages refound, and returned to Europe.' But Ireland would never be part of Europe. An earlier historian noted: 'Thus separated from the rest of the known world, and in some sort to be distinguished as another world.' One female slave for three milch cows or six heifers. Between bouts of harsh coughing, Casement wrote: 'Individually the Englishman might be a gentleman, but has no conscience when it comes to collective dealing. Collectively the English are a most dangerous compound and form a national type that has no parallel in humanity.' Waiting for him at their hands: the hangman's noose, Pentonville lime, posthumous disgrace. He like dressing up, adopting disguises, travelling on false passports. He whitened his face with flour, buttermilk, travelled in a German U-boat with a cargo of sanitary pipes, was over-fond of his body-servant Adler Christensen, a man 'of atrocious moral character' wanted by the New York police.

Yesterday I watched a jackdaw being buffeted on a bough of the sycamore in Johnny O'Toole's well-set windbreak, cawing in annoyance or delight, who can say? Today, a loud assembly of crows are there.

The low black devil-dog up the road, who had barked and run away, today crept onto the wall and suffered itself to be patted on the head—an even odder-looking beast when seen close up. A little girl emerged from the model Connemara house. Was it her little dog? Indeed it was. Its name? Elvis.

The O'Tooles were weeding in the windbreak. 'What's this ugly-looking thing growing over here?' Lucy asked her husband, the publican, raconteur, chain-smoker, historian, horticulturist and Fine Gael man. 'Nothing that grows is ugly,' he came back with.

True enough. But little enough grows in Connancht (at least three-fourths of which is less that one hundred feet above the level of the sea) barring ancestral grievances. Lucy's father was a publican too, O'Connor of Salthill, doubtless related to the old ruling sept of O'Conor, former masters of Connacht.

'Whiskey,' the Connemara pony, stands all night sleeping in the frozen paddock, tail to the wind. In a remote bar in bouderstren Drim, I was searched by three youths who said I was an armed UDA man, and they were Provos. Or Cowboys. The door was thrown open, I saw the darkness without. They pointed. In this out-of-the-way region, Ireland's old grudges take on some reality. But who is friend and who is foe? Where is Iar-Connacht, the Celtic Katyn, does the old resentment end? 'Shoot the fucker!' a tall fellow stinking of draught Guinness bawls into my ear-lug. 'Down with the fucker!' The small devious smiling barman who had spoken with some feeling of

King Herod's maggoty corpse, says 'Shussh!' but doesn't mean a word of it, taken with this display of patriotic ire.

'Shoot him! Shoot him!' howls the patriot, pint in hand, safe in this region of Provo sympathisers. The humid smoke-filled bar is in uproar. Cromwell and his dragoons ride down the unfortunate Pierce Ferriter, dispatch him with a sword-thrust through the third rib. Falling in slow motion, Gibson of Ulster is tackled by a group of English defenders. Ireland trained, cooler-headed, calculating, building their attacks. 'Get the boot in!' The narrow old bar by Lynch's Castle is as steamy as a Turkish bath. Ward of Limerick is too late to take the pass, and down goes Gibson, of the North.

Then breaking free from the ruck, the giant Kerry footballer Moss Keane takes possession and sets off alone for the enemy line, felling Sassenach to left and right; an awesome sight, and the bar goes wild. The dense air is friendly yet hostile, a *distilled* hostility. I drink hot toddies with cloves, half pints of Guinness. The rugby players seem to be struggling underwater, scrums agitating the seabed.

Extraordinary clarity of the firmament above the little pier; in our Galaxie those remote small stars do reel in the Skie. In the morning the two hunting seals will come with the incoming tide. At night the air is pure crystal, good as oxygen into the lungs.

Old Brendan Long of Dingle spoke of 'air current.' Tommy Durkhan said that when the sun went down in clouds over Lettermore Hill, it would rain tomorrow; and so far has proved right. In the sodden west the low clouds constantly discharge rain on the land, swans are upended in the small tarns that become lapis lazuli before the stupendous sundowns, created by God or the moisture-laden Atlantic seaboard air.

There is a wren at the door. The place is cold but wholesome. There is a young bird on the water. The man is generous. God is generous. Una is well. The hound is young. The well is clean. Leave a big stool at the door. (Simple Lessons in Irish.) Wishing to be well when not exactly ill. Wishing to be ill when not exactly well. Fog and mist mixed, darkening, and as far out as the wind that dried your first shirt.

Now, framed eerily in the small inset window, a greenish face appears behind rain-bespattered glass, under a greenish pork-pie hat at least one size too small for the head, and long–suffering grayish eyes look sorrowfully into the early morning obscurity of the odorous bedroom where the hessian-covered wall by the bed-head hides the stains caused nightly by the previous owner, a bachelor farmer, in violent projectile vomiting of Guinness over an extended period of time. The window is open a foot, the morning cold comes in. A fine rain falls like some distress of the viscera.

'Your brother!'

We had arranged to meet by the bridge. The Morris Minor needed attention from the part-time mechanic who worked below the bridge in a graveyard of rusty car-parts. A pig named Emily was eating cow dung. Scraping with his fingernail on the glass, greenish-tinged, my brother was so kind as to inform me that one of the cows was bleeding from an udder. I saw the sad profile, the unfortunate sodden headgear; a rain-drip depended from the narrow ill-coloured nose. Under one arm he carried a roof-slate. Behind him the needles of rain.

Well, as a matter of plain fact I had no intention of even venturing out. The rain was slanting in against the thatch, the Maamturks had quietly betaken themselves elsewhere, with flocks of sheep reduced to the size of lice on their flanks. In the sodden west the overhand of clouds was once again leaking rain. Am I or am I not the same person whom I have always taken myself to be? A hundred times no. Brother Coman (the Dote) had as a child a fancy to be a bird, a crow say. We had tamed a jackdaw, converted a biscuit tin into a bird-bath, and in this the fastidious creature bathed daily. Now the rats were frolicking at night in the kitchen until one big buck rat electrocuted itself in the fridge. The stench beggars description. They were carousing on the dregs behind An Hooker, sole owner and proprietor Johnny O'Toole, a man with an acid tongue, when he cared to use it.

The Mental Health Week in Ireland would end, as per advertised programme, at the Great Southern Hotel in Galway, with a Medical Ball. Charlie ('Hot Lips') Haughey, Minister for Health and Social Welfare, would attend. By a chain of accidents, I found myself in the thick of it, having dined that night in the Claddagh Grill on the sixth floor, with a view of Galway Bay through the steamed-up bay window. Some Americans were dining there. Warm white wine, poor service, tasteless fish not fresh from the bay, stained tablecloth, the tally not cheap. I went down in the lift and found them gathering downstairs, the medical clan, the wives and sisters and friends. Below the bust of a cantankerous Roderick O'Connor in the lobby the typed notice was up.

DEPARTMENT OF ANAESTHETIC
HYPERBOLIC UNIT

A demonstration of the Decompression Chamber would be held, God willing, at 10 a.m. on Saturday, October 22nd. Re-compression [sic] Chamber.

By midnight the lone diner who had polished off his dinner with an Irish coffee (*de rigueur* for the *arriviste*) was thoughtfully blowing his nose into a large clean linen handkerchief under the clock in the lobby, Paddy in hand, confused by the hubbub of the medical convention now in full assembly. The excited wives, smoking like paddle-steamers, were getting into their stride. The bearded bust of the patriot O'Connor thoughtfully studied the carpet design, two harps emblazoned on a field of green. Wined and dined elsewhere the wives were already in great form. A serious father carried his small son, in pajamas, up to bed. A group of merrymakers were flabbergasted to run into a group of friends.

'Patcheen!'

'Hairy!'

'Aw Jaysus.'

'Dja know Pechunia?'

Observe the provincial social mill, Irish among Irish, all friends here begob.

'Vinnie, ar ya goen upsteers?'

'Whass upsteers?'

'Dancen.'

Sober men smoking Sherlock Holmes pipes occupy the lounge, amid the gilt and green. The ice will give out long before midnight. Constricted about the hip and bust in Hellenic-style ball-gowns that expose white backs and arms, the wives appear to be in a perpetual froth of excitement, riggish charmers, knowing the minister to be there; rushing from lift to lobby, from bar to lounge, they might just run into him. (But someone was already having a word in his ear; the hooded ophthalmic eyes, vote-catching eyes, looked elsewhere, the head angled to receive a confidence.) Never trust a man with double vents. An employee in green uniform carried a zinc bucket past.

'God forgive me, that's all I'll say.'

'There's no sparks in my lighter!'

The country doctors, no strangers to women in distress, imperturbable men well accustomed to visiting ladies' bedroom, pass nonchalantly from foyer to bar, or from bar to lounge, ball of malt in hand. Later a glass in either hand. Bareback ladies in geranium and raspberry chiffon, with great shoulders white as statuary, faces flushed with spirits and high excitement, take up strategic positions. The minister (smaller than imagined, dapper as George Raft) would surely pass. He was a ladies' man.

Male hotel employees whisper to female employees in green as they pass into a darkened dining-room. A backless strawberry chiffon speaks to a grass chiffon (monumental). Men in dinner jackets walk on the balls of their feet. Green and raspberry chiffon mingle with the mauve and cowslip yellow (a mistake with orange hair), one lady carrying what appears to be a bicycle pump.

'Dermot Kelly—Ann Seymour.'

'Wouldja like a glass of something? . . . a glass of orange or something?'

An old-style hooded pram, with a baby asleep in it, is pushed from the lift at 1:45 a.m., well past a baby's bedtime. The reception lounge is emptying. Roderick O'Connor stares down morosely on emblazoned harps. Chiffon and escorts begin to ascend a long flight of stairs leading to the ballroom above. A buxom wife with fur draped across two-tone off-green hurries through, all business, after the manner of Garbo striding to the elevator in Grand Hotel, preceded by bellhops bearing floral tributes. An employee in morning-bluejacket and black trousers with razor creases carries through a full bucket of water. The doctor with the Don Ameche moustache, who had not moved all night wedged between chiffon and chiffon, is still drinking vodka and orange. A red bow tie meets a suavely affable priest. 'The great bulk of the faithful are ineffable.' The hooded pram is pushed into the darkened dining-room. The last of the dancers have disappeared up the ascent. Frisky music issues thinly from the ballroom. Since ten past midnight, when the minister, summoned by an aide from without (someone was whispering in his ear again), had departed unobtrusively for Inishvickillane, the Medical Ball has been gathering momentum.

'Don't attempt to go, Eugene!'

'Second row? Ho-ho-ho!'

'Second row for Ireland.'

'Aw Jaysus.'

Lobby and lounge are emptying. The women rock on their high heels as though tormented. Room 133 is flooded. A foreign-looking beauty with brown back and fine shoulders is twisting her hips on the sofa, adopting dangerous Theda Bara poses. The Irish-coffee man, still alone, is downing short ones.

'It's never happened to me.'

'He was with you an Tony.'

'The last dance or was it the first?'

'You haven't seen my Kathleen have you?'

'Noooo . . .'

'I'm interested in all Kathleens but my own Kathleen would do.'

A heavy wife has capsized onto an empty sofa and seems in need of air. It's her room that's flooded. A fubsy widow stands before her. 'My room's flooded as well.'

'No!'

'I'll go straight up.'

'You'll do no such thing.'

The spoilsport with legs outstretched is fit to be tied; her complexion high, this has happened before.

Ah, Galway.

The town was founded by the de Burghs in the thirteenth century. In 1498, the curfew was introduced. In 1641, the townspeople were all English. Lord Mayor Richard Brown assured Bingham, the governor of Connacht, that the loyal citizens would 'until the last gasp sustayen all miseries and distresses' to defend it. Cromwell's dragoons stabled their horses in the empty houses. The plantation was arranged by ghosts. Rent had always been high there.

'He told me he was interested in buying a house. I told him no way, there wasn't a chance.'

'How about you an me haven lunch?'

'White socks?'

A press photographer, a seedy Dick Crossman who had

arrived late and half-cut, is now carefully arranging a group of smirking ladies and laughing gentlemen against a wall, for a commemorative group photograph. Though none are too sober, the men are careful not to touch bare female flesh. Four pints of Harp are carried through by two stout drinkers, frowning with concentration.

'We're dyen to see the dance.'

'Is Hilary there?'

'You're crooked.'

'Andy will sort ye out.'

'Mebbe.'

'No maybe about it.'

The ball is ending, the reception desk empty, the hotel staff gone home. It's difficult to get a drink. Mad Meg Magee has arrived, a mighty figure of flushed outrage, come late from some brisk business in Kells. The head waiter is in a huff and refusing to take orders. The bar seems to have been squirted with water. The barmen look as if they have been wrestling, the place deserted but for the usual last carousers, deep in some argument concerning horses. Lobby and Lounge are slowly emptying. From an armchair a lady in astonishing electric blue wishes to discuss amateur drama with me. She come from Nenagh (opening wide her basilisk eye). Nenagh, haunt of dreams!

It's raining in Eyre Square as if it would rain there forever. In the old days the gypsies fought there. In O'Flaherty's B & B, where the Aranmen stay, the beds are hard as penance. The pickpockets too have gone home. Glistening blackly, two powerful cannons point at the ivy frontage of the Galway branch of the Bank of Ireland, the handsomest in the land.

'Oh dear God, it's spillen out of the heavens!'

'See you next year.'

'Be good now.'

Ronda Gorge and Other Precipices

From *Ronda Gorge and Other Precipices*,
Secker & Warburg 1989

SEX MAGAZINES ATTEST to contemporary glut; clipped to the kiosks the toothy photomodels expose a good deal more than their gums. The ancient mossy trees are still in old disarray near the dry riverbed where the last public garotting took place in Málaga. An empty taxi careers past with its indicator raised: 'OCUPADO'.

The passing of the Generalissimo has seen Spain pass, rather awkwardly (there is no other way), into the latter part of the twentieth century, with strikes, pornography and terrorism. Porno movies featured the Fallen Abbess, Anne Heywood, she also feature in *Buena Suerte, Miss Wyckoff* (dir. Marvin Chlomsky). Charlton Heston *[sic]* bares his teeth manfully in *El Desesperado* at the Zaybe. On an old wall in an alleyway near a dusty door is painted 'TOD DEN JUDEN', in a street only fit for pogroms. There is a place for everything, even misfortune, in the Capital of Sorrow.

The very ancient port of Málaga stands for the past; here nothing essential ever changes. Pigs' blood flows into the gutter by the market. Time passes slowly at Portillo, in the shadowy bar Antiqua Casa De Guardia (*fundada en 1840*) Black-clothed widows of Spain walk about in their day of perpetual mourning. Bulky men in gray uniforms convey packages to and from Banco de Bilbao, veritable *postillons d'amour*. In the woodsmelling

wine-bars, stout men in braces are taking their first drink of
Muscatel: '20' is chalked again and again on the knife-scarred
counter, 20 pesetas for a shot of *dulce*. Everywhere I hear that
sad sounding ordinary word: *siempre*. Around the *mercado* by
night there's a dreadful smell of old prick. Málaga is full of fruit.
Admision del Rector! Athens and Málaga are oily cities.

Delicate touchers of cash registers and balancers of scales;
something fresh and fishy is being weighed judiciously. And
always the talk of money, *'dinero'* in the mouths of the pasty-
faced Latin men—*millone*s! King Juan Carlos himself looks
permanently constipated on the stamps. Men are blowing their
noses gustily into clean linen handekerchiefs, while having their
shoes polished. Market women squat on the steps by the bus
terminus for Nerja,

Offering Scotch whisky and French cheese, Calle Córdoba
smells as always, of open drains, dissipation, mournful numbers:
an abattoir stench in the streets of pickpockets, male prostitutes.
Watch-sellers lie in wait near Portillo, a coach is pulling out for
Cadiz. But little by little the pleasing things are going: Hotel
Cataluna closed the Café Español reduced by half.

Ciné hoardings are explicitly horrifying; a naked girl bound
to a stake is fearfully impaled, a wooden dagger protruding from
a mouth pumping blood, watched by bushmen or cannibals
who crouch watchfully nearby. Some artist has rendered a pair
of convulsively clasped hands, naked as fornicating nudes.

Andalucia, Talmudic as anything alive, is made up of
contradictions: ciné advertising become inverted Catholic
iconography outré as ever (the Fallen Abbess); blood still
flows. While a fat fellow with sunken breasts in a Jaeger jersey
stands idle in the doorway of Viajes Marland, not expecting
much in the way of trade. It's going to be another hot day in
Málaga.

After dark in the Cafe Español nine ladies arrive carrying
Menefis plastic shopping bags, dressed in moleskins, with one

fox-fur; rather Germanic in mien, grim of mouth, with blue eyeshadow. Draping the furs over the backs of their chairs, they order Coca Cola and Cognac. An old-style waiter (Wicklow Hotel, Dublin, circa 1946) places a bottle of Cruzcampo at a judious remove between a nervous young couple, having removed the cap with a wristy one-handed pass, looking elsewhere: a polished gesture of exquisite tact.

The grim-mouthed Ingebabies are now joined by three other dressed in more expensive woolen jackets, which they throw over the backs of their chairs. Is it a Counsciousness-raising session at coffee-break or Málaga wives out on the town?

Cat-fur is worn aggressively by the gum-chewing transvestite whores at the Bar Sol y sombra near the market. Vermilion lipstick goes ill with hair dyed off-yellow, saffron wigs, heavy makeup, stiletto heels and deep bass voices. They adjust false bosoms, study the effect in the mirror, eyes flash like Semiramis, ignoring the snickering of the young male barmen. Traffic is heavy to and from the *Señoras*. None of them are being picked up—transvestite whores wild in appearance as pro-footballers at a drag party.

Are the blind lottery-sellers really sightless, or have they induced blindness upon themselves by an act of will? They circulate about the cathedral, tapping with heir white canes. There's much to be seen in Málaga; a strong sense of *déjà vu* permeates it; shoe shops for spastics, religious candles for funerals, china cats stare from shop windows; within— candelabras, dire reproductions of landscapes; casseroles and glassware, dinner-plates in opened crates of wrapping stuff. A fellow is artfully arranging a large fish on a slab. Smell of drains and dust; English faces scored by the winter sun, a last opportunity to swagger a bit.

In the hotel bar above the Alcazaba overlooking the harbor and the bullring, von Stroheim, bald as a coot, riding crop under one arm, sporting spurs, is throwing back double whiskies. A pale-faced barman at La Campana wine bar is deeply immersed in a pornographic magazine printed in Madrid. The evening trade is drinking *Seco Montes, P. Ximen, Agte, Seco Anejo and Málaga Dulce* tapped from the large barrels ranged behind. The *servicio* is as old as all human ills; a dank place with water dripping from above. Málaga always meant the past. Snails are in. Service in the stationary shop is slow even by Andalusian standards; an unseen transistor plays 'Roll Out the Barrel' in a muted way. Girls in school uniforms with hockey sticks pass by. A powerful horse is being played over a path to keep down the dust. The city never changes. A bird sing in a cage. Sallow-complexioned businessmen are ordering *sombras* with *churros* in what is left of the Cafe Español. The Bar Baleares has become yet another shoe shop. Málaga is obsessed by Yo-Yos. Victoria draught beer hard to come by.

Small sailors are propositioning the *chicas*, who parade in pairs giggling; their long hair freshly washed. They are all a-titter; the attentive tars getting nowhere. A collection is underway for the *Asociación Protectora Malaguena de Subnormales*. Landaus drawn by carriage-horses in foolish hats proceed half asleep down Travesia Pintor Nogales, carrying tourists. Saigon has fallen, the English pound is dropping. American public opinion rising. 'TYRANNIQUE OU TROP CONCILIANTE', cry the kiosks. 'SAIGON PANICS AS LAST AMERICAN LEAVES. ANGRY PICKETS LASH TOP JOCKEY WILLIE.' And in a heavy Dutch accent, *Algemeen Daghlad* announced: 'KANS OP CRISES BLIJFT!'

To keep up with the rest of Europe, the crime rate in Málaga has risen; port of call, furlough, of blind men, of graveyard statuary, ornate chess sets. In La Sirena fish-bar by the harbor, the well-heeled clientele are flashing 5,000-peseta notes, not bothering to count the change. The barmen move as elegantly as dancers. Bar Pombo is closed for good. The lottery-man is whistling the opening bas of Beethoven's famous Fifth, the so-called Symphony of Destiny. Blind men go tapping around the cathedral; inside the *Orquesta Sinfonica de Málaga* are offering *Ars angtiqua* (R. Diaz) and *Sinfonia sevillana* (J. Turina). Resident organist: Christian Baude.

When the offices empty, the port hums like a beehive. A vast Soviet tanker lies to in the bay. The wine-bars open. Deviants lurk in the groves of the Alcazaba. In certain tall hotel rooms overlooking stairwells you would suppose yourself back in a previous century. Port of curious chess sets, stonemasons, shoeshine-men selling lottery tickets on the side, vendors and deviants, blind men, operatic traffic policemen in navy blue uniforms with white gloves and white pith helmets, sunglasses *de riguer*, even in dark bars. *Quiosco los Periquitos.*

Black swans with red bills paddle the dirty pond in the Alameda Gardens where a child dressed as a diminutive bride is being photographed by her adoring papa. It's time for lemon tea. Awkward soldiers with close-cropped heads are walking their girls. The sun coursing through the luxuriant overhang of tall palm trees light up the inverts who watch from public benches. Not a crestfallen buttock insight! ASPIRINAS ASPROMANIS! The cathedral bell at midday. EXPLOSIVOS RIO TINTO! Drawn by repetition of clever moves, White cannot escape the check without letting the Black rook join the attack. And if his king tries to hide on 93, we may expect trouble. Platonou and Minic wiped off the board. Adios Quinteros and Browne! The *mariposas* are in a perpetual froth of excitement in the clever mazes of the Alcazaba; lured by the stagy decor, the sudden appearance and disappearance of like-minded lads. *Todaviá no me acostumbro estar frustrado.* So much, as Plato politely phrased it, for such matters.

While modern Spain sprawls along the Mediterranean, busily going to Hell, the ascending new road to Ronda is as extraordinary as the southern approaches to Barcelona. Cut off from the mess of the coastal 'development' and deep in the off-

season, Ronda (850 *metros de altitud,* 32,049 *habitantes*) offers
herself as a kind of Sparta. A bullfighter's town. From here came
Pedro Romero and the great Ordoñez.

The coastal stretch from Málaga to Marbella is as ugly as
the urban development from Salthill to Costello Cross on
Connemara's Atlantic seaboard, allowing the Spaniards slightly
better taste. Up here men with windscorched faces are talking
intently to each other. They are addicts of circles and shades of
green, with the habit of contradicting you ingrained, a Moorish
trait. In Ronda your thoughts fly upwards. Walk on the windy
walls. To live here would be to marry a very strict but beautiful
woman.

The surrounding countryside of undulating hills and far
vistas rivals certain valleys in Yugoslavia near the Austrian
border, or the Transvaal. Beyond the gasoline station (*Zoco
500 metros*) lies the veldt; land the colour of puma, Africa.

And do they love green! Oxidized bronze bells, washed
and bleached army uniforms of Thai-like neatness, worn with
panache under tasseled forage caps, introduce touches of green
everywhere. Into the Bar Maestro—just wide enough for you
to turn around—twitches a grievously afflicted beggar, calling
'BOOoojijjji!' In an alleyway off a nameless street a bar is
crammed with soldiers in green uniforms. PENA TAURINA
ANTONIO ORDOÑEZ, the sign says, swinging in the wind.
A torture-picture: the sad comedy of a reunion of friends.

In Piccola Capri, open at long last, the recorded voice of
Bob Dylan sounds like an unhinged aunt, singing sadly over a
sensational view of the gorge by night. Down there flows Rio
Guardiaro.

I saw a line of hanged victims carved in stone. In the
pedestrian walks I see the finite gestures of bullfighters, jackets
draped over shoulders in torero manner when the weather
permits. The wind sets its teeth into the toreros to be, the Ronda
girls rumpy as *rejoneadores*. Thin shoulders protrude like flying

buttresses. Mauve slack are worn by these addict of *alegría* who spit pipas in the street: flashers of mil peseta notes, dislodgers of preconceptions, relishers of large mushrooms sautéed in garlic, child-lovers, they themselves somewhat childish. A chess competition takes place in what once must have been a Moorish palace. Pena: J. M. Bello'n. *Torneo Social Ajedrez*. For three days the Levant blew a half gale.

Men with convex eyebrows frown thoughtfully into their coffee and cognac. '*Poco diferencia,*' they say, always ready with the qualifying clause, the caesura, the direct contradiction. I have two eyes, I say to the man in the late night bar (we are discussing the 'invisible villages'). No, says he, you have four. It's true, I'm wearing *gafas*.

An old church, I say to the old man in the corner of the *libreria* where I buy carbon paper. No, he contradicts me, not old, only two hundred years—of *Iglesia Nuestra Señora Del Socorro*.

In the Germanic Restaurant Jerez near the bullring a distinguished grey-haired man arrives with a lady in furs. The owner seems to know me, hovers about our table and stares pointedly as if at a long-lost son who refuses to acknowledge his own padre. The noble-looking Frenchman in the neck-brace, hair a sable silver, pulls up his expensive tweed trouser-leg to expose a calf of corpse-like whiteness to the lady in furs who bends forward, slowly removing her sunglasses—'*Ouch, cheri!*'

In the long bar overlooking the plaza a stout man in a Panama hat set at a bullbreeder's angle sits at the counter, plunged in thought. He is joined by men in expensive leather jackets with the swarthy faces of impresarios. A posse of purposeful men with bursting bellies now arrive, roaring for cerveza.

A calm nun in a powder-blue modern habit is transacting some business at the Banco Central. The waiter with the scorched face above his red jacket is playing in an old Simenon thriller, as is the lovely girl who sold me carbon paper in the libreria, as is the contrary old man sitting in the old corner. A thin bell is tolling. The cold in hot countries is absolutely poignant.

The bullring is the largest and most dangerous in all Spain. The New Town is a mess, a sort of Arab shantytown. A ring of towns with odd names face Portugal: Estepa, Eciza, Arcana. On the winding road to Marbella and the desecrated coast lie the 'invisible villages'; not to be missed on any account.

Soon the eastern coastline from Estepona near Gibraltar to Gerona near the French border will have gone the way of Marbella and Torremolinos, and it will be left for hardy souls to move to Pontevedre or La Coruna on the Spanish Atlantic coast. American bombing colonels out from the air-base at Moron de Frontera drink cognac like beer.

From Numina to Nowhere

Paper read at The Importance of Being Elsewhere
festival, Swansea, Bloomsday 1995 (The UK
Year of Literature), with John Banville and Jugo
Hamilton, Ty Llen (National Centre for Wales)

THE WELSH AND the Irish were always elsewhere; isn't that part
of the fabled Celtic charm? Otherwise why the Little People,
semi-invisible Gentry? Why the gorgeous Gaelic? Why song?
Why ancient raths? Why ancestral bores? Why anti-English?
Why magic circles?

Wilde himself, on account of proclivities that would land
him in prison, was "apart" all his life. And who was it saw the
unconscious James Joyce carried out of his Zurich home in a
stretcher, "struggling like a fish" and . . . "apart"? Torn apart.
But hadn't he been "apart" all his life? As Beckett after him.

The writerly function is to see and not be seen, hear and not
be heard. So what are we doing here?

A friend of mine, a congenial sort of chap by the name
of Mooney, a dry-fly fisher on Lough Arrow and Lough Key,
wandered into a Copenhagen bar that specialised in Country &
Western. In his breast pocket a tape of The Chieftains and the
latest Van Morrison fresh off the presses, which he offered to the
woman behind the bar, thinking he was doing her a favour. The
tape-deck was playing some old Danish film music.

'Would you like to try this?' says your man. She took a look
at it, gave a sniff, handed it back, saying: 'Vee don't play that
diddly-diddly shit in the afternoon.'

You will get no diddly-diddly shit here this evening in the very heartlands of Welsh culture, for the trio you see before you are arch anti-traditionalists.

We cannot go on writing novels in a traditional Irish way for the very good reason that one would be poleaxed by a stupor of boredom; although this does not seem to deter some of our contemporaries (whom it would be invidious to name) from ploughing the same old furrow that has been ploughed since O'Flaherty stuck his ploughshare into the old sod.

Don't you expect any of that malarkey here. We are creating a new tradition, and see farther than the old one.

I have lived half my life out of Ireland and would still be living out of it were it not for the cnuás, a living allowance I and some eighty-four other aspirants in the arts receive from a government sponsored annuity disembursed by the Irish Arts Council every quarter, worth £8,000 per annum in 1993. It rises in increments as the cost of living rises. The only stipulation is that you reside in Ireland and produce good work.

The reason I left Ireland in the first place was for much the same reason that the young W.B. Yeats gave up French lessons at Bedford Park in London. The model student was encouraged by the compliments of an aged French mistress, that is until W.B's father sent in his two sisters. Whereupon Willie walked out, never to return. 'How could I pretend to be industrious and even carry dramatization to the point of learning my lessons when my sisters were there and knew I was nothing of the kind?'

A Welshman long ago perceived conquered Ireland as a halfway house to nowhere, a lost misty place stuck out there in the Irish Sea at the back door to the Atlantic.

You must know the man I mean. Geraldus Cambrensis, Gerald of Wales, King Henry II's scribe and factotum, whom I see as tough and wiry and as hard to bring down as Gareth Edwards. It was the same Gerald who wrote famously of Ireland:

'Thus separated from the rest of the known world: and in some sort to be considered another world.' The Celts were the people who came out of the darkness. They brought it with them; it still clings to them. And how can one live your life in such darkness?

I come to Somerset Place by forced marches from Kinsale, which is twinned with fashionable Antibes and that strangely named port called Mumbles, Victoria village and Gateway to Gower. So if there be any from Mumbles here this evening, I bring greetings from your twin across the channel. Hwy!!

We have a dire warning for Mumbles. Two ruthless Kerry Property Developers have bought up the Old Head of Kinsale and are in the process of building a golf course on it, which is rather like building a handball alley on the hill of Tara. The land is infested with theme parks. Now we walk on the Old Head under sufferance, provided we stump up a quid a head. I had stopped going there before the JCBs moved in.

So look out, Mumbles. Hold on to what you have. Hold on to Mumbles Head and Dinosaur Park.

As part and parcel of a general Americanisation, Yankee uplift and hygienic overhaul of the Old Sod, they have a sort of Disneyland Supermart in Portlaoise, of all places (where the Provo freedom fighters are imprisoned, awaiting a free Ireland all in one piece, which they have untidily bombed into shape). The boys will have their sport.

To the matter in hand. Our topic this evening is 'The place of Europe in our lives'. I have lived under a number of dictatorships: Dr Strydom and Verwoerd in South Africa, Franco in Spain, and I am tempted to add de Valera in Ireland of the forties and fifties, operating a rigid Catholic paternalism that had some of the formal elements that make up totalitarianism, beginning with the name of the party. Shin Feign, "Ourselves Alone". Roughly translated from the original Gaelic, it means 'Who-do-you-think-you're-codding?'

Fields Afar, Greater Latitude Antic Hay

Paper read at 10th John Hewitt international Summer School at Carnlough, Co. Antrim on 30 July 1997

I WAS TAKEN aback yesterday listening to Professor Kearney's brilliantly allusive paper, with its references to eight-winged swans as insignia for a united federated Europe and ideal French communes of ten souls, which made my paper seem very flimsy in comparison.

But no matter. It was after all only talk; and had I not once attended another such seminar on the same theme, the troubles in the North (the subject we are still debating), and that was all of twenty years ago at the University of British Columbia in Vancouver.

At the luncheon up stood a stout, apparently sober Professor to deliver the keynote address; which turned out to be an all-purpose paper used before, pointing out deficiencies and educational drawbacks in Chairman Mao's Red China. This is, I believe, what is known in soccer circles as 'action off the ball'.

Dr Conor Cruise O'Brien—not one man but three, his enemies averred—had been invited to speak but did not show up. Roy Foster stood in for him.

Last Saturday *The Irish Times* carried a plug for the John Hewitt Summer School, informing its readers that the theme this year was 'Beyond the Planter and the Gate.' Is this the gate that won't open? John Hewitt was certainly a Dissenter, but

Montague, who spent years in Paris attempting to turn himself into a convincing Frog, seems to me a most unlikely Gael.

What is my nation? Shakespeare asks.

Bloom, one man living all his life in one place, was a one-man nation, sneered at and abused by the rest of the nation because he wasn't Jewish. The smaller the nation, the bigger the neurosis.

My old friend Arland Ussher, Ireland's last philosopher (who had no philosophy), wrote 'History's pomps are toylike.' We learn mortality from our father and civic virtue in the form of good manners from our mother, and learn our history—always long and cruel—in the nursery.

Down south, where I come from, we have two languages at our disposal: an official one that few understand, on street signs and on official notepaper, and a secret language that appears to be standard English but is not; its Gaelic roots are betrayed by certain very un-English formulations and constructions that were more evident in the 1930s when I was young, before that rough beast TeeVee slouched into every home and began to take over.

We do not live in an ideal world and it would be intolerable if we did; the burden of the past is a heavy one which all must bear.

'Beyond the Planter and the Gael'

My credentials are that I've published ten books in forty years of episodic labour and lived under three dictatorships in three different countries—four if you count the land-island called Berlin in the seventies; a land-island a hundred miles deep within the GDR, up tight within one of the capacious pockets of the USSR. The dictatorships were: Ireland in the 1940s and 50s in the time of de Valera and Archbishop McQuaid; South Africa in the time of Verwoerd and Strydom, Spain in the time of Franco. I was living in Johannesburg at the time of the Sharpville massacre in March 1960 and in Munich in September 1972 at the XXth Olympic Games and the slaughter of eleven Israeli atheletes.

South Africa was a true ethnic mess. Afrikaaners mistrusted the English, both oppressed the African, whom the Coloureds did their best to cheat. English-speaking South Africans who voted for the United Party in the shape of the absurd Sir de Villers Graaf mounted on his high white horse, spoke of the 'goold old Yew Kay' as their ancestral home; but Afrikaaners who voted for Verowerd and Afrikaanse Nationalism and nationhood had no such delusions about ever returning to Holland. South Africa was their home.

For Berliners in their walled and divided city, it didn't feel like the city they had known; they couldn't take a stroll down Unter den Linden nor take an outing to Potsdam nor make a phone call into the GDR, over the Berlin Wall. Our landlady, Frau Meinhardt, a foursquare Hausfrau from Wiesbaden with a husband killed in Russia, said the heart had moved, away from Unter den Linden, moved westward to be away from the Russians.

I was brought up in Dev's Ireland; a period of a benign paternalistic dictatorship brought to a farcical close when Archbishop McQuaid took it upon himself to ban *The Dark*, John McGahern's most innocuous novel. The author was subsequently sacked from his teaching post in the National School at Clontarf; McGahern had compounded his offense (written a dirty book) by going through a form civil marriage with a Finnish lady in a Registry Office.

A sequel to this ban took place some years later when *The Dark* was brought out in Braille, making it possible for blind Irish to read prohibited matter deemed too unwholesome for "sighted" Irish, out of whose hands it was wrenched by the irate Archbishop.

Dev and his appointee, McQuaid, the former Dean of Studies at Blackrock College in my father's time, between them were determined to keep Ireland pure and uncontaminated by European filth; we had our own gas-cleansing stations and cleaning up operations just as effective as those put into operation by the Nazis on the Soviet Russian Front.

In the 1950s I travelled through South Africa and what were then the Two Rhodesias, now Zimbabwe from Namaqualand to Ndola, and Zambia; a period that came to a close with Sharpville, an action that sounded the knell of doom for apartheid.

Public benches in Johannesburg were marked BLANKES or NIE-BLANKES, European or Non-European, depending on colour and race, either Aryan, African or Asiatic—what were called Cape Couloured, the shopkeepers of the Cape Province. Non-European was an euphamism for 'non-person', non-existent, that is except as female cook or washerwoman or a male refuse collector. The voteless Africans and Coloureds perambulating the streets of Pretoria, Bloemfontein and Port Elizabeth were invisible to their White overlords passing in large air-conditioned limousines; as were the Africans digging drains under an African ranger supervised by a White overseer, as his White shadow, his minder. As far as the Whites were concerned, the Blacks didn't exist, although the streets were full of them, forbidden to beg, squatting along the pavements, the more ambitious ones studying law books.

I was browsing in a Johannesburg bookstore when an African sidled in and asked the haughty lady at the cashdesk had they *This Gun for Hire,* one of Graham Greene's Entertainments. She couldn't refuse to serve him, so she affected not to understand what he was saying; or perhaps she didn't know what he was saying. If he wasn't talking English, he shouldn't be in a bookshop, so she couldn't help him. He was a stroppy Munt, and she wouldn't serve him.

Blind Borges of Buenos Aires wrote that the absence of

camels in the Koran was a sure proof of its authenticity; for a fake Koran written by an imposter would have droves of camels in it. Similarly the fact, the indisputable fact, that White South Africans could not see their Black brethren whom they contemptuously dismissed as Munts or bleddy Kaffirs, was a sure sign that they were there (even as anti-matter that has mass but cannot be seen) in their teeming millions, abjectly present as a rank-smelling obscenity in the fastidious nostrils of all Whites. For nothing is less visible to the naked eyes of the well-heeled than the destitute of another race whom they don't wish to see, or even smell.

Now to take a great leap back into history: Aubrey in his *Brief Lives* tells a pretty story about protocol in the court of the first Elizabeth of England. The story goes that while making a deferential obeisance to the throne, the feather of his cap sweeping the floor, one elegant leg thrust out, Sir Walter Raleigh broke involuntary wind all too audibly, which the Queen affected not to notice. Raleigh, who consorted with whores before breakfast, was of course deeply ashamed of himself. He took ship and sailed away as far as possible out of sight and hearing of his Queen, and stayed there, taking 'purchase' and prizes left and right on the high seas; until he judged that it was safe for him to return again with his spoils as presents and peace-offerings to the Queen, before presenting himself at court where all had long since been forgiven and forgotten.

Little did he know his Queen!

In he marched, putting as brave a face on it as he could, preceded by sackbuts and trumpets playing and ladies-in-waiting batting their eyelashes at him, to once again make a cautious low obeisance to the Queen, who greeted him roundly: 'Welcome back, my lord. We hath quite forgot the fart.'

In those free and easy days if a Queen disapproved of your politics or perceived you to be a threat, she could have your head cut off, the fate that befell the luckless Mary Queen of

Scots. Her last interrogation, taken down on the spot by a scrivener, has been recovered and is up for sale. She proclaimed her innocence to the end; she had never acted against Elizabeth.

A Russian-American lady in Texas told me that she, Mary Queen of Scots, had hidden her favourite Skye terrier under her crinoline as she knelt at the block and begged Almighty God to take her soul into His hands.

'Every family has its secret word,' wrote Harold Nicolson, the diplomat and author, dismissed as 'soft & domestic' by Virginia Woolf in one of those acid diaries of hers; his son Nigel fares no better—'the bolshie with dirty feet'.

What Harold had in mind, I think, was a pet name, a fond nickname that would also be an endearment, combined with an endorsement and guarantee of worth in the constant replenishment required by People of Substance; and itself a reflection in the sheer delight of being fine and setting an inordinate value on the pedigree; the worth was that emblazoned upon the family escutcheons of the Nicolsons and the Sackville-Wests of Sissinghurst.

Writer and sceptic Paul Theroux touches on this, when referring to Samoa and Robert Louis Stevenson: 'Fiction has the capacity to make even an ordinary place seem special. The simple mention of the name of a place can make that place become singular, never mind what it looks like.'

The secret word was a coded term known only to initiates, those gathered intimados within the family circle, the all-knowing inner ring of the privileged.

Elizabeth Bowen, aged five, was walked by her young English governess in the purlieus of Herbert Place in a fashionable part of Dublin and spied above the rooftops 'a sky for the favoured', Irish Anglicans and Roman Catholics would see different skies, as would the rich and poor of Dublin, and in those days the poor were indeed very poor and wanting; that impoverishment meant living on the rim of subsistence. For Catholics and Protestants the very air was different.

Many of our Anglican opponents from Campbell College and Portora Royal School, Beckett's alma mater, had this distinctly sallow or olive complexion.

I tried to recall what Chateaubriand had said of Emperor Napoleon on horseback—the olive skin of the Corsican had a hint of oxidised copper green, as though the Emperor were already turning into a bronze equestrian statue fit for some town square in France, already a public monument.

The Protestant complexion par excellence is the colour of watered-down maple syrup or weathered walnut; the product of a sound diet, good regular meals and exercise (exaggerated in the case of the cricketers by the unfamiliar squandered peaks of cricket caps striped transversally in school colours, the pink and white of Peggy's Leg or Bullseyes) which seemed to go with fierce double-barrel names (Blood-Smith), togged out in spotless white flannels with razor-sharp creases and haughty I-don't-give-a-damn accents of Douglas Jardine, skipper Brown with-neck-cravat, Ted Dexter clouting sixes over the sightscreen. A rich patina betokening Substance and Privilege, as the gaze on fruit in the market, the down of fine skin.

Who can say but that these sallow-skinned Protestant fellows found us Catholic cricketers (a contradiction in terms here) as peculiar and unsettling as we found them, and they read in our school caps not Clongowes or Castleknock or Belvedere but the dark confessional, the Latin Mass, Jesuit casuistry, priests in alpaca gowns with wings, rising incense, open air Benediction and the Stations of the Cross—archaic forms of worship prior to the time of Henry VIII. And this, mark you, in a batting list that included Kelly, McAllister, Lynch, Mooney, and McCann.

Gray and even black Protestants have always featured in our simple-minded rural mythology, as do lamb-killing scald crows and the black flocks of predators that take wing of a morning to raid the young wheat and barley.

The Reverend Riversdale Colthurst, a retired Anglican divine and honorary member of Greystones Golf Club, was the bane of my life when I lived in that Protestant enclave and was a member of the same club; Greystones, Co. Wicklow being the preferred place where Protestants retired to die.

Edwin Lutyens, Ned to his bosom friends. was the most eminent of Edwardian architects in his day and fell madly in love with Lady Emily Sackville, bossy mother of the distraught daughter in flared riding britches who had a crush on Mrs Woolf.

Ned and Lady Emily conducted an correspondence, she signing herself 'MacSack' and he 'MacNed'.

Word games, gnomic utterances favouring one's kith and kin (and belongings and pets), fanciful names—all are forms of high-minded play-acting. As are buying presents, remembering birthdays, inviting friends to stay, sacking servants, buying stuff for dresses, croquet on the lawn, charades in the conservatory in inclement weather.

The lower orders of course do not play games, being much too busy working cut their own miserable destinies, performing endless chores, toting wood and coal. Servants, observed Virginia Woolf with acute disdain, smell (unless it was the dog Pinka she had in mind).

And was there not some choleric Colonel or Brigadier in the British Army who was taken aback to see his men in the buff swimming in a river and all of them white as slugs, when he had expected them to be covered hair?

My parents were what is called non-practising Catholics, though my mother took Holy Communion in her bed every five years or so, serviced by an obliging Parish Priest who came on his pushbike from the village a mile away.

Pet names are a guard against loss, like primitive music. Songs and tunes unsung and unplayed drift away, fail into abeyance: and if unplayed and unsung for long enough can only return in strange and hard!)' recognisable forms.

You may recall the ancient Indian brass band that played in the movie Pather Panchali, S. Ray, one of the great Apu trilogy. The wrinkled ancients played this antiquated broken-down music, apparently Indian music but Indian music with a pain in its gut, a dirge for summoning snakes; they seemed to be playing it undewater or deep in the jungle. The old familiar tune came back in bits and pieces that seemed vaguely familiar but now shattered like broken teeth. But it had come back—it was, it surely was Tipperary!

You must go a long way from home in order to feel free to write. Forty years ago in King Williams Town in the Eastern Province of South Africa, under a fig tree in the sloping garden of my wife's parents, he German and she Welsh in the time of Verwoerd, drinking gin and tonic and reading Gibbon in the shade, in blistering summer heat, I thought myself liberated enough to write about sodden Kildare where I had been born and brought up. For no one could see me under the fig tree, having come across God knows how many time zones and meridians and lines of latitude; free at last to write as I pleased, just to do as I pleased.

Thirty and more years later in Kinsale, when I was working on *Donkey's Years*, the key that unlocked the door that had been locked for so long, as long as my parents lived and longer, was by calling my mother 'Mumu' and my father 'Dado'. Not Mater and Pater, nor Mom and Pop, nor Mum and Dad, nor Mummy and Daddy, nor Ma nor Da, nor any of those clinging endearments by which children seek to bind their parents to themselves.

For had I called them Mum and Dad, they were likely to be Anglo-Irish Protestant, and had I called them Ma and Da they were certain to be Roman Catholics, but by calling them Mumu and Dado I had freed them and myself too. and created an impossible pair in the Celtic Garden of Eden—an Irish rural couple who were neither Protestant nor Catholic, I let them be themselves and judged them accordingly; and the children turned out to be just as non-denominational. my three strange brothers.

If every family has its secret word (every privileged family with primary and secondary education followed by university), the same is true of languages: every language has its secret word.

The Spanish have a very beautiful secret word for something that slugabeds will never see, what the maddened prizeman James Joyce called 'the deletful hour of dungflies dawning': *madrugada*. In the Iberian peninsula where things grow prodigiously, they have more than one secret word. They have Lorca's word: *duende*. A word for the spirit that dwells in or around a thing, be it animate or inanimate. A matador fighting a bull can attain *duende*; it's something that exists in the arabesques and sarabands that bull and matador in dancing pumps make in the scuffed sand by the barrier or out in the middle of the bullring, and is as visible as valour for those with eyes to see.

In Andalucia they have an even more beautiful word— *Querencia*, which is the area in the bullring where the bull mistakenly believes itself to be safe when in fact its fate is already sealed by the long lances of the picadors mounted on their knacker's yard nags; as during the Civil War the citizens of Madrid mistakenly believed that a certain part of the city was safe from Franco's bombs dropped from the air by the Condors; or as the daughter of my amigo Tony Kerrigan believed her bedroom in Dos de Mayo in Majorca to be a safe refuge, her own *querencia*. A child's 'secret place' is the *querencia* nonpareil.

The older way in Irish writing, so prone to please, was to show a world where everything was familiar, if mundane; an indulgently upraised forefinger, mark you this. The modern style attempts the opposite: to discredit all such complacency and show a world where virtually nothing is secure.

Unfolding history (the cry in the street) is now perceived as a tattered concordat, all dying fails, like Murphy's mind, the younger Beckett's too. That melancholy man Adorno argued that today it is part of morality not to be at home in one's home; for 'wrong life cannot be lived rightly'.

I read somewhere that all thought, all successful thought, all language that grips and the words whereby we then recognise the writer, are always the result of a compromise between a current of intelligence that emerges from the writer and an ignorance that befalls him, a surprise, a hindrance. The rightness of an expression always a remnant of hypothesis. Riviere writing to try and curb Artaud's demented ravings put it like this: 'In order for the mind to tap its full power, the concrete must serve as the mysterious'.

John Beckett. Sam's cousin, but earlier in the book Jonce asked him what it was he valued most in his own work. Without batting an eyelid, Sam said: 'What I don't understand.'

Sir Joshua Reynolds stood before his sitter as if standing before unexplored territory. Kandinsky loved circles and what he termed 'the spiritual perfume of a triangle'. I once heard the pianist Arthur Rubenstein in a BBC interview refer to a link between the thing played and the thing recalled: 'It's a bit dryish you know. A bit dry at first. But suddenly the piano begins to smell. Perfumed you know.'

When Rubenstein played a Chopin Nocturne (the piano 'a disguised percussion, instrument') he released the trapped perfumes of Poland, the pale creepy sick Pole with the long fingers who had a way with the ladies.

Once in New York Rubenstein was getting out of a yellow cab outside Madison Square Garden where he was to play that night. Rehearsals had not gone well and he was in a vile mood, paying off the cabby, who asked "Is there a fight on here tonight, Mister?"

'There sure is,' snapped Rubenstein. 'I'm going to fight the piano.'

'The Pianna,' cried the cabby. 'Say, mister, ain't that the Mexican champ?'

Rubenstein, now in a thoroughly good humour, tipped handsomely.

'You said it,' laughed Rubenstein. 'It's going to be a tough fight.'

Anthropologists tell us that the savage's idea of a piano is: 'You fight'im, 'e cry!'

Speaking of savages, the world wherin he found himself must have appeared inconceivably strange and threatening to the eyes of Prehistoric Man; for no names had as yet been assigned to anything and that included himself, the first Wee Man, numero uno setting out on the long journey from Numina to Nowhere. All else was amorphous protozoic slime, depthless and repellent, as all that moved on the earth or slopped about in the mud or swam in water or flew overhead or lurked in jungles, all were seen as potential enemies, always ravening and raving.

Nursery rhymes, the laying on of curses, prison jargon, the trance-speech of spirit mediums, the last words of the dying, the little language of lovers where the loved one is likened to monkey or snake, all are secret languages. In Franco's Spain in the time of the little Generalissimo, the one word you never heard on the lips of Spaniards (unless it was a Guardia Civil), the taboo word that must never be spoken aloud, was 'Franco'.

In the officers' mess in the time of the Indian Raj the name of Gandhi was taboo. Writers should learn to keep their traps shut. For a writer's life is no more intrinsically interesting than that of carpenters, plumbers, lathe-turners and window cleaners; and rather less so than those of burglars, cardsharps, sword-swallowers, snake charmers and nocturnal poachers.

Cantraps of Fermented Words

Paper read at the Cheltenham Festival of Literature, 12 October 1997

As YOU MAY know, Mr James Joyce was an uncommonly over-wrought type of person, a past master of discursiveness, who in his youth had written a turgid short novel called Stephen Hero. For almost two decades towards the end of his life, he had occupied himself assembling the component parts of *Finnegans Wake*, that baggy monster to end all baggy monsters, with all its intestines on view, inside-out like the Pompidou Centre in Paris. It was an enormously difficult jigsaw puzzle; a mosaic laid out on the table, an insoluble conundrum.

Mr James Joyce of Trieste and Paris was a great bamboozler, a magician with rings on his fingers and bells on his toes and a mouthful of rotten teeth, who with patent dishonesty displays that he is hiding nothing up his sleeve. *Finnegans Wake*, the prototypal do-it-yourself novel, asks of the puzzled reader that he or she join him in complicity to put the thing together, reassemble it, unravel it, decode it.

Mr Joyce's first disciple was Mr Sam Beckett of Foxrock, a solitary withdrawn man, ever the prodigal son, ineffably detached, Master of the Leopardstown Half-lengths, master of brevity, who had written a couple of ersatz novels, Synoptic Gospels that were a gloss on the 'authentic weakness of being', dispensing in a lordly way with characters, chapters, paragraphs, punctuation.

L 'Innomabie and Comment c'est (*The Unnamable* and *How*

It Is) were intended as a test of the slovenly reader's patience; severe works with this in common: the author's adamant refusal to try and amuse us.

The Good Lord did not put us on this earth to be amused.

It all boils down to a question of words. Eudora Welty wrote a story set in the Old Natchez Trace during 'the bitterest winter of them all' in Mississippi in January 1807. A deaf mute of twelve years shocked into dumbness by the death of his parents, is astonished to see speech made visible in the freezing air:

> He saw the breaths coming out of people's mouths. It was marvellous to him when the infinite of speech made visible in the freezing air: speech became visible in formations on the air, and he watched with awe that changed to tenderness whenever people met and passed in the road with an exchange of words. He walked alone slowly through the silence and let his own breath out through his lips, pushed it into the air, and whatever word it was took the shape of a tower.

A writer who shall be nameless for the moment, with three novels published which had failed to make any impression, found himself at the age of forty-three struggling with a fourth novel provisionally entitled *If I Forget Thee, Jerusalem*, which gave much trouble during the seven interminable months of a painful gestation, to be conceived and delivered to the publisher 'in anguish and travail'. He wrote to his editor, uncertain whether what was being offered was 'drivel' or 'absolute drivel':

> It was written just as if I had sat down on one side of a wall and the paper was on the other and my hand With the pen thrust through the wall and writing not only on invisible paper but in pitch blackness too, so that I could not even know if the pen still wrote on the paper or not.

I may say that the author concerned was not one of your crafty practitioners who never had the slightest doubt as to the true commercial value of merchandise that sold well, nor the least qualms in energetically promoting the stuff.

Random House accepted the novel, the 'absolute drivel', changed the title from *If Forget Thee, Jerusalem* to *The Wild Palms*, rearranged the chapters to make the whole incomprehensible to the astutest reader and brought it out in 1939, which I don't have to tell you was a bad year to bring out anything.

The chastened author, William Faulkner, had to wait another thirteen years before it was published on this side of the Atlantic, and another twenty-two years before the contents were rearranged as originally intended, by which time he was eight years dead.

Not long before this, he had moved to Charlottesville, Virginia, leaving behind him Frenchman's Bend and Sutpen's Hundreds, Jackson and Jefferson and the hotbeds of Memphis brothels and the appropriated Chickasaw Indian land that he had made legendary.

I have made stabs at writing a novel and published five works purporting to be novel, at least three of them miserable failures, absolute drivel, duds, dead stars. I spent eight years on one that died the death; all that remained carbonised in the refinery was what Joyce called 'cantraps of fermented words'.

When I began using words in German, Danish and Spanish, three languages I cannot speak, and then inverting those words, I knew I was in trouble, and had come up against a dead-end wall.

Whether contracted or expanded into infinity, the novel by and large is good for nothing unless it's bursting at the seams, as a stout party frustrated and irked by braces or corset. Faulkner himself admitted that he never knew where one of his novels was leading him until it took off of its own accord around page 70.

Nabokov would not accept the hoary old truism—that characters take over and write the novel—which he declared was a lie 'old as the quills'. His characters would never take over; they were mere galley slaves.

Suffice it to say that behind every text of any value lies a sub-text; lurking behind the superstructure of the ultra modern Ulysses, with all its shabbiness intact and still ahead of its time—lies old Homer's ultra-ancient Odyssey, the model of models and numero uno amid the Master Plasters.

In writing, either autobiography or fiction, as with painting or Pelman Patience, we have one of the very few silent occupations left to us; an occupation as silent as fishing or burglary. The text composed by the author in silence apart from heartfelt groans and deep sighs is read, partaken, by you, the silent reader, in search of an ideal insomnia. And to have this silent stuff read aloud to you by the author in person, can be a dire experience akin to being clapped into the stocks and pelted with rotten garbage, shat upon by civit cats, or being introduced into a roomful of strangers you do not know.

That world-besotted traveller Paul Theroux has some unkind things to say of British literary festivals in general and the Cheltenham Festival in particular, in his artful pseudo-autobiography *My Other Life*:

Cheltenham—a tea party as big as a town, books as theatre, writers as performers. Dogs walking on their hind legs were what I thought of. It was bad for everyone. The people watching should have been home reading, the writers either should have been writing or else doing something equally dignified—anything except blabbing and making faces.

On the Rack

A paper read at the Cuit International Festival of
Literature at Galway on 24 April 1999

IF A PROFESSIONAL jockey were to admit to you that he didn't
like horses, no doubt you would be much amazed. Perhaps you
would be less surprised were a professional writer to tell you that
now he never sets foot inside a bookstore, whether or not they
display copies of his books there, because such places depress
him.

Some thirty-three years ago I was living in Dublin as the
beneficiary of a small retainer from the publisher Calder which
would be just enough for me to live on in Spain with a wife and
three children to support.

One morning, judge of my delight upon receiving galleys of
my first novel, *Langrishe, Go Down,* from Grove Press which was
to publish it in tandem with John Calder, the canny Scot. The
highly paid New York publishers who had already set up such
malodorous metropolitan fizzbangs as William Burroughs's
Naked Lunch, Hugh Selby Jnr's *Last Exit* to Brooklyn, Alexander
Trocchi's *Cain's Book*, and last but not least in malodorousness
Henry Miller's *Tropic of Cancer*, had little interest in Irish
country matters set in the 1930s. At the top of each galley,
not pasted on but printed out, appeared their idea of a more
appropriate title, punched out 280 times:

LANGRISHE, GO HOME!
LANGRISHE, GO HOME!!
LANGRISHE, GO HOME!!!

As an ex-Catholic, I couldn't imagine a stranger surname than Langrishe. Beckett, as an ex-Anglican Dissenter, couldn't think of stranger (to his ears) Catholic surnames than Murphy, Molloy and Malone, odd-sounding to Anglican ears at least, as the Dobbs and Pearsons of the Trinity quad to my Catholic ears. Prods all.

A year before this (in 1966, the year my mother died) *Langrishe* had come out in London to some little acclaim; Book of the Month selection and praised by Penelope Mortimer in *The Observer*, condescendingly so by the other known critics of the posher Sunday blatts. Beckett happened to be in London, rehearsing one of his plays, and I asked him as a great favour to come to a friend's house in Camberwell to meet a few ardent admirers of his.

McGahern, ever modest and thinking himself unworthy to unloose the latchet of the great man's shoes, slipped off. It was like having an eagle-owl or even a great vulture in one's living room, when Beckett arrived with a small entourage. It had been a tiring day for him and he was exhausted. He did not say much, rustling his feathers and fetching up heavy sighs, as if weighed down by captivity. Of course he was frightfully polite, answering questions and staring at guests with his fierce eyes. But no questions were asked; photographer Goldblatt kept his Leica well out of sight. My wife, somewhat importunate, pressed him for his candid opinion of *Langrishe*. He said he had only read half of it so far and didn't wish to give an opinion. When she still pressed him, wine speaking, Beckett, in exasperation (feathers rising), finally burst out: 'If you want to have my opinion, I think it's literary shit and he knows it!'

Well, talk about backhanders!

Next morning I said to my wife: 'Let's go down to Zwemmer's and see how the literary shit is selling.' So we sallied out. I had never actually seen anyone purchase one of my (two) books. It might be as exciting as fly-fishing on the banks of Lough Key with Mooney, or fishing for salmon in the Corrib. We took a bus to Tottenham Court Road and in Zwemmer's left-hand window, lo and behold, nice as ninepence and resplendent in puce (not snot) green stood a clothbound copy of *Langrishe*.

There was another copy on the display rack for Recent Fiction. "Let's hang about a bit", said I. Presently in sidled a stout, shifty-looking fellow wearing a loose-fitting pea-green naval-type duffel coat, still favoured by some of the London intelligentsia and Michael Foot. He began browsing about by the Recent Fiction rack and soon enough—trout risen on the Nore—laid a chubby hand on *Langrishe* and (trout swallowing hook) began turning over paces, enraptured, eyes bugging out of his head.

Not wishing him to catch me staring, I moved to the back of the bookstore, keeping him in view all the time. He kept turning pages; he was caught! We watched him loiter near the pay desk and then stroll out with his hands in his pockets, cool as a cucumber, whistling. There went a happy man: he had nicked the single copy of *Langrishe* from the rack.

I approached the gentleman bookseller, who was gazing over our heads as though he had better things to think of, and inquired politely how *Langrishe* was doing. 'We have it in our window,' fluted he, 'and one copy in the Recent Fiction rack.'

'You *had* it in the Recent Fiction,' I told him, 'but you don't have it anymore. Look for yourself.'

Well, talk about bluster! His face dropped, I can tell you, and we left him rummaging about amid the non-fiction, just in case it had got mixed up in the stock.

That evening at the Calder launch, high up in New Zealand House and sponsored by a dry martini company, the man from

Zwemmer's sidled up to me and was at pains to tell me that I'd 'got it all wrong'.

'How so?'

Why, the mysterious browser in Zwemmer's had been one of their own reps sent hotfoot from another branch, which had sold out and needed copies for the window display. It was selling well enough.

'Was he wearing a duffel coat?' I asked.

It is a truism, though perfectly true in this case, to say that writers have only one book in them, and keep on rewriting it, like bores who drone on and on, until it becomes a parody of itself. The better the writer, the more blatant the parody. You're not going to sit there and tell me that William Trevor doesn't parody himself, as did O'Flaherty before him, as do McGahern and Banville after him, bringing out parodies of previous books with every new one they publish, stuck with their particular themes, their *idée fixé*.

I dare say that Roddy Doyle and Frank McCourt began parodying themselves as soon as they put pen to paper. Even Faulkner and Hemingway blatantly parodied themselves in their later work. It is almost agreeable to read bad Faulkner, Bill gone wrong (*A Fable*), but bad McGahern gives me stomach cramps (*Amongst Women*, the publisher's title; McGahern was stuck for one, and no wonder).

When I myself began writing, I found I could write about Ireland only by pretending that it was Germany; Howth had to become Heidelberg. Fiction, I found, was always a sort of disguised autobiography. Now that I have turned resolutely towards nature and write only pseudo-autobiography, I find it becomes more and more a disguised fiction of sorts, a stream of fiction thinly disguised as fact. One should swallow a toad every morning, said some wise old Frenchman, in order to be sure of not encountering something still more disgusting before the day is over.

I may be writing pure fiction, or as pure as fiction can get. I have just finished *The Whole Hog*, the hindquarters of the panto-horse that began with *Donkey's Years*. The mid-section was *Dog Days*, and the brothers who were formerly swans have reverted to type and turned themselves back (or been turned back), all become umbrellas again. For a brother, as James Joyce said rather cruelly, is as easily forgotten as an umbrella.

Gertrude Stein, that heavy totem figure of the nineteen twenties, wrote somewhere that fathers were depressing. 'Mothers may not be cheering but they are not as depressing as fathers.' But one's father is not so easily shaken off as that, not off the son's back anyway. There he belongs and clings, as the Old Man of the Sea clung limpet-like to Sinbad's back, an insufferable burden to be carried all his life. Amos Oz wrote of the father living in the son, something to be borne.

Don't you abhor novels with strong fathers in them? I know I do; they wear me out, particularly Irish fathers. Elizabeth Bowen gives a lovely picture of her father in *Seven Winters*. The Russians saw fathers as familiar demons—old Karamazov. A power of Irish fiction pullulates with bogus fathers.

Can it be that one writes in order to contain or symbolically kill the father in one, do away with him? Samuel Butler did it in *The Way of All Flesh*, and Paul Durcan, the Irish Villon, has a stab at it in *Daddy, Daddy*, one of the most subversive short works we have. Durcan is killing the Judge (who happens to be Judge Durcan) and screaming for mercy at the same time.

Alright, alright . . . perhaps not even to kill (we have far too much of that in Ireland); to pry loose the father, who holds tenaciously on in order to confound him, prove him wrong. My own father, if he was anything, was a loving father, but have I not all my writing life attempted to show that even love cannot be trusted? Love Irish-style is a sort of roundalay of family psychopathology, a simmering Irish stew.

News flash! Forget about fathers, the sequel to *Angela's Ashes* will be toddling along any day now; 'tis called *'Tis*. Yes, *'Tis*. As in *'Tis a Godawful Long Way to Tipperary*'. Except 'tis poor Limerick about to get it in the neck again, when the hype gets going, like a thousand bomber raid on Dresden. What is it about this man that so fascinates? I have a feeling that the punters, who read the frantic publicity, do not read the book.

The French and the Americans have always swallowed great dollops of lies and distortions about our fair land. You get the Hollywood lies about the Old Sod and the stock-types who occupy it in Ford's embarrassing *The Quiet Man* rivalled in vulgarity only by David Lean's *Ryan's Daughter*. The English and American notion of Ireland is not so much a land of cockaigne as a cockeyed land. But, goodness me, you can't wear the Irish public out; never, when dollopping out the grossest flattery.

The common man or the common woman certainly cannot bear very much reality. They, expecting to be entertained, the he of it and the she of it, have an inexhaustible appetite for the meretricious; even the third and fourth rate will do. Else why should 600,000 punters (suckers, dupes of the conmen in sharp publicity) run out and buy *Angela's Ashes*?

Nuala O'Faolain's *Are You Somebody?* sold 700,000 copies. I doubt whether two volumes of my tripartite pseudo-autobiography sold 4,000 copies between them, having been swallowed up three times by ever bigger consortia and conglomerates: Reed Books swallowed Secker & Warburg, and Random House swallowed Reed and the German Bloatermann swallowed them all, though Slicker & Windbag is still there, silent and motionless in the great whale's belly, and I am inside the smallish belly of Secker, Jonah studying his fingernails.

Should you detect a hint, a small hint, of sour grapes in all this palaver, you would be right. I was reared on sour grapes, a sick person's preferred treat. The Germans have a saying: the father has eaten sour grapes and the children's teeth are put on edge. One finds oneself in that ineffably sad Neverneveryever land of the book retail warehouse of returns and remainders, a place unknown to McCourt, the misery-maker of Limerick.

Payee No. 2201452 in the Secker & Warburg royalty listing is one Higgins, with two titles remaindered and four more not selling and destined to follow them. More than likely to go that way, into remaindership, the Valhalla of all scribblers who put things off.

I declare myself the implacable foe of the Sob Sisters; I am ever on the side of the Fabulists. Oh for God's sake hand me the smelling salts!

Musing

Paper read at The Lord Kingsale,
Kinsale, 30 March 1998

PUBLIC READINGS CAN be tricky affairs. There is nothing more calculated to cause a gritting of the teeth, a shudder of the spirit or even a rising of the gorge than to be voluntarily confined in a Function Room to endure an hour-long ranting by the author in person, of pre-digested matter now regurgitated, delivered in a monotonous drone. It is enough to make a cat laugh or a dog throw up.

Since there are no limits to the depths into which a downrightly bad reading can sink, neither are there limits to the heights to which an outstandingly good reading can ascend. I have heard both.

That most modest lady Alice Munro of Canada, with eight great collections of short stories behind her, was reading in the Y in New York, and did she wow them? Sure she did. The auditorium was packed.

The other side of the coin was Brother Antoninus, a Beat poet togged out as a Dominican, atrociously vain, reading his drivel with cast iron complacency at Amerika Haus in Berlin, where they don't take fools too gladly. It was a cruelly lit room, with neon strip lighting, and the audience were leaving as fast as they were arriving, and Brother Antoninus was counting them and sweating, in between delivering his awful verse. It was an experience through which one would not willingly go again.

So the stuff you seem to be receiving may not be the same stuff I'm giving out. Adolf Hitler never knew what he would say until he felt the mood of the huge crowd at one of those monster Nuremberg rallies; the mood of the crowd lifted him up and carried him on, the wind that shakes the barley.

You can embarrass an audience by being very vain, like the late Robert Graves, or very shy, like Marianne Moore. The best recorded performance I ever heard was of James Joyce himself reading from *Finnegans Wake*, late one night when twirling the knobs for different stations on the wave-bands on an old wireless set and getting some European station, maybe Italy, and hearing for the first time Joyce's voice, the voice of a dead man which didn't sound at all dead, reading extraordinary material, which before I had taken to be nonsense. You couldn't hear him reading it and ever consider it nonsense.

I lived once on the top floor, the fifth floor, of a flat in north London overlooking Crouch End playing-fields. I left something cooking in a saucepan on an electric burner and went to the other end of the apartment, turned on Radio 3 and got the voice of Robert Lowell reading from 'For the Union Dead'. Ten minutes later he was still reading and the whole apartment was filled with black smoke; as I ran back to the kitchen through this battle-smoke, I could hear Lowell still reciting himself. Nothing could stop those great American heroics, those brave cadences—truly the authentic voice of America. Gritty.

We had a builder in the other day to do a job. On the same day some copies of one of my books arrived from the publisher and I gave one to the builder for his wife, said to be a great reader. He read the title and the blurb, neither of which conveyed much to him, and inquired politely what kind of writing I did—musing, was it? I'd never heard it described in those terms: 'musing.' Was that what it was?

I found this question impossible to answer. Writing without beginning, middle or end? Writing that won't sell?

'You mean like Addison and Steele?' I said. 'Little essays.'

'Yeah, geezers like that. Daft geezers.'

'Dull geezers, you mean?' I said. "Dead geezers?'

'Yeah, dull.'

'Well not exactly. I aspire to be amusing. A bit of a laugh you know. Never did anybody any harm.'

I never heard what the wife made of *Flotsam & Jetsam*, and I don't believe her husband read a word of it. He was a hard-headed, practical man bringing up a family, and to him writing must have seemed a feeble sort of activity, hardly an honest occupation like plastering or painting walls and doors. The more serious the aspirations of those who wrote, the more futile and useless it appeared to him. Fiction writing is a game for fools and I should know, having spent most of my life at it. In lieu of life as it is lived, we have something supporting on the page.

What I have done is to compose an answer of sorts to this sceptical builder, who is probably known to some of you; for it's a viewpoint shared by many. He is an Englishman, born in Purley who brought his wife and family over here for what he calls 'the better quality of life' found in windy Kinsale. Like your humble servant, he is a blow-in, an honorary citizen. Here, then, is the open letter: 'An Open letter to a Certain Sceptical Builder who Maintained that Serious Writing is a Foolish Occupation.'

Dear P.J., One of the heaviest prices we paid for our neutrality in WWII was the strict State censorship imposed on books, films and even paintings. Roualt's *Crucifixion*, refused by the Fathers in Maynooth, springs to mind. It was the scantiness of the Lord's loincloth which offended the Reverend Fathers, although I myself have seen scantier ones in seventeenth century Mexican churches.

When Neville Chamberlain discovered that Herr Hitler

wasn't much of a gentleman, he thought he had discovered his weakness. Au contraire. Hitler was no gentleman and had no intention of ever being one, nor of keeping his word; which is surely the first requisite of a genuine gent—his word is his bond.

The war, in any event, was not going to be fought by gentleman; it was not going to be another Charge of the Light Brigade. If Chamberlain had remained in office, Britain would have lost the war, and Ireland become an offshore colony of Nazi Germany, used for pig-breeding.

The hatred that Churchill inspired in Hitler was proof of his effectiveness; he was a dangerous enemy. We kept the ports but were stuck with Dev and his satrap Archbishop McQuaid, panic legislation and sterilisation of the mind.

James Joyce invented a sly neologism to describe the ineffectiveness of Chamberlain, concentrating on his rolled umbrella, his gamp. Joyce's new-minted word for Chamberlain's futile foreign policy of appeasement was 'umbrology', which suggests both rolled umbrella, an inability to make up one's mind, perhaps a proneness to make fatuous gestures ('Peace in our time' while waving a scrap of paper at the dupes), dithering, and taking umbrage. All that was umbrology.

When Sir Harold Nicolson of the Foreign Office declared to Mussolini that 'rearmament no more produced war than umbrellas produced rain', the Dictator was only too pleased to agree with him, and, depend upon it, they both laughed heartily at such ready wit. Meanwhile, on the emerald-green island strange things were happening: *Brief Encounter* was banned because it seemed to encourage adultery, Chaplin's *Monsieur Verdoux* had an offending blasphemous exchange cut out of it.

In those days we were afraid of our shadows. The Dublin booksellers conducted their own secret censorship and refused to stock certain titles or else hid them under the counter like cats hiding their excrement. Miss O'Flaherty of Parson's

Bookshop on Baggot Street Bridge refused to stock *The Ginger Man*; Donleavy's brand of dog-roughness shocked her. Parts of *An tOileánach* by Tomás Ó Criomhthain of the Blaskets was excised from the English translation put out by The Talbot Press. The cuts were made I suspect by 'An Seabhac' himself, a Mr Sugrue who had published a number of delightful tales in the language of West Kerry.

The Censorship of Publications Board had become a sort of minor Catholic Inquisition set up by Archbishop McQuaid in the middle of the Irish Sea. 'Suggestive material', in Catholic theological jargon, led inevitably to "sinful thoughts". This continued into the 1960s when the miniskirt put an end to it.

A haughty Protestant bookseller of Hodges Figgis in Dawson Street, Dublin, when asked by me to explain their under-the-counter policy said: 'If we don't approve of a book, we might stock it but won't display it', an extraordinary way to run a bookshop, like advertising cigarettes but advising smokers that smoking can kill. Under-the-counter books produced a nation of gropers; not gripers or grocers but gropers,

The young Beckett, whose first collection of stories, *More Pricks Than Kicks*, was banned, wrote a piece of virulent bile entitled 'Censorship in the Saorstát' which had to wait years before it was published.

Bellow refers to the Hidden Prompter, which I take to mean something akin to Proust's 'involuntary memory', that which delves into the past, to dredge up a line, a phrase, even a word, urging 'Divulge! divulge!'

Perhaps it's something that begins in childhood, or used to begin; for now that the big TV screen, ever agape, ever chatty, has replaced the mother reading to her children by an open fire, that impulse must be much weakened or even atrophied as the world becomes noisier, and silence seems critically hostile.

Writing, the impulse to record, comes from reading itself, listening to someone reading to one; hearing one's mother reading is like listening to her breathing, sensing her bloodstream's flow, and all those pauses and verbal mannerisms become part of the story; the mother becomes part of the story, an involvement impossible with the TV screen which after all is only a machine, a tube.

Perhaps I overstate this a little, but not much.

Reading began for me when I was down with measles as a child, followed by my younger brother, and in those days that meant six weeks in bed in a darkened room. My mother bought a copy of Hans Andersen's *Fairy Tales* and read it all to us, with our hair standing on end; first in the darkened bedroom with the Venetian blinds half drawn and later under a yew tree on the edge of the tennis court. After Hans Andersen, we asked for the Brothers Grimm to really alarm us. If Andersen's fairy tales about swallows and frogs were coded messages about the author's secret life he couldn't lead or even write about; the Grimms' tales were coded messages from the vast German forest where all the offensiveness which shouldn't be mentioned or seen was hidden away; a place of lost children, witches, gnomes, criminals.

The Germans were dangerous because they dreamed collectively, Count Ciano told Il Duce.

This may account for my later obsession with all things Teutonic, from Emil Nolde to Günter Grass. And later when I came to live in those great cities, Munich and Berlin seemed like home-away-from-home to me (although I never bothered to learn the language).

A German friend of mine, who died five years ago, had his ashes interred in a bluebell wood in Sussex. It was on the Ides of March. A walnut tree was planted in his memory and two firecrackers (in memory of his childhood in China) laid at the foot; a boy called Bertie lit them and out of them what should shower but confetti! Is it not pure Grimm?

My brother and I, cured of measles, could never get enough

of these chilling yarns. We pestered our mother to read us more; until one fine day we began to read for ourselves, C A T finally definitely meant cat, the furred, tailed creature that moved about so silently, one suspects that the average reader, the normal know-all fed on TV and daily doses of newsprint, can take in only just so much 'serious' reading, and that in a cock-eyed way, impeded by all manner of distractions, of which the least worry is the so-called Political Correctness.

Similarly, the Freudians can see only a Freudian text; the Feminists, permanently het up, are looking only for further pretexts to be offended—again!—by gross male piggery. The Magic Realists are ever on the lookout for the heavy influence of Gabriel Márquez; and the Postmodernists read a text all their own. While the reviewers, the hacks of the book pages, affect to know more about the book under review than the authors themselves, and know better ways of writing the books they so patronisingly scan.

I am not alone in seeing a levelling out process which seems to accelerate as we approach the Millennium. Walt Disney is an entertainment machine, producing those godawful winsome animals turned out in hundreds of thousands with tireless proficiency by his animators; McDonald's is a sausage machine; Colonel Sanders Kentucky Fried Chicken a chicken-processing plant; and the murky Murdoch a tabloid machine for extruding yet more tabloids. All are busily engaged in a flattening-out process, from the ever-chummy 'Uncle Walt' to the more sinister media magnates with their global markets, their designs on our hearts and minds. Soon we'll all be mixed up together, we Irish, in Dr Tony O'Reilly's *Independent* meat-grinder machine, our new Irish stew.

What, you may ask, has this got to do with the written word, the word we are talking about, the good word? Very little. And the gap between these two kinds of writing widens, yawns, daily, for the ideal reader in search of an ideal insomnia. 'Perhaps all that the masses accept is obsolete', wrote Yeats. [see p.150]

Today everybody reads *Angela's Ashes* and sees the movies hyped to hell, *Michael Collins* and *Schindler's Ark* or whatever it's called, and of course *Titanic*. The great public at large know that Tiger Woods is big; everybody knows that. Everybody has become the same—as shopping malls and drive-ins and filling stations.

My mother knew and cultivated a number of minor Irish writers, among whom figured Crosby Garsten and Oliver St John Gogarty in a wasp-yellow waistcoat and tan boots, who had nonchalantly removed Brother Bun's tonsils, as he had those of W. B. Yeats before him. I didn't know then that the first character to appear in Mr Joyce's *Ulysses* was the self-same 'Stately plump Buck Mulligan' of the tripping dactyls, seen strolling about our garden familiarly addressing my mother as 'Lily.'

She read us many books by Irish authors which in a vague, uncritical way I found disappointing, among them Frank O'Connor, Maurice Walsh, Francis McManus (what improbable heroics took place in Candle for the Proud and Men Withering!), Brinsley McNamara, Kate O'Brien (*Without My Cloak* and *The Land of Spices* were banned) and the oft spoken of, well-thought-of Lynn Doyle, whose real name was Leslie Alexander Montgomery, a bank clerk who is remembered, if at all, as the author of several volumes of droll stories set in the fictional Northern village of Ballygullion.

A dead dog was floating down a river, passing under a bridge in the moonlight. Two old codgers stood gossiping on the bridge. It was an Ireland I didn't know or wish to know, supposing it existed other than in their addled heads. I thought that the middle of Ireland must be a mighty strange place; Longford, where my mother came from; Cavan, where her nurse came from; Roscommon, where my father's people came from—all were mighty strange places. 'Here be dragons' wrote the old map-makers of blank areas where no white man had ever set foot. They might just as well have written "Here be monsters".

For me as a child growing up in the 1930s, the middle of Ireland was Terra Incognita. And I may say that the later old-fashioned novels of John Broderick and John McGahern and Pat McCabe of *The Butcher Boy* fame, failed to make this central void any more appealing than it had first appeared to my childish eyes.

With these rays of sunshine I'll leave it; an uncontrollable mystery, my dear PJ. Watch out for falling joists.

Yours,

Rory of the Hills

Lord Nelson, the Ladybirds of Muswell Hill Broadway, Alexandra Palace in Flames

Dublin Writers' Festival, 15 June 1998
Reading at St Patrick's Hall, Dublin Castle with Carol Ann Duffy and Seamus Heaney

ON A WINTER afternoon in London, one of those gray lifeless days you get there, I was making my way through Trafalgar Square and, looking up at the gray sky, noticed a small flag flying on top of Nelson's column.

Other pedestrians seemed to have noticed it too, for they were looking up and discussing it as they passed along, and I thought *How amazing—people are becoming observant and taking note of their surroundings at last.* But hold on, this was back in the bad old days when the other Nelson, Mandela, was still breaking rocks on his penal island. It transpired that two intrepid South African climbers had scaled the tall column and stuck a South African flag on Horatio's high hat as an anti-Apartheid gesture. There was a photograph on the front page of the *Evening Standard* to prove it, and this is why the people were staring up, confirming what the newspaper had shown: an anti-Apartheid flag was stuck on top of Nelson's foppish yet natty naval hat. It took the British Army to get it down, for the engineers to remove it.

My three sons were raised in north London, in Muswell Hill Broadway where they attended schools within sight of

Alexandra Palace, which had been set on fire thrice, the last time during a parents' meeting held in a house overlooking the park and palace, as a wing of the palace went up in flames. The kids rushed to the window and shouted 'Hey look, Mum, Alexandra Palace is on fire!' They wanted to run home to see it on the six o'clock news. The planting of the flag on Nelson's hat, a symbolic gesture, a metaphor, wasn't real until confirmed by a photo on the front page of the *Evening Standard*—and a palace going up in smoke wasn't real until the kids had seen it on television news, to authenticate it.

One summer the pavements of Muswell Hill Broadway were crawling with ladybirds and nobody noticed them. Muswell Hill was the home of The Kinks; they came from there, The Kinks, Ray and the other brother whatshisname? There's always a lost brother somewhere. Ray and Dave Davies, they were the Kinks.

Now we can go on.

A German fellow went to England to try and improve his English, taking up quarters in outer London on the Uxbridge Road down Ealing way, where all the Irish go. He thought he was doing fine, could salute casual acquaintances with 'How's it going, mate?' 'Sick as a parrot', 'Moving the goalposts', 'Over the moon', and those other patented ready-made phrases that pass for rational conversation over the water.

Until one day, perusing his paper, he was flummoxed by the arresting headline 'Shepherd's Bush Combed for Missing Model Girl'. A simple declarative sentence on the face of it, you might think. But was it? Wasn't he missing something? Had he got the hang of it or had he missed the boat, lost his middle stump? Did he take sugar? Was there some subterfuge at work here, some nicety of thought, subtle British badinage working to confuse simple-minded foreigners, to throw dust in their eyes? Like a piece of grit in the eye, the English language was peppered with subtleties and riddled with ambiguities, the German thought, rather like the English themselves.

Perhaps the German was unaware that Shepherd's Bush was one of those curiously named parts of London, like Swiss Cottage or Burnt Oak or White City or Elephant and Castle. He probably knew that 'bush' was slang for pubic hair; if so, what was the shepherd doing in London, why were the police combing his pubic hair, and where was the missing model girl? The day the British Navy sank the *Belgrano* in the South Atlantic, those poor Argy

Bargies were given scant time to say their last Paternosters. *The Daily Mirror* fairly gloated, splashing 'GOTCHA!' all over its front page in twenty point bold, hot as a projectile vomit. The jingoistic fervour was a classical throwback to the times of Desperate Dan and the Boys' Own heroics of The Dandy and The Beano; all the lofty patronage of colonial days when Great Britain had been in control and nignogs knew their place, namely at the foot of the social laddere.

In our own more scarifying times, the razzmatazz sports section of a mass-circulation tabloid shouts out "GAZZA AZZA BONK II" And this enigmatic 'headline' is crystal clear to all hot and heavy *Sun* subscribers: 'Gazza' is Paul Gascoigne, the fractious footballer who famously couldn't hold his place on the English team for the 1998 World Cup and was once again reduced to floods of tears after he was deemed unfit to perform 'at the highest level'. Manager Hoddle told the press that he had 'gone out on a limb' for Gazza; as though he'd found the drunken midfielder up a tree and tried to coax him down. And by God now he was after the bimbos. Bonking was something that bimbos did, particularly with such a fine stud as Gazza, commanding astronomical fees and well able to show a girl a good time.

'GAZZA AZZA BONK!!' howled the headlines. And the lads shouted it out, howling their delight to high heaven, capering about and displaying their adoration from the terraces. There the great Gazza's supporters were caged, in fighting trim, shouting abuse at the referee, employing restricted vocabulary with no names for many things but one name—coyly referred to as the F-word—for most things, used as a imperative in a very fierce way.

Jerkish is the name of the language developed in the US some years back for the communication between people and chimpanzees; it consists of 225 words, and Ivan Klima predicts that, after what has happened to his own language (Czech) under the communists, it can't be long before Jerkish is spoken by all mankind.

Nature as such is disappearing, has already disappeared. I say that which is is, I say that which is not also is. You'll have to believe me. I have never been here before.

The first inkling that a novel could be more than just a story told came to me on reading Joyce's *A Portrait* where the miserable Dedalus-Joyce family life was on the page, exposed for our inspection. It seemed to have been written with me in mind by an author not long dead, published when Joyce was thirty-six, read when was twenty-two. The Shock of the New turned out to be something very old involving an impoverished family in Dublin. Fiction, when it's any good. tells more than a story, transforms the mundane, So that a place, that place then, any place anywhere at any time, if written of by a writer with eyes to see, will never be the same again.

The young Beckett found the work of the ageing Proust more heavily symmetrical than Macaulay at his worst and jeered at the first Gallimard edition of the great editorially botched novel brought out in 'sixteen abominable volumes'.

The old Matisse, shown the work of the young Bonnard, said: 'Well, I can't say that I like it, but I will say this—when you apply black, it sticks.'

Now to come a little nearer to our time and place, let's look at Patrick Kavanagh's work. The laborious honesty of his novel *Tarry Flynn* is a poor sort of model, a poor reflection of life lived from hand to mouth by the poet who was so socially maladroit, then scraping a meagre living in and around Morehampton Road. Kavanagh was to drink amid company with Beckett once in Paris. Awed by the Master of the Boulevard Saint Jacques and uncomfortable in polyglot company, he knocked back whiskey after whiskey, 'one lung and all'. Beckett marvelled—'They couldn't bring it to him fast enough'—and soon poor Kavanagh was 'blathering'.

Today on the racks of the better bookshops you will find peasant novels just as dated as *Tarry Flynn* and Kickham's *Knocknagow* sold as modern Irish Classics. I'd feel ashamed to go in there, to be mortified by what I might find. More blathering.

One mustn't speak too ill of the dead now. It's considered unlucky. But Paddy Kavanagh rarely spoke anything else but ill of the living and the famous dead; he could not abide coevals, presumptive rivals. Bad-mouthing others and belligerent cadging were the forte of this man from Mucker; joyless by temperament, permanently aggrieved and disgruntled, he hadn't a good word for anybody but himself.

Kavanagh saw himself as a failure, the stay-at-home who cultivated only grievances, bore only grudges, always impoverished, always cadging, unable to free himself from the encroaching mess of a contingent world, drinking Bovril in McDaid's. The crusty and cantankerous pose adopted in any company was perpetuated in print: in the ghastly *Kavanagh's Weekly* paper of which he was both editor and main contributor, or the ill-tempered diary he contributed to John Ryan's *Envoy* magazine. The lonely and embittered bachelor of *The Great Hunger*, who scatters his seed into the ashes of a dying turf fire, is a figure symptomatic of this sorry state of stagnation that was Ireland and Kavanagh then, during our Emergency.

Kavanagh was one of the hazards to be encountered between his setting-off point at McDaid's in Harry Street via Doheny & Nesbitt's and Toners and the numerous pubs scattered along

Baggot Street and Leeson Street until they petered out at the less posh end of Northumberland Road. He was to be met proceeding on his ruined feet along the Grand Canal towpath where today a statue of the poet seated in bronze tranquillity, in 'tremendous silence' as he said himself, has been erected to his memory. I must say my memories of the man are not particularly fond. The critical success of early work could never compensate for later failure; failure in life too. He had a soft spot only for himself and what he perceived as his own miserable failure. Beckett, the low-church Protestant highbrow, cultivated misery too, but his was an exalted state of misery, something known to martyrs and saints, austere ascetics, Simon Stylite in the burning desert.

When, as an aspiring young penman, I sought models that might serve, I found only *Green Rushes*, and such predictable stuff—some of it banned by the Censorship of Publications Board which had deemed them unwholesome, unfit for the common Irish reader, the ideal reader in search of an ideal insomnia.

Perhaps these are the sort of novels that Joyce himself might have written or been obliged to write had he stayed at home in the rancorous capital or moved to Mullingar and was stuck for a subject-matter, had to make do with the russet bog, the brooding peasantry, the dark Central Plain, the pint of plain that is your only man, the snow on the barren thorn.

You may recall the old man with red rheumy eyes from the west of Ireland mentioned towards the end of *A Portrait Of the Artist as a Young Man*, who, on being told of the universe and the stars by Mulrennan, marvelled 'Ah, there must be terrible queer creatures at the latter end of the world!' The latter end of the world would begin for him just across the Kerry border.

If you were a 'well-thought-of' Irish writer, you were in; if not well thought of, you were out. Joyce was not well thought of and was definitely out; Beckett's turn was yet to come. 'You'll never lose money by underestimating the bad taste of the public' is a truism that no honest person can deny. The awful conception of a rolling news service that runs non-stop, like a chemical factory belching toxic fumes twenty-four hours a day, is an abomination; if you consider that news generally means bad news, like tuning into a dreadful hour of your life, watching Bob Geldof on breakfast television. An organ-grinder's monkey would entertain just as well.

On the Dublin-Cork afternoon train the cellular phones are red-hot approaching Limerick Junction.

'Dis train terminates at Cork City. Thank you,' Guard Moriarty announces over the spluttering intercom in the strange new Service Talk to which we must become accustomed if we are to get around at all.

'Please stand clear a da doors; de doors are about to close!'

The levelling-out process goes on apace, accelerating as we approach the millennium;

Murdoch and Mammon. Richard Branson will fly you anywhere on Virgin Air; Dr A.J.F. O'Reilly, the Heinz beans kingpin, wheels in his mobile meat-grinder to set before us a steamy half-raw Irish stew calculated to put hair on our chests, bring a flush to Irish cheeks and a twinkle to every Irish eye.

And the hearts of the great common Irish public, beat as one: think the same easy shallow thoughts, dream the same common dream.

Seán agus Sinead become Damien and Kylie, become Brad and Tracey, become Rocky and Moonbeam, soon to be Heavenly Harani Tigerlily.

Where are they heading? Where are we going? What are they up to?

I have lived half my life in Ireland and the other half out of it. The first part spent in childhood and boyhood as an anxious simpleton, an aimless non-participant collecting impressions. When out of favour with my testy father, I was the brat or the whelp; when in favour with my mother, I was her dotey.

The party you see here before you is assuredly no spring chicken but a fellow well advanced into the sere and yellow, twice married and a grandfather four times over, now returned to a homeland as unlike the one I knew as Ithaca to Odysseus.

When I began writing seriously for a livelihood a lifetime ago with Calder, I had the mistaken impression that what I was writing was fiction, when it fact it was autobiography, thinly disguised. And now that I am writing autobiography, or aspire to, it turns out to be fiction; perhaps disguised fiction but fiction nonetheless, though so not so blatantly fictitious that my younger brother ('the Dote') wouldn't take offence and threaten me with the full rigours of libel law. I had to buy him off with an expensive lunch in Wexford, with three bottles of Chilean white and the best brandy in the house.

On being invited to speak here this evening in such distinguished company, I decided against reading either fiction or autobiography but to make a fresh start on a blank page, airing certain matters which may be of abiding interest to keen readers like yourselves.

Part Two

Of People and Places

Flann O'Brien the Semi-invisible Man

AT A TIME when the faces of Dermot Bolger, Billy Roche, Colm Tóibin and the likes of Roddy Doyle, our suddenly famous ones, are as familiar to us as the morning bacon and eggs, it behoves us to step backward for a moment, to a time when Irish writers tended to be invisible, wanted to be invisible, living very poorly, ill-paid for their efforts and with hardly two pennies (old currency) to rub together.

In the early 1950s in Dublin Flann O'Brien was a peculiarly invisible man. Tony Cronin says that he wasn't as invisible as he thought he was; but he was still fairly invisible all the same.

Some great writers have faces that you are not permitted to see: Dante and Joyce were two, Shakespeare another; Voltaire and Céline. Was it not said famously of the Nadar photo of Baudelaire that the eyes glaring out of it belonged to another man? I am thinking now of certain writers who want to make themselves invisible, will themselves to be invisible, and almost make it. Their faces are like masks and their real faces hid behind these.

'Cruiskeen Lawn' had been running for years in *The Irish Times*, yet few in Dublin knew what Myles looked like. When the column appeared in Irish, ninety per cent of the readers didn't understand it; the stout Protestant editor Bertie Smyllie certainly didn't. On weekends Smyllie liked to potter around the hills and dales of Delgany Golf Club with his equally corpulent obituary writer, Eamonn Lynch.

The first photo I tracked down of Flann O'Brien hung in

Delgany Golf Club. It was a group photograph of a Diplomatic Corps outing with Smyllie and some of the *Irish Times* journalists lolling about on the grass. And, lo and behold, in the back row, a small-sized, roundish, dark-featured man in a gangster hat, and one roly-poly jowl scarred with what appeared to be a duelling scar or knife wound was the man himself: Myles of the Ponies. The first and indeed the only time I was ever to meet him in the flesh—such as it was—turned out to be a suitably bizarre occasion.

I had been invited to participate in an early TV Arts programme in monochrome to or into which Ben Kiely, Anthony Cronin in a bow tie, the pale publisher Alan Figgis and Myles himself—well-oiled already and inclined to be cantankerous—had been summarily roped. The proceedings commenced bizarrely enough in McDaid's when Cronin (dressed in complementary shades of nutty brown corduroy) retired to the Gents belowstairs to divest himself of his day-to-day clothes and change into his studio gear, which was all ready in a dry-cleaning plastic parcel; only to, reappear presently dressed in identical suiting, his *Traje de Luces*.

The plan was to get a sober Myles into the studio; a plan scotched—if that's the right word—when in he strolled in the convivial company of none other than Ben Kiely, who had just discovered that they were twenty-fifth cousins thrice removed; the tyro from Tyrone and the oracle of Omagh—the Mookse and the Gripes.

The gangster hat was tilted at a contentious angle and I seem to recall the alcoholic's tongue darting in and out to moisten the thin dehydrated lips, monkish in their severity; and a ball of malt appeared at his right hand as if by magic.

Once he had had a few snorters and was given his head, the jig was up; any further discussion could neither be contained nor controlled. Myles the Clobberer was let loose, and on his chosen subject, and began to rant—names were about to be named. The unseen Controller became alarmed and presently a note on yellow paper was passed down to the flustered linksman and the programme abruptly cut short, to my intense relief. Though I had remained as silent as humus throughout the proceedings, contributed nothing and was never seen on camera; and now the arty crowd were taken off and substituted by something safer, which turned out to be The Dubliners.

Meanwhile my mother, in a high state of excitement, had gone to a neighbour's house to watch her famous son on television. She had never seen TV before, for it had yet to get a grip on Dublin; she sat transfixed watching Ronny Drew twanging his trusty old guitar and belting out the rattle of the Thompson gun. 'Oh,' said my mother, 'I never knew Aidan could play the guitar!'

The proceedings ended as they had begun on a suitably surreal note back in McDaid's. I was not to know that Myles was almost ashamed of *At Swim-Two-Birds* and would not hear any praise of it, when I ordered him up a double whiskey and said how much I admired the book.

The trembling hand was just again raising the little chalice to the thin parched lips and the fly-catcher's tongue just about to dart in and out, moisture breaking out about the small pinched nostrils, and I received a very leery look for my pains. 'You should have known better,' sneered Myles, 'and you a Christian Brother's boy yourself.'

I don't know who he was confusing me with or who he thought he was addressing; but whatever else I may be, I certainly am not a Christian Brother's boy.

Hidden behind three or more pseudonyms, the secretive and semi-invisible author instructed his new publisher, O'Keefe, that no biographical details whatsoever, or any photo of the author, were to be released with his second novel, *The Third Policeman*, that came out in 1967, a year after his death. He had looked askance at a photo of himself that had appeared on the reissue of *At Swim-Two-Birds* six years previously and seemed doubtful whether it was himself or not. Would that the present set of vain practitioners had a little of that becoming modesty.

The Plumber from Palmers Green

WHILE ON THE subject of misunderstandings and cognate matters, may I be here permitted to state categorically that *Langrishe, Go Down* is not a Big House novel, nor was ever intended as such. I had transformed my three brothers and myself into elderly spinsters, and the interloper, the German gamekeeper, was introduced as an afterthought; as a foreign agent used to disrupt the vegetative state of the four old biddies, a fellow who would ask awkward questions. I was also, I suppose, poking fun at *Lady Chatterley's Lover* by that deeply absurd English novelist D.H. Lawrence with his stale rhetorical devices and his fatuous attempts to demystify that which by its nature is uncorrectable—the sexual clinch; whereas fiction writing as I perceive it has nothing whatsoever to do with helping people over that particular stile.

When my first novel came out in 1966, I received a letter from a reader in Palmers Green who identified himself as a working plumber, objecting to two ballcocks in the lavatory on the upper landing of Springfield House, referred to as 'musty dinted ballcocks' in an overflowing cistern. One ballcock is plenty, wrote the Palmers Green plumber.

I wrote back to tell him that it must have been a Freudian slip. 'No symbols where none intended.'

A somewhat vainglorious Jewish writer whom I knew in Spain years ago, with one novel to his credit, highly praised in the *New Statesman & Nation*, was complaining one day of being stuck in his second novel. He was making no progress and wanted to sleep for six months, wake up and find the novel finished—but it had to be a good novel. My wife that was, the mother of my three sons, said helpfully that she had the very thing. She had pills that would put him to sleep. 'Spanish pills?' he asked. No, they were German pills. No, thanks, he said, no German pills for him. If he swallowed them, he might never wake up.

I knew an American writer of sorts called Lyle Joyce who lived part of the year in Greece. He was disturbed in his mind and used to book himself into a mental home when he felt more mental disturbance coming on.

With no money in Paris, he had presented himself at the offices of Olympia Press and sat in the waiting room reading a Chinese newspaper not from the top down but from the bottom up, until Girodias asked him what he wanted. He took out of his pocket a few typed pages of what he claimed was a little-known fourteenth-century Chinese pillow-book, which he was in the process of translating into American English.

Girodias read the pages and said he would commission a translation chapter by chapter. The book was published in due time and sold well. A couple of years later it was taken up by Barney Rosset of Grove Press who wanted to bring out a deluxe edition, where it was in the company of *Langrishe, Go Down*, which Grove was attempting to market as a dirty book along with Henry Miller's and *Last Exit to Brooklyn* by Hubert Selby Junior. Rosset said he wanted illustrations for the second edition. Lyle Joyce said no bother, he knew a little-known fourteenth-century Chinese pornographic illustrator who happened to be resident in the Bronx. Get him, Rosset said, delighted.

The author's name was given as Yu Li. Eventually it was unmasked as a fake. Girodias said: 'I don't give a damn. It sold well. I don't grudge him a yen.'

Anthony Burgess at the London Savoy

1980

IN THE DIMLY expiring late October afternoon light a family of imbeciles huddle by a traffic jam, viewing a poster for the Ken Dodd Laughter Show. Idiot smiles fixed and upstanding, hair stiff as yardbrushes, they cry 'Tatty-bye! Tatty-bye!' in high freak voices.

My taxi-man can speak four languages. Rain begins to fall as your correspondent enters the rich precincts of the Savoy Hotel, where famed soft-porn authoress Erica Jong has not booked in, following a murder on the top floor. Air-conditioning keeps the flowers fresh in the vestibule where floorwalkers and house detectives in dark suiting move as sombrely as undertaker's mutes. A great coal fire burns in the grate. The PA machine is tirelessly extruding news of world-wide calamities and the latest war news: ISRAELI JETS ATTACK tackatatackata LEBANON COAST tickeytoc DUPONT'S 24 MILLION LOSSES ticketyboom.

Mr Burgess, whom I have already met at the Hutchinson launch, arrives with entourage exactly seven minutes late. Effusive apologies.

We ascend slowly to a high suite overlooking the Thames and a vision of never-ceasing traffic headlights moving through the murk. A broad bridge seen through an open window. A leg-brace supports itself against one wall. Mr Burgess orders strong coffee, offers Scotch; the entourage retires to another room.

Anticipating a blustery manner and possible truculence, judge of our surprise to encounter a tall handsome man in liturgical shirt set off by red tie, hair a sable silver, manicured nails, no discernible accent, the slitty eyes of a fellow inured to a hot climate (Malta, Malaya, Borneo); a reserved affability. Most happy to be interviewed for the new *Sunday Tribune.*

The dollar millionaire has just published his twenty-sixth work of fiction, *Earthly Powers,* for which Messrs Hutchinson stumped up a rumoured £75,000 advance. Already 9,000 copies have been subscribed from an initial print-run of 15,000. Michael Korda, editor-in-chief of Simon and Schuster, paid a rumoured $400,000 (say £170,000).

The Booker Prize went to the sage of Bowerchalke, William Golding, who came up to Stationers' Hall from rural Wilts. Agent Deborah Rogers is said to have sold movie rights of *A Clockwork Orange* for a paltry £400 four years back; but there again the English rights of *Waiting for Godot* went for half that.

Mr Burgess himself was not too happy with Kubrick's explicitly horrorful angle, and was alarmed by the resultant murders, following screenings. CHAOS ODER ANARCHIE, the wall graffiti proclaimed. LEV LESBISK. CLOO IS LUVE. Gobbledegook was on the rise, the eye radiantly preparing for death.

Mr Burgess, unsolicited, recalls early days of poverty, as if it had not been his very own bread and dripping. Schoolmaster Devar brought two copies of *Ulysses* into Manchester, secreted upon his person in order to pass undetected through the customs, the same customs that burnt 2,000 copies in 1922.

In 1959 Burgess was given a year to live; overwork had taken its toll, a suspected tumour of the brain. He had brought out five novels at the rate of 2,000 words a day in one year. 'Fecundity is not a good sign?' The eyes narrow behind a cloud of Daneman cigar-smoke. You've got to write—keep at it.'

He was teaching in Borneo then, couldn't find a job in

England, pensioned off. 'A thousand pounds was a lot in 1957.'
He believes in the Word. In 1965 his first wife died. He soon
remarried, the Italian contessa; they make their own deals,
rumoured to be stiff. His work—some fifty titles now—goes
into translations. Publishers may speak of a continuing slump,
but Mr Burgess goes on churning it out, novels, oratorios,
reviews and articles, screenplays. Prolific as Arnold Bennett.

He had thought to take a sabbatical in Dublin, show his
Italian wife 'another kind of Catholicism'; nothing came of that.
He accepted no state grants, Arts Council handouts; all revenue
came via his strong right hand. He was with Jack McGowran
on the day before he died, of a heart attack in the Algonquin. A
fund for the Irish actor was started, funds collected, but it was
'too late anyway'.

He would like to write a play about John Calvin; tried to set
up a film based on John Hawkes's *The Lime Twig*. Composed
music for the bassoon, spoke with Borges in Middle English to
baffle the Peron spies. He is sixty-three but doesn't look it, fears
his memory is going, but it isn't. His son Andreas wears a kilt,
wants to be a Scotsman, doesn't wish to write.

Cranks phone in the middle of the night—another
Clockwork Orange-type murder—your comment? 'People like
war. It's like art, has a beginning and an end.' The ghosted book
on Ingrid Bergman was just a rumour; Anthony Burgess is no
ghost. I complain that there are no meals in *Earthly Powers*;
a real book of fiction must have a meal in it. He reaches out,
finds a page, shows me a meal; well, a list of stuff to eat. It seems
ungracious to dislike the novel but the author does not much
concern himself with this. It was a year's work, discarded before,
taken up again, finished; there are other books to be written. I
pick a page at random:

'Hellsmoke curled from the gratings. Red and yellow light
flashed on and off faces of gratuitous malevolence.'

He admires the gentle Svevo, Corvo's *Hadrian the Seventh*,

Faulkner's 'harmonics', Joyce for his everything. The T. S. Eliot Memorial Lecture the University of Kent was delivered extempore, *con brio*, broadcast. I heard it; the audience was dominated and could only titter. He set out to prove connections between linguistics on the page and tonal structures in music, compared 'The Wreck of the Deutschland' and *Finnegans Wake*. A witty defence of obscurity.

He can be witty, but the fun comes rather grimly. The host is standing now, fingers clamped rigid like Beckett's on the cigar (Beckett's brand too), the noble head enveloped in Daneman smoke. A kind man withal, considerate of others, with few bad words to say of his fellow scribes. He fell afoul of Professor Ricks and Saul Bellow, for reasons unclear. Mr Burgess shows me politely to the door of his high suite, offers a firm handclasp, specific advice. 'Work! . . . Work!' his last words on the slowly closing door, the narrowed Burgess eyes. The entourage are silent still in another room, holding their collective breath. In the murky Strand a peevish voice cries out: 'You flash cunt you, I 'ope yow wreck yow fukken caw!'

I wish Mr Burgess well in the rough times ahead. Our times.

Marcel Marceau at the Olympia in Dublin

To WHOM CAN we compare this extraordinary man from Limoges? He works in darkness, a man going over Niagara Falls in a barrel. He glows out of darkness, as a white moth at night, his arena restricted at times to a rectangle of illuminated studs set into the stage floor. Even what he omits has meaning, like Hindu calligraphy.

None of his 'normal' actions are expected; he 'sleeps' like a sundial, one leg cocked in the air, the angled legs of the Isle of Man insignia: Le Rêve, Le Fabricant de Masques, Cain and Abel. He gives you the creation of the world in nine minutes flat, with prehistoric fish; in Les Mains he demonstrates the nature of perfidy, the sick dictator. He carries no Harlequin's wand, for his own hands can manufacture solid objects out of thin air. Unlike Pierrot, he comes stripped for action, jointed like a wooden dummy, the artist's model with jointed limbs. Watching his performance, you must discredit what you are seeing, for he shrinks and expands, now David, now Goliath's victim slain, David still alive, Jack and the Beanstalk.

His art is as sad as those parks full of parading pedestrians now dead in the Italian movie *1900*. He walks along burning buildings, plays a firehose over stalls, dress-circle and pit; up into the balcony drenching the nobs in the parterre; or dragged about on the leads of powerful but invisible dogs who yet appear in the corner of one's eye, just out of sight.

The effort to survive with dignity distorts him. Chaplin,

menaced by a maniac gold prospector in *The Gold Rush*, must sleep with one eye open, like a partridge; his head where his feet should be.

Sometimes Marceau's features stiffen, narrow, as a fencer at parry and thrust or Ordonez preparing to dispatch a bull. The features narrow, a warning that the horse is about to kick you, kill you if he can. Like all great ones, he is not house-trained. There is a turmoil at the centre of his stillness, the stillness of the matador holding himself braced, about to plunge the sword over the horns into the hump. An extraordinary moment: behind the chalk-white face of the mime appears for a split second a swarthy sailors throat awash in sweat. At times the face resembles that of Emperor Napoleon in the Abel Cance movie, at others it's the aquiline features of Dante; the face swells up or shrinks away, the features 'play' yet remain still, locked, like a flame fanned by a sudden breeze, as the spirit moves him. A man lost in his dream, he defies comparison, this incredible mime. What can he live on? Lightning? Electricity? White light? Parsley?

Zbigniew Herbert in Berlin

Born Lwów, Poland in 1924
died in Warsaw on 28 July, 1999, aged 75

He had the build of a welterweight boxer, barrel-chested but
nippy on his feet, somewhat abashed to admit that his wife was
a Baronin, which went against his Socialist principles. It didn't
mean what it meant in other countries, a title like that, he told
me. He had fought in the Polish resistance, was to become Poland's foremost poet.

'If the key to contemporary Polish poetry is the collective experience of the last decades, Herbert is perhaps the most skilful in
expressing it.'

Czeslaw Milosz

1. K'nang!

Early one gray afternoon, when least expected, the Zbigniew
Herbert's, Pan Cogito in person, called and the host slipped out.
Joint get-togethers with the Higginses, Herberts and Hollerers
had not proved too fruitful and had by mutual consent been
discontinued. For after politely bidding their hosts the time of
day in English, the guests reverted to German and continued to
speak German to each other for the rest of the evening, leaving
me quite in the dark as to what they were discussing with such
animation, with Jill bored stiff, translating episodically.

I was all set to depart via the kitchen window as the
unexpected guest could be heard in the living-room roaring
masterfully for strong potions.

'You are leaving us?'

'Looks like it.'

'Well damn you then and go.' Jill Damaris (née Anders, so
there must have been some Polish blood somewhere) responded
with eyes positively smouldering. 'God is good, Jack is earning,
and everything is nice in its own time. So fuck off!'

She looked daggers at her estranged bedfellow, then added
an inspired afterthought. 'I hope that whore gives you some
frightful disease.'

Stepping closer, lowering her voice, looking dangerous, 'A
good dose of *Raptus* to shrink that overactive prick of yours.'

I fell back, stunned at the virulence of this.

'Thanks . . . Most kind of you I'm sure. You will entertain
our guests?'

I was already on the window-ledge, like a bird, was to meet
Lore in twenty minutes outside Podbielski Station, had dropped
from sight. Jill stuck her head out the window. 'And fuck you
too!' she screeched haggishly.

But I, silently letting myself out the gate, was already flitting
away, bathed in an amber light and head down as if advancing
against imminent storm. The light was near-umber, as if torn
from unhappiness. *Dominations first; next them, Virtues; and
Powers the third*; thus spake sapient Carey.

Jill (what had gotten into her?) was developing new
techniques of intimidation and retaliation. I might be immersed
in Pavese (*Among Women Only*) which I had come upon in
Margot Schoeller's bookshop and, raising a casual right hand
for a glass, might look up from the printed page to find my
spouse staring at me with an intense basilisk stare (or glare) of
probing and purest hatred.

Or again, encountered going through a doorway, she would

make a quick unexpected lunge, with a karate hand angled at my face, throwing up my hands to protect myself; and then the cat-like counter-lunge at my unguarded privities, the gloating cry *'K'nang!'* and then the fire in the crotch, as I doubled up, gasping, holding on to the doorway. The Queen of Air sailing off upstairs, calling down 'Serves you right, you dirty bugger.'

I was nonplussed by the tactics deployed, and the new crudeness of the language used, and for self-protection and a quiet life took to occupying rooms other than those occupied by my wife. If she came in, I would move out. We were like opposing small wooden figures in a Tyrol clock. If she came to watch a television programme that I was watching, I moved away. Then she would sail in: 'If I sit down, will you get up?' up stood contrary husband, bridling.

'I might.'

'Skunk!' (The threatening edge, the rising intonation.)

I (rhetorical): 'Tell me, when is this bloody nonsense going to end?'

Jill (brightly ironic): 'Oh so you begin to see it's nonsense? You are coming to your senses?'

'I am going out,' I said, and I did just that.

As I came out of Podbielski Station, Lore ran across the road with her hair flying and we kissed like lovers in an old French movie, Gérard Philippe and Madeleine Robinson in *Une Si Jolie Petite Plage*, an old sepia print the colour of happiness.

Jill, wringing her hands, her face twisted and ugly, being diabolical: 'Ah, you are leaking? Are you sober yet?'

These latter tactics (*K'Nang!*) I put an abrupt end to one day, when attacked once again in the kitchen, by forcibly bringing down the heel of my fist on the top of her bowed head with such violence that two fingers were dislocated and to my amazement I found the lethal Sabatier in my right hand which I instantly plunged into the breadboard and left the kitchen with fluttering heart, feeling murder in the air.

Thereafter, she complained of a ringing in the ears and thought to consult a doctor ('I will simply tell him that my dear husband has gone insane over another woman and likes beating me insensible') but did nothing more about it. Then her teeth were giving her trouble. She and Nico made sorties across town to visit a handsome Polish dentist who was adept at his job. I was advised to go and see Dr Slobodanka Gruden.

'No thanks.'

Of course it was not always open warfare.

Drinking alone in a Spanish bar opposite our old haunts near the Hotel Bogota, she had fallen into conversation with a stout sweaty oleaginous umbrella manufacturer from Bruges who tried to get her drunk enough to say *Je t'aime.* He was a simple soul but could neither get her drunk nor persuade her to say *Je t'aime*.

'Suck a big fat wobbly *mercenary* Belgian!' cried she gaily. 'Just imagine.' 'Mercenary' was a very bad word in her vocabulary.

'Oddly enough,' I said, twirling the ice, 'friend Herbert's Baronin, quite unsolicited, said that to me at one of Peter Westler's dos. I may say it was a little embarrassing.'

'Said what to you?'

Je t'aime. Isn't that soliciting? She seemed quite sober.'

My caring wife showed her intense interest by not revealing it, not showing any interest.

'And what did the fierce Resistance fighter say to that affront to his Polish pride and honour?'

'He was at the other end of the room killing off the vodka supplies and not available for comment. I wouldn't care to mix it with old Zbigniew—or all that pent-up Polish rage. I bet he fights dirty, probably carries a shiv.'

I suspected that Herbert rather fancied Jill. He had called upon us once when I was away, burst his trousers and had to go home for a new pair. He returned to take mother and Nico out boating on Schlactensee.

How did he burst his trousers, pray?

Her reply: 'He has a pot belly.'

Was that an answer? I smiled, thinking of female fickleness and their own perplexing anatomy. Perplexing for the owners. Once at dinner with the Herberts and the Hollerers, Herbert the wild Pole had leaned across the table as if to kiss my wife's cheek but taking hold of her nut-brown tresses began pulling her across the table until her eyes filled with tears; and nobody said a word, least of all the husband. The host had been drinking vodka all day.

Pan Cogito became waggish in his cups, but it was a Polish waggishness that had sharp edges to it, unpredictable elements that made for uncomfortable fun. I did not understand this wit delivered in German, French, part Polish and Yiddish. Zbigniew Herbert's grandfather had spoken only in English, his mother was Armenian, his father a lawyer and professor of economics—'hence my syncretic religion—Orthodox from my grandfather, Catholic from my father and all-round evidence of Hasidic culture.' But he never spoke of the war, his time as a Polish Resistance fighter.

'How do you say Resistance in Polish?' I asked him.

'Opór, Résistance, Notsstand.'

'What is one to think of Katyn?'

'One doesn't,' he answered, blessing himself.

He had a most princely air, came from the rough olden times. What I didn't know then was that his uncle, son of an Austrian general, had received a Russian bullet in the back of his head at Katyn in 1940.

He now joined Professor Hollerer, the ex-Luftwaffe liason officer, embracing him, and the pair of them were soon sitting cross-legged on the floor, the best of friends.

Jill in her cups could be most amusing; inebriation seemed to release some hidden joy and she became flirtatious like a scheming tease in Restoration comedy—Mrs Bracegirdle? Only a good-looking broad could have carried it off. If booze made other women contentious and dull, it enlivened Jill Damaris: she positively sparkled.

2. He Puts the Wind up Two *Hausfraus*

One day when short of funds, I was walking by the Paris Bar with Lore, and put out of countenance to see approaching Pan Cogito and the Baronin, no less already making preliminary gestures of greeting and delight.

I kissed both round tight cheeks of the Baronin inclined for this homage, and introduced Lore.

'You are coming out or going in?' Herbert inquired civilly.

'Well, neither,' I said shiftily. 'Actually we were walking.'

'But you will have a drink with us?' Pan Cogito proposed.

I looked at Lore and Lore looked at me.

'Well . . .'

'Perhaps just . . .' Lore equivocated.

'. . . the one,' I amended easily.

'March in then.'

So we trooped into the Paris Bar, I scraping and bowing, wondering whether I could hit my fellow Daadite for a small tiding-over loan of say DM 50. Within the week another cheque would be in. We had the same paymaster in Bonn. Zbigniew was in a sense the dark angel or hidden intermediary, for had he not been the guileless agent mediating between us and Fate, we might never have met. Without Sepp Walser's misdirected phone call we would not have attended the same party. Unless Lore had known Sepp Walser, we might never have met.

The Herberts ordered coffee and brandy, Lore a glass of house red, and I a draught beer and Steinhäger.

'The last time I was in here, I ran into Reinhard Lettau,' I said. 'You know him?'

'No.'

The poet crossed his stout Polish legs (bursting like sausage-casings) and looked around with a pleased expression, for the proximity of strong spirits always put him in a good humour. He, who at first glance had seemed the very soul of afternoon sobriety, was now seen to be in that pleasant state between moderate and immoderate insobriety where everything struck him, the relaxed observer of human foibles, as being highly entertaining and amusing, a time of pratfalls. In particular, the antics of a pair of stout *Hausfraus* at a nearby table who were steadily putting away plates piled with *Kuchen*, seemed to engage his closest attention.

He watched the two *Hausfraus* and I covertly observed him. Here was a delicate situation that called for tact. An operation was required that I was only too familiar with: The Touch, 'as delicate as the turning inside-out of an eyelid'.

Saucy Mr Cogito was staring rudely raptly at the slowly descending stiffly corseted determined no-longer-young rump slowly heavily yearningly descending (heavy as a heifer on a cowpat or the shadow of a helicopter on its landing pad), a great questing lump of sentient female matter. As it (the rump) was just about to meet the wide seat ready for it, up sprang Pan Cogito with a most extraordinary smile fixed on his face, and offered one gracious hand (the right, or sword-hand) to the lady, who (in mid-air, as it were) responded for her part with an answering smile frozen on her lips; while the gallant's free hand was laid most gently and circumspectly on the stiffly corseted rump, hardly stroked before it had cleared imaginary crumbs and dust from the seat of the chair, to make all in readiness to receive her bum. It was a hidden gesture of extraordinary affrontery and recognised by the three who watched, and by the participant himself, now holding the hand of the graciously subsiding but slightly embarrassed *Hausfrau*, with a fixed smile of gracious thanks fairly glued to her lips. Hand in hand now, however briefly, they might have been in some kind of a slow stately dance, a pavane, not a mazurka.

She was gustily breathing her thanks to him through her nostrils, fluttering her eyelids at him; she must have sensed he was a foreign gentleman (although he would have passed for a German). The smile fluttery, going on and off, the two hands just barely touching, he (the male partner very serious) with the 'ghost of a smile' on his lips, Pan Cogito as he might have led a dance with one of the kitchen staff (the cook?) in a manor house in Poland in the country before the war.

The expressions on the faces of the Baronin and Lore were sights to behold. The Baronin might have seen something vaguely similar before, when a furious husband had watched before brief words were exchanged and a dueling ground chosen, somewhere near an early morning wood in Poland. The Baronin was *alight* with pride in her man. In those quick glances she threw, I seemed to detect cocked pistols and swords raised to lips, blood drained from faces, the caped seconds standing like statues, a surgeon at the ready; for honour had been besmirched and a wrong would have to be corrected, in a land where affronts to ladies were answered by bullets, sword-thrusts, thrust and parry.

Lore looked as if she might rise up in her Prussian wrath (inside she was on fire) and fetch him a resounding buffet on the earhole, to teach him some manners and how to conduct himself properly with *German ladies*, even if they were *Hausfraus*.

It seemed to me, no participant, but a mere observer, that actions like these had been going on for a very long time in Europe and I (as a mere Irishman) had no part assigned; it was out of my ken, a code of honour that was lethal, blood speaking to blood; defending something obsolete as honour with forms of reprisal (the early morning duel) as obsolete. I thought of the

German waiter standing stiffly to attention outside Kempinski's or was it Alexander's, the crimson cloth, the coffee and brandy, the cigars, the two Frenchmen coldly insulting him. Or the Spanish barman who had broken two dozen eggs deliberately on his kitchen floor because his hospitality had been abused by another Spaniard; to attempt to pacify him, I laid a restraining hand on his chest and it was as if I had touched a wall, hard as a castle wall in the sun: *Andalusian honour impugned! Banners! To arms!*

'May I?' the poet breathed with outrageous impertinence.

She was a four-square Berlin *Hausfrau* in a corset of chain mail and with an amiable social manner as impregnable as chain mail. Pan Cogito, the ex-Resistance hero, must have recognised at once the mother of a *Wehrmacht* soldier, one of the field-gray ones who had run shouting *Raus! Raus!* across Poland for six long years of burning and raping and killing, a veritable orgy of destruction against all things Polish, from unborn babies (murdered in their mother's stomach), to grannies and all their homes burnt down. She might have bred three or more of such furies, released them to go *Raus! Raus!* through Poland, lining up the Jews before long ditches they had commanded them to dig, and dispatched them out of hand as if killing rats, which is what they had become in Nazi eyes, for Jews had ceased to be human. Special 'treats' were arranged for Resistance fighters captured by the NKVD, SS and Gestapo, and Pan Cogito had been such a fighter, a brave one.

He must have known in his Polish blood and heart that here she was, the mother of all Polish misery, for his short hair was standing on end. Here was a Polish mastiff about to spring at the throat of his enemy. But of course he would not spring, he was much too much of a Polish gentleman; and the mother of his enemy, her soldier son killed twenty-seven years before, was about to stuff herself with rich *Kuchen*, for which she had a weakness, slowly easing herself down, rump foremost, on to the spacious seat that he had so thoughtfully wiped clean for her; all was in readiness to receive that purposeful stall-fed complacent German bum.

Now he looked younger than his years or his gray hairs would admit, smiling that inexplicable fixed smile, a smile caught in the camera lens for a pose that was intended for his Polish mother, who was dead.

She was subsiding, a descending shadow, on a patch of clover already darkened by the great descending cowy shape, well uddered, soft and pendulous, she was *Die Rose von der Alm*. And he, no polished Polish peasant but a rough cowhand in dirty leather jerkin tied about his middle and sweaty old hat worn back to front, for easy milking, was softly rubbing and stroking her great milky belly, urging her to a better yield. A *very* dirty sweated-into crumpled hat worn back to front to facilitate milking when pressed against Rosi's side and he could hear (with a halfwit's glad, sunny smile) the deep rumbling of milk as within a great deep Polish churn and his fingers were squeezing pint after pint of creamy milk into the bucket, and he was adjusting his sweaty hat on his round peasant skull, Rosi and himself pestered (for it was high summer) by swarms of eager Polish flies.

Judging the time to be ripe now (for no one had suggested a second round), I took out my yellow Spanish Bic retractable, snapped it into firing position and swiftly scrawled on the back of the Paris Bar menu: *Temporarily embarrassed and need some of the readies.* I was about to add: *Can you do the decent?* But wrote instead: *Can you oblige?* Signed it DAAD and pushed it across towards him, who had now turned his attention away from the Great Milker Rosi (or was it Heidi?) and the smile was gone from his face. Rosi (or Heidi) with shoulders bowed and arms moving with contained power, as if breast-stroking, was wolfing into the heaped plate of *Kuchen*.

Here Zbigniew Herbert was stumped. His French was

fluent, his German more than adequate, he could get around in Italian, knew some Greek, but his English was poor and this seemed gibberish: what were readies? He stared at the scrawl and then into the hazel Irish eyes with his blue Polish eyes. You are *embarrassed*? Do you suppose I am *not*, old fornicator? (his glance seemed to say). He practised a calm dissimulation. For he was not being asked to subsidize (not only subscribe to) DAAD cuckoldry—*another* cuckoldry, for this was not the only one, marriages were breaking up like ice floes in the spring all over Berlin. Were Poles openhanded like the Irish, I wondered, I who never had much of the readies. Certainly, he (Pan Cogito) was not too happy about it. Was he already worrying about getting it back? The amount (a modest DM 50) would not bankrupt him.

He studied the scrawl, his hand cupped about a cigarette, but could make nothing of it, shrugging and muttering 'Nyet', and pushed the menu back to me, who stroked the Bic through this message and tried any tack: *Sine pecunia* [how do you say 'I want . . . I need' in Latin?]. *Can you lend me DM 50?* And pushed it across. Pan Cogito took out a pair of old spectacles, cleaned the lenses with a tissue, affixed them on his nose and studied this carefully.

'Ahhh,' he said, 'aahha, *now* I get it. That might be arranged,' he said in a tactful aside, but vaguely, as if the matter did not greatly concern him, staring abstractedly at Rosi, who was still munching away.

So that was that. No subvention, no round. It was time to leave. He summoned a waiter with a swift hand signal.

They walked to the car, Pan Cog talking torrentially. The small car, a battered Lada, looked as if it had been driven all the way from Krakow.

'Where do you walk to?'

'Oh, around you know,' I said. 'Around and about. The Tiergarten probably.'

'Hop in,' cried the Baronin, adjusting her motoring goggles. 'I drive at *prodigious* speed, my dear husband map-reads. We are safe.'

'We are not,' said he, climbing into the passenger's seat beside the Baronin, who was puffing out her cheeks and pulling on motoring gloves.

But they had not gone far when he cried out to stop.

'Stop. I must urrr-inate.'

Then he was out with a hop, skip and a jump, running for cover and already undoing his flies, and had presently vanished into the high drenched bushes, for a shower had fallen while they were inside the Paris Bar.

The vinyl seating at the back had gashes in it as though it had been attacked by knives, a plaid rug was stretched over the front seat, a small memo pad (blank) was clipped to the dashboard. The Baronin was observing me in the little mirror with an amused look. Then she looked out towards the drenched bushes into which the urinator had disappeared.

'My husband . . .'

'Is a dear man,' I finished for her.

The Baronin laughed, stroking the plastic steering wheel with one finger of her gloved hand. 'That was not *exactly* my thought,' she said, still holding my eye in the mirror. 'My dear husband is a madman. Sometimes I wonder what he would have been like without the horrible war. Perhaps quite dull. Another man.'

'There is always war in Poland,' I said after a silence.

'That is true. Sadly true,' the Baronin agreed. 'There will always be war in Poland,' nodding.

Presently, he reappeared apparently headless, carrying a huge bunch of drenched yellow-and-white laburnum before him; and this with some difficulty was forced in through the window and onto the back seat, beside Lore.

'Drive on!'

Now they came to a roundabout and the two stout Hausfraus of the Paris Bar were about to leave the pedestrian precinct and make the crossing to the island in the middle and from there across the perilous way to the far pavement, but had not counted on him who urged the Baroness to accelerate about the roundabout and, sticking his head and great bully shoulders out of the window, he was howling some of the more rousing staves of the Polish partisan song (*'Jak nie Teraz, to Kiedy?'*) at the two hesitating *Hausfraus*, now marooned on the island in the middle and having misgivings about proceeding any farther, because of the madman howling abuse at them in Polish or Russian, as the Baronin drove at a methodical thirty-five mph three and then four times about the circle. The two *Hausfraus* were now thoroughly frightened, for the brown Lada went around and around like a toy stuck on its circuit, and the lunatic leaning out the window and making rude signs now, with a hydrophobic foaming at the mouth, looked and sounded demented.

'On,' said he, smiling a tight smile. 'We mustn't alarm them. Drive on.'

Now began the struggle to catch and release the bumblebee. The pollen-glutted bee had crawled out of the drenched laburnum and propelled itself towards the windscreen and the light between Baronin and Pan Cogito, sunken into his seat and brooding, both of them staring straight ahead in catatonic trances as though speeding at ninety mph, and not a steady thirty-five mph. A page of the blank memo pad was used to induce the bee to climb onto it and from there be released into the open through the front window.

And that was that.

On parting (no DM 50 denomination note slipped discreetly into my hand), the Baronin offered Lore a tiny frozen smile (the rarest of Polish orchids) and the back of her hand for me to assay a gallant *Handkuss* (does one fall on one knee?) and then the Herberts drove away in high style, with much hallooing and

valedictory hand-waving out of side windows. The back window
was still blocked up with a great pile of drenched laburnum.

'Now what?' Lore asked. 'I cannot ask my father to lend me
money.'

'And I certainly cannot beg favours of my wife.'

'No.'

'Do we get credit from Luigi of Rusticano?'

'We do not ask, dearest Schmutz. We do not *need* money.
Let us walk through the Tiergarten.'

So they walked hand in hand, without a pfennig between
them, through all the bronzed and burnished boscage of the
Tiergarten.

Günter Grass in Amsterdam

IT MUST HAVE been winter. I recall snow on the ground outside Templehof, Berlin West as it was then, on the flight back from Schipol. It may be that I confuse two different occasions, two visits to Amsterdam. It was a *Bookenball*, a *Buchfest*, in the late 1960s, or early 1970s, when 'happenings' still took place.

Grass joined Mary McCarthy on the podium to read their speeches on the subject of 'Literature and Politics'. Would I care to join them? I said that I could see no connection between literature and politics, and they said, 'Ah, but that is already a political statement.' 'It may be so,' I said, 'but it's not a subject that I am qualified to speak on. Politics is not my cup of tea.'

Grass, as you might expect, made a very good stab at it, telling his Dutch audience, mostly young, that his young sons deplored the fact that he wasn't left wing enough for their taste and this from the man who had stood on the hustings for Willie Brandt and written *Die Blechtrommel* and *Catz und Maus*, already well on his way to telling German audiences what was what.

Up stood a patriotic young Dutchman who began truculently enough: 'Well I, thank God, am not one of your sons.'

The speeches were supposed to continue through the lunch. Mary McCarthy made a diplomatic sort of address calculated not to upset Dutch or German sensibilities.

My Berliner guest was Hannelore, who had said of Grass: 'He looks as if he eats iron.' He spoke in the same manner and ruffled a number of feathers. The Happening happened, as was obligatory. Bezije Bif, a Resistance publisher, hosted the luncheon and some such gesture would be expected.

The first course was served up a number of times. A lamb was to be slaughtered in the kitchen and one of the serving girls took hold of the microphone to make a protest whereupon plates flew through the air and broke up at the feet of the orchestra. Grass gave a wolfish grin. Things were livening up. Mary McCarthy never stopped smiling. The pushy contemporary of Jan Cramer, Harry Mulisch (very mulish indeed) seized the microphone and made an impassioned appeal. Plates continued to rain down on the floor and broke up in the vicinity of the orchestra, who were beginning to look distinctly uncomfortable.

First course followed first course with timed regularity. The serving wench had handed in her notice. Grass was speaking to Mary McCarthy, even if he disliked speaking in English.

'Would you care to meet Herr Grass?' the beautiful Berliner, Hannelore enquired.

'Does Herr Grass want to meet me?'

'But of course he does. Are you not the first Irish on the DAAD?'

She went to the podium and Herr Grass inclined a civil ear to her. She came back, stepping over broken crockery, to say that Herr Grass would consider it an honour. So I made my way to the Great Man.

Nikolassee was too far out, he said; I must move closer to the centre of Berlin. He was in the phone book and we must get together one day.

The first courses continued to arrive, the plate throwers had desisted, Mary McCarthy's smile was fixed on her face. Hannelore and I decided to leave.

Günter Grass said 'You are leaving so soon?' 'We go for lunch,' I said. No lunch served here. Pleased to meet you. Will be in touch.

But I never did. Walking back to the hotel, Hannelore slipped and fell on the icy pavement.

I took a shower when we reached our room, cut my foot badly on the shower stall, bled like a pig all over the room.

Unless you stop bleeding, I am going to kill you, Hannelore said, at her fiercest.

Then the flight to Templehof, thin snow on the ground, the return home to Beskidenstrasse, the more than cold welcome.

Pinter's Pad

1. Calligraphy; such delightful copulatives

Calligraphy can be as revealing of character as a stutter or a limp handshake or halitosis. Pundit and pedagogue George Bernard Shaw had developed a crabby old man's hand when dispatching yet another of those interminable postcards of his to strangers all over the world. His vanity was boundless. He became a crabby old man in his advanced years, the only sign of light-heartedness or liberty in his autodidactical character was revealed as he danced on the avenue of Ayot St. Lawrence when his wife died. Hitler, another vain and humorous man, danced when Paris fell. It was not exactly a dance but a mock version of goose-stepping all-conquering *Wehrmacht* in their victory parade down the Champs Elysée.

Faulkner, as with Leonardo da Vinci before him, used a private code known only to himself, as I discovered when shown the MSS of *Absalom*, in the Harry Ransom rare collection at the University of Texas in Austin. The handwriting was singularly neat and meticulous where you might expect a splashy much-corrected text with numerous addenda, all dashed off in the white heat of inspiration in the hotbed of a Mississippi summer.

Yeats and Joyce had somewhat similar handwriting to one another. The varorium edition of *Ulysses* is as scored over as a war map, with addenda reaching out into the margins to accommodate the overload of afterthoughts. Bloom's member in the bath is memorably described as 'the limp father of thousands' as marginal addenda.

Some can write as they speak and to read their letters is to read their minds and hear their very voices' intonations, witticisms.

Rounded curvy linear handwriting with curlicues in it is generally feminine—the rough angular style with straight up and down strokes is male handwriting. If the downstrokes descend lower than the vertical ascend, you are dealing with a depressive, a melancholy soul. If the signature (Arland) dips downward like a ship sinking in the distance, it means that Ussher is in poor health again. The Usshers lived hard by Sandymount Strand and every winter they went down with flu.

Simple words can 'give something away', particularly signatures.

Here is a tall tale. Once in a high apartment overlooking Table Mountain in Cape Town I was invited to draw a tree by a man who boasted that he could read my character or innermost thoughts from a drawing. So I drew a tree of no particular species which was all roots and heavy foliage. He studied this decoy tree and said 'You love your mother'.

'Naturally so' I said. "But I thought the house was the mother and the tree was the father.'

'Well, not in your case,' he said.

I never met him again, but a month or so later when we were living in Johannesburg I received a letter from London informing me that John Calder of Calder Books and Barney Rosset of Grove Press had both accepted my first book, *Felo de Sé*. On the publisher's notepaper the Calder logo was the tree I had drawn.

My first wife has a copy of *Ficciones*, signed by Borges himself, an unusually assured signature from a blind man, following a public reading in London.

Beckett's handwriting had a distinctive individual cast to

it, punctuation resembling the French circumflex as if stabbed into the page. His first handwritten letter to me in the Isle of Man was incomprehensible; the only line I could decipher was 'despair young and never look back; for wisdom see Arland Ussher', giving an address in Sandymount Road. Thereafter he did me the favour of typing his letters.

What have Joyce, Beckett and Pinter got in common apart from uncommon handwriting? A love of white wine. Joyce preferred Swiss white wine with the significant name of San Patrice which he likened to 'white electricity'. Pinter followed Beckett in his preference for Sancerre. Calder, Beckett's publisher and friend used Sancerre in his conquests of the ladies and boasted of 300 by the age of sixty, so it must have served its purpose.

Pinter's own calligraphy is not what you would expect of a dramatist so laconic, and given to brevity. He speaks as you would expect such an author or dramatist to speak, sparingly. He is vague about his background and origins, except to say that the da Pinta's were Portuguese Jewish, possibly traders or ships' chandlers. His letters would surely be typewritten, dashed off at speed on an old manual long in service—but no such thing: handwritten epistles! The calligraphy develops along 'strange geometric hinges' (Webster), neither crabby linear nor upright, but a mixture of both. The words themselves are unusually large in his A4 white notepaper which can accommodate only a mere four or five words per line. They do not sprawl across the page but proceed in an orderly fashion, written with a fountain pen or perhaps the fat green rollerball I noticed on his desk. The contents are as brief as brief can be. The signature is huge.

It is an odd kind of unjoined up writing with words separated from those preceding and those following. The spaces between the lines are generous. The effect is of hieroglyphics. Isaac Babel too had this widely spaced-out style but the lettering was much more diminished, the words small and neat. When he began to make money from movie scripts, he had to support many poorer Babel relatives. When imprisoned by Beria, all his papers were destroyed and the great Jewish author of *Red Cavalry* with 'specs on his nose and winter in his heart' was shot out of hand.

Oscar Wilde the classical Greek scholar, had generous spaces ('leading') between the lines of his epistles and what can that mean? Kafka wrote his letter to Milena Jesenska as you would expect Kafka to write. He regretted a letter he had once written her and wrote a follow-up begging her to destroy the previous intemperate missive.

The first time I met Pinter was in our rented house in Beskin-straße in the Nikolassee area of West Berlin at a time when the wall was still up and you couldn't phone into East Berlin. He came with his Jewish producer, Max Rosenberg, to discuss the movie possibilities of *Langrishe, Go Down,* which Pinter was to script. We had to wait thirty-three years before it appeared on the big screen. Pinter asked for whisky but was happy to accept German beer as a starter and white wine for dinner.

'You know', said I, 'the von Ribbentroffs lived in great splendour in Dahlem not far from here. Albert Speer and his family lived in more modest style at Wannsee. He passed our local station, Nicolassee S-Bahn, in his open tourer en route to his office in Berlin. He was Hitler's architect; wasn't even a party member nor wore a uniform before Hitler appointed him Armaments Minister. One morning he noticed a crowd of Jews on the platform above but went on his way without thinking any more of them.'

'How did he know they were Jews?' Max Rosenberg inquired.

'How do I know that Harold is Jewish?' I asked.

'Well, how do you know?' Pinter asked. 'What is it in my work that tells you I am Jewish?'

'Victims', I said. 'Not even the women are spared.'

Pinter gave me one of his hooded looks and Max Rosenberg sipped his wine.

The second time my wife and I supped with the Pinters was in London when he was married to the actress Vivienne Merchant, living in an imposing Regency mansion in Regent's Park in a terrace of such dwellings within earshot of the London Zoo and may even have heard the bloodcurdling roar of the lions in their dungy cages, mad with captivity, bored out of their skulls. We were to eat out at a restaurant run by an Irishman.

Pinter threw open a door to reveal a steep flight of stairs leading down to a basement. He told us that their elderly housekeeper or cleaning woman had fallen downstairs and was lying there when they had returned from a night out. Again we were in Pinterland where awkward confrontations and calamities are commonplace. When we were about to be seated in the restaurant, Pinter suggested that the guests sit facing inwards towards the other diners which I thought showed evidence of a courtesy that had not occurred to his wife. In any case common courtesy is not too common nowadays. Or perhaps he, as the host who paid the bill, had the say in the seating arrangements. They had been to this place before and Pinter wished to show it off at its best. My wife left her Borodino hat behind in Pinter's pad. Old father Freud declares that leaving something behind is evidence of one's wish or intention to return again. Next day Vivienne Merchant took her to the bedroom and threw open the hanging cupboard to reveal a line of hats, among which were some Borodinos, and asked her to take her pick. Was this a subtle put-down or evidence of exquisite politeness? I cannot say. I do not recall anything Vivienne Merchant said in the course of the evening. I noticed a framed picture of Pinter propped up on his desk. The Emperor Napoleon exiled in Longwood House on St Helena had many statues, paintings and reproductions of himself at various stages of his career in the hallway and in every room of the house. Was he a vain man? Probably. Was Pinter? I think not, within reasonable bounds. He liked to get his way, demanded due respect, having come up the hard way from Hackney, like Chaplin from Kennington Oval. Both had made themselves into another person. Chaplin never acquired an

American accent, despite all his years in Hollywood. Pinter dispatched one of his succinct missives to me praising *Dog Days* as 'a bloody marvellous book' and inviting me to drop into his pad for a few jars if I was ever passing through London. Some time later I took him up on this offer.

***

The approaches to Pinter's pad are authentically Pinteresque. We stayed overnight with an old friend and were driven there by a sedated schizophrenic in a black leather jacket and head-gear which he never removed. He preferred to remain silent. A heavily built man with a bull neck who dropped us off at the mouth of the road where Pinter had his atelier because the entrance was blocked with branches of trees, like hastily thrown up barricades before the onset of some civil disturbance. Our silent driver was indeed a real life version of tough drivers in *The Room* and *The Homecoming* who silently indicated the interference and drove off. We made our way on foot up a short hill, coming to a house with a window open on the first floor from which viewing platform Pinter was looking out anticipating our arrival at the hour specified. As with Kafka and Klee before him, Pinter is a great starer-out-of-windows. 'Higgins' he called down. The face vanished from the window and presently the door opened on to the street and Pinter stood there vaguely outlined against a dark interior. 'Grand to see you again,' said I, though I couldn't see him with any clarity. 'This is my wife Alannah.'

What would be the proper subject to speak to Pinter about? World chaos, the mess in the Middle East, American Messianic or murderous imperialism, cricket, the eternal verities, the present state of the stage in London. As I recall, we spoke of the lamentable state of the Middle East, Clinton-Blair's bombing of Serbia and matters germane to these world horrors. The seating was arranged in a triangle with the host facing Alannah and the husband relegated somewhere to the rear left near a bookshelf where *Dog Days* was prominently displayed. It was the set of a Pinter play cast and directed by the dramatist himself. I suspect that had Alannah been a plain Jane, she would have been seated where I was sitting, cast in a minor role, so to speak, with not many lines to deliver. I kept my mouth shut, confining myself to a nod or two when Pinter glanced keenly in my direction. My wife, journalist and novelist, kept her end up splendidly, so much so that Pinter took an immediate fancy to her.

He had never heard the name Alannah before, he said. I told him it was a Gaelic form of endearment meaning 'my dearest one'. What does Pinter talk about on these social occasions? He hadn't met my wife before, so what subjects suggested themselves? A certain amount of protocol had to be observed. A reserved formality as when granted an audience with the Pope.

When Orson Welles shook hands with Pope Pius XII, the Pontiff clasped Orson's podgy hands for a quarter of an hour in both his and questioned him closely about the rumours of Irene Dunne's impending divorce and enquired what was Tyrone Power up to? He seemed well informed on Hollywood gossip, while the fate of European Jews did not seem to concern him overmuch. At least the subject was not broached. Perhaps that would have been inappropriate—Vatican politics decided otherwise. He had a pet goldfinch which he carried about on his forefinger. Welles, being an observant type, remarked on the scaly feel of the papal handshake (like holding the hind leg of a tortoise or the foreleg of a lizard). Pius XII was said to levitate about the Vatican gardens, possibly with the goldfinch fixed on his finger like a fat gold ring.

Could he not have opened the bulging Vatican coffers to alleviate suffering in Europe, excommunicate Mussolini and

Count Ciano, order priests not to hear the confessions of
Fascists, instead of levitating around the Vatican gardens with a
goldfinch stuck to one finger?

The forays into the next room continued, another bottle
uncorked, the genial host continuing to draw his lounger ever
closer to the charmer sitting opposite him. 'May I use your
facilities?', I asked at last, fearful to leave him and Alannah
together. In the toilet, a blown-up photo of the dramatist
glowered down at the pisser below and my member shrank
to nothing under that imperious stare. Was he not a mixture
of Shelley and Byron, the ladykillers, with an admixture of
Ted Hughes in the modern era? Hadn't one of Shelley's wives
drowned herself in three feet of water in the Serpentine and
Byron in the bedroom of a hotel in Italy had thrown himself
like a 'thunderbolt' on the chambermaid, according to Dr
Polidori? Rumour had it that a young actress had 'gone off her
nut' when Pinter discarded her. Perhaps Lady Antonia had put
her foot down put a stop to such cavorting. We had hardly
seated ourselves in identical black leather loungers, somewhat
similar to the black leather casting couch below, glasses in hand,
when the phone rang. Pinter picked up the receiver and said
'Higgins is here' and replaced the receiver. Presumably it was
Lady Antonia on the line. Pinter's recorded messages do not
belie his reputation for brevity. He growls, 'I'm not here.' Pithy.
Derek Mahon has even improved upon this brevity: 'Speak.' I
heard somewhere that Pinter will not be crossed, criticised or
contradicted and certainly not in matters political. He is very
fixed and steadfast in his attention to you, doesn't fidget nor
use his hands to emphasise a point, very concentrated keen eye
contact leaning forward. Only leaving the workroom to uncork
another bottle of Sancerre.

Wishing to change the subject and knowing of his interest
in cricket, I told him that I had played for Phoenix as a lad
under Jimmy Boucher, and fielded in his leg trap. Pinter said

that he had seen Boucher bowling at Lords and had been very impressed. "Do you know the best line you ever wrote?" I asked him.

'No,' he said.

'It's from "Hutton and the Past"' I said. 'Donnelly had made 180 for the Gents versus the Players and you wrote, "He went down the afternoon with his lightening pulls."' Pinter leant back, plucked the book from the shelf, checked the quotation was correct and returned the book to its place.

I told him about the late B.S Johnson, a disappointed writer had once interviewed me for the Overseas Service of the BBC at Bush House. On the way there he kept kneeling to pick up paperclips off the pavement discarded by those going in to broadcast. When the interview was over, he invited me to a wine bar to sample some of the master's St Patrice which Joyce had likened to 'white electricity'.

2. On Meeting Janusz Sikorski

My eldest son Carl works as film projectionist at Screen on the Hill and begins work at midday. I called on him and we had coffee in the foyer, then I made my way on foot up Roslyn Hill to Hampstead Tube Station and from there with some difficulty by Tube to the Angel Islington where I walked some distance to the Almeida Theatre to collect two complimentary tickets.

Tickets in pocket, I passed an Italian pizza place empty but for one diner and no piped music. I stepped in and ordered a Four Seasons Pizza and a glass of house red. The other luncher was a businessman studying documents. When he was sipping his wine, I called across, 'Have you seen the two Pinter plays running at the Almeida?' He said he hadn't but intended to. I was served a pizza as sticky as chewing gum and a glass of red wine and was then presented with a bill for £40.50. I walked across to my fellow diner and said 'I just got a funny bill. How is yours?' I showed it to him.

'That's a funny sort of bill all right', he said.

'Funny for one glass of house red and a poor sort of pizza', I said. The waiter was hovering near. I handed him the bill and said, 'Would you kindly adjust this. I'm a lawyer and could if I wished put you out of business for this chancery.' He took it with ill grace and went away. Presently he came back and presented me with a bill for £29.50.

'I hope you are not expecting a tip on this', I said, preparing to leave. My fellow diner collected his gear and walked with me to the door. 'I don't believe you're a lawyer' he said.

'What am I then?' I said.

'I think you may be an Irish playwright.'

'Not a bad guess.'

'What nationality am I?' he said. We were now standing outside the pizza place.

'You speak very good English,' I said, 'but you are not English. Do I detect a faint Scots burr?'

'I work in London and live in Bromley and have been doing so for many years. I've been to Scotland. My name is Jan Sikorski.'

I told him my name and we shook hands. 'Are you by any chance related to General Sikorski?' I asked.

'I'm his grandson.'

'Well, I'll be damned," I said. We had taken to each other at once and exchanged addresses.

'Can you lunch with me here tomorrow?' he said.

'Alas, no,' I said. 'I'm flying back to Cork this evening'. So we parted company. I was to receive postcards from destinations as far apart as Poland and Palm Beach and one evening the Sikorskis came to supper in Kinsale and we all got on famously. They had bought two or perhaps three bottles of excellent wine. They were devout Polish Catholics. I said I didn't believe in either damnation or eternity. He took me to the window and pointed to the sky above Kinsale. 'That's eternity', said he. Then he took me to the sliding door, all glass, overlooking the garden and pointed to the sky, 'And that's eternity'.

'Didn't the clever Egyptians, or perhaps Arabs, invent the zero in mathematics?' I said. 'Well, I believe in that even if I never understood mathematics, or ever wanted to. I still don't believe in eternity, or damnation for that matter. Where does Christian charity or forgiveness come into all this? Eternity is just another of those big empty words signifying nothing,' I said. 'I don't believe in it any more than I believe in damnation, as I once had the gall to tell Bishop Buckley of Cork.'

'Is Cork a city?'

'Does a bear shit in the woods?'

'I believe in Satan before I believe in saints and I don't believe in them anyway or any more than I believe in fairies or Santa Claus. In fact, I probably do believe in fairies and was told on good authority that they exist in Roscommon to this very day. Albert Schweizer is no more a saint than Archbishop Tutu or Mother Teresa, that bizarre trinity of holy shows. Nelson Mandela is the nearest you can hope to get to a real saint. Imagine breaking rocks for twenty-seven years on Robbin Island under Afrikaaner guards and coming out sane. If Gandhi was a saint, he was a foolish sort of saint who did nothing much for India— offering passive resistance to the cruel Raj and spinning wheels and goats in order to keep India pure, i.e. backward, like Dev and his bostoons and colleens dancing jigs and reels at every crossroads. Why do holy men and holy women always have to be simpletons or half-wits? The blessed, we are told, become pure spirits and are promised an eternity of heavenly bliss while the damned become impure spirits consigned to hellfire for ever and ever. This is surely chemically impossible. Even volcanoes have their periods of rest, even the Nazi crematoria. What in God's name are we dealing with here? Paltroonery, ignorant bloody apes, blind superstitions, the delusion of loonies and nutcases, dickybirds, or just heavenly whimsy? There's a statue of the Blessed Virgin on the outskirts of Baliinspittle, County Cork. Some years back she is supposed to have moved. The grotto has since become a shrine, but she hasn't stirred since. I was in a psychiatric ward with a fellow called Long who 'fervently believed' that he was the Holy Ghost. What we are looking at out there is just sky and bubbles, the troposphere above that, then interstellar space and then the endless void beyond. Not Eternity. Have you seen the two Pinter plays yet?'

'No. Not yet'.

'I asked Pinter what they made of *The Room*, his first play. He said with relish 'It frightened the shit out of them.' A blind negro is kicked to death by a character called Bert Howard, the delivery man. The audience seemed a trifle cowed. They refrained from guffaws at *Celebration* in case Pinter was having them on again. Better stay mum. Pinter was still too far ahead of them. Elliott's prim and proper cocktail party seemed as remote as Hackney Wick from Johannesburg, the Jo'burg on the Witswatersrand. *Celebration* had the waspish sting of Webster's *White Devil*. The weasel has crept back under the drinks cabinet.'

The Bosky Dew

Patrick Collins 1910–1994
Catalogue note for the Patrick Collins exhibition
at the Douglas Hyde Gallery, Dublin 1982

ULYSSES WAS HIS Bible. He called it Uley-says, liked to quote two lines from it: of Stephen 'rear regardant' and of 'The weedy watemays of Ireland.' These were the lodes, the fern seed hexagonals, the Cephalanthera and Epipactis, the bosky dew.

He knew Elliman (onto whose surname he insisted on grafting a third syllable), showed him where Bloom might have pitched from Ben Howth, tore the great ensuing biography in two, all 842 pages of it.

He lived in Ireland for most of his life, went abroad reluctantly, took Ireland with him. In a London restaurant he gave his order in atrocious French; waiting in the reception area at breakfast time was appalled to see one hundred identical men come downstairs in dark suits, bowler hats, with rolled umbrellas, carrying briefcases. In Turkey once on the steps of the station (Istanbul?) he saw a strange bug, studied it all day. He was a lover of the visible world.

His letters when they came were much like his conversation: tart, the telling phrase (he wanted to be a writer; I wanted to be a painter), a sort of Irish Degas; once in Normandy he had threatened to knock me down for dismissing the Frenchman's work. Self-educated, his mind was not narrow. He liked to talk, liked French wine and tobacco (Diskey Blew), congenial company, preferably Irish (the major and minor premise). He always had plenty of words when he wanted them, appeared to know a lot of people but had few close friends; whom his *intimados* were I never knew. He saw things that others less perceptive would have missed.

Once in winter after a shower when we were crossing transversally the wet Ranelagh triangle, heading for James Russell's godless pub, a thin young beauty in high heels stepped off the curb, seen for a moment in the act of crossing a narrow-road-become-stream-after-shower, and he glancing quickly said: 'Sandpiper.' He liked the jenny wrens in the low Normandy ditches.

Once he whistled a robin-hen out of a bush on the Howth Road, pretending to be a cock-robin at the start of the mating season. In his youth he affected a Latin Quarter hat, sunk deep in Celtic gloom, was Stephen Dedalus. He loved wild birds, first and last light, mystical nature who is commanded by obeying her (Bacon?); he fancied a spicy brand of Findlater's rasher which he cooked by throwing it into an open wood fire. He was rarely in low spirits, or hid it, never morose, a traveller who had remained at home. He liked the company of women. Once in a bosky wood with a tall lady, his nostrils dilated. After many years of confident bachelorhood he came to late fatherhood in middle age. He was never stingy, did not go in for our national sport: mudslinging.

His fragile art had something of the *muscae volitantes* to it, threads seen before the eyes, opaque fragments floating in the vitreous humour, flying clouds. He painted Howth Castle as though adrift on the outgoing tide, in unnerving hydrotherapy. He should have been a sailor in Melville's day. His art was circumscribed, as the Eskimos', but not for him le Brocquy's white spaces. His palette was feminine, pink, gray and faint blue, early morning sky colours. He admired the work of Cézanne, Léger, Pollock, Bacon, wild men with oils, his opposites. And

Nano Reid, Camille Souter, his familiars. He had something of
Izaak Walton in him ('Everything is alive . . . birds and animals
are as interesting as men and women'), or witty Charles Lamb
in a boisterous mood. There was something of the dandy there.
No shrewder judge of character ever trod shoe leather. He was
(still is) his own man. 'Any painting I did in my life,' he told
the *Irish Times* lady, 'has got forty paintings underneath it . . .
or maybe only five.'

He was touched by the sight of the prehistoric standing stone
in a brake of trees in Howth Castle grounds, as later by the
menhirs of Brittany. Underneath them lay the everlasting forms.
He painted the shadows of things, avoiding the direct face, the
later lies of Rembrandt. Opposites greatly appealed. He introduced me to Donne's poetry, the stories of Eudora Welty, Chief
Ikkemotubbe and Yoknapatawpha County, Flagstad singing
Wagner's *Liebestod* on an old 78, Flamenco music, Maire ní
Scollig, bottled and draught Guinness. When thickheaded he
could be brilliant. We walked on Sunday mornings in the damp
Howth Castle grounds, smoked Disque Bleu up in trees. He had
a grand laugh, low and personal, the Stuart love-locks nodding.
He had, one shouldn't wonder, something of the Shane O'Neill
nature: hot royal blood; yet he was good-natured. False position
induces cant; of both he was singularly free.

When I knew him first in his Howth Castle days, he was
working in an insurance office in O'Connell Street, and spent
six months or more on a painting, reworking over it with a
dry brush, layer upon layer of paint with little or no geometric
perspective, like the inside of a faintly luminous box; the
outside, the damp countryside, was all flux and flying cloud. A
technique like the lacquered nature painting of the Edo period
in Japan, long after Musashi the champion painter-swordsman,
or Jakochu who spent eight years on a series of thirty dyed silk
scrolls called 'The Colourful World of Living Beings'. One

looked into the details for a sight of Basho bound for some secret shrine, his stomach shrunken, ill with dynasty, living on black rice and sake. I was in my middle twenties, the savant-painter in his middle forties. His landlord was a Lord, related to a great Catholic family expelled into Connacht by Cromwell. Another attendant Lord lived in the bird sanctuary on Ireland's Eye. You spoke of the difficulty of getting any breakfast there, the profusion of daffodils in the grounds.

I first met Paddy Collins in Arthur Power's hospitable house behind the monkey-puzzle in Sandymount; 1950 it might have been. I'd met Power through Arland Ussher, whose name had been given me by Sam Beckett. The Powers had said: 'Higgins must meet Paddy.' A monk, Doris said, a mystic, who lived alone in a wing of Howth Castle: Kenelm's Tower. It was arranged. It must have been winter, I recall a coal fire burning in the grate. Brinsley McNamara was there. Collins arrived later with a gorgeous Spanish girl named Carmen. I knew no one in Dublin in those days, had written Beckett in praise of *Murphy*, and he had given me Ussher's address on Strand Road.

Lord Talbot de Malahide allowed him the dead timber in the grounds. I took to spending weekends there, sawing and hauling wood, sleeping on the sofa before the fire at night, listening to Collins speak. His boyhood had been spent in some strict religious teaching institution, he had been to Paris. Early on Monday morning the door banged below and he would be away. I put some of that time into a story called 'Tower and Angels' (from Donne's 'Aire and Angels') ten years later, and some more into a novel (*Balcony of Europe*) twenty years later, and more again into another novel (*Scenes from a Receding Past*) twenty-seven years later. For Heidelberg read Howth, for Neckar read Liffey, for Fishback read Millionaire's Cove, for Schloss Park Schwetzingen read St Stephen's Green, for 'Pastern' (the man who came to look at a horse and stayed as tenant) and 'Ruttle' read Collins, with an admixture of Ussher—the former objecting to the 'emaciated buttocks' of the latter. The Yeats family had once lived in Balscadden Cottage, John Butler taking Willie into Amiens Street and across to his studio on the Green. Collins had walked in the opposite direction across the Green to his office in O'Connell Street. I have come across a Merlin Revue (*Trimestrielle*) of Winter 1952/53 which he borrowed. *Godot* had just opened in Paris; corpses were being exhumed from 10 Rillington Place. Collins was living in Kenelm's Tower.

Of those finished times and friends, now so many gone to ground—Ussher, Terry Butler, Dillon and Campbell, Knudsen and Gerda Schurmann, Ralph Cusack, Behan, McNamara, Billy of Davy Byrne's—what remains? These canvases offer some kind of testimony. Painting, that most rigorous of arts, attempts the impossible: to arrest time. Now for a while the episodic labour of a lifetime is gathered together here; but its creator, I trust, has not yet finished.

Collins himself is not by nature a modest man; he knows too well what he has. He already praised in print Hone and Paul Henry (the latter 'a modest man who painted Ireland like an Irishman'), strangely omitting Orpen, but more gifted Irish landscapers (seers of sorts) were to arrive later—himself, Nano Reid, Camille Souter (an eerie Grand Canal in the Municipal Gallery as fine as Corot).

Jack Yeats in his later years applied oil paint thickly with a knife as if spreading butter, and his human figures are treated as sentimentally as any by Keating. As for Paul Henry, he had much to be modest about; instead of painting what was there before him, he seemed to be employing knitting needles (large wooden ones), and worked it out in gray-blue wool; not painting but woolgathering. Those absurd clouds and uninhabited cottages existed only in his head. The fierce cirrocumulus towering over Mayo, lit from within and behind, was beyond him.

But Collins's landscapes are quite another thing—the real thing, his own, and yours and mine, thankfully. Those remote images brought close seem to emerge from a hypodermic superfine. But you cannot take his Stations of the Cross too seriously. He was never a figure painter.

From Johannesburg I once ordered a Collins landscape from Ritchie Hendrick's Gallery on the Green; it arrived in due course at Jan Smuts Airport, with an old copy of *Ulysses* strapped onto its back. Back in Dublin and again throttled by pecuniary limits, I was obliged to sell it, the artist himself kindly finding a buyer in Sir Basil Goulding.

Paddy Collins has come a long way from Dromore West, from George Collie's Life Class, from Dermot O'Brien's old studio in Pembroke Lane, from Kenelm's Tower; from *Rain Lake* and *Moorland Water, Children in a Legend, Stephen Hero*; and yet not so far. This roundelay makes it all contemporaneous. The good things are not gone yet. Painter of *plein air*, paint on!

West Berlin Diary 1970

ONE MINUTE IN the life of the world is going by; hear it as it goes (says the musician). Paint it as it is (says the painter). *Muss es sein. En muss sein.* Café Funke on Martin Buber Strasse. Huge copper beech trees at the end of the road, road workers digging in a drain. Erlin Busch Park, Dahlem.

Five war veterans were seated on a park bench, four in the shade, one blind man in the sun, a blind man's stick between his legs. He removed his Panama to wipe his forehead, the crown of his head, his armpits. One day he sat on the bench with me, could feel me sitting there, maybe could feel I was not German. He had a wooden leg and chain-smoked cigars. He offered me one. He told me his parents were killed in Auschwitz.

Chestnut trees outside the Landhuis. Pacelli Allee, Podbielski U-bahn, Spanischeallee, the tennis courts.

Chinese children play in Schwartzer Grund. A sunny morning at Schlachtensee. Jagdschloss, Grunewald.

Do you recall the times, Hannelore, when we were afrolic like Antony and Cleopatra on the seashore, being the Nordsee sand transferred to the Havel shore where the swans hissed? I see you looking down from your high apartment where you live with the Blue Beast; I cannot exactly see you thereabouts, looking down on the Havel or the restaurant with tables outside. Didn't we go there once or twice? It rained. We walked to the motel in the rain and had coffee and cognac downstairs in a gloomy dining room. We spent the weekend there near where the tough Hell's Angels in black leather liked to congregate, gun the motors of their Harley Davidsons, the parting hogs grunting.

'Don't fuss.'

London Diary 1978

RITA WAS NAMED after Saint Rita, patroness of lost causes. She once saw Fred Rondel in the Serpentine Lido. Employed by Rachmann to clean his Rolls-Royce, Fred is a man of superhuman strength and as a result of maltreatment in a concentration camp, an excitable nature. He once bit off a man's ear and, on the spur of the moment, swallowed it. Posses of policemen have quailed at the thought of arresting Fred. He has a pointed head where he was hit with an iron bar.

February 10, Friday.
Blank until May.
May 3, Wednesday.
10:45 Sheil's office.
11:00. To Maschler at Cape, re *Colossal Gongorr & the Turkes of Mars*. Large dark old-fashioned publisher's office, Maschler in pink shirt coiled into swivel chair, asked me had I
written it. Considering it for Cape.
7:30. Harry's bar. Foss.
Damp drizzle. 'Enough to give you the pip,' says the bakery lady.
June 13, Tuesday.
Colossal Gongorr accepted by Maschler of Cape for £1,000. 2300 on signing, £400 on agreed text, £300 on publication. Fifteen per cent of first serial rights to Cape, control of US edition (if any) with agent. Publication in Spring 'probably'.

Dublin Diary

June 16, Friday (Bloomsday) Dublin.

Taxi to Heathrow from terminus for fiver to find automatic loading system out of order, flights delayed, boarding for Dublin delayed, faulty step, sitting in front with woman bereaved and small son of eighteen months, a Glasnevin woman and this her first time home in four years a sad occasion, the brother's funeral. Drank two gins and helped the bereaved woman with her baggage.

Sunny windy day in Dublin. Dinner at Nico's. Light on in Rough Deal (formerly) in Essex Street.

June 17, Saturday.

Sunbathing on patio, Protestant church bells ringing merrily, Catholic bagpipes played over the wall, coming on the breeze, the sparrows in the overgrown hedge, the high seagulls wheeling above, connection al fresco on a rug in the sun, Martini with ice, mint. Christine came by bike, long joint, Bustaid, sun all day, Christine departs. Roast chicken and brown rice salad, out to Phoenix Park, the herd of deer, the blue distant hills, the elderly jogger, the path, the official residence of US Ambassador Shannon, lager in Cheerio Ryan's pub, the red house on the Dublin quays, few cars, fewer people. Tedious film on TV, a highly improbable Hollywood romance, wine and then vodka, lights out. The clink-clink of the weighing-scales outside on the window ledge all night.

June 18, Sunday.

2:20 depart for Straffan. Two litres of white wine from Tommy. Sunny Sunday. A hitchhiker trying to get to Prosperous. Swimmers above the weir, school sports heard across the river, a loudspeaker, going monoplane flying out from Weston, the great beech tree fallen into the river, its foliage still growing, picnic on the bank. Straffan Inn. 'How he was makin' out I do not know. He was like a god to her.' Rosita in slashed shorts with one buttock exposed goes to change in Ladies. The guarded ways, accents of middle Ireland, the ugly housing development, the huge Esso signs. What Protestant church? What Celtic tunes? And where?

June 20, Tuesday.

François Truffaut married Madeleine Morgenstern.

Christine called third time for bicycle. Invitation to Eddy Delaney exhibition in Dun Laoghaire on 21st. Overcast, cold.

June 24, Saturday.

Rosita leaves for Kilkenny.

Reading David Jones's *Dying Gaul.*

Wrote review and posted it. Out with Mac Intyre to Searsons', Goggins, walked home to supper of cold chicken, wine. Rain about. Rain: 'the constant weather of this city' (McGahern dixit).

The garden destroyed. The pink in the cement. The disturbed boy. Harris the Gaelgog. The woman who shares two weak men. They beg to be chastised, she obliges. razor blade hung about her neck, tight-fitting, skimpy dress. The screeches of the man being beaten. Both lorry-drivers but weak men, no match for the fierce Punk. Little girls in white worsted stockings coming from school, already with the legs of teasers.

Aggressive girls are likely to become teenage mothers. Do girls make good mothers? Yes they do, yes they do. No they don't, no they don't. Do battered ladies ever bloom? No they won't. No they won't. Time alone can tell.

July 21, Friday.

Phoenix Park races. Won £70 on two races. Encountered Cronin in his tout's outfit, cloth cap, tipster's slouch. Therese in bed all day in darkened room listening to radio.

To Nico's to spend winnings. House empty at last. Denis Johnston on TV, of Blake: 'Death is the crown of life.' Good and evil intermixed in one and all. Death is the end of life. Poxy philosophy.

July 22, Saturday.

Overcast, threatening rain, phoned home. J. out of hospital on Wednesday, weak. Flattering Broderick review of Ussher's book of aphorisms, *From a Dark Lantern*.

Richard Harding, glazier, in Artane from age of four to sixteen, father abandoned family of eight, mother an alcoholic, makes movies. UCD student called with query about Balcony. Boucher or Fragonard? Writing thesis on Stuart, McGahern, Banville, Higgins, Moore, living in Australia.

August 4, Friday.

Duffy's Circus at Booterstown. French film music (theme for *Un homme et une femme*) emanating from Big Top as if from under the sea. Smell of dung. Horse-shoe shaped entrance, Est. 1775. Miss Maureen Francis all the way from Budapest. The Ringmaster, not dressed up but in suit, blows a whistle. Three Hungarian trapeze artistes, the clown Oxo on the rope.

August 6, Sunday.

Carl's 19th birthday. At 8:15 all the clocks stopped in Hiroshima on that hour and day of 1945, 100,000 Japanese died on the instant or within the hour, and a further 100,000 died thereafter. In clear round figures 200,000 corpses.

Smell of dust. Windstorm, a few drops of rain. Her face to the wall at siesta. 'I grew up in this kind of weather. I can't tell you how like King Williams Town it is.'

This terrible heat reminds me of you. That passion, that futility. Julien returning, probably unsober, after tiff 'concerning money.' *Mi casa es mi refugio* (?).

August 24, Thursday.

Up all night playing cards with Carlos until he retired to bed at 3:00. Two games of chess. Time-call for 4:45 am, taxi to Luton E 10, Monarch flight to Málaga.

The obnoxious young English family, wife with short hair dyed red, handsome husband and doted-upon brat of a daughter, in a squalid nest made up of scattered sheets of *Daily Mail*. Husband bears brat off to toilets. Young mother agog on their return: 'Did she go? Did she do it?'

From 1978-79 Diaries, London and Cómpeta

JANUARY 1979

4 Thursday

Some recipes for a freezing January.

(1) Basic Ale Flip

Heat the stove up merry.

Three or four pints of ale in a pan, a generous spoonful of butter, biade of mace, a clove.

Boil, set aside. Use a spoonful of cold ale to mix with beaten yolks of two eggs and the white of one.

Mix for all you're worth, with one of those French metal whisks if you can get it, and then mix more, adding the ale potation to that of the eggs. Pour between two jugs so as to froth. Might serve five persons.

Drink it all yourself, say I.

(2) Negus

A quantity of port to add to a double quantity of water. Sweeten the mixture with lump of sugar, some lemon and grated nutmeg, and the merest touch of the lemon's rind. A drop of ambergris. Or ten drops of the essence of vanilla. Serve smoking. Drink every drop.

Prehistoric Mnemonic Device

Captain Cook's Tahitian interpreter Mahine kept a journal in the form of a bundle of sticks.

Duel in the Woods

On a circle of old fencing-ground on Hampstead Heath near Kenwood, I saw two men from another century, fencing, watched by coal-black disdainful negress, who strolled off under the trees, dressed all in black. The villain in cape and knee-britches fenced with the dwarf Carlos Pavlidis. Were you to meet a man from another century, who would seem the stronger, you or him? *Le Grand Magic Circus* had played in Roundhouse—*500 Years of Adventure & Love*—and the great elm tree, 250 years old, still stood; to be blown over a winter or two later.

This vision for 'Students of the inexplicable, Perhaps more of Jerôrne Savary than Chateaubriand? 'He was the showman of grand tat of spangles, broken buttons and pluckable G-strings, and his rough artistry snatched up epic subjects.' Rehearsing with red scarf seven foot long about his throat, puffing a cigar a foot long,

6 Saturday. Epiphany

The rats are out in Mayfair, in a West End of uncollected garbage, industrial strikes and foul weather as Agatha Christie's old *Mousetrap* enters its 27th year at the St Martin's. But Jerôme Savaryz *1,001 Nights* is running at the Shaftsbury, Far removed from *Anorexia Nervosa*, Celia Gore-Smith displays melon-sized breasts tipping from half-bra, larger ones behind, above fishnet stockings, plays Pretty Lady, donkey Morgiarne, Mrs Sinbad, dances with the Spanish dwarf (Carlos Pavlidis) well aware of the power of her charms, regarding the audience through half-closed eyes, now dancing with the dwarf in her arms, she is fleshiness incarnate. With a bright smile she demands the Eiffel Tower as a present, to be set down in the desert; and when the curtain rises again, there it is, at dusk, sparkling in the desert. The small-time gangster in two-tone shoes is all twitches, his shoulder pads up like a ruff. Standing in the desert the kilted dwarf stares through a telescope at the distant glowing Eiffel Tower, then at the parterre, as at a spectacle just as strange, then up the skirt of the huge Scheherazade.

TinTin screws Princess Sultana on a sand dune, As he comes, his mouth spews blood, cries 'I grew rich by robbing corpses!' The concubines of the absent Sultan make merry; his soldiers kill the rutting partners who persist in their copulations to the bitter end. The show, which lifts one up and bears one away, like the grinning dwarf in Celia's arms, is dedicated to the *Gastarbeiters* of Europe, those unhappy men torn from their families and obliged to go to work in a foreign country whose language they do not know.

One rainy day we waited in Aranjuez in a café full of Algerian *Gastarbeiters* en route to Germany, those strong family men torn from their families; they tried not to show their pole-axed wordless misery. Is life thus? Then it cannot be lived.

Foss tells me of night-sounds in the Wandsworth kitchen. The sizzling of nocturnal cooking and the brisk clatter of cooking utensils announcing a night-feast in progress with their Anorexia Nervosa girl guest who will eat nothing during the day.

On the topmost flat on Muswell Hill Broadway, overlooking the dirty pool of the Broadway, the old spayed cat has been put down; the aged poodle whines all day behind locked doors or craps on our balcony. Miguel Baraddas is away again in Germany with the steel band. Tracy Goodman, his stupid mistress, wants to kill Miggy Junior, who is making her life a hell, 'ruining their relationship'. Uncollected garbage is piled up in the hall, where the post is delivered in an arbitrary sort of way, left on ledges, on the stairs; the garbage reeks to high heaven. This winter seems already endless. Life does get excessive, that's its way. Now the grave-diggers have gone on strike, downed tools, the dead left unburied.

12 Friday

Sunny morning. Julien has used up his pocket money and 'can't go to school'. Electricity and milk bills overdue. Accumulated mountain of garbage being most reluctantly collected, black plastic bags hurled into garbage truck, much detritus left behind. Borrowed £2 to pay for this diary in which I hope to record good news in coming year if I am spared. Passing the St. Martin's theatre one morning, saw some anxious punters looking for tickets to *Mousetrap*. Uniformed doorman (loftily): 'Not until ten o'clock in the morning is the box office open.' Like one of Dr Kakfa's doormen. The anxious punters have half an hour to wait, as I pass by.

Two gossipy queens in G.M. cafe in Museum Street. 'Ah'm very straightforward . . . verrry straightforward.' Eating cakes opposite leggy Pretty Polly hoarding of great persuasiveness. 'For girls who don't want to wear trousers.' 11 dernier. Premier Pickle. The madman carrying dry cleaning through the Broadway traffic that whirls around, avoiding pavement and making perilous progress. Glancing back with affronted stare constantly, head screwing on his neck, dancing on.

Saturday 13

Small bar on Rosslyn Hill in Hampstead.

Sahib masterfully drinking pint from pewter mug. With lofty patronage addresses uppity Indian not quite sober: 'How long have you lived here?' Rather puts him in his place, Hampstead or not. Not drinking from personalised pewter but from common pint glass.

'Fifteen years here and you criticise the country! My pedigree is two thousand years old.' As a grand oak casts its shadow, one can hear the unspoken prefix, 'My good man'.

H'rrrrrump.

Another Indian arrives, very polite greeting. "How are you? How is the family?"

'How's yours?' (*frostily*),

Sahib, mollified by invitation to drink, graciously accepted, 'I was down in Dorset. That's where you meet the British, broadly speaking, You're from Burma, aren't you?'

"First Gurka Rifles."

'Sterling virtues.'

Indian has begun to grovel a little (old bad colonial habits die hard), the Sahib (purple-faced) becomes more masterful by the minute.

14 Sunday

Irish pub in King's Cross where horses and form are discussed, stout punter like Scott Fitzgerald in houndstooth suiting with braces being desperately affable in a recognisably Irish way, Regularly spaced set of false teeth. Nicotine-stained fingers poring over *Irish Independent*, one of the most bigoted newspapers ever put out. Pub clock with Gaelic casualness a quarter of an hour fast. 'Commere till I tell ye.'

Devil Bar, Grosvenor Hotel on Park Lane. Irish barman in green jacket: 'In actual fact . . .' A formulation that used to amuse poet Kerrigan. Piped music, scent, Mike O'Meara of Rainbird Publishing collecting dry-cleaning after having his hair trimmed in Curzon Street emporium.

Wednesday 17

Foggy overcast on Broadway, *Hibernia* with Delmore Schwartz review, Brenan review today, gas on, paraffin heater, electric light, hungover, rail strike, truck strike, intimidatory picketing, twenty per cent or more pay demand, fifteen per cent offered, £90 or more brought home each week, Sheil phoned—departs tomorrow for ten days as cook on safari into Sahara.

Freshwater men called to examine damp patch on bedroom wall, Health Inspector complaint, could hardly believe that it had been leaking since 1970. Will send man around and phone before. Cheque bounced, error. Stink from below, Xmas garbage uncollected three weeks tomorrow, phoned refuse collection, tomorrow they say. We come tomorrow.

Reading 1971 diary, same situation. Back from 14 months in Berlin, rent overdue, rent and rates cheques bounced, two Freshwater repair men on roof.

18 Thursday

Grisly morn, foggy and cold, lights and heating on at once, refuse collection as promised, hurling black plastic bags into maw of refuse truck.

The IRA are back. At 12:46 a.m. in Blackwall tunnel in Greenwich a bomb exploded on gasometer holding seven million cubic feet of natural gas. 'This is the IRA. For God's sake do something about it.' The call came just before midnight to Press Association in Fleet Street, using IRA code. 20 pound bomb, 33,000 residents evacuated. Warning that Kensington gas works would be next target.

Lorrymen pickets, one man killed in Scotland on picket line, run over, salt scarce. No state of emergency says PM Callaghan with stiff upper lip, as flames leapt 300 feet into the sky.

Snow, freezing conditions. Mario the cat missing.

19 Friday

Colder, J. complaining of injury or pain in foot. No post. Nuala phoned. Mahon has not received paperback *Langrishe*. I have not received Hibernia package of last week. Wants me to review *Nightwood*. Post it now. Delays out at Heathrow, snow, icy runway. Brady 'fit' after attack. Arsenal midfield player set upon in Tube because of his Irish accent. 'They called me an Irish bum and blamed me for the bombings. It has nothing to do with me. Can I help it if I'm Irish?' reports *Evening Standard*.

20 Saturday

Wretched weather continues, wretched dreams, or more properly nightmares, water rates final demand £17.

21 Sunday

Muggy overcast, milk delivery at first light, collected wash, woman bellyaching about lost blue bag, so back through the murk, 3:10 on clock face just visible in the fog. Paulette and son around 5:00, supper, she shows a card trick learnt from St Exupery. Her tyrant mother hard with servants. Exhibition of her famous father's books in Paris. Lefebre. [sp?]

22 Monday

Phone Bank Manager or write. Mail again deposited in stinking hallway below, five stories down. Half of Inner London's 1,100 schools shut their doors because of shortage of teachers. NUT members were told not to cross picket lines, back caretakers and dinner servants out on strike action, some 'indefinitely'. London hospital strike of porters, ward orderlies and catering staff. A council spokesman for NIJPE said that 3,000 council workers were on strike in Southwark. 'It is an indefinite strike.' Ambulance men refused to answer calls in defiance of union pledge, those grievously ill are not taken to hospital, the dead unburied (gravediggers down tools). Barometer falling, England going down the drain. Prepare for the longest and grimmest of winters. Postal and telegraph strikes begin mid-February. Britain in the last third of the XX century.

23 Tuesday

Drizzle turning to sleet or snow, maximum temperature two centigrade, continuing cold, further sleet or snow forecast. Lighting-up times: 5:02 p.m. to 7:23 a.m. Irish Sea moderate becoming rough. Channel and North Sea rough. Barometer falling in Truss City. A handful of dustmen clustered around a brazier outside a council depot. NOPE pickets stood guard outside the gates of the Royal Free Hospital. Of the 76 stations of the London Ambulance Service (LAS) only 15 were taking calls. Phoned Tim O'Keeffe anent *In Night's City*—being read by his US associates. Phoned Faber anent *Nightwood* publishing history. *Gongorr* galleys arrived First Class Urgent from Cape. Phoned Mary Banks in Cape. Checked galleys in office and back through the slush. Two gallons of paraffin 93p. Some queries to Rosemary Goad of Faber.

'The women we encounter excite our imagination rather than our hearts. We love the world they represent and the destiny they make out for us.' Joseph Roth, *Flight without End* (*Flucht Ohne Ende*, 1927). The year I was born. That sad word, *Ohne*. Ineffably so. Thought for today. On, on.

28 Sunday

Widley Road with Leitch. Glenfiddich in bar, friend came, Corcoran, lunch. Recall little of this. Driven home, collected some wine. Slipped and fell awkwardly against gas fire in Elwin's room. Pain very sharp. Threatened to jump out window.

29 Monday

Less painful if I don't move. Brenan review for *Hibernia*, dictated *Nightwood* review to J. who typed it up. Emergency medico came, Indian, said I had four cracked ribs, gave painkiller.

31 Wednesday

Much pain yesterday, immobilised, difficult to breathe, today worse. Doctor called in morning, said he could do nothing. Ambulance called Hospital. Back here by 3:30 and soup and toast in bed. Relief that nothing worse happened, that I sent off review. Next lot of *Gongorr* proofs will include illustrations. Mahon inside institution in Belfast, drying out, says Leitch. Wants to go to US. Heaney was there, goes to Harvard for six months. At 7:00 Pam Presho called, had heard of accident from Elwin. 'You can't go in, the patient's having a

piss,' J. says. To her (outside). To me (head in door, eyes roll):
'It's your Old Flame.' 'Enter, Old Flame,' I said, making myself
decent. 'I just happened to be passing,' she said, widening her
nostrils. Wearing cast-off boots from War on Want which gave
off someone else's foot odour, old style coat with racoon collar.
Long black hair, fine eyes, left grammar school at age of 15. In
front room with Jill. Going she calls out good night.

1 Thursday
    Sunny morning, J. with toothpaste on brush, urging me to
rise. Telex of yesterday crossed with this today. Calder royalties
and cheque for £387 all titles, J's tart letter demanding payment
paid off (seven items unaccounted for).
    1 *Asylum* £400 from BBC (Trodd), half paid on signing.
    2 Ullstein *Langrishe* paperback advance?
    3 De Barra film option (£500)?
    4 David Jones BBC TV: 22,000?
    5 RTE 2 £200?
    6 Bourget Scenes French advance (£200)?
    7 Hanser advance?
    8 My Irish expenses (see letter to Davidson).
    Inexplicable items: Italian (Feltrinelli) advance on *Balcony*
only paid now?? Italian royalties for *Langrishe* only £3.07? Irish
Foresters quote £2:50 ??
    Paramol. Take six a day and two days of the week vanish.
Happened four times before. Whittington Hospital. Beautiful
young Pakistani woman vomiting black blood. Sounds like
an old woman behind the curtain. In a bad way. The husband
watching, listening, later seen outside the X-Ray room near to
weeping.

3 Saturday
    Sunny morn. Woke in pain, turning in bed. Clear sky. No
post. Tim Truss, Carl's friend, here as usual. Julien now sleeping

late, 3:30 and still comatose. J: 'Oh why am I not in Spain?'
I take to such complaints as a matter of course. Her tail of
Tampax. And then again, then again, her lack of freedom, no
space to write in, be composed in. Emergency doctor said I had
4 fractured ribs and inflammation of the lungs, an alarming
diagnosis. 'You are a smoker?' Of course. Frowning, writing
out prescription. Awkward night, loud stereo and cries from
drunkards on the Broadway. Regular twosome arrive at 11:00
p.m. to spend night on Carl's floor. Mario and Truss, two
Damon Runyan gangsters. Truss & Mario.

5 Monday.
    Deposited £387 in National Westminster. Buy *Waning
of the Middle Ages*. Typewriter ribbon (black), envelopes and
stamps. Write Calder to query missing items, about £2,000
unaccounted.
    Phone devious Calder, who 'cannot remember' what was
paid in TV rights for *Langrishe*, 'cannot recall' if any cheque
came in. Same for *Asylum*. Ullstein pay Hanser no royalties 'for
a long time'. What of French advance? Bourget remains silent.
'I got your small cheque,' I tell him. Silence as he digests this. 'It
wasn't a small cheque,' he says. Devious accountancy.

14 Wednesday (St. Valentine)
    J. cries of more snow, the window clogged up, the temperature
dropping, Kevin Keegan's birthday (Elwin's hero). Elwin sends
him present (harmonica) to Volkspark Stadium in Hamburg.
Huddled against window in djalaba. Elwin out to see friend
Anthony, posts letters to *Hibernia* (Heath and Lash reviews),
Hamburg (the harmonica). Hibernia owe £100. Postal and
telegraph strike begins Monday, so Dublin revenue terminated.
May go on for months. More snow by mid-morning. Front
room now too cold to work in. Silvie Butler's Bologna address.
The late Terry wrote March 3, 1969, ten years ago on my

birthday. We were in Nerja. The dead are receding from us; we are receding from them.

Cold continues, increases, Broadway silent, no buses running. J. 'not funky' leaves before lunchtime, buses now running, back before six. 'It was an ordinary day; it bared its teeth at me.' Dr Franz Kafka of Prague.

17 Saturday

Shifted furniture out of bedroom into freezing front room overlooking frozen Broadway and bus terminus, public toilets. Converted bedroom into living room, overlooking snowscapes beyond Express Dairy before Queens Wood, distant dome of St Paul's.

Uncomfortable night. Freezing air gnawing through the walls. Seagulls flying around in the fog. Front room not used now, being too cold to heat. Cat shat on mat, under impression it was fine river sand. Walked out for first time in weeks, ribs still trouble me, injury happened over three weeks ago. Ski-slopes below Alexandra Palace. Emergency rubbish tip along venue, odourless in the cold. Poverty means 'to have no choice'. A continuous fight against beastly circumstances, against others in poverty, always.

Foss phoned, to meet in Princess Louise in Holborn at 6:00. The Shankill Butchers sentenced in Belfast. 11 sentenced. Leader Moore is credited with 11 murders or attempted murders, his friend 10 murders. I read in *Evening Standard*, drink fresh squeezed orange juice in Italian place, waiting for Foss, a most punctual fellow. Must tell him that Paulette knew St Exupéry when she was a child in St Amour. A heavy man in leather leggings, had one card-trick as a party turn, which she has taught her adopted son Kieran.

Up bright and early. Sunny morning. Embrace from the two lads. Julien's *Adios, mi padre!* from the door, Carl abed, not working today. Draw £30 from bank. Buy Surfacing by Margaret Atwood for journey, Virago Press. Heathrow Central, Terminal 3. Air Canada flight for Vancouver already boarding. To Sands Motor Hotel on English Bay at Stanley Park. Sylvia Hotel (first choice) was full up, receptionist phoned Sands. Pain of decompression, descending (ears); pain of Mayo knee excruciating, after sitting for hours. View like Hanna's flat on 16th floor facing Málaga harbour. Here the open Pacific, the riding lights of the ship moored in the bay. The long brown legs of the joggers. No Disque Bleu, the light going. Phoned University of British Columbia but Philip Moir out, expected back soon. A couple jitterbugging in a 4th floor flat by big windows. The light going. Trolley buses leave for Main. Lilac horizon, lights of ships at anchor, the narrow view of sunset between high rise apartments. The air of the bay. Uncertain of exchange rates, supperless to bed, nursing knee, after powerful shower, ?? chlorinated white water.

28 Saturday

Meeting Parry at Drury Lane pub. To Spread Eagle in Wandsworth until closing time. Hot food in Indian restaurant. Parry departed for Elmers End. Dossed down with Calnek on Foss's hospitable floor. Up at 7:00 a.m. to Saturday drizzle. Away after Calnek before house was stirring. A No. 19 to Centre Point, 134 to 'home.' Not sweet. Sour reception by herself. 'Don't wake me up, I must have sleep,' ominous; as proved to be correct. 'Oh so it's you.' Maximum acid, then tears and recriminations etc as per formula, all within hearing of Julien, who is having party tonight. Saturday.

Calnek phones. He and Angela. But party here. After much phoning and rearranging of plans, end up in Harry's bar in Hampstead, Angela arrives late, 7:00. Calnek, sour, about 9:30. Double brandy for Angela. Closing time. To Indian restaurant. Protocol of ordering. Waiter will not allow two main courses divided three ways. Calnek rises up in fury. 'As far as I'm concerned, you can shove it up your ass,' and marches out, followed meekly by us, to bad meal at Polish place, no difficulty with ordering. A pattern begins to emerge. Salting his meat when told in dumbshow by elderly bearded Arab of Tangier that salt was bad for him. Head Waiter insulted in Copenhagen hotel. Trouble with free drinks on the Tangier-Málaga flight. Horses for courses. Long wait for taxi at Round Pond, Calnek simmering, humours ill, 'this is no true capital city'.

Return by cruising cab to dog's dinner that is Muswell Hill Broadway, expecting to find Julien's party in full swing, but only burst balloons, peanuts shells. Party was fiasco, only seven turned up, got Julien drunk. Poured bucket of water downstairs after departing guffawing guests, shouting 'You bastards!' Gallon of cider almost untouched. Jill returned to find him on sofa with balloon on his chest, 'like twelve year old'. Sewed on buttons, packed suitcase, all sweetness. Angela slept in Elwin's room, Harry in front room, both had departed when I rose at 4:00. Bon voyage.

24 August 1978.

19:13 from Málaga Station. Barcelona tomorrow evening, hotel in the barrio. I haul bags from point to point, misinformed of departure times. A bus leaves at 2:00 am from back forecourt. Back forecourt? Two Iberbuses arrive in front of station when I had decided to wait until ungodly hour for wrong bus at rear. Relief to be away. Norwegian queer courier. Return for private filming of *Langrishe* at White City, script by fastidious Pinter close to original.

16 September Saturday 1978.

Reach London, God willing, around midday. Departed August 24th.

London

Shared taxi with Doyles who live near Muswell Hill and have a house beyond Cadiz, Jerez. Dropped off at corner of the Broadway, sunny breezy day in London, warm. Met Carl at door, he astonished as I, was not expected until tomorrow, flat in disorder. I had bought bottle of Scotch.

Told them of wild life in Ramblas, riot-police standing about in camouflage gear, sallow complexions, armed with bazookas. Transvestite prostitutes at street corners. Drinking with Sven who runs an ice cream business in Torremolinos, another gaudy metrollops.

19 September, Tuesday.

Private showing of *Langrishe*. BBC Television at Wood Lane, White City. Ask for Stuart Griffith at Reception. 6:00 showing for 8-10 persons. Foss entering masterfully. Angela arrives later in the bar. Huge bearded security guard takes her under his wing. Names given, also double gins, all ushered into small projection room. My three sons.

Jill's comment: Story told by Otto, not Helen, otherwise very faithful to novel. Even Oscar the dog was in it. Sheil's comment: "Hardly Anglo-Irish.' Catholic Ascendancy looked like Czarist Russia, a Dacha in Odessa.

20 September, Wednesday.

The small black poodle (one of two devils) who prefers to deposit knotty dry turds on our balcony is howling next door in Miggy's flat.

September, a season of wasps.

Chinese couple black-berrying on the banks of the old railway line to Muswell Hill, a station long demolished as the race track of Alexandra Park.

Uncollected garbage on Archway Road. One cannot throw open windows in front room overlooking the dirty pool that is the Broadway, because (1) rising toxic fumes, (2) thieves on the scaffolding outside, pretending to be working.

Archway Road, that squalor. Sheridan Quality Butcher. A sea-chest outside the Peacock second-hand furniture dealer. Pit-Stop Exhaust Centre.

Collected *Gongorr* typescript from Susannah Clapp and gave her some drawings.

Phoned Leitch. Saw *Langrishe* again, at his place. His derision. No, no ! Sandra' s rage. 'You sneer at everything.'

The Orange yoke. The crab apples small and sour.

Wasps everywhere. *Wongor*—hoax book supposedly from Australian aboriginal, discovered (reputedly) by Yugoslav talent scout whose name when translated from Serbo-Croat into English means Happy Christmas. If the stories are good but the whole thing a hoax, can it be taken seriously? Answer: Yes, if it makes money.

Maschler in two minds, confused, smiling tightly.

22 September, Friday.

Carl is 'doing up' his room. All woodwork stripped, even skirting boards, and a pale imitation-woodwork wallpaper affixed to the walls. He is attempting to tame four young mice ("mices"). Bill Swainson sends proofs of *Asylum*, due November with advance copies mid-October *Langrishe* 3rd printing. *Scenes & Asylum* for Riverrun Press in New York. Frankfurt Book Fair? Kluger's translation of Scenes for Hanser? Pile of junk and empty wine bottles emptied onto the balcony. He is also "fixing up" the outside coal-hole.

24 September, Sunday.

Walked out with J. early, around former racetrack at Alexandra Park to Hampstead Heath, third lovely September day in a row. You read the notices to me under a tree on the heath. Clive James critical of Pinter, Denis Potter ecstatic, Philip Purser moderate.

29 September, Friday.

Mary Banks phoned from Cape. Last queries about *Gongorr*, text now ready for printers, preface approved.

Letter from Rosita. Miserable. Needs £100 urgently.

No review in NS.

J. arrived late with Callus and two bottles of red wine. Callus on best behaviour, moored barge in Chelsea Reach, saw advertisement for relief barman, marched in, said 'I'm your man,' got job on spot. A fiver for 11-3:00 p.m. New shoes £17. Clothes in dry cleaners. No longer taps left toecap on ground (compulsive tic), touches left thigh. What would Holmes make of this? Shaggily looking into *Houses of Ireland*, muttering 'Dismal. dismal.' Lack of people? Chess with Carl. 'Give you a game, Trevor!'

Next morning found bed tidied, bird flown. Stink of cat-crap (Mario) to bless traveller on his way. Angela thought to be working in antique shop in Notting Hill Gate area, calling tomorrow.

30 September, Saturday. First wintry day.

2 October, Monday. Week 40.

Wallpapering in Carl's room. Bath. Invitation to Philomena's. Walk as far as Highgate Wood gate with Julien. The fat white goat Clancey, tamed and frisky, gallops through Queen's Wood like some heraldic beast, or a regimental mascot, over the mass-graves of the Plague.Philomena under threat by threatened sale of house. She would not find another apartment for £10 a week. The Chelsea Girl Grace Johnson died of cancer, left all to her girlfriend, an old love, wanted to see *Langrishe* film before she died. What's it all about?

She knew, Philomena said, knew she was dying.

The dead: Terry Butler (in Bologna),

Gerard Dillon (in Dublin),

George Campbell (do.)

Peggy Keenan (in London)
Grace Johnson (somewhere in the shires).

3 October, Tuesday.

Stanley Spencer at War for review for *Hibernia* (a request), after Grass: *The Flounder* (*Der Butte*). Anthony d'Offay Gallery of New Bond Street showing drawings and paintings by Spencer the mystic. 47 Downshire Hill. Richard Carline, brother-in-law of Hilda Spencer. Letter to Theocharis re lost *Vanishing Heroes*. *Asylum*—what's it about? About a man going mad on the Isle of Man.

7 October, Saturday.

Sunny morning, cloudless, breezy day. Posted 'Down the line' Spencer review to *Hibernia* with Grass review. Pain in lumbar region gone but poor sleep. Another dream about Springfield: wrote radio drama, crowd strolling down to kitchen to hear it, brother B., all windows fogged up, deep winter. 'The Ritual of Death' or some such portentous title. *Colossal Gongorr & the Turkes of Mars* from Cape in Spring. *Aslyum & Other Stories*. *Langrishe, Go Down* 3rd printing in November.

The coal hole refuse can only be collected by special collection on November 9th. Just another gesture of bourgeosie impotence? Angel Cake.

12 October, Thursday.

Anton Felton lunch postponed. White Elephant, Curzon Street. Elwin to Whittington Hospital for knee. No X-ray, no school. Sunny day. Voice of Grass on Kaleidoscope. Speaks of a lost Danzig.

13 October, Friday.

To meet David Jones in Harry's bar. Bald, he says, over 6 ft. Met Grass in Berlin. 'No playwright.' Producing Babel play.

Tancred Dorst movie on Hamsun that Jones (Somerset Welsh) would like to film. Hadn't read *On Overgrown Paths*. Gave him copy of Delacorte Press *Balcony*, get Ken (Pennies from Heaven) Trodd interested. To contact Trodd when he has read *Balcony*.

14 October, Saturday.

Third or fourth day of fog. Saw von Sternberg's *Scarlet Empress* with Foss at Everyman. Dietrich & Sam Jaffe (1934). Borrowed £3.

15 October, Sunday.

In 18th century all believed, as did Dr Johnson, that swallows lived in ponds all winter, their wings folded and in trance under water. Only one man sceptical in England—Dan Defoe stood on coast and saw swallows fly away to warmer climes.

Now the rubbernecks gape up. Today I took taxis around to cash £300 less commission £268. The day the pub was overflowing, J. not there anyway, I went to 'quieter' bar, three gins, gazed about.

16 Monday. Full moon.

Sheil's office. Felton luncheon engagement with Sheil and Rosalie. Foss advises caution about taking civil actions against publisher, no possibility of winning such actions. Seven publishers owe him about £20 each. Felton requires any correspondence on last Arts Council grant.

Trodd in Belfast.

Rosalie will arrange luncheon when he returns, has read script of *Asylum*, second treatment due from Ruth Carter.

Brief session with affable sharp clever Jewish lawyer Felton, no lunch. Stood at street corner. Dived into pub. No money. Rosalie never finished her whiskey. Asked Sheil for £300 less commission. No change from Scots flower-seller. Was to meet J. in pub near Covent Garden, taxi blocked in traffic.

18 October, Wednesday.

Julien (at Barnet since Sept 11 when I was in Spain) brings his big drawing book home, drawings of cauliflowers etc, shows great improvement.

Sharp pain in lumbar region gone, replaced by ache in gums. Beard-scratching, no exercise, no will.

19 October, Thursday.

Post: Felton requesting paperwork of financial relationship with Calder, to link in to Sheil paperwork. £267 cheque from latter representing last *Gongorr* payment, Cape cheque in Spring to go to Sheil. £60 due from *Hibernia*, gives £50 to RS. Say £28 in hand. £75 to lads in £25 portions. £20 dairy bill. Calder (per Swainson) in hospital (pneumonia), having lost voice, now coming back. Carl abed until 4:00 pm.

£45 due from 3 *Hibernia* reviews, sent to RS. £15 due to me for Spencer review published. Loud truculent knocking on door from truculent dairyman (Irish) with bill for £25 outstanding. 'I can count.' Previous debtors escaped down fire escape. Sunny day. Flat cleaned. All in readiness for the great day tomorrow.

21 October, Saturday.

J's 49th (?) birthday, wedding anniversary coming up on 26th. Philomena, Leitches, Sheils, Derek Mahon, the O'Farrells, Foss and Jenny, Fiona and Goldblatt.

22 October, Sunday.

In bed until 4:00 reading *NY Review of Books*. Gave £25 each to three *Gongorr* authors.

23 October, Monday.

Sunny day. Walked out by Alexandra Park, first day of half-term. Guy Fawkes coming up, Queen's Wood, Highgate soccer players, ground covered in acorns, two squirrels in a chase, buy long bread from courteous Indian, Marmite. The keys cut at Shepherd's still do not work, he re-cut the wrong key. J. upset, second letter from boss, trying to get rid of her. Carl buys new suit in Tottenham Court Road for £39. J. drafted stinging reply, phoned Fiona, her lawyer advised. Disturbed night, wake to overcast gray day.

24 October, Tuesday.

Leon Edel: Rivalry between James brothers.

The Waning of the Middle Ages. Huizinga. Dillon's.

Life in the English Country House. Mark Girouard. Yale UP.

The Garden & the City. Maynard Mack.

A Week on the Concord and Merrimack Rivers, boat trip by brothers Thoreau.

Walden—nine years after taking up residence—a quest for the recovery of self, as the extremity & precariousness of mood generated by its inwardly spiralling from an illness—sentences.

Thoreau d. 44—wrote over 2 million words or between 10,000 & 15,000 words a day. Brother died of lockjaw.

25 October, Wednesday.

Jacket designs of *Asylum & Other Stories.* £5.95 1000 copies cased.

£2.95 $11.95. 2000 paperback

UK & USA (Riverrun Press Dallas).

& *Langrishe* £2.95 $6.95 paperback only

Photostat of Felton letter to Calder asking to see his books. £45 to RS. 'Am in love with you without putting a tooth in it.' H'mm.

Several thousand cased *Langrishe* in hand per sloth Cresey, Not much demand following Pinter-Jones TV film.

26 October, Thursday.

23rd wedding anniversary.

Afrodita tar Hjem from Gyldendal, Nanna Jeiner, dedicated to her suicide sister, J. drafted letter, defence, adrenaline flowing, enraged with her boss. Today decides not to write letter, not defend points made, must accept that she is getting on, slowing up.

1 November, Wednesday.
Cumberland Stores Saloon, Beak Street.
Neil & Vivienne Jordan. They have lunch with Sheil. Back by 3:00. J. in woods watching autumn leaves fall.

2 November, Thursday.
Whittington Hospital Out Patients' X-Ray for Mayo knee, giving me trouble; a cripple in Central London. Swainson phoned. *Scenes* reprinting September 79 in paperback, only 200 copies sold since January or total of around 2,000 in a year of trading, less than LGD in a couple of months in '66.
2 advance copies of *Asylum*, bulk of printing in tomorrow. 500 sheets of *Langrishe* went up in smoke at warehouse fire. Third reprint ready. Trodd to discuss *Asylum* as Play for Today series. David Jones reading *Balcony*.
Arnold of Hanser Verlag wrote: 'The advances from Ullstein were accounted with the advance we paid to Calder (for *Balcony*). So Calder should inform you on this matter. I have just received translation of Scenes from Martin Kluger.'

13 November, Monday.
Phoned Swainson and Calder himself answered, 'all alone' in office, sounded baffled, said review copies had been sent to *Tribune*, then contradicted himself saying LCD copies not ready yet. This does not exactly inspire confidence. Bill on vacation this week.

15 November, Wednesday.
'Gas in the Decompression Chamber' until 5:00, caught No.

134 rounding corner in the rain, fare not demanded as usual, walked in fine drizzle from Warren Street to Duke of York in Charlotte Street, under new management, redecorated, and Foss seated before half pint of Bass. Northumberland Arms & girl in combat jacket with insignia reading *Plexus*, face invisible, straw-coloured hair, very hot. Still drizzled, under Foss's lady's umbrella or brolly to Museum Tavern, American Hot & bottle of Valpolicella at pizza place, cognac at Plough, near-blind man reading letter at end of bar, pages close to eyes. Foss held forth in praise of Coleridge, even *Ancient Mariner*.

16 November, Thursday.

Hangover, sunny morning, Carl abed until 3:00, J. in bathroom preparing to go out at 6:00, left before 5:00 after varnishing heater.

Phone call from Sean V. Golden in US, 30 pp of Schoneberg to be cut to 12 pp. Went on working on 'Gas in the Decompression Chamber'.

Bill Webb of Guardian has not received *Asylum* or read my letter or knew about publication date, not contacted by Calder office. *Tribune* knew nothing either.

Chimney sweep to call & Gasman after, to fix gas heater in front room. Painting kitchen. Sunny day becomes overcast later, with drizzle.

19 November, Sunday. Week 46.

Up till 4:00 am last night. Ravel, Berlioz, slow chess with Angela Vernon (the way she likes to play), Foss phoned re O'Meara lunch Tuesday.

Did not venture out all day, late breakfast, Julien bought two bottles of wine, Angela cutting out skirt of Liberty print. Lost 4 games of chess, won 5th, Angela affecting exhaustion as I recall before, continuing to play with Carl whose voice breaks back with excitement.

Exhausted, retire after 12.

21 November, Tuesday.

O'Meara lunch 12:30, 36 Park Street.- Grosvenor Hotel rear entrance.

Tagebuch einer Velorenen by G.W Pabst with Louise Brooks at Goethe Institute, 50 Princes Gate SW7. 6:00 pm. Not great.

Trinka puppet exhibition at Reed House, Piccadilly. O'Meara told of sitting on Barbara Cartland's poodle. Chinese restaurant with geisha girls in pyjamas slit to the crotch, O'Meara very familiar. Bill of £41 gives £14 a nob. O'Meara treating as usual.

24 November, Friday.

Sunny then chilly, letter from Philip Haas, assistant to Clifford Williams RSC 'admirers of your novels & short stories—would you consider a commission for the writing of a play?'

29 November, Wednesday.

Cape party 9:00 pm in the Graham Greene Room.

Party assembles in Maschler office & annex, red and white wine. Heard Ian Craigh introducing himself to someone unseen. American woman who farms in Gloucestershire likes sheep. Sheil came after Pinter play with Mary. Met Ian McEwan, influenced by Alan Burns he admits. Music playing upstairs, trio or quartet. Maschler in open-neck shirt. Tall brunette of surpassing beauty coming downstairs with packet of Gitane open in hand, disappeared. Susannah Clapp in off-the-shoulder black being approached by drunken fellow with American accent. J. dressed for the road sitting on bottom step. Taxi home.

30 November, Thursday.

Publication of 2nd edition of Felo (*Asylum*) & 3rd printing of *LGD* & in Dallas, Texas, *Scenes & Asylum*.

Foss phoned. Calnek sent him about 40 pp to read, wants me to read. (Why send to Foss first?) May have to leave for Canada, harassment from Roman lawyer, not working too well on book (I imagine lonely). Too depressing to go into, Angela has details. Always this mystery. Contact so-and-so for details, harrowing.

1 December, Friday.

BAFTA. Robert Cooper of Belfast BBC wants original radio play from me. Bar on second floor. Rosalie Swedlin all day in BM researching cookery book, lives in Islington, car parked somewhere.

Ken Trodd. Stuff suspended from about his neck, I Am a Security Risk badge, look of Scotsman (Trocchi?), shirt open several buttons down, reluctant to meet your eye. Third version of Ruth Carter *Asylum* script going well. Director may or may not be available in March.

Otello, Old Dean Street, Soho. Cooper asking for narrative play. Said no, then suggested Glimpses of the Great Micky. Freezing night.

Dream: Unknown thin girl shows front tooth missing, says much stuff was drained off, pus, her fans collected it. I asked will you have a new tooth? Will you be able to sing? (She must be a singer.) Oh yes. She fits in very white false tooth, longer than the rest.

Earlier today an ungracious loan, ungraciously dispensed by J. (sourly) 'We are not going to support you.' The royal we.

2 December, Saturday.

Freezing night. Return after midnight, feeling ill.

Skinhead on No. 134 was upstairs among the smokers, ordered his buddy to sit behind, doesn't like to share anything, shambles off at Broadway, heavy Bovver boots. Lumbering off to catch No. 7 starting for Finsbury Park.

Dirty frozen tarmac. Soho full of drunks, piss, assembly of men outside Sauna Parlour trying to pluck up courage to enter.

Dream: London bridge, say Vauxhall, wide low walls, no traffic or pedestrians, I am crossing right to left towards Elephant & Castle, Oval, see Miriam Makabe in shorts in middle of bridge being chatted up by two admirers, gabby American tourists, lowsized but insistent. I call over, 'I heard you sing in Johannesburg.' She doesn't believe me. What theatre? A four-letter word, begins with G. She looks sceptical. I say: I heard you singing, admire your singing very much. What theatre? She asks again. Then I remember the name. 'King Kong' at Wits. Now she believes me. Her leading man worked at J. Walter Thompson, where I worked, if you can call it work, hiding behind a pillar in the copy department.

I follow (in the dream) Miriam Makabe into a kitchen where lights are low. Carl is there looking very tall and brushed. He says he must retire. I am in the dimly lit kitchen with Miriam Makabe in very brief shorts cut in V at thigh.

3 December, Sunday.

Pinter is now writing script for *French Lieutenant's Woman* (the faker Fowles).

Chris Davidson, Calder's stooge and front-man or Chief Sloth. I can never get anything out of him except depressing statistics. Systematically everything goes wrong.

Phoned Trodd. Will arrange luncheon with Ruth Carter, who lives in country. She has visited Celbridge. 140 scenes: 70 minutes. Director: Giles Foster. Better begin March as more daylight for shooting.

4 December, Monday.

Phoned Calders secretary. Davidson not in office. Swainson and Calder in Texas. LCD paperback not yet in. Spot check of half dozen London bookshops reveals

1. Zodiac: Some copies of LGD available, no *Asylum*. 'We will not be getting it in.'

2. Dillon: No copies of either, not subscribed for; 'your best bet would be Hatchards'.

3. Hatchards of Piccadilly: Some copies of both.

4. Belsize Bookshop: Neither in stock. To order either would take about a fortnight.

5. Zodiac (2): 'Let me just check if we have any Higgins on the shelf. No.'

6. High Hill Bookshop, Hampstead. Not in stock but on order.

Foggy, chill. To Barnet College yesterday evening to see first year Design Course exhibition, two of Julien's among them. Roger Butler. Charlie the head teacher.

7 December, Thursday.

Trodd phoned after lunch. Luncheon engagement next week at White City to meet scriptwriter and director. Haas phoned to say Clifford Williams out of town, himself off to New York for three weeks, will contact me mid-Jan.

All Day on the Sands, Giles Foster, Alan Bennett. the *Old Crowd*. Lindsay Anderson. Walked to Castle Bar. No sign of either title in Hampstead bookshop full of Xmas shoppers. Rices arrived after me, J, was there first. Drunken Irish fellow goes four times to toilet. Tasteless turkey.

10 December, Sunday.

J. away to Seven Oaks. Fox called at 6:00. 6:35 at Hampstead, rain heavier, two drinks in Duke of Hamilton opposite Mile End Hospital where I first met you, visiting Michael Morrow with Mad Meg. Harry's bar relatively deserted. Jack Trevor Storey not present. University yobbos and their girls gassing around the false gas fire in the other section. Closing time 10:30, back home. Chess until 2:00 am. Calnek's text: the stink of artifice.

Why sent first to Foss?

J. in Seven Oaks. Woke at 8:30 am, alarm in Julien's room did not go off, Carl not working. Tim Truss asleep on floor under overcoats No post.

14 December, Thursday.

Hibernia (Nuala Mulcahy) phoned to apologise for botched setting of review. Looking for someone to do reassessment job.

Neil Jordan unwilling to undertake it ("not good enough"). What about old Jordan? No. Casey? No. Montague? No. Nuala O'Faolain? God no. 'Have you so many who are against you.' Yes.

15 December, Friday.

Trodd appointment on at White City. No. 134 to Warren Street, not asked for fare, 36p. saved, borrowed £1.50 from Carl, walked to Oxford Circus, connection to White City. Beer in pub and arrive late. Find Trodd, unlaced, and Ruth Carter, very gabby, in cafeteria, an oldish waitress bullying them to order, as Giles Foster arrives, but leaves soon after.

They keep typed notes. Foster suggests Estragon and (Lunatic and ward on Isle of Man). 'Relationship,' Ruth Carter (East London Jewish) suggests. Two in a cell, I say. Two mates in a cell doing time; birdlime.

Had to borrow £1 from Ruth Carter to get home, again finding I was 5p. short on fare. Smell of piss and pot in Finsbury Park, lines of plucked turkeys. John Baird pub on Muswell Hill and fellow complaining about his badly topped pint to overbearing barman. Went into Lounge Bar for flat pint, gaped about, then home. Damp street, sodden sidewalk.

16 December, Saturday. Week 50.

Awful night, bleeding period ending coitus. Clear morning, real coffee, brushing and floor washing, Carl abed until 3:00, the weekend begins with Mario phoning. Eyesight weakening.

Wishing to be well when not exactly ill. Wishing to be ill when not exactly well. Accidie. No inclination to walk out, papers blowing about amid eager Xmas shoppers.

28 December, Saturday.

Overcast foggy after night of screams below & breaking of wooden crates, cries from the foggy without. Went down and bought some books. Fog and mist mixed, drizzle, darkening by 3:00 pm. No post. Guests departed.

30 December, Saturday.

The weather was neither good nor bad. An overcast gray day and a frugal grudging daylight such as I recall very well from the days of my youth—typical London weather you might say.

Last day of the year.

Cómpeta Diary 1978

Málaga airport charter flight terminal after midday. Taxi to Alemeda[sp?] Gardens 200 pesetas. Dust on the palms, flat Victoria beer, bus to Cómpeta. Our neighbour Antonio Fernandez got on at Torre del Mar. Elwin asleep. The ramp. The silly movie people. Cold beers. The ascent. The casa shrunken after three (four?) years' absence.

Dusting and sweeping, it comes alive a little again. Drinking whiskey on terrace. Angela Vernon seen at bar by Elwin, who misses nothing. An Alsatian flattened by the heat, birds die in their cages, the grape harvest poor. Daylight going, eyesight going, the dark coming on fast, to sound of gunshot, cries of children, evening meals being prepared. Life out-of-doors in Cómpeta up in the hills, that's home.

Feeling wretched entering; will feel worse leaving. How a house (long unoccupied by the family) makes its demands. *Lo mismo. Bienvenido.* Mackerel sky over Mediterranean away in the distance, the fucked-up coast.

A thought from Spandau Prison: 'How much strength the bourgeoisie derive from the decor of the world. The security that environmental reliability gives one. The bourgeois's home is the last line of retreat from the outside world'. (Albert Speer, serving out a 20-year sentence).

In Connacht with Rosita it was the wettest winter in living memory (since 1840?) and the old postman came drenched across the bridge, and I was taken for an Englishman. In Cómpeta in the *sierras* with Jill it was the hottest summer in living memory (110 degrees in Málaga in late August and birds died in their cages, water ran out here) and I was taken for a Frenchman. *Au contraire* on both counts.

August 24, 1978 Thursday. First day in Cómpeta.

August 25, Friday.

Walk to Angela's *cortijo* in the great heat, past the cemetery, the wilting vines on ridges of dry earth. Workers around the *cortijo*. Part the bead curtains and there is Calnek in black cords, Angela in yellow bikini, her casa transformed, new ceilings.

J. sunbathed.

Heated argument with Calnek on relative merits of Babel and Singer, Harry's new find. Departs huffily.

Angela and Harry to call at nine; former arrives at 10:30, latter (hates this unfurnished house, and no wonder) showering, downed by two bottles of Clariña. Royal Spot blend with coffee on the roof. Whiskey refused by Calnek who arrives late, showered and spruce. Poole's brand.

August 26, Saturday.

Nine strokes from the church bell, roseate light suffuses the high wall, the darkness of its unfinished Windows, thunder in the hills an hour before. Dinner at 10:00 for Harry and Angela. Evening commotion in the *medina* below not yet begun, the last heat still in the walls, on the patio. Then the lights come on. The coast obscured in heat haze. Dinner for 100 in Baptism celebrations at 7:00 at Café Bar Espejo (The Mirror Bar run by Placido and Nieve Espejo, Calm Mirror and Snow Mirror respectively).

Elwinisms: 'I have only one English friend here and that's Phil. He eats grossly'.

'All the boys ask me sophisticated questions and all the girls think I'm funny.'

Bought trousers at market on square for 700 pesetas.

Angelaism: 'She told me that she fancies you again.'

Wire clothesline rattling in the night wind rising at daybreak over the sierras. The flies arrive with the sun.

Calle Rueda, Cómpeta.

The sound of the weighing-scales tipped by the wind on the window ledge at Emor Street. First flight crossing into Dublin airport (leaving?), sound of early traffic on South Circular Road.

Angelaism: 'I'm finished with this man-woman thing. (*Pause*). It's been going on too long.'

August 28, Monday.

Alan Tobias called, come from Frigiliana around 200 bends and curves, always ascending. He ran off the road coming up here, counting the ridges. Two-stroke broke down on return, taxi man demanded a couple of thousand pesetas, but accepted 300, all he had on him.

August 29, Tuesday.

Philip called. To mule men's bar again. A teacher in Palma, tried to get post here. Teachers earn 40,000 pesetas a month or about £60 a week.

The French-Canadian in his wheelchair. Pulls himself along to chess contests in Nerja, around 200 descending curves. And how to get up again?

August 30, Wednesday.

Day at beach this side of Nerja. Nose running. Sardines *a la plancha* and two bottles of chilled red, a salad. for 840 pesetas or thereabouts. Called on Tobias outside Frigiliana. Shown work for New York exhibition and illustrations for a book. My disappointment; his abuse. Leaves on 12th via Madrid. Skinny Jenny learning typing.

Rafael's teak-like indifference, Antonio asked for Trevor. Piscina. Made the *playa* at dusk. Julien on the darkened shore.

Great fires on mountains as we ascend, Angela hurling Calnek's old car into the bends. Two sleep-well gins at Espejo. Rafael tried to call Carlos in Londres, but Málaga couldn't get Madrid. Madrid kept silent.

Harry sold his car to Angela for £200, not safe for her to walk home. The fires on the mountains along the opposite valley, the mad village. Family nervous in back seat as Angela drove wildly, too fast, too fast, around 200 bends.

Slept on roof, starry night, you were wretched, fearing mosquitoes that never arrived. Windstorm. Wind rising like a great sea behind the high sierras.

August 31, Thursday.

Up at 9:00, down to market for orelli, the great heat continuing. Post. J's extended siesta. *Gongorr* contract from Sheil.

Letter from Nanna. Will be in Jutland or Bornholm mid-September. Copenhagen flat too small and noisy. Book of lyrics due out October 1st, bought by Book Club. Posted yesterday. Misses *knepp*.

A projected sequel to *Gongorr: Bood*.

September 1st, Friday.

To Nerja with Angela, changed 260 in bank for less than 8,000 ptas. Paid for expensive dinner at Bar Jesú (2,200 ptas.) and then abused by pampered bitch for not being able to stump up 200 ptas. for gas at filling station, being cleaned out. Miss Angela Vernon.

The outlines of windows marked in pencil on the walls of two upper rooms. The Alsatian chained to the door. Dolores in widow's weeds.

September 3rd, Sunday.

Walk to Fabrica de la Luz. The Mariposa creeping by with his crooked eyes. My sons turn into Prehistoric men banging oleander bushes with sticks, bowing and paying homage to the harnessed mule tethered to a tree, as cavemen were prone to do, carrying large stones up from the pool, gaping at mule in close range, giving brute roars, cave-men inchoate. Return at 5:00 in the heat, Indian music from drop-out's *cortijo* over the stream, a cock crowing, to Bar Espejo for cold beer.

Here everything is fiercer, intenser, even the fires; the flames go straight up into the dry clear air, shooting rockets to the Virgin. Pall of thick black smoke from *barrio*, gray-white smoke dispersing from Carmé's fire, children howling at dusk, the moon in its first third, a shooting star or failed firework dropping towards Torre del Mar, over Corumbella, smell of smoke over Cómpeta.

Elwin saw snake on way home.

The father's name: 'Seldom there.'

September 7th, Thursday.

To bed by 2:00 am, alarm set for 6:00 am, last coitus. My family away in the dark. Hacking coughs of early risers about plaza. From terrace I watched the two buses depart, horn sounding at first corner, barely light at 7:15, the church bell rings the quarter hour from belfry, sickening sensation of their going, departure's sweet sorrow.

Dozed for an hour and then away to pool by fabrica, showering under waterfall, sickening absence. To pool below Santa Anna, still ghosts of sons, back by 5:00. Out at 6:00 for cigarettes, Clarifia, walk to *cortijo*, Calnek asleep, fires for harvest festival, chess, beat him in first game. Played Fisher game at 13, Capablanca, heavily defended King, coffee and cognac at Espejo, another bottle of wine. Fires. Children playing with fires in the drains. Up late. Long day. You said the fortnight felt like a month. Looked rested, less strained.

Washed sheets, dry in half an hour on terrace, in the heat. Slept in *cortijo*.

September 8, Friday.

Up before 9:00 am. Walk down to Cómpeta. The landlady's sister in black mourning amid the vines speaks of the terrible heat of Málaga. Uncomfortably hot already here on the ridge, in the breeze, cold in the nose persisting. We decided against long walk on Sunday. Buy long loaf. Water garden front and back.

Nanna wrote of '*refugios*' in Jutland, they speak a curious dialect, a wet cold place. Ellen said to be prostituting herself in Copenhagen, Hanne studying to be a teacher, the formidable Anna Steinmetz living with a black man. Boy on way to *cortijo* asked of Elwin (Elwee). Londres! Carmella with crate of Cokes for Labradors. Cold in the nose persisting. as the insufferable heat. Concerned about non-arrival of ticket, money just about not enough, want to hold on to £25 for London. Possible to look into their bedroom without too much pain. Fires on hills around, as last night.

September 9th, Saturday.

Spent night on terrace, too cool for comfort at times, then flies. Black coffee, yesterday's bread, last of the grapes. Watered garden and front, cold in nose still persisting, cough, last *suppositorio* (*Edusan fuette*), the last El-wee! squeaked once by passing boy, memory of your 'Come back well.'

Sopa de Ave con Fideos

Gallima Blanca Aquadar nueva ebullicion

Chica COSMO Karen Valentine

¿Pór qué una mujer tan INDEPENDIENTE debe casarse?

EL IMPULSO SEXUAL: Cual es la frequencia normal y buena?

Con cuanta frequencia lo hacer los damos? Dr Wendell Pomeroy, homeopathic medicine

man. Diario de una gesposa infiel, por Edna O'Brien.

Afrodisiaco humano: Robert Redford.
Cuatro Buenas Razones Para Casarse.
Overweight, eyes blasted.

September 10th, Sunday.
Wrote in 2 notebooks, two bottles of *vino* at eventide, walk in cool of evening, path in shade. Two gins at Mule Men's bar, numbers of cerveza and cognac, hearing bead curtains parting. Only 'was' permitted, never 'is,' per Calnek, of reverie over beginnings. Optical illusion in sand dunes of windy Jutland knows Bornholm, 'many good bars'.

September 11th, Monday.
Workers start before 9:00, shirtless Calnek supervising, a regular Musso among the *fabricantes*. Shower, tea, grapes and away to phone Viajes Málaga or call on Casa de Correos. Hot day. Elwin at comprehensive in north London, Julien at Barnet School of Art, Carl in projection box. Walked back here, cleaned up casa, packed, washed sheets, got all in readiness to depart. Bottle at Espejo, walked back. Light meal, chess. Lovely moonlit warm night, the scents rising from the valley. Very tired, slept at once. Conserve funds, feeling awful.
Playing chess with Calnek some nights ago, Maude caught and ate a snake, then a bird, consumed all but feet and some feathers. I kicked what I took to be a coil of rope on the floor. The snake corpse! Played Cuban Grandmaster's famous games, defeated another Grandmaster when he was twelve.

September 12th, Tuesday.
Cuatro fabricantes working cheerfully in the sun before nine. Tea, tuna and bread. Walk to Elwin's pool; sun not yet in it, dipped, dried out on aqueduct wall, boulders warm. Walked back through Conellias *alpagata* (almost new) gave out, gave up walk to Third River, to see the valley scalped by last year's great

fire. Tuna dry, bunch of grapes fairly good, though not much flavour in them, ripe enough. Ran into Dolores. Invited Calnek to Last Supper tonight at 8:00 at Espejo. He says he has papers of mine, possibly more *Gongorr* material, drawings.

Casa empty and cleaned as for departure did not repel as expected, sleep here tonight, perhaps on terrace, for the last time. Feeling better for the first time. Cough almost gone, nose not running. Three weeks here on Thursday. Season of *pichoichos* (Rafael's name for them) twittering and warbling in the air. Brought up foam-rubber mattress (it sweats) and sunbathed a short while, reading Vonnegut, a mixture of vanity and tedium.

Down to *Bar Espejo* at 8:00. Raffo handed over envelope from Viajes Málaga like a courtier at Versailles handing over a missive to the King. Departure from Málaga as from London about E65 total fare excluding what's spent en route on coach. French-Canadian couple at chess. Rape and red wine, coffee and cognac, over 500 ptas. Calnek thinks someone fingered him in Rome. Walked a minimum of three miles a day up and down exercise yard at Regina Caeli durance vile. Retired at midnight having emptied basura.

September 13th, Wednesday.

Night on terrace. Open sores on second toe of either foot, heard imaginary door being opened, woke early, heard seven strike, did not rise until water came into cistern, turned off butano. Arrival of flies.

Graces of Spain. Handsome *campesino* with his brown hand on throat of beautiful *amadecasa* with her back to wall below, smiling absently, but far from absent: tableaux. Half-smiling?

A little girl singing below. *¡Alo Paloma! Alo Paloma!!*

The breeze on the terrace, in the olive groves. Bunch of grapes from the vine, cold water from the cooling jar. Had last drink with Calnek outside *Espejo*. My bags at his casa. Did not offer to tote them down to bus. Dread of journeys begin for me before the journey starts. Uncertainty of whereabouts of *Tourafrica Iberbus* in forecourt of station, is it front or back? Is departure at 3 or 4? Officially.

1979 SEPTEMBER

28, Friday.

Nobody coming down until next May.

Bar Espejo. Had hoped to hear of your presence. Alone?

How long? Half year? How good!

The Morgensons due in October.

Wallace Stevens' poems. Your bedroom. This bedroom. 'I am tired.' Canillas. The valley, the bridge, the girl's arms in the olive tree. The thwarted one walking away. The insistent bells. Night. Small Placido whom I have offended (it is difficult to offend Spaniards but it can be done). I addressed him as Rafael (his barman and factotum). The drunken Danes staggering away. Huge wads of notes. In summer you said 'I am alone.' Another Stevens poem. What does it say? J's epistle: "Today the last day & have only got your letter dated the 5th. Very sad to go. Visited the old haunts of good times where you are included & went to the beach, with the tent, for three days. We were taken to Nerja one evening. When we arrived the fishermen were bringing in their catch. This went on all night. In the morning we found a pile of fish on a plastic sheet for us. Two fishermen still remained, tidying up. I went over. There was Paco, Carmé's eldest son. Thank you I said for your present. I recognised you last night, he said, Jill, Spanish friends para siempre. He went off, walking home. The rounded shape of his mother.

You seem to see yourself clearly. Perhaps that is a start for you. Not with me. Hard to go over old ground, all being said. Julien very interesting company. I am pleased to compare him to Julia who has had a superior education. In fact she has no delicacy of behaviour & sees little beyond the vicissitudes of her anatomy. Julien long past such trivia & into better things.'

The bell, the bell! The motorbikes groaning by, like bees into the village. Look at me. The young.

Idle to lament. Passive grief, cold the first night, woken by plaster falling from beams. Early morning and Antonio the mule-man croaking.

'*Tóma cojónes!*' The goats being driven out to pasture, kids bleating, the herd dog moves among them.

Absented entry of young men into Bar Espejo, stroking their members. Meaty palm-beating outside.

The quiet milk-drinker. The hand flung out in salutation. The darkness falling. Twice in stout Luis Montes's bar I failed to invoke the ghost. Where are you?

The deepening silence. Light in French-Canadian's casa on the hillside opposite, lame gemnologist and chess player, Louis by name, surname not known. Reputed to have gone by wheelchair to chess in Nerja. Tottilla outside Bar Espejo. The crude Danish couple return to Copenhagen tomorrow. Movie on stout Luis' television above the counter, Marilyn Monroe astride the manhole, the drinkers gape. The deep sea, fish as birds, the whale. The silence here. Deepening. The demands of the campo. The Danish lady in the plaza. The church steeple. The operatic behaviour. The fellow whose name I can't recall. Pointing. Rafael. A pregnant woman passing.

You (who is not you) with children under olive tree near the rich man's mansion. You (turns out to be elderly German Frau) passing me on the narrow path to Canillas. '*Guten abend,*' a civil salutation.

A letter in the cellar. My middle son to my eldest: "Dear Carl, having a great time here in England, & I hope you are enjoying it down there in Spain. I was very disappointed to hear they killed Juma & the two cats, I am now taking my O' levels at school. I've been getting dizzy spells, which Jill informs me that you used to have. The frost has already come, unluckily enough we did not have any fireworks this November. Jill is mending clothes as we are short of money. Many trees in Alexandra Park are being chopped down because of some sort of disease. Jill would like to know if you would like gloves for hristmas or what would you like? love, Julien, snap.'

September 1979
29 Saturday

Out at dusk. Luis's bar. Brown child shirtless on counter, gaping at TV. Bar Espejo and Antonio Jimenez in cloth cap greets me *'Carlos!'* (Andalucia cannot pronounce Aidan).

Four years. In Portugal. *Adios, Cómpeta, adios.* Invitation to lomo. Before that went to Antonio's bar. Black six-foot exotic girl in pink jeans with escort in ecstasy over tapas. Moro? Espejo until 2:00 a.m. Good night's rest.

Note on door, coffee in plaza. Ran into Angelino last night, says that Morgensons are due. Away at midday. Posted letter to Jill, postcard to Nanna. Third River seems very far, with bad (Mayo) knee. Secret place desecrated by new campinoes. Dip. Fag. Return. Halts. Midway bar. Left stick (caña). Antonio's bar, gin tasting of mouse-droppings. Read Theroux. Home at dark. Evening skies. Red half-moon on its side, on her side, last night, 2:00 a.m. Now silver. Mute in Mule Men's Bar.

Yesterday a funeral for an old woman of 70, today two more go. *Cemetario* business. In the midway bar an old decayed man massages his stomach and groans, cannot drink after operation. Returning, the sound of goatbells, the piney air. The Pope arrives in Dublin.

Sun going down in Antonio's bar. Gin. More mice droppings. Reading *The Great Railway Bazaar*, for review. The deaf mute crowing. Notice on the door awry. The images defaced. Apprehensive on the walk, would knee hold up? Longer distance than imagined, you think you know it but you don't know it, the Second River far away, the Third farther still. Those names of mountains that Paco gave me. Secret place, what you call the grassy place, our wedding ground, marriage-bed, almost desecrated. Stayed only a short while and then returned slower than going out. The burnt trees. The little hopes. Chill in the air walking with Angela, before leaving for Málaga. The man from Estremaduro who invited us to taste fine wine in his finca. The valleys. The wind in the fir tree humming. Breeze. Sunset. A bat.

30 Sunday

Ends of yesterday's stale bread, cannot get butano to work, dine on grapes and glass of water. Back room after shower for Theroux in Ceylon. Room below cool, air from the front, the roof hot. Morning fragrance of honeysuckle, one o'clock hunger. Restless night. Tank three-quarters empty, turned sprocket, it begins to fill. Tried butano again. it works. Miracles. Went to shop above, found it closed, bakery closed also, bought milk, tomatoes, goats' cheese and four sardines below, cooked meal. Coffee. Recovery of composure, or partially.

You on telephone, no word, annoyed, returned to Jutland. Peeved at silence that Christmas. I think today. No word. Tired after long walk, years of no exercise, in all day, finished *The Great Railway Bazaar*, began thinking of an Irish journal.

Loud party nearby. The lights go out. Moon over Cómpeta. Lights come on again. A dog barking, eleven sounds from church, might only have left Gatwick now. Sunday rates £30. I phoned on Monday morning, 24th, your Copenhagen reading on previous Thursday. Promised to try and get away as soon as possible after that. German Nescafé. Caca and windblown straw before the casa. Swept it clean, watered the honeysuckle. Its scent in the morning is the breath of life. An unusual sight: Franco the postman, letters in hand, hurrying down the hill, carried by the slope. Nothing for here. *Hoy nada*, Laureano used to say with prophetic gloom. Midday delivery?

Living in perpetual fear (*miedo, aprension*), of what, then? Knee giving out on mountains, *gafas* breaking, being object of contempt and derision, as when I was a lad, fear of going mad. Fear, the basis of all nastiness.

O C T O B E R 1979
3 Wednesday
Nanna arrived six days after me.

Woke at 5:30, rose up at six. Tea & grapes. Watched sunrise. Thin smoke rising from bakery. Cleaned kitchen, emptied basura, all neat and tidy against your imminent arrival. Tired, wrote letters to Jill, Mulcahy, Marilyn Edwards (had forgotten Feltrinelli, of foreign publishers), Brian Fallon (proposed 'A Wet Exposed Place'), dozed on bed. I slept, was asleep when you spoke my name. I woke, saw you on top of stairs, out of breath. You said 'You're here' I said: 'I don't believe it' (meaning: you being there). You had waited seven hours at Málaga airport but I didn't show up. You had waited for the bus to Cómpeta, & I wasn't at the bus stop.

You spoke to some Danes outside the *Espejo*. You left your baggage there, told them to watch it, said you would just have a look. And there I was. And there you were. I said 'Take a shower. I'll get the baggage.' You slept for a few hours. The sky teemed with swallows When I went onto the roof. My symbol for happiness, swallows in flight. I went down and found the remains of the wine drunk and you sitting up smoking in bed, smiling, naked. Mateus Rosé. Omelette. Night on roof. Near full moon. Explosions in space 'like milk overflowing,' you thought. A second moon declined to nothing much over insane village. Because you had arrived.

You spoke of 'the antique fuck,' the Bornholm fisherman who wanted the city girl (you), thick accent, tell me what to do. Raped by Faustus, by Andersen with his green eyes, first you and then his beautiful redheaded wife, all in one bed, in a creaking wooden house in the country. You spoke of Hakim Stangerup, just dead, the former Nazi collaborator. A long novel by his son, Hendrik, whom I had known in Nerja years before. Living with a Bergman actress.

4 Thursday

Awoke at seven. Market at ten. Posted three letters. PO closed. Two fine mackerel from Fish King. Walking from the market with you I saw how poor and shabby was the pueblo, sky becoming overcast. Walked out at midday to Fabrica de la Luz. Blue tent by the stream and boyscouts being scouts, swung across on pulleys. Showered in waterfall on returning, at sunny corner, your drenched bush. The dirty-minded owner of Canillas bar dozing under his spreading walnut tree. Ordered up Victoria Grande (lukewarm) and tapas. Walked home in evening light. Raffo nursing infant on his thigh, Placido among clients. Bottle of 103 and white wine for Calvary, the punishing steep ascent. Cooked Fish King's fine mackerel. Midnight feast. Our first day. Hardwon happiness. The night sky glowing. Saw you last on May 15th in happiness, in Copenhagen.

Encountered Antonio *septulero* (the grave-digger and arch-gossip) in Canillas bar, under the walnut tree, who observed you in a doggish waggy way. Every bar we enter has a postman standing at the counter, or the ex-postman, or both together.

The night you wept for your suicided sister.

6 Saturday

Walk to pool in valley below Canillas by smouldering dump that you name Gahenna. Intimacy in the long grass, you almost fainted in the 'dirty bar'. Antonio of Walnut Bar playing dominoes, sprang up to offer lovely lady an invitation. Two cognacs, dark 103. Bought chicken for Coq-au-vin from Lydia with bottle of Vino de Cómpeta (dark as cascara, which it tastes like), your 'smashed potatoes', beans. *Vino corriente* being undrinkable, went for two bottles of Clareniña, ran into Miguel ('Franco') the postman, telling me I owed him eight pesetas for under-stamped letters, two awaited in casa.

The pool behind Santa Anna, your near-faint in the dirty bar, the stink of Gahenna, the beauty of the pools, hidden away. Outside a Copenhagen restaurant Knud Jensen (the mildest of men) struck Hermann Bang, you told me. You told of someone starving in Granada, in a room full of flies. Plaster fell from the back room ceiling as you spoke. Post is being delivered (flung) through either window below. We find mail in odd corners.

7 Sunday

Cold remains of coq-au-vin with stale bread, being Sabbath. Walk to Third River. The fountainhead, the deepish pool before the little waterfall, the burnt trees, wind . . . sighing through the branches, you wore only espadrilles on the hot path miles from anywhere, in the hot sun, we had the cold chicken, the white wine chilled in the pool, starting back at five. Darkness fell as we came off the path, luminous, to lights of village below, and uproar in Mulemens' bar. *'Mira! Mira! Mira!'* Gin and beans to stem exhaustion. No moon. Galactic Way. Starry night sky, barking dogs, coffee laced with 103 and so to sleep.

Some pages of London 1982 diary

AUGUST

24 Tuesday

Knock of postman with Hawkes symposium. 8:00. Sun.
You prepared to go. Coffee. Julien's Cómpeta tape.

23 Wednesday

Julien continues to play tape. Away to Alexandra. Gin sans
ice. Bar at East Finchley. Webster & Burton. Grouse. Nat West
branch. Peas. Walk back. Red wine. Cooked meal. Unchanged
world. You unsober. Front room changed. Dream of Dublin.
These strange (?) factors: A breast perhaps removed? A young
negro disappointing. Belton's amazement. Now calmness again,
Gerd resigned, ten years of misunderstandings, inability to say
what's wrong; he wouldn't listen to you; you slept on sofa, made
a new room. All of that. Morning. Coffee.

12 Wednesday

Zoo Station. 45 minutes stereo Radio 3. West Berlin locations.
Your story of some Somerset uncle who hanged himself not
with rope but wire.

Carlotta last night in kitchen: 'We're young.' Carl: When
sick in a foreign country. Our stuff. Head down, injured at
table, embraced by 'my wife'.

Heard today J. P. Donleavy interview, in tweeds, explains
difficulty of adapting *Ginger Man* for stage. *Beastly Beatitudes*:
based characters on real people but wasn't saying who they were,

no names. Unpleasant character, not American voice. Ireland despite TV unchanged, the Irish character.

Prepared spuds, chops, carrots. Elwin awoke at 3:00, bread, left in shoes, came back with Carlotta, they left for her place. He returned 10:30. Good meal. Julien just after. Foss phoned to announce Max Frisch being interviewed by Ronald Hyman. *Montauk* rewritten four times. Girl of thirty-one. 'To stand for a while more or less naked.' Work changed after. Briefer. 'We're always fictionalising, we can't avoid that." Brecht in Zurich. Helene Weigel—'after all she was a good cook." Of Brecht: 'He gave me the measure of good work.' *Montauk*—'Very private stuff- Russians liked it. Lindsay Anderson's *Fire-Raisers* at Royal Court best production. Hyman inquired of atomic mushroom. 'No, not that.' No film or TV—'Would have to learn it."

'Impact too strong.' Lives in New York. 'I'm not so sure why I'm there . . . l need those forced chances to keep myself alive.' *Man in the Holocene, Bluebeard*, almost all dialogue. A court scene he saw. His diaries. Architect. Writing another diary, would leave it for fiction. Not to repeat. Hyman deferential, *'Herr Frisch.'*

11 Tuesday

Onan thrice for disturbed night, your disinclination, disturbed after court that morning, no bus even, then phone call from Piers Plowright. You said alright even if I didn't mind absence of . . . heart is it? No thanks. Yet turn you over & you would have been hot. Buss in the small of. Part the spheres, feast the eye, treat the tongue, moisten & enter as before. You'd come, as before. Is it all the way in? one teaser asked. Oh it's good! another tease said in another place. All wettish dreams. You decided to return to Louisa. Phoned from here. I on balcony, uneasy, watched you walk slowly below, from car, up by fire escape, I in front room, unpeeled *New York Review of Books*, banging pots and pans in kitchen, I crept out, No.

134 to Archway Road, walk in wet leaves to Prince Of Wales, a pub in Highgate Village. Chris & single drinker. Southgate & 'butch clarinettest' tonight. Two White Shields, two Bloody Mary, three gins, small Ann or Anna, Gerry with Susie, talking, mother still recovering from operation, upstairs. Mohican Indians with moist eyes of rats fixed on plump Ann or Anna, Southgate with pipe clenched between teeth, intermittently tuning up, Jazz going simultaneously on transistor above, no one notices, Glen McAllister's brandy voice, no offer of a drink, knows I know what I know, takes off jacket & then tie, attacks crossword puzzle, rounds with two friends, affable, puts on tie & jacket. I leave. C&C in kitchen with Mum drinking Valpollicella. Nick all night. Woken at 4:00 am.

9 Sunday

Quiet here, din of traffic, wintry feeling with slap of tyres. Up to your open door, double bed tidily made up, away in your heated car. No post. Toomey pacified? NS cheque on its way. Will you come? Phone as promised. No Elwin. Julien's light already burning. Work today? Yes, off soon after. Elwin elsewhere. You phoned at 1:00, 'Just opposite,' 'a fright' with hair cut short. Door ajar, no wine, coffee. Morning in courts with Lucien. Black charged has since assaulted a Greek boy, warrant out. GBH. Police phoned at 8:00 a.m. Defendant not in court. "Jolly Irish drunks" were there. No touching, hardly consent to sit on lap, went out for Diamante, £10 in hand (Julien paid back on request), smoking like furnaces. Phone at 4.00. Plowright to say 'Zoo Station' commissioned, we go to Berlin with sound recordist, needs list.

No review of Wic[??] which is 'sure to be repeated.'* But when? 'You pleasure in my good fortune at last, not like to

---

* *Winter is Coming.* Broadcast BBC Radio 3, 23 September 1983. Directed by Piers Plowright. Location recordings by Antonio Jésus Fernandez.

see me cast down, embrace' you can now if you want me. No thanks. All or nowt. Celebration? Where? Louise injured her back riding on Sunday, in school uniform, but crept back. Gerd away weekend. Never asked what you are up to, why so late, sleeping out in Alexandra Palace ruins, all-night Scotch at Cheryl's.

10 Monday

Phone. Mahon. Mrs Higgins thinks. No togetherness. Cheque en route. £50 for sketch in due time. Art Editor miffed. Julien in Poole's two-piece suit. Overcast, drizzle, hungover. Early October swallows skimming over trees in Alexandra Park. Screeching of drunken or drugged girl, bellowing of escort, in back of new buildings last night, Elwin returned late. Four Lanterns lit up. Marie the Cornish woman studying law. Piscean. Swifts too above the trees, still foliage, feeding, gray sky overcast. Dream: You, hand, almost there, period, behind, instant, taken, tremulous. Your face. Vas. Period, anointed, inwards. Four Lantern talk: Wanting Knapp because you 'become dowdy' without it. Colour gone. Needed it. Gerd drunken before, more seriously now, 'heavy stuff,' abed you said, too drunk to know. Books on Four.

Rushdie interviewed. *Shame* second novel. Flat in North London. Victim's shame after attack. Hermione Lee. Kingsley Amis in bruised brogues going on about SF, rugger, more bruises. Japanese XI. Stand-off wearing white gloves. Slippery ball. So. Diplomatic letter to Toomey, by hand. £250 NS. £250 Calder. BBC. A&B. Fiction Magazine. Barnet window-cleaner got the word. In Christ there is no East or West. You meet people from all walks of life. Coach road to St. Alban's in the old days. Countryside.

Locks herself in the WC and refuses to come out. Eamonn threatens to break down the door. Healy persuaded Eamonn to relent and the sister, greatly relieved, stayed.

At midday Mick makes his way to a Pimlico pub, having been up drinking last night until three in the morning. His huge Alsatian is baying, his Polish wife fell downstairs.

The Corkman whose wife died of cancer has four nine-year-old linnets singing in cages. The wife of the rich Irish landowner wanted to write poetry, showed her efforts to Healy, later did away with herself.

Widower Seamus drinks at Brady's, has two heavy sons in the National Front, sitting heavily together in Dorset. The wife died of some incurable disease in Korea. I asked him where her soul was now. 'At No. 6 Caldwell Street in the Oval.' His wife's ghost occupies the upper story and can be heard moving about and sighing.

Now read on.

A thought for today: Those who believe in fresh starts never have 'em (fresh starts, that is). The diary has to achieve its rhetorical effects (flourishes?) with an audience of one, a theoretically perfect readership where writer and reader become one (wasn't it Murphy who considered the closed circle pure?). Or a device to shut the common clay out? This is for specialists and neurotics only. Now read on.

A visit to Caldwell Street, WC 12. Bizarre tale of little Maire in her shift pinned to kitchen sink by Irish wolfhound. The animal's head in her crotch, growling, salivating, she terrified to move an inch.

Cheeks on fire always, as pippins in late summer, that ardent glow. In the darkened back bar of Brady's Irish pub at Oval-Brixton, her admission of 'being far from happy with Healy'. An odd husband by any standards for anybody, anywhere. She thought herself a slave to his bidding. Irishmen! Pah!

The perfect host brings fresh orange juice of two oranges for his guest in bed. Healy and all whom he consorts with seemed tarred with the same brush, thrive on the outré; for them near-chaotic discomfort is habitual and mess acceptable, normal.

What the normal English mistrust and indeed fear in the Irish is that disorder. The Irish themselves do not see it as disorder.

Take the juice of two Jaffa oranges . . .

Anne Marie, aged thirty, being the first wife and mother of his eldest son, came downstairs to make breakfast and took it back upstairs to her twenty-year-old lover, the young artist. She lives on the premises with him. Marie the second wife in Ireland with Little Moonbeam, does not care for London or Brixton and will not return until the ex-wife has her own flat.

Eamonn works for Mick the builder. Anna the sister of Eamonn doesn't want to return to Ireland and is being forced to do so by her brother. She threatens to slash her wrists.

Envoi

Finnish White Knights
For Professor Anna Kokko-Zalcman of the Sorbonne

THE DELIGHTFUL WEEKENDS in the *stugas* on the lakeshore or on the seashores of the Baro Sound, in those villas that the French, ever boastful, called chateaux, and the Finns, ever modest, more simply call *stugas*. They are old country houses built of wood and stucco on neo-classical lines inspired by Engels—the Doric order of the portico covered by a slight green mold.

During the white nights of summertime the people of the North are a prey to a queer restlessness, to a kind of cold fever. They spend the nights walking by the sea, or they stretch out on the grass in the public gardens or they sit on the benches by the harbour. Later they walk home skirting the walls, their faces turned upwards. They sleep only a few hours lying naked on their beds, bathed in the cold glare that penetrates through the wide-open windows. They lie naked in the nocturnal sun as if under a sun lamp. Through their open windows they can see moving through the glassy air, the ghosts of houses, of trees and of the sailing boats rocking in the harbour.

Princess Louise von Preussen, whose father had been a younger brother of the Crown Prince, and Ilse were to meet me that evening at the Potsdam station. 'We shall bicycle over from Litzenss' Ilse had phoned.

Speaking in Potsdam French: 'that peculiar Potsdam French,

self-conscious and shy . . .' There was a shade of cold severity in her simple grace, that cold severity, so peculiar to Potsdam and to its baroque architecture, its neoclassical pretensions, the white stuccos of its churches, its palaces, its barracks, its colleges, its houses—a severity both courtly and middle class, supported by the thick green dampness of the trees.

From *Kaputt* by Curzio Malaparte, translated from the Italian by Cesare Foligne. 1948

Potsdam 1974

Seen from Berlin-Ostende train, crossing over a hundred miles of DDR, ossified as if under water. Seen trembling in the depths there: a copper dome, a deserted sportsfield, a rifle-range, an officer with elephantine posteriors riding a bicycle down on its rims, soldiers moving around in Red Army uniforms.

'The sinister light of defeat. It was necessary now to carry everything a step further.'

From *La Nausée* (1938) by Jean Paul Sartre, translated from the French by Robert Baldick.

'There are a lot of people walking along the shore, turning poetic, springtime faces towards the sea; they're in holiday mood because of the sun. There are women in light-coloured dresses, who have put on their outfits from last spring; they pass by, as long and white as kid gloves. There are also big boys from the lycée and the commercial school, and old men wearing decorations. They don't know one another, but they look at one another with a conspiratorial air, because it's such a fine day and they are people. People embrace without knowing one another on days when war is declared; they smile at one another every springtime. A priest walks slowly along, reading his breviary. Now and then he raises his head and looks at the sea approvingly. Delicate colour, delicate perfumes, springtime souls. 'What lovely weather, the sea is green, I like this dry cold better than the damp.' Poets!

'Bankes and Tansley, beef triumph, the beams of the lighthouse, 'Luriana Lurilee' the silence of the hostess, the end of the meal.' *To the Lighthouse* by Virginia Woolf (1928)

Scene in Potsdam, 1948

We walked towards the centre of the town; I was walking beside Louise who was leaning on her bicycle. The rain had stopped; it was a warm, clear, moonless night. I felt as if I were walking by the side of a girl through the suburbs of my own hometown; as if I had gone back to my own boyhood in Prato; in the evenings when the girls left the factories, I would wait for Bianca.

We stopped on the bridge . . . A boat with two soldiers was gliding under the arches, sweeping down the stream. We came to a restaurant not far from the bridge and went inside. The large room was full of people; we took a table at the end of a smaller side room were a few soldiers sat silently around a table and two girls, mere children, were having supper with an old lady, perhaps their governess. Their long blonde hair was braided down their shoulders, and they had starched white collars turned back on their gray school-girl dresses.

Perhaps because her mother was English, it occurred to me that Ilse was a picture of innocence such as Gainsborough might have painted. No, I was wrong. Gainsborough painted women as if they were landscapes, with all the candour, the proud sadness and the languishing decorum of the English landscape. *Kaputt* by Curzio Malapanta (1948).

Nordland Spring, 1855

It was quiet and hushed everywhere. I lay the whole evening looking out of my window. An enchanted light hung over field and forest at that hour; the sun had set and coloured the horizon with a fatty red light, motionless like oil. Everywhere the sky was open and pure. I gazed into the clear sky and it was as if I lay face to face with the depths of the earth, and as if my beating heart went out to those depths and was at home there. God knows, I thought to myself, why the horizon clothes itself in mauve and gold tonight, or perhaps there is some celebration above the world.

A slight fragrance rose from the earth and sea; there was a sweet sulphurous smell from the old leaves rotting in the woods.

No, I had not shot anything, I was staying at home in the hut until there was nothing left there to eat.

Well I did not shoot to murder, I shot to live. I might need one grouse today, so I did not shoot two, but I would shoot the other one tomorrow.

Soon there began to be no night; the sun barely dipped its face into the sea and then came up again . . . How strangely I was affected sometimes these nights; no man would believe it. Was Pan sitting in a tree watching to see how I would act?

Pan by Knut Hansun

Part Three

Mnemonic

Introduction to the Minihan Portfolio

(Introduction to Samuel Beckett Photographs by John Minihan, Secker and Warburg 1995)

I

JOHN MINIHAN AND I have collaborated before. I wrote the text to his photomontage of the last wake held in Ireland, in his County Kildare hometown of Athy, not too far from my own rustication. (It surfaces again in Joyce's *Portrait* as the answer to a puerile riddle.)

His footage of Beckett rehearsing *Godot* and tasting a drop of Guinness in the bar is as dramatic as anything Tisse ever shot for Eisenstein's *October* in the way of grainy atmospherics.

Sam Beckett, that Terra incognita ever receding, was never an easy subject to entrap. Here is a record of the last of the living Beckett and the final resting place in Montparnasse. Beckett wrote of matters that few before him had attempted, touching the essential boredom of human life, human imbecility, so testing of the Deity's much-tried patience, with a candour that went far beyond candour. A rippling, peremptory prose that was—what was the word?—illuminated, rock-steady with faith. That was Beckett.

For a writer working in Joyce's wake, it was difficult to get out from under the shadow, thrice difficult if you were an Irish writer, unless you ignored his work, as did X and Y. The Joycean savoir faire was uncommon, a matter of musical cadences, living falls. The Meister's shadow darkened—lightened?—Beckett's early work from *More Pricks than Kicks* onward through *Dream of Fair to Middling Women* to *Murphy* (1938), before the influence was finally shaken off, exorcised.

A special torment was reserved for Beckett, an appropriate fate for a favoured disciple: to be crucified upside down. He saw our life out of alignment and in a special way; overseer of the mush, the stench, the deeps. The great precursor had set up the theme: wayward inwardness. Joyce himself had died of a surfeit of disappointments, famous himself yet his work considered obscure, as old Melville in the obscurity of the Customs and Excise office. His (Joyce's) last ur-novel had been almost two decades in the making, the arduous time-consuming erection of scaffolding, no routine job but a chronicle of the Celtic Unconsciousness itself in all its unplumbable murkiness. He regarded it as his best work, saw it with a specially favourable (if purblind) eye; as the 'unusualness' of a mongoloid child is said to solicit a special mother-love, this was to be the father and mother of an impossible love. It was an equally impossible novel.

Beckett too was to become diverted into a far-from-Celtic mist (nothing clearly seen from *Echo's Bones* (1937) to *L' Innommable* (1952)) until his eyesight was corrected and the mitts cleared; whereupon he advanced from strength to strength, His radio and stage work brought him into contact with professional Mage people who helped bring his characters to life; a nature austere and withdrawn learnt to accommodate the crowd.

For a fellow famously reclusive, refusing to give interviews and hating to be photographed, he has left behind him a memory of warm friendships: and a body of work less cloistral than is supposed, accessible to browsers of all persuasions.

The venerable Irish mirror held up to nature must needs be not only cracked but a distorting mirror. There are, to be sure, good times and bad, But you cannot do much in a dead place, and Ireland in the 1940s was stone dead, a moribund island buried by Dev for his anointed one (Archbishop McOuaid, with whom he had gone to college) to whisper the last rites over.

The two decades dating from the publication of *Ulysses* in 1922 to the death of Yeats and Joyce produced some work of exceptional liveliness, which included Beckett's *Murphy*, Flann O'Brien's *At Swim-Two-Birds* and *An Beal Bocht*, in a bucklepping Gaelic that mocked the sometimes oleaginous manner of the original (*An tOileanach*).

Taking the mickey is a venerable Irish custom, like droning away on the bagpipes, drowning the shamrock, not casting clouts before May is out, casting aspersions on you know-whom, or the practice of dropping in uninvited on 'friends'. I once asked the late Alex Trocchi what Beckett's French was like, what was he up to, and why write in French since he managed so well in English?

'Sam's taking the mickey out of the French language,' Trocchi said.

The Irish surnames look out of place in the French text—Malone, Macmann and Molloy, lost amid the murr and myrrha of things French. But no odder than Beckett felt himself to be as a solitary, low-church Protestant highbrow amid the Catholic antiquarians and zealots. In due time, Molloy would be converted into a faintly Latinised English with the help of the South African Paul Bowles, which left the author dissatisfied, as did the later translation help from the American Dick Seaver. He could not wholeheartedly endorse alternative versions at such a remove. *Watt*, in his own English, he dismissed as 'execrable'.

Joyce's archetypal mummies were superseded by Beckett's retarded and half-witted men and women come down in the world, in a narrative fuelled by Godlike (or *Godot*-like) uncertainty and doubt. Where now? Who now? When now?

II
A Storm Blowing from Paradise

A mutual mistrust of what Joyce called the 'wideawake language of cutanddry grammar and goahead plot' lead Joyce and Beckett off in different directions. The lapsed Roman Catholic believed the more the merrier and put in everything: incremental stockpiling, addenda piled upon addenda, until he went too far in *Finnegans Wake* (sans apostrophe). Whereas the sceptical ex-Anglican made it his dictum that the artistic process was a contraction, not an expansion. This can be checked by a glance at the published proof corrections on Ulysses and the abridgements displayed in Beckett's working notebooks. Reductio ad absurdum led to unimaginable departures, 'an unspeakable trajectory'.

What both writers had in common was a playfulness, a scepticism and exuberance, a rhapsody of verbal energy; an art of a different order from any achieved up to that date. Art has always been bourgeois, when it could be something grander. The first inkling that a novel could be more than a story came to me with the reading of Joyce's *A Portrait of the Artist as a Young Man*, published when Joyce was thirty-eight, read when I was about twenty-two.

Kate O'Brien's *Without My Cloak* (1931) and *The Land of Spices* (1941) were both banned by Ireland's Censorship of Publications Board. Beckett rejoiced to be found in the category of those authors 'deemed from time to time unwholesome', with his lexicons of wit's brevity, by one (seemingly) at his wit's end.

'Success and failure on the public level never mattered much to me,' Beckett wrote to reassure Alan Schneider, 'in fact I felt much more at home with the latter, having breathed deep of its vivifying [*sic*] air all my writing life up to the last couple of years.'

A prey all his life to a foreboding that never abated, for him the gray air was 'ever aswirl with vain entelechies'. There must have been a bitterness in the gray, grim air of occupied Paris that Beckett was alerted to; disguised as a Frenchman, cautious as a spy, acting as a courier for the Resistance. They didn't want Sartre, who talked too much, was swayable, blind in one eye.

Elizabeth Bowen as a child of five, prevented from reading, being walked by her governess from 15 Herbert Place in the fashionable part of Dublin, saw 'a sky for the favoured': 'Early dusks, humid reflections and pale sunshine seemed a part of its being. I used to believe that winter lived always in Dublin, while summer lived always in County Cork. By taking the train from Kingsbridge Station to Mallow one passed from one season's kingdom into the other's. When they first made me understand that I had been born in Dublin I said, "But how? My birthdays are always at Bowen's Court." A house where a child no longer must be virtually rolled up and put away. So by having been born where I had been born in a month in which that house did not exist, I felt that I had intruded in some no-place.' (*Seven Winters*)

The very air is different for Protestants and Catholics.

The air of occupied Paris was gun-metal gray, the field gray of the Wehrmacht officers who occupied all the best seats outside the cafés. Beckett had said famously that he preferred France (Paris?) at war to Ireland (Dublin?) at peace, and had returned there to save his soul, and to make himself as a writer. The 'fallen' city, the whore that had put up such a feeble show of resistance, could be forgiven. The Anglican lady who was to inherit Bowen's Court had the dead air of blitzed London in her fastidious nostrils, poet Mahon's 'unventilated slopes'.

III
After Embers

The existences of Anglo-Irish people . . . like those of only children, are singular, independent, and secretive.

> *To most of the rest of the world we are semi-strangers, for whom*
> *existence has something of the trance-like quality of a spectacle.*
>
> Elizabeth Bowen, *Bowen's Court*

In Irish writing could there ever be an authentic Protestant note, unmistakably that, pure and simple? A diminuendo of sorts, a sorry Anglo-Irish *Schultzmusik*, a *De Profundis* fit for the Pale? And how would these same Protestants view their Roman Catholic neighbours? The natives like to see themselves—even if only in a very poor light—as they had always imagined themselves to be (from the lies perpetuated in *Ryan's Daughter* and *The Quiet Man* on to the Wicklow simpletons of *Glenroe*, the long-running soap opera that would have astounded Synge, who had tramped through the Wicklow glens and knew the people) mutatis mutandis, Nappertandywise, as . . . gas cards.

The bog poet Paddy Kavanagh of mucky Monaghan, ever boggish in his ill-humour, refused Synge any insight whatsoever into the poor Aran islanders (even if Synge had Irish, which Kavanagh hadn't), for Synge was a gentleman and, worse still, a Protestant gentleman of culture who had gone to Trinity and had travelled in Europe. Joyce himself could not but be caustic at the expense of the two Dublin society ladies of Protestant Ascendancy stock whom he transformed into the grotesques, Mrs Bellingham and Mrs Yvelton Tallboys, about whom Bloom (or his more active subconscious) had erotic daydreams, a sort of onanistic counterplay to the invisible Martha Clifford. The dreams were sado-masochistic in character; the urgent need for a jolly good hiding.

Myles na Gopaleen of *The Irish Times* objected to the Joyces speaking Italian (no doubt Triestine argot) among themselves. That Beckett wouldn't read *At Swim-Two-Birds* because of a slight the greenhorn author had made against Joyce means that we have come full circle.

Possibly it takes a near (or neo-) outsider to catch the

plangencies and bitter wit of the oppressed insider; for a Protestant writer to examine it without any condescension is next door to impossible.

Beckett, for whom the impossible would always be a challenge ('I can't go on') does it magnificently. Nothingness does not confront another nothingness but implies something opposite to it and in highest contention, to keep the void from pouring in. Such contention in the skill keeps the void away, stays the mulligrubs. Though Beckett's fellowmen may be jocularly addressed as 'fellow bastards', individuals as 'swine' and humankind at large as 'the sniggering muck', the accumulated energy of the verbal strategy and frolics cannot but endear the dullest browser or the most muddy-minded casual reader to the works of this peerless penman, 'frozen by some shudder of the mind'; always with a new surprise in store around the next corner, over the page, the verbs taking off and the pronouns dancing afrolic; even if the persistent whisper in the head says 'Thou fool thy soul'.

'. . . that time in the end when you tried and couldn't by the window in the dark and the owl flown to hoot at someone else or back with a shrew to its hollow tree and not another sound hour after hour not a sound when you tried and tried and couldn't anymore no words left to keep it out.' *(That Time)*

As with a new and difficult music as yet unperformed, the texts can be read as flawless as they stand; only dud performances can flaw them. When asked what he valued in his own work, Beckett replied 'What I don't understand'. It is perhaps no coincidence that the two actors who professed themselves baffled by Beckett gave outstanding performances—Peter Bull as a very testy Pozzo (the absentee landlord in extremis) in the original Criterion Theatre production; and the peerless Paudge Magee growling away in any Beckett-staged Stuck. Give a dog a bone.

Regarding the modern hero of fiction as a shadowy personage

(Proust's bedridden and effectively nameless hero, the guilt-ridden heroes of Kafka and Camus, or the retrogressive Oskar, who never grew beyond the age of three in *The Tin Drum*), you may well ask:

Q: Why heroes so spectral and shadowy?

A: The hero of gigantic appetites, of journeys to the ends of the earth, had been replaced by the hero as multiple consciousness, who does not (cannot?) travel at all, except in his own head. The perceiver has taken over from the participant.

Joyce (who was going that way anyway) invented a multiple consciousness which he called 'Leopold (Poldy) Bloom', a much-cuckolded seller of advertising space, son of the suicide father Virag, of Hungarian Jewish blood who had married Mary Higgins. Assembled craftily over a period of seven years, he (Bloom) was intended to represent or stand in for the Collective Celtic Consciousness, or CCC, that was thought to be injured, the sense of déjà vu that invested the land itself; the sense of strangeness, of both belonging and not belonging, of being hard-done-by, of being betrayed, of alienation, which I take to be the trademark and sorry plight of the 'mere Irish', their status quo—an island race obliged to live close to itself on no matter what terms. The smaller the island, the bigger the neurosis.

Brian O'Nolan, the speaker of Tyrone Gaelic, would pay grudging homage to Joyce, but in the next breath would have to disparage him, and to Beckett of all people, who would in turn refuse to read *At Swim-Two-Birds* because of the imagined slight to Joyce, and would in turn tell it to me in the Giraffe Restaurant in Klopstockstrasse in Berlin. 'Joyce,' spat out Myles the begrudger, 'that refurbisher of skivvies' stories!' It may have gone down well as a public sally in the Scotch House or as an acid aside in the Pearl Bar, but it didn't go down well with Beckett, deviser of the voice and of its hearer and of himself. Most certainly not.

James Joyce, dare one say, was in a sense a refurbisher of

skivvies' stories—this is truer of *Dubliners* than of *Ulysses*. Irish art was, Stephen Dedalus said, the 'cracked lookingglass of a servant'. Joyce, outside his own land, was to be the oracle for the Unsaid, the Unspeakable, the silent generations. Not that they were silent—that was not their nature, among themselves; but unrecorded, unknown outside of themselves.

I once asked Beckett his opinion on Joyce (the awe-tist ne plus ultra, not the man) in one word. He didn't hesitate: 'Probity,' said Sam stoutly. I have heard it defined as a ferocious application to the task in hand. The begrudger, Brian O'Nolan, being a civil servant, had to invent a number of aliases to write under. As Myles na gCopaleen (Myles of the little horses, the ponies) in his *Cruiskeen Lawn* (or The Full Jug) column of *The Irish Times*, over two score years, he had invented perhaps his own best character; a conglomerate being called The Plain People of Ireland, as stand-ins for the entire Celtic Unconscious that was well aware of itself, if unrecorded; the Volk of the Irish Ego, the yolk of the Gaelic egg.

It was not exactly invented, because it was there already. The real hand that wrote *At Swim-Two-Birds* belonged to a nameless pseudo-narrator, the suicide hand that had scrawled in blood thrice in German: Goodbye, Goodbye, Goodbye. The Red Hand of Ulster? The dismembered extremity clutching at 'the bare, hard, dark, stinking earth' that is home, must be home.

In 'real life' (so called) the 'uncle' had been the real father of Brian O'Nolan, sometime student at University College, Dublin and bane of the Literary and Historical Society. The brother—I mean one of his real brothers—Kieran O'Nolan, spoke to me about the composition of this flush oddity with a kind of grudging admiration, or admiring horror. For it was sucking back everything into itself like a humming Hoover eating dust and dirt, and he considered himself a lucky man to have barely escaped the insuck, the inflow.

Cuckoo operations are carried on in *Gulliver's Travels*,

Murphy and *At Swim-Two-Birds*. A large egg is laid in a small nest and the innocent hatching out of the false chick (already, in the egg, twice the size of the putative mother) carried on by the innocent parent-bird, the pseudo-mother.

In *Gulliver's Travels* the poor condemned Irish—'old savage Irish' wrote Swift to his friend Pope—are seen alternately as giant and dwarf, controller and controlled, master and slave. Gulliver either striding about in seven-league boots and dragging the Blefuscudian fleet off its moorings, or carried about in a box like a ferret, tied down by the roots of his hair by creatures the size of his thumb and interviewed by a midget queen who insists on correct protocol.

The nameless hero of O'Nolan's (hereinafter Flann O'Brien) first novel will become a nameless hero with a wooden leg in the next; a murderer by proxy who descends into a revolving Celtic hell manned by his deadly enemy, the rozzers (Civic Guards, offering bags of sweets), in *The Third Policeman*, written soon after.

I first encountered *Murphy* in Greystones circa 1950, when his cousin John Beckett loaned it to me. He sometimes came home to Greystones to see his widowed mother. Both spoke familiarly of Sam, who had visited them when deaths occurred. Sam loved the countryside, loved Bray Head, the bright yellow 'ling'. Beckett relicti abounded in Redford Cemetery, overlooking the harbour.

Murphy, which I swallowed whole at one sitting, is one of those once-in-a-lifetime novels that cannot but inspire affection. It is lit by a special light, a loving favour, and the kite-flying hill on Hampstead Heath became for me a special place on that account. The opening is unforgettable:

The sun shone, having no alternative, on the nothing new. Murphy sat out of it, as though he were free, in a mew in West Brompton.

The opening two sardonic clauses are as dumbfounding as unthinkably masterful moves in chess. It reads as a much stouter novel than its 158-odd pages (and odd they are) would concede; Celia is Beckett's most sweetly realised female character. I was later, through Arland Ussher, to meet the original of Ticklepenny—Austin Clarke—who was not prepared to talk about Beckett.

The markedly anthropoid Miss Counihan has a bust which is 'all centre and no circumference'. I had to wait some years to get the point of this joke, until it was revealed to me in *Otras Inquisitiones* by Borges, the blind Argentinian seer. He quotes Pascal: 'Nature is an infinite sphere whose centre is everywhere and whose circumference is nowhere'. Borges set out to hunt down the metaphor through the centuries. He traces it to Giordano Bruno (1584): 'We can assert with certainty that the universe is all centre, or that the centre of the universe is everywhere and its circumference nowhere'. But Bruno had been able to read it in a twelfth-century French theologian, Alain de Lille, a formulation lifted from the *Corpus Hermeticum* (third century): 'God is an intelligible sphere whose centre is everywhere and whose circumference is nowhere'. He finds the metaphor again in the last chapter of the last book of Rabelais's *Pantagruel*, in Empedocles (who casts all things about), in Parmenides, in Olaf Gigon (Ursprung der griechischen Philosophie, AD 183), who had it from Xenophanes six centuries before Christ, when he offered to the Greeks a single god. And I found it again in Beckett's *Murphy* (1938):

'Not know her is it,' said Wylie, 'when there is no single aspect of her natural body with which I am not familiar . . . What a bust! . . . All centre and no circumference!'

Metaphysics as a branch of the literature of fantasy? The Borgesean sources are innumerable and unexpected. He saw Lord Dunsany (!) as a precursor of Kafka: Browning's poem 'Fears and Scruples' also foretold Kafka's work. In this correlation, the identity or plurality of the men involved is unimportant: 'The early Kafka of Betrachtung is no less a precursor of the Kafka of sombre myths and atrocious institutions than is Browning or Lord Dunsan'.

Murphy had boasted of conducting his amours along the lines of Fletcher's Sullen Shepherd. Professor Neary and his henchman Wylie discuss Murphy. What is it that women see in him? Was it his surgical quality?

Oh no.

The comic novel, operating in some zone outside History and Time, writes itself, discovering its theme and form largely independent of its author; rather in the hit-and-miss manner in which Alexander Fleming discovered penicillin; with the help of mucus from his nostril, saliva, tears and the whites of eggs.

Murphy. Slang. 1881 (Use of common Irish surname). A potato. Murphy('s) Button. A device invented by J. B. Murphy, an American surgeon, for reuniting the parts of an intestine after complete severance.

Both Beckett and O'Nolan had independently admitted to me that they could see no virtue in their first novels.

The young Liam Redmond returned from Paris with two volumes of the Shakespeare & Co first edition of *Ulysses* secreted in his baggage. He lent one to his friend. When he had got through one volume, O'Nolan asked for a loan of the second, protesting that he was 'only half educated'. In later life he liked to disparage Joyce, as did Nabokov.

Beckett came out of Joyce like the cuckoo out of the Irish egg. ('There's no end to the earth because it's round,' marvelled Bloom.)

IV
Fistula and Cyst

In the first letter Beckett ever wrote me from Paris, the line occurs, but I couldn't decipher it. The calligraphy was a beast: the hasty hand of a hard-worked doctor firing off prescriptions.

Eventually Peggy Beckett, the mother of John, deciphered it as: 'Despair young and never look back.'

Oh most excellent sack! Get your own suffering in order early, stow your gear and buck up, messmates. Excellent advice for one setting out on life's journey. Anticipate squalls. I first met Beckett during the Criterion production of *Godot*, which had effectively bowled me over. He was coming down from Godalming with Peter Woodthorpe (Estragon) and a lady who had been at Trinity with him. John and Vera Beckett were then living on Haverstock Hill, and invited my wife and me over for a supper (silverside of beef, as I recall, done quite rare) to meet Beckett.

The party from Godalming arrived maybe an hour late. I wondered whom I would meet, Democritus or Heraclitus. Well, in the event, neither. It must have been Sunday. The murmurous Dublin accent was lovely to hear; he was not assertive, taller than I had expected, carried himself like an athlete. He had a copy of *Texts for Nothing* in French on the mantel, stood with me after the meal, asked my wife's name and inscribed this copy.

The following evening we accompanied the Becketts and Michael Morrow to Collins Music Hall in Islington, where the young Chaplin had performed in Fred Karno's troupe. A nude chorus girl was pushed across the stage on a bicycle, but what affected Sam Beckett was the row in stitches at Mr Dooley, who gave a rapid-patter monologue on what the world needed, which was apparently castor oil. It was in essence Lucky's outpourings at the Criterion. Beckett was leaning forward, looking along the row. On the way out my wife and I [who?] ran into Mr Dooley and introduced him to Beckett, of whom he had never heard; Mr D. was chuffed that Monsieur B. had liked his patter. It was all good clean fun.

Vaudeville appealed to Beckett. The farcical had to be given its head, the hats briskly exchanged. Brecht called it 'crude thinking' (*das plumpe Denken*), a device to liberate the metaphysics. Pratfalls, skids, banana skins.

The austere playwright, thought to be so reclusive, wasn't so reclusive after all, as close and enduring friendships with actors testify; as did the business of conducting much of his social life in cafés and bars. He seemed to be well aware of what was going on in the world at large, lived in no ivory tower.

He himself was not cold and inspired warm affection in others.

'When you fear for your cyst think of your fistula. And when you tremble for your fistula consider your chancre.' (*Murphy*)

Watt (225 pages), datelined Paris 1945, written in English, resumes from where Murphy left off in 1938, composed in bursts to keep his hand in when hiding from the Gestapo in deepest Roussillon, and finished in Paris when he was searching for the knockabout vaudeville style of Godot. It has its quite deliberate leaguers. *Mercier and Camier*, long suppressed by the author, contains preliminary intimations of the interrogations of *Godot* ('They didn't beat you? . . .') and already there are echoes of the great radio works ahead, the dramacules for the air. Nothing would ever be wasted.

Sloppiness, blur, was anathema to him; he brought a new astringency into writing. He was opposed to stale innovations, the time-honoured usages and abusages of the antiquarian Gael. He was a caution. He was his own man.

George Moore of Moore Hall, Mayo, the 'genuine Irish gent' lampooned by the younger and malicious Joyce, was only playing at being a Frog, the boulevardier and Parisian aesthete ('Life is, au fond, so limited, so diabolique, n'est-ce-pas, between cocktails and thé?') was a mask behind which one recognised a cherubic flushed face. The honed style was honied with high aspirations.

A thinner and more authentic Hiberno-Gaul came with Monsieur Beckett's progress towards acceptance by Editions de Minuit. He had paid his dues, stabbed once by a clochard, he had shed his blood for France. France proud, fallen, occupied, freed; and Beckett himself was part of these operations, even if he shrugged off his Crux de Gaulle (*sic*) as 'Boy Scout stuff.'

But you don't play games with the Gestapo. In his evolution as a writer in English and French, a whole world separates *Murphy* (1938) from *Molloy* (1951). A world war separates them, a way of viewing life, the acceptance of one's lot, one's tenure here on earth.

Up ahead are the mourning figures, robed and nightcapped, 'bringing night home', in the starless, moonless heaven of his later work. The funambulistic staggers of *Play* (1964), *Not I* (1972), *Footfalls* (1975), *Ohio Impromptu* (1981), *Catastrophe* (1982) and *What Where* (1984) cannot conceal the fact that the Gestapo weasels are at work in the long burrow again; in Nacht und Traume more specifically.

Certain hidden factors of the Occupation festered in his mind, with the knowledge that an authentic torture chamber was operating in Paris at X. In those years he lived in the sixteenth arrondissement at Y, and would have passed it on his way to Z. If the Gestapo noticed Beckett in the street, they saw only another emaciated, thin-featured Frenchman passing by. He had reduced himself almost to nothing.

'Where were we. The bitter, the hollow and—haw! haw!—the mirthless. The bitter laugh laughs at that which is not good, it is the ethical laugh. The hollow laugh laughs at that which is not true, it is the intellectual laugh. Not good! Not true! Well well. But the mirthless laugh is the dianoetic laugh, down the snout—haw!—so. It is the laugh of laughs, the risus purus, the laugh laughing at the laugh, the beholding, the saluting of the highest joke, in a word the laugh that laughs—silence please—at that which is unhappy.' (*Watt*)

The dreamer and his dreamt self. Sun long sunk behind the larches. Fade out dream.

Blind Borges had a theory that all the great books of the world might have been written for children, that all story-telling tended towards the conditions of the fairy tale.

Ideal reader in search of an ideal insomnia, hear this: Our life is a story told. Perhaps that is why children love to hear stories of the beginning of the world. We were weaned on terrifying yarns, it came with our mother's milk; from her lips we heard the saddest stories for beginners: Dick Whittington and his Cat—banishment. Rapunzel—gruesome intimations of the coming sexual combat. The girl imprisoned in the tower becomes Mary Queen of Scots kneeling to the headsman with a Skye terrier hidden up her skirt; becomes Joan of Arc watching the faggots being lit, and the greatest faggot of them all, Jean Genet—assuredly no saint—the man who had supped deep with horror, said that her menses had come the night before and she had to ascend the scaffold steps with a 'rusty stain' at crotch level on her virgin white smock, and had that humiliation to endure along with the taunts of the English soldiers.

Many stories and novels carry on their backs a load of atrocious bad news, as the bucklicht Mannlein (little hunchback) his hump. Indeed, the implication inherent in our readings and interpretations of free-floating texts is that we knew it all along, for even the oddest and cruellest fictions had a familiar ring to them. Beckett praised de Sade for his style. Winding its serpentine way through all fairy tales (fabled by the Daughters of Memory, the Misses Mneme) is the legend that we cannot forget, that hurt and upset us long ago, even before we could read; all those variations of the theme of banishment, from the home, the hearth, the heart, the homeland, the bed. The Fall.

The cruel stepmother becomes the witch in the forest, the brothers have turned into swans; before Adler and Jung were Bruder Grimm and Hans Andersen, the gentle giant, the frustrated man: and before them again Brentano and anthropology. And long before them, the Dark Ages and the yarns of illiterates never committed to writing but carried in the head before parchment and vellum, before the city, the nursery, the little lie of solicitude, the big lie of 'caring'. In a word, Inglenooknarration, gruntings and groanings and gushy whisperings; Gobbledegook.

And before that again, a much more numerous company, our true forbears, the Frightful Ones: the vast multitude of our speechless and indeed repulsive ancestors warming their bloodied hands before a communal cannibal fire.

Out of these depths rises the story. Varying from country to country, from language to language, down the centuries, offering innumerable versions of the one yarn that would change; story become interdict become precept—the story of the Fall, of the expulsion from paradise, of the angel with flaming sword.

Consider the multiple stories of exile: Jean-Jacques Rousseau, who invented the Noble Savage, locked out of his walled town; Dante in exile; Joyce and Beckett in their chosen exiles. Life is a story told.

When told well enough, the story outlasts the storyteller, triumphs over oblivion. All the best stories in the world are about dispossession; of lovers in full flight, couples eloping from an angry father, from the cuckolded husband. Our Diarmuid and Grainne, Isolde and her fancy man (who had bad halitosis), Jim Joyce and Nora Barnacle (whom some said could hardly spell her own name), Willy Reilly and the Colleen Bawn. Paolo and Francesca whirled about and about in their cloud. The flight of secret love into the unknown.

Our abominable past.

Nietzsche spoke of the void eternally generative. The abyss itself has rarely been subjected to such close scrutiny since the sour grapes of the great Jacobeans. Hear the melancholy Irish cadences come throbbing through the French and English texts, mournful as sea-warnings from the Kish.

The angle of attack was always unusual and unexpected,

a pincer-movement directed at the heart. Nothing seemed to reduce Beckett's characters, male and female and mostly getting on in years; they cannot be put down, for they themselves can descend no lower. The seedy solipsists get great mileage out of their misery; unceasing monologues tending towards the condition of unanswered prayers. Misery, with them contagious, never seems to reduce them; none plead, though close enough to abject misery to grovel. There is a continuous Court of Appeal in session.

Instant vagitus recorded, cry, then silence; the prescription is a little daunting and would quickly reduce itself to preciousness in hands less assured. Doddering old Democritus, setting forth to seek misfortune, encounters whom do you suppose but the young Heraclitus just arriving, grinning from ear to ear.

By some extraordinary means, hard won in a hell of private grief known only to himself, Beckett, from his retreat in the Marne mud, had issued directives more or less undecoded and direct from the psyche itself, that silent lover of suffering in silence. All lead back to the Self, where all ideation has its seat, in the brain. Lemuel Gulliver can put the King of Laputa in his coat pocket.

Beckett never succumbed to the merely anecdotal, nor was he too free with messages.

> . . . alone on the end of the stone with the wheat and blue or the towpath alone on the towpath with the ghosts of the mules the drowned rat or bird or whatever it was floating off into the sunset till you could see it no more nothing stirring only the water and the sun going down till it went down and you vanished all vanished . . . (*That Time*)

The paradox is that the story swamps the storyteller, outlives (outlasts) the author. The voice crying out 'Arise, ye wretched of the earth!' has only that message and cannot stop crying it. The idea behind the story is perhaps to rid the Duree of its ancient horror, its fixity of purpose, its hostility, its baleful intent; the drift being that Time itself must have a stop, that our lifespan here on earth must end.

All dreams turn into pointless stories as soon as we tell them to someone. But dreams are by their very nature extraordinary; the true nature of the dignity of man is that all is extraordinary, at least potentially. The core of the story is never quite found, the centre never quite arrived at but gestured to, from a safe distance. Anna Karenina is forever coming downstairs, Ulysses is forever sailing by, his ears blocked up with wax, the Sirens cannot stop singing, the fireworks are always rising up over Mirus Bazaar, the Good Fairy (safe in Pooka's pocket) is always losing that hand of poker (the stake: a simple soul just born).

Samuel Beckett kept himself to himself in an even more cloistral way than his austere mentor Joyce, who had after all his family as a bulwark against the herd, an inner ring of bonding that expanded with the years on the arrival of grandchildren; though he (Beckett) could unbend with Magee and McGowran, no intellectuals, who had some intuitive understanding of what he was after. Despite his frigid bearing and frosty mien, there was something warm and endearing about him. Few if any ever called him Samuel; it was always Sam. If he liked you, well and good, you were instantly accepted into the closed circle, the enclave. He gave with an open hand and had to be taken with the same reciprocal spirit, as unstintingly. Was it this that inspired affection, or was it his work, so affecting, or was it a combination of both? One was privileged to know Sam Beckett, for his like will not come again; such generosity of spirit was rarer than radium.

With Sam Beckett you could never envy the genius because it was housed in the man; no writer had ever done less to conceal the treachery of that shelter.

Tellers of Tales

Introduction to *A Century of Short Stories*, Book Club Associates, 1977

'A phrase', wrote Isaac Babel, 'is born into the world both good and bad at the same time.' And, a stiff corollary, 'no iron can stab the heart with such force as a full stop put just at the right place.'

The combination of letters is not something to fool around with (pace Isaac Bashevis Singer). An error in one word or one vowel accent can 'destroy the earth'. In the beginning was the Logos. The imagination, avoiding the hegemony of the banal word, goes in search of a fabulous world.

Stories have their oldest roots in folklore, the common dreams of all language: an oral tradition. The West of Ireland stories that open this collection may belong more properly to Paddy Flynn, not to Lady Gregory or even to Yeats, who later transcribed and retranscribed them, searching for a purer diction. The poet saw the storyteller asleep under a bush, smiling. The prescription 'he dreamed' tilted the Tower of Babel. Some stories have no beginning, others no middle (*Mosby's Memoirs?*), and there is a Gogol story that has no end. Transcribed, because of Gogol's defective memory, the pages were baked into a pie.

Nursery rhymes, laying-on of curses, trance-speech, the Little Language of lovers (*Journal to Stella*) where the loved one is likened to monkey or snake, are all perhaps akin; as are rhyming slang, prison argot, all secret languages. The sedulous dreamers always refused to be psychoanalysed. Hence

Nabokov's obligatory sneers at the Viennese witchdoctor and Freudian 'mystics', Joyce's dismissal of Dr Jung and Freud as Tweedledum and Tweedledee. The Bruder Grimm were always anthropologists.

Here then is an idiosyncratic collection of middle and early twentieth century short stories and apercus published in English during the period 1890-1970. Eighty years, a lifespan. A look askance at people and things perishing, talents and vanished cities, the slow decay of manners, time's afflictions. From the groves of US Academe, Nabokov sees a lost white St Petersburg, a misty Fialta, written at a time when his talent was perhaps purer. Djuna Barnes invokes a Berlin that no longer exists; Singer, another Warsaw. James Joyce, starting out on a career of notoriously straitened circumstances, looks back from Trieste towards Dublin at the turn of the century.

Some of the American stories might be regarded as post hoc European writing; a branch that sank underground for a generation, transmuted into a newly entangled language. Bellow might have written in Russian; Singer's English is coloured by its Polish-Yiddish origins; Beckett's work in French has to some degree modified and pared his austere English.

Behind the London clubmen, the swells and hearties, rowing men and athletes with single sticks and boxing gloves, dukes and baronets, names to conjure with, racehorse owners and scoundrels, lawyers and surgeons, sinister non-English persons, criminals and low fellows, wronged women, 'Penang lawyers' (a stick that could fell an ox), growlers, nice bits of blood between the shafts, that infest the pages of Conan Doyle, in a London of cabs and Bow Street runners or an unspoilt countryside sometimes luridly lit, lay another England: a land of dead bare-fist champions, ostlers and seconds, more Penang lawyers, and the hangman; and behind them stood the Empire, Bloemfontein, India, Gurkhas and the Raj, Sir Arthur Conan Doyle's land, boys' land. An exhumed Egyptian mummy sprints down an Oxfordshire lane, after Abercrombie Smith of all men. Elsewhere, a gigantic hellhound roams the moors.

Unmasker of the outré and the bizarre, Doyle's work is tinged with a certain Edwardian bluntness and brutality. A text teeming with the minutiae of keen observation is notable for the energy of its verbs and the marksmanship of its adjectival clauses ('A spray of half-clad deepbreathing runners shot past him, and craning over their shoulders, he saw Hastie pulling a steady thirty-six . . .'), combined with an inventiveness that is hard to resist. His output was huge, Balzacian; the sheer energy prodigious. H. G. Wells had it also (he once played a game of fives against Nabokov's father.) Human dynamos.

V. S Pritchett's writing has the mark of the just, decorous, law-abiding English mind. Passion induces responsibility. How English couples interact, the men shady, the women a cross between boa-constrictor and angel. ('They spend half their lives in the bathroom.') A self-effacing talent that does not draw attention to itself.

William Trevor, like Pritchett, and Dickens before them, is a sly recorder of London, its inner life and outer fringes. Very good on middle-aged despair ('The English Disease'), progressive inebriation of cocktail parties, the fog of cigarette smoke and the warm smell of brandy, the fearful Mrs Fitch ('that man up to his tricks with women while the beauty drains from my face'), the edgy diction of distress is well caught. Dukelow, Belhatchet, Angusthorpe, Dutts, Miss Efoss, Matera, Marshalsea, Abbott, Da Tanka, the Lowhrs, Digby-Hunter, Wraggett, Buller Achen ('reputed to take sensual interest in the sheep that roamed the mountainsides'), no telephone directory can hold them. Echoes of early Eliot. Curious congeries. 'I looked in a window,' admits the halfwit dwarf Quigley, 'I saw a man and woman without their clothes on'. Voices as garrulous as Mr Jingle, as sinister as Quilp. His characters talk because they are unhappy. Stories of Ireland too, refreshingly free of the turgidity and rank complacency that characterise the older Cork School; free too of the insidious self-pity that mars much of the work of his juniors. Born Cox, of County Cork.

John Hawkes is a crafty manipulator of chilly details, not in the contemporary American grain, but more 'European' in approach. The Sicilian Vittorini (*Erica*), the German Robert Musil (*Tonka*), or the Austrian Robert Walser (*Kleist in Thun*) spring to mind; mordant ambience of Bierce or Poe, among the illustrious dead; or the surrealist Harry Mathews among the living. Admired by Bellow.

Saul Bellow's own dramas of ideas (*Herzog, Mr Sammler's Planet*) show the anecdotal and discursive held in a vice-like grip. Exegeses proliferate. Imbued with fluctuating hope, the short declarative sentence has rarely been worked to better effect. Recapitulative epistolary forms, letters to the dead. Updated versions of *Les Liaisons Dangereuses*. Chronicler of sexual intrigues and vexations, generally Jewish. A touch of Chateaubriand; Laclos. Few writing today can match his descriptions, both acid and tender, of the tarnished Modern Megalopolis and the dire condition of its citizenry. The trembling energy of the modern city (tumescent Chicago, rotting New York): 'a strip of beautifying and dramatic filth'. A keen ear for argot and slang has gone into the making of an abrasively idiomatic high style. Hemingway, by comparison, is ill-mannered, when not insane (*Islands in the Stream*).

William Faulkner, after a false start as poet, came to his main theme early on: the back country and woods of Mississippi, its garrulous habitués and clientele of 'freed niggers'.

Exhumed from the *New Orleans Times-Picayune* files, 'The Liar' (July 1925) is one of sixteen signed stories and sketches marking Faulkner's debut in fiction, written at the age of twenty-seven during a six-month sojourn in the Vieux Carré French sector of New Orleans. The story, the only one not set in the Vieux Carré, but in the back country, may have been written aboard the freighter *West Ivis*, bound for Italy and mailed back to the *Times-Picayune* office from Savannah. Like all Faulkner's best work, it reads as though written on shipboard, adrift on a tempestuous sea.

Faulkner made early supererogatory claims to being 'sole owner and proprietor' of Yoknapatawpha County, Mississippi. Here already, escaped from chronology, is one loose horse troubling Mis' Harmon as its brother would trouble Mrs Littlejohn in *The Hamlet*, dispute right-of-way with Ratliff himself, and a whole herd of wild spotted horses go rampaging on through Frenchman's Bend. Gibson's store, give or take a prop, would become Will Varner's, all ready for the usurping Snopes dynasty.

Faulkner was already at work on his first novel, *Soldier's Pay*, to be published by Boni & Liveright through the agency of Sherwood Anderson; the same publishers would bring out Hemingway's *In Our Time* and early work by Djuna Barnes. Faulkner was travelling in Europe that summer.

The second story given here, 'Delta Autumn', is from *Go Down Moses* (1942). 'The Liar' is notable for much preliminary spittin' and whittlin', the 'prodigious' yellow of an outbuilding, the description of a pistol shot, with other intimations of latent powers ('the others sat in reft and silent amaze, watching the stranger leaping down the path'.) Only in the back country would his imagination take off. Those Mississippi farmers and traders spoke Elizabethan English with a tinge of Baptist fatalism. Faulkner's English would always be odd and curious, a vocabulary replete with archaisms ('yon', 'ere' 'dasnt') and Bible tones. 'Myriad', 'doomed', 'avatar', 'apotheosis', 'redeem' and 'chastisement' recur and recur, particularly 'doomed'. 'God knows I hate for my own blooden children to reproach me,' says the father in *As I Lay Dying*. Jefferson is 'a fair piece'. In rural Ireland it would be a fair stretch, or step. Where a metal sign designates Jefferson, Corporate Limit, the pavement ends.

It is curious to compare Faulkner's early work with Joyce's, both into their first novels while engaged on short stories. Office girls took home seven shillings a week, a deck hand a pound a month, porter cost a penny a pint, and it was possible to dine on peas and a bottle of ginger beer' (twopence halfpenny, old currency), in Dublin at the turn of the century, when James Joyce came of age. Little evidence here of the later all-in-oneness of *Ulysses* (1922) or the wholesale discarding of the 'wideawake language of cut and dry grammar and goahead plot' as discovered in *Finnegans Wake* (1939). Language topples as Europe itself topples. A sequel to *Dubliners* (1914), Provincials' was never to be written.

Sponge cakes, raised umbrellas, old gentility, dusty cretonne, waltzes, unheated rooms, poorly paid servants, foul weather, crestfallen daughters, tedious aunts, craw-thumpers, *Mignon*, *The Bohemian Girl*, descant singing, the human voice, music, tenors, the dead, these stories, written at the suggestion of the middle-class mystic George Russell for *The Irish Homestead*, and later included as the third and ninth in order of composition of the fifteen that made up *Dubliners*, were rejected by thirty publishers; the 'blackguard production' must since have been reprinted in as many different languages.

Written mostly in Trieste when Joyce was working on his first novel, 'Stephen Hero', *Dubliners* reads today more like *Little Dorrit* than Chekhov. The ground already seems exhausted. Jack Mooney climbs upstairs for ever and ever, with two bottles of Bass under one arm. Prototypes of Gerty McDowell proliferate. Dublin circa 1906: a circumscribed area in which to settle old grievances.

I remarked their English accents and listened vaguely to their conversation.

O, I never said such a thing!

O, but you did!

O, but I didn't! (*Dubliners*: 'Araby'.)

A gap of some twenty years divides *La Fin* as written by Beckett, in French, and its appearance in English; thirty-three years yawns between some minor retitling and rephrasing in the two Barnes stories subjoined here.

Whatever happened, it happened in extraordinary times, in a season of dreams. These stories, begun at Rosses Point and ending in a rowing boat on Dublin Bay, have gone almost full circle, in three-quarters of a century's patiently accumulated recording.

Our Hero, After Babel

Introduction to *Colossal Gongorr and the Turkes of Mars* by Carl, Julien and Elwin Higgins (1979)

JUST BEFORE THE publication of *Ulysses*, James Joyce was walking in the Bois de Boulogne with his wife and Djuna Barnes, when a man brushed by them muttering darkly, whereupon Joyce turned pale. Questioned by Miss Barnes, he said that the Unknown One had muttered in Latin, 'You are an abominable writer!' A dire omen on the eve of publication, James Joyce feared.

Nine years later he persuaded George Moore to read some pages of the book in a French translation; but Moore could not go on. 'It cannot be a novel, for there isn't a tree in it,' he complained to Janet Flanner. An odd demure. Family trees abound in it. He would not have known that the Irish alphabet is made up of the names of trees; the eighth letter ioda (i) signifying yew tree. 'Fik yew! I'm through!' (Finnegans Wake).

Joyce admitted, 'I'd like to have seven tongues and put them all into my cheek at once.' He did his best, knew many languages, could speak a number fluently, though not all simultaneously ('The chief spoke his native tung'). He loved and understood children and thus could not, as is sometimes claimed by the Irish, not the least vindictive of peoples, be a Bad Hat. He battled with language all his life, married one of the Barnacles of Galway.

The child, who knows nothing, invents the world, and is haunted by it. A child's secret scribblings and scrawlings are a vatic spreading of the inks. Early terrors, induced by reading, are perhaps premonitions of later realities, rendered in symbolic form; the form of the Tale. The movies and television, the latter regurgitating the former in an insatiable greed for perpetuation, are poised to destroy story-telling; and story-telling may be the base of language. The Noun today can no longer name (nail) its Object; verbs, the energy of a sentence, are machine-made.

The text here was firmly founded on a general ignorance of the English language, the rules of its grammar and the generally accepted usages of spelling. It seems to be in a hurry. Where? To tell its tale. Just beyond lay the murky, depthless region of Unthought or whatever lies beyond the realm of Words.

The later fierce story-telling freely dispenses with punctuation as we understand it, commas and periods are dropped, along with paragraph spacings (useful for breathing purposes), as sense outruns syntax, in an effort to say the impossible, and the whole races on towards its close, multiplying its own multiples forever, with heroes and heroines reduced to lowercase versions of themselves. The method employed: The Continuous Overflow.

The icy wastes are testing grounds for valour and extraordinary deeds. The monsters may be ill-defined but are true monsters ('There wos this ophill creature who could eat people'). When a sheet of paper is being burnt, Baroness Blixen observed, 'after all the other sparks have run along the edge and died away, one last little spark will appear and hurry after them.'

The Floating World, the kingdom where children play, seeking astonishment but menaced by monsters, is reached by crossing the line at noontide, entering the Land of the Unicorns. The path progresses sometimes through the mother (Proust?), sometimes through the father; the signposts to it are marked Solicitude.

Jean Genet wrote:

The ryefield was bounded on the Polish side by a wood at whose edge was nothing but motionless birches; on the Czech side, by another wood, but of fir trees. I remained a long time squatting by the edge, intently wondering what lay hidden in the field. What if I crossed it? Were customs officers hidden in the rye? Invisible hares must have been running through it. I was uneasy. At noon, beneath a pure sky, all nature was offering me a puzzle, and offering it to me blandly.

If something happens, I said to myself, it will be the appearance of a unicorn. Such a moment and such a place can only produce a unicorn. Fear, and the kind of emotion I always feel when I cross a border, conjured up at noon, beneath a leaden sun, the first fairyland. I ventured into the golden sea as one enters water. I went through the rye standing up. I advanced slowly, surely, with the certainty of being the heraldic character for whom a natural blazon had been shaped: azure, field of gold, sun, forests. This imagery, of which I was a part, was complicated by the Polish imagery . . . When I got to the birches, I was in Poland.

An enchantment of another order was about to be offered to me. The 'Lady with the Unicorn' is to me the lofty expression of this crossing the line at noontide. I had just come to know, as a result of fear, an uneasiness in the presence of the mystery of diurnal nature, at a time when the French countryside where I wandered about, chiefly at night, was peopled all over with the ghost of Vacher, the killer of shepherds. As I walked through it, I would listen within me to the accordion tunes he must have played there, and I would mentally invite the children to come and offer themselves to the cut-throat's hands. However, I have just referred to this in order to try to tell you at what period of my life nature disturbed me, giving rise within me to the spontaneous creation of a fabulous fauna, or of situations and accidents whose fearful and enchanted prisoner I was.

The crossing of the border and the excitement it aroused in me were to enable me to apprehend directly the essence of the nature I was entering. I was penetrating less into a country than to the interior of an image.

The Thief's Journal (First published by Editions Gallimard in France (Journal du Voleur), 1949. This translation by Bernard Frechtman, first published in Great Britain by Anthony Blond, 1965.

Early terrors: Noah and his Ark in the Deluge (the nightmare of being born), Jack and the Beanstalk (falling nightmare), Three Blind Mice (disguised infanticide?), Dick Whittington and his Cat (banishment, exile), Dr Hoffmann's Struwwelpeter, much of Hans Andersen, most of the Brothers Grimm, Rapunzel in particular (nightmare upon nightmare).

The child has not at his disposal the adult barrier—the barrier of forgetting—what are you doing now and something identical in the past. The child has no past. Today the past has disappeared, while the future has never been so close, within touching distance. Or, better still, future and remote past merge into a present of irredeemable decadence: apes from outer space mounted on horses drag human infants through the streets of New York in A.D. 2022. Conan.

As parents spend less and less time with their children and are replaced by serial television, 'living memory' must lose much of its meaning. What meaning, if any, will 'living memory' have in the minds of our grandchildren? Every family had its terrible sentence. Not any more.

The child too feels the growing emptiness about him. 'Around the shore of the pool a bundle of apes were jumping.' But a rustle in the bushes is often a signal that help is nigh. A handful of phrases gather and the lightning strikes. 'Suddenly there was a loud shout from the shore.'

The furious Christ who expelled the buyers and sellers from the Temple two thousand years ago has returned, whip in hand, to chastise wrongdoers—'in the graspe of their hands was pistols'.

I say that that which is is. I say that which is not also is. The remote past and the future have never been so close together and the present has disappeared as the world shrinks and the imagination of man dwindles away. The weakening began in language itself. Maybe it continues, roughly, in the din of Rock; certainly no other century has been as loud as ours. Meditation ('think-tanks') becomes more difficult by the hour.

The disturbed child (the modern urban child?) makes a baboon in plasticine, then a snake-charmer, then a man dressed in animal skins with a parrot on his shoulder and a fowling-piece cocked by his knee, with an umbrella also made of skins for protection against the fierce island sun—Crusoe. Somewhere, just out of sight, the savages are howling.

Heraldic beasts guard the fictive way to come—Kafka's martens, leopards, jaguars, the tiger in Bursen's training cage. A hero becomes a cockroach overnight, sickens, expires, is thrown out on the refuse-dump. Gone are the old source books—Wynken de Worde's *A Lyttel Gest of Robyn Hode* (initiation rites), Finnemore's *His First Term: A Story of Slapton School* (ritual flogging), *The Giant Mole*, or *The Mime of Mick, Nick and the Maggies*, to make way for Hergé's faceless boy-detective, Jean de Brunhoff's *Babar, King of the Elephants* and his court, Pom, Flora, Zephir, composed and illustrated in a Swiss sanatorium by a man dying of cancer, as a memoir for his children.

The brink, the abyss itself, is very close in a child's early feelings, experienced as a condition of convalescence. The blue-shadowed wall towards the end of a long summer's day, the emptied city and the deserted home; the sense of dread, things in abeyance. In the silence that settles over nature, human cries go straight up like hair rising on a terrified scalp.

A word about the composition of these yarns. They were written in English after three years' schooling in Spanish and one year in a West Berlin school. The stories have been filtered through strictly limited vocabularies in these two languages, and were written in four different countries by my three sons at ages varying from five to fifteen, covering a period of perhaps ten years. I assembled them from Spanish cuadernos and Berliner Hefte, retitled here and there and put together in the Connemara Gaeltacht during the worst winter in living memory, through weeks of penitential rain, looking out of a cottage window at the Maamturks, and they have afforded me more pleasure than any of my own enfeebled labours.

To convey something straight from the heart in a familiar tongue—in this case Hardiman's 'comen English tong'—is no easy matter. To convey something strong and straight from the heart in a lost tongue (one's own) is more difficult. From the pre-verbal chaos of unnaming, go on without false emphasis or hesitation to the later exemplary truths of the Primer. Why do children love to hear stories of the beginning of the world?

I first saw West Berlin, that half-city, in 1956 when touring with a marionette group out from London, bound for Rhodesia and the Copper Belt; then a father to-be. Sixteen years later I returned, now the father of three sons, and in the dark cellar Quasimodo next to the Delphi Cinema on Kantstrasse, spoke to Martin Kluger of a possible children's book that would be different, a Boyes Buke for Grown Boys. This is that book, eight years on. No, twenty-three years on. I have lost count of the years.

Jonah Mackol suffering for Linda, and in a POW camp at that, assumes the old form of the knightly vigil, chivalry. Slay the dragon (or the ape) and the reward is not Linda but 'all the proteins of a good square meal'. After the raw fish and water, the beatings. The Tarzan-Linda saga is a re-working of *The Sleeping Beauty*. The illustrations are by the three authors.

Why, asks Eleanor of Worms, does the child forget? Because if he did not forget, the course of this world would drive it into madness, if it thought about it in the light of what it knew. Children might just as well play as not. The ogre will come in any case. Dia guive.

Extracts from Colossal Gongorr and the Turkes of Mars

Stories written in Nerja, Andalucia, by the three sons of the author, Carl, Julien and Elwin Higgins

Thomas Wills

'My name is Thomas Wills,' said the stranger in a low voice. Wills was sertainly a stranger but he had come through the wood and not the path. He had a thick black beard as well as hair, and blue swade shoes, his jacket looked like a jumper and his trousers were black and white. He carried a black suitcase, [about] which I wondered and intended to see inside. He had taken up the stable (or to put it in a more spaced way) the barn. That night I crept up to the barn window and peeped in. I saw nothing. The whole barn was completely empty. I quickly ran back to my home, after a while of thinking where the stranger was, I ran out of my house and went to the 'Sea Lion' which was a bar.

Tatoonie

She noticed his unabanished stare, but this time she only smiled. She ran upstairs, still liking him.

A week later Luke woke up in his bed and yawned. He approached the window and looked across Tatoonie.

Tom Spring

'I will NOT tolerate disobedience in my school!' Said the headmaster, and gazed around the pupils in the class. 'Now who smashed the gymnasium window?' The pupils were speechless. Suddenly Tom Spring raised his hand from the midst of the crowd and spoke. 'I did it sir.' The crowd burst into mutters and whispers. 'Silence, I will have NO muttering,' said the headmaster. 'Tom Spring, come to my office.' Tom spring Emerged from amongst the crowd and stepped onto the Platform where the headmaster was standing.

'Follow me to my office!' he said angrily and strolled Ahead in dignity. Tom spring had the urge to run away. He had never had the cane before. And He didn't want it now. The headmaster swung a brown mahogany door and turned to his desk. Tom knew this was it. But Instead of the headmaster taking a cane from the cupboard he took out a file. 'Now' he said with a smile.

A Story Without Beginning or End

Chapter 1 Arrival

. . . jonah hit the ground, he had landed In A forest. jonah Rolled up his Parachute and hid it in a bush, he looked at his hands they had been badly burnt he put his Right hand under his left shoulder and his left hand under his right Shoulder and ran through the grass. he stopped and listened, Suddenly a hand covered up his mouth and a machine gun was put to his face. 'Who are you' Said a young lady, in a french acsent 'my name is jonah I'm in the R.A.F.' Replied jonah.

The young lady walked in front of jonah 'It is true' said the young lady admiring jonah's medal. The young lady Was

Wearing a black jumper a brown pair of jeans, A pair of Plimsels a leather belt strapped with bullets. her hair was long and black and came down to her shoulders. her eyes were hazel Brown and her lips cherry red. 'Are you french' asked jonah, Rather puzzled. 'oui, monsieur' che Replied With a smile. 'you are admiringly beautiful' Said jonah with a close look. 'Merci' che Replied 'but now you must come with me' che said. Jonah stopped 'Where are you taking me' he asked. 'Why to our hideout' che said.

'Who's our hideout' asked jonah with a puzzled look.

'Let me explain' che said.

'I should jolly well think so' Said jonah sitting on a log.

'My name is linda tennis, My father used to be a banker until the germans Invaded france, my father was killed, everyone Ran away and hid iff they could. The germans tortured my mother to the death And I am Revenging their deaths, I have friends In my hideout, now will you Please come with me'

'yes' Replied jonah 'but my hand theyve got blisters'

Suddenly there was a shot linda and jonah stood still. A german voice came out of the woods: 'hauben Krau lotze un bieren' (the voice said, meaning stop where you are, the wood is surrounded).

'It is an ambush' Said the young lady, quickly Run.

Linda Ran but jonah still stood, not knowing what to do. Linda staggered to the ground. Then there came the sound of Machine guns. 'oh my god' Said jonah covering his face. then the german voice spoke again: 'harben zi gnitze' (meaning do not try to resist).

A minute later the germans came out from behind the trees with rifles and machine guns. The leader spoke

'Get up.'

Jonah did not stirr. the leader kicked jonah on to the floor. jonah stood up in a rage and yelled 'murderer' jonah tryed to strangle the leader but was knocked out by the end of a german Rifle.

Chapter 2 Imprisonment

jonah awoke to find himself in the back of a truck with 3 germans with machine guns standing by him, jonah's hands and legs were also tied up, so that made him helpless.

'Where are we going' asked jonah.

'Stuttgart' Replied a german. Stuttgart was a german Imprisonment for British prisoners everyone knew the place or either had heard the name.

'hotze uf Naken irr' said one of the germans (meaning have you a cigarette).

'ja Kaultze urr laten' (meaning yes here take one) the other german Replied

The german handed an open packet of cigarettes over to the other German and then passed the packet on to the third german.

'grassias' he said (meaning, thank you).

After many hours driving the truck finally stopped, the three germans dragged jonah out, the light blinded him for a second. When jonah slowly opencd his eyes he looked around.

Stuttgart was a large Prisonment. On jonah's left were the generalls quarters and the ammunition hut for the sentries, on the right were the sleeping huts for the prisoners and behind jonah the sentries sleeping huts and not too far from that the cooking house.

The soldiers dragged jonah into the generals hut. The general was a fat man with a desperate look he held a cane in his right hand.

'Vat is your name' he said coughing a little In Between.

'my name is jonah Mackol R.A.F., squadron 8.'

'zearch him' said the general.

The sentries searched jonah. they found a packet of gum a

compass, a picture of his family and a knife in his Buckle.

'Do you know anything Of the British Plans' said the general.

jonah didn't Reply, then the general struck him across the face.

'Anzer me' said the general.

'I Do not' said jonah Rubbing his cheek in a fury.

'I do not believe you' said the general. 'Put him in the concentration camp for two months' he said with a laugh.

Chapter 3 Lonelyness

jonah was led down corridoors, there were doors and doors on every side, the german in front of jonah stopped and unlocked a door, the german behind jonah pushed him into it. And the door was locked again. jonah looked around, the room was small but uncrowded a small bed lay in the Right hand corner and near to the barred window was a table with a chair.

Jonah Stood on the chair to look out of the barred window. he saw the British prisoners lining up, they all looked very weak. Suddenly one of the men flopped in-to the floor, jonah saw one of the germans kick him but the prisoner did not stir.

'Take him away' said the german.

jonah climbed down from the chair and lay on the bunk. The hot sun turned the place Into an oven. Days passed jonah becoming weaker all the time the only thing they gave him was Raw fish, Bread and water. They gave him injections trying to force him to tell the British Plans. On the last day jonah was practically dead his legs could not move he could barely move any of his body the german sentry gave the prisoners jonah to take care of. jonah felt water treacle on to his dry mouth and flow onto his neck 'thank you' said jonah very slowly and then fell uncunsious.

Chapter 4 Friends

Two days later jonah felt Better, the prisoners had taken good care of him, feeding him on meats starch and all the proteins of a good square meal. Bob one of the young men had taken more care of jonah than any of the other men. he had stole some of the food that Jonah had eaten for the two days from the generals food store in Stuttgart iff you were caught Stealing food the penalty was death. When jonah awoke he found four men around him 'you look Much Better today Whats your name' Said a tall man with a small moustache. jonah Rubbed his eyes. 'My name is jonah.' 'hye' said Bob smiling. Then the fellow with the small moustache spoke again:

'My name's clark stairs this is stephen mayday that is

A Polar Bear's Last Roar

Chapter I

We Stocked

The year was 1874 an aqua plane was crossing the North Pole inside were 4 tourists except for one Jason kong who was driving the aqua plane the rest were tourists there names were Jonah Mackol, Linda tennis, and Stephen mayday. Suddenly Jason spocke 'wer'e running out of fuel'. 'Look a enormous Iceburg' shouted Linda 'we'll crash into it were bound to' said Jason Jason pulled the Geer on to full power the aqua aeroplane lifted into the air 'Phew well be safe for a while' said Jason they whent a little way and the the phropeller stopped 'Oh no were going to crash, hang on' said Jason the aqua aeroplane dived down and smashed on the ice there was a silence and then the aqua aeroplane whent into flames. Suddenly a arm stretched out of the door of the aeroplane. then the figure came out it was Stephen he pulled out the rest and spocke 'Run, the aqua aeroplane is going to blow up' 'I can't, said Jason, my leg is injured' Stephen picked up Jason and they all hid behind an Iceburg Just then there was an explosion bits of the aqua plane flew everywhere and then the rest disepeard down the ice cold water. Just then Jonah notice a chunk of ice falling above them. he pushed the rest out of the way and then he dived to them the chunk of ice hit the icy bottom. 'Jonah you saved our lives' said Linda 'I'm afraid I did' replied Jonah 'I'm afraid my right leg is cripeld' said Jason Just then there was a Roar 'What was that' said Linda then a Polar bear came around an iceburge the polar bear roared again he roared at the four then Linda spocke 'Keep still' then Stephen spocke 'we can't were all chivering WERE ALL CHIVERING shouted Stephen he ran at the polar bear and the polar bear ran at him. Stephen ran into the polar bears stomach the polar bear teared Stephens jersey and picked him up. then Jonah rushed at the Polar bear he's head buded into the polar bear he grabed a pointed Ice burge and plunged it into the Polar bears chest the Polar bear made a last roar and crashed on the ice. Now Stephen and Jonah had made fur coats for all so they moved on. As they whent along Jonah saw some Penguins he spocke 'LOOK penguins' they all stopped on their track and Jonah pointed them out Soon they whent on Later they stopped 'Well stop here for a minute' said Jonah they all lied down and whent to sleep. While they were sleeping they didnt notice a wallruss come up to them it's fangs Pricked Linda che awoke and said 'a wallruss' then che patted his slithery head the walruss whent up and rubbed his cheek against Linda's. che cmiled then he turned and jumped into the icy water. Linda lied back and whent to sleep.

Chapter 2 An Aeroplane in Sight

Jonah was the first to awake he chivered a little and then shacked Linda a little later everybody was on their feet and were on the way as they walked along Jonah heard the noise of propellers then he spocke 'Lizten is that the noise of propellers' 'by god its the new aqua plane specialy designed to go under water Id no that noise anywhere' said Jason Just then they all saw the aqua aeroplane it was enormous The four shouted and yelled HErP! HErP! but the aqua aeroplane didnt notice. It Just flew around and around then it flew away. 'We couldn't get it to come, down, we coudnt' said Stephen 'dont worry sooner or later somebodys bound to find us' said Jason the four turned and continued walking later Stephen stopped 'I Cant carry Jason any longer' Im warned out' 'Picke his feet up Im warned out to but we have to move on' said Jonah 'I cant said Stephen 'Off course you can' 'I cant Im tired' Picke him up we cant stay here well starve 'I cant' said Stephen Jonah slaped him across his cheek 'Now do as your told' 'Nobody slaps me and get's away with it' said Stephen he ran up to Jonah and picked him up above his head then he threw Jason at an iceburge he crashed on the Iceburge and then he got up he ran toward's stephen and grasped his hand into a fist he swung it and it landed in Stephen's Jaw Stephen fell on the ice a little blood poured down his chin 'okay, you win' said Stephen he got up and lifted Jason's legs 10 hours whent and the four lied down 'Now, we need food' said Linda Just then there was a snort and a ΛEEOOW and a walruss appeard it was the walruss Linda had patted he had fish speard down his tusks he made a kind of a smile and whent up to the four Linda spocke 'he's the wallruss I saw last time' che put out her hands and patted the wallruss he shacked his husks and the fish lay on the ice. 'but we need more then this' Linda said to the walruss he turned and dived into the ice cold water a minute later he appeard with a fish the size of half an arm stucke in the two tuskss they pulled it out and some matches and other things cooked the fish the last fish'es skeleton was thrown on the ice they all got up. They were full of cooked fishes Linda saw the wallruss jumpe into the ice and disepear 'that was a lovely meal' said Jason 'it sure was' said Linda looking at the walruss go down.

Chapter 3

as they whent On they didn't notice thin ice in front of them there was a crack 'HELP!' shouted Linda che saw the ice part and then che fell into the ice cold water 'AAH!' she said and then che disepeard under the ice cold water and che appeard again Jonah let go of Jason's arm's and took a rope out of his trousers he lassood it to Linda che grabed hold of the rope and che was pulled to Jonah then che spocke '~~~m CCCOLD' Jonah raped his fur coat around her's 'thank you' said Linda chivering 'wev'e got to find a way of signalling some one' said Jonah 'Ive an idea how about carving an enormous letter S :O: S' said Stephen 'a great Idea' 'has anybody got anything usefull' suggested Stephen 'Ive a pen' said Linda 'NO that's . . . Ive got it' shouted Stephen he took a pointed Iceburge out of the ice 'this will do the trick' after that he made the leterr S.O.S. as big as football pitches they waited for a plane for days 'I dont thinck we'll make it' said Linda Just then there was the sound of propellers 'an aeroplane' shouted Jonah 'HOORAY' shouted Stephen and by god it was the new built aqua Plane.

the aqua aeroplane flew down on the ice and the propeller's stopped out of the aeroplane came three men one of them ran up to Jason 'your leg is Injured' he said 'Yes, it is, Im an aeroplane driver' said Jason 'Im doctor martin' 'Will I be able to drive an aeroplane doctor' said Jason 'Yes said Martin but youre going to have an operation on your leg' 'I dont mind' said Jason meanwhile Linda, Jonah, and Stephen were talking with the other two men 'my name is Stephen Philips' said one of them Im a television Reporter tell me how did you survive in this bitterly cold place' Well said Linda I saw a wallruss and patted him and he speared the fish with his tusks and we cooked them' 'do you know why he did this' said Stephen Philips nearly eating his tie with anxiousty 'NO' said Linda then Jonah spocke 'can we get out of this place' 'Yes certainly' said martin they all hoped in and drove off

Linda saw a speck of the wallruss and che thought che heard a faint EEEOOOW and a snori and then che whispered bye bye my friend.

THE END

Paper read at Hemel Hempstead October 17th 1999

SOME COME LATE to their true vocation, whereas others never find it at all. I knew a number of painters, most of them now dead who came late to painting. But few came as late as Carl.

Jack Yeats was twenty-six when he painted his first work in oils. Kandinsky had to leave Tsarist Russia, land of snow and bells, to discover painting in Germany, when he was thirty years of age. The painter whom you see before you, whose work adorns these walls, had turned forty when he began working in oils. I can tell you a little about him, for he happens to be my eldest son.

He was born forty years ago in Johannesburg on the 6th of August 1959, fourteen years after that bomber Enola Gay dropped that terrible egg on Hiroshima. He was reared and sent to school in Andalucia and came to speak the language like a native, the hard brittle lingo of Cervantes and the Moors of Spain, became a sort of Spaniard, drew in coloured pencils, wrote stories to please himself.

We moved about. From Dublin to Nerja, from there to Berlin, then to London. Carl had to learn some German. He lived for a time in Mexico City where, it is said, 'Surrealism runs through the streets.' His imaginative life was, I suspect, more real to him than his real life. He hates things to come to an end. Perhaps he does not belong to this century, but to the time of the Troubadors, Queen Genevieve, knightly gallantry, jousting, favours worn in the bonnet or in the helmet, chivalry, deeds performed for a shy lady who swoons in a tower.

He undertook lowly ill-paid jobs. One as a tea-boy or factotum in a Covent Garden warehouse where his workmates amused themselves by trussing him up and sealing him in containers and tea-chests. He occupied his lunch breaks trying to get out.

He was learning the hard knocks of life, a useful noviceship, like Buster Keaton's daddy teaching the young Buster how to take pratfalls.

In Cómpeta, up in the foothills of the sierras, he worked for a plumber who played the piano in his basement, Manolo of the Banda Pastoral, who played the piano and the mandolin in an attempt to curb an ungovernable temper. Carl became a sort of surrogate son.

He (Carl) walked enormous distances by night over the rolling hills between Cómpeta and Frigiliana. He wanted to throw in his lot with the poor goatherds who set off at sun-up for distant grazing grounds and returned at sundown. I advised him against it. In General Franco's day, everyone in Spain was accountable to the Guardia Civil—even goatherds, prehistoric men armed with slingshots. They could communicate with the goats in a very glottal lingo known only to goats.

He spent a third of his life cooped up in the projection box of the Odeon Cinema on high Muswell Hill, where the Kinks came from—probably the highest point in London. Of the miles and miles of garbage that flowed endlessly through the projector, he saw only what he wished to see, what appealed to him, pure things, miracles; for you cannot mask or blind the visionary eye that sees only miracles, teeming subatomic life.

Carl had no formal art training. All he can paint is what his eyes have seen, taken in, whatever his memory has retrieved from the mess and chaos out there.

He saw Sylvie Kristel, the soft porn star, taking off her clobber in the movie *Emmanuelle* eighteen times. He had a push-bike on the fifth floor of our London apartment that had fourteen punctures in one rear wheel alone. He named our cat after his best friend, Mario from Madras.

If he led a life like that, how could he not but paint like this? In order to be free, painting must borrow from what Jack Yeats called 'the living ginger of life'; boosted by fantasy and imagination. Genuinely felt painting perhaps comes from not knowing, from innocence. That point which the painter is trying to arrive at already exists, waiting to be discovered, waiting for the painter to arrive.

Style can be as varied as our thumbprints, that all differ, and make their individual marks on a gigantically reduced scale, and all the imprints different. Carl has the magnifying-glass eye of Richard Dadd, who painted his one masterpiece in Bedlam madhouse.

The lad who escaped from the tea chests, from the clutches of the maddened Spanish plumber, from the hours and years in the Odeon Cinema projection box, has liberated himself in Hemel Hempstead Old Town Hall.

It's my particular pleasure to welcome all the old friends assembled here; and I now declare this exhibition open.

Interview with Ursula Mayrhuber, University of Vienna

2 May 1989

Can you remember when you first knew you were going to become a writer? When did you first start writing and when did you first publish?

I began at an early age. I have always been fascinated with the word. I wanted to be a painter, studied art as a profession and discovered I was a bad painter. So I thought I'd better stop being a painter. Writing for me is a kind of drawing. I can draw but I can't paint; I do it with words. When I travelled in South Africa with the puppets, the first time I'd been travelling in strange parts, I began to write more seriously then, trying to break free from working with the puppets. And then I began to put together these stories, *Felo de Se*, and discovered after about two years that I had the makings of a book there. Since I knew Beckett, I sent it to him, and he said, 'I like it, with modifications, quite a possible start', and he recommended it to Barney Rosset at Grove Press. Rosset was connected with Calder, and Calder took it, and Rosset brought out the stories at the same time.

So you started out as a painter?

I wanted to be a painter and went to the School of Art in Dublin. Quite soon I discovered it was all copying. Maybe the teachers were not so good. If I had had a good teacher, I might have gone on to be a painter. A friend of mine, Paddy Collins, is a painter and he wanted to be a writer. I'm a writer, and I wanted to be a painter. The two are similar kinds of operation. You can read in Beckett's work that he had very bad eye trouble once. What's that eye infliction that you've got to be operated on without anaesthetic? Glaucoma? Anyway, he was as blind as a bat in Berlin when I met him at the Akademie der Kunste. You can see in the end of the trilogy that there is almost nothing seen there. The beginning of his works is highly pictorial, *More Pricks than Kicks* and *Murphy* are very pictorial works. And then in the trilogy, *The Nameless One*, you cannot see anything, it is all mud. And that's Beckett's blindness. And when he had the operation, he began to see things again.

What drew you to German references and locations in your writing? Do you speak German?

I was finding Irish writing in those days very boring, very predictable. And I wanted to write about Ireland in a new way, and I found by changing the Irish scene to a German scene I could say things about Ireland I could not say if I was calling it Ireland. I wish I could speak German. I spent a year in Berlin. I'm not good with languages. Irish, too, I missed that.

How do you feel being an Irish writer writing in English then?

It's very useful to be an Irish writer, like being a Jewish writer, because you've got two languages there. There is a hidden language behind the way people talk. They do not talk here as they speak in England. So you have the muscle of Irish in the way people talk and the circular way that the Irish mind works. It's very useful to have a hidden language behind your real tongue. My mother read fairy tales of Grimm and Hans Andersen to me when I was a child. I wonder how many mothers read to their sons nowadays? My mother put the idea into my head that I might be a writer. I liked reading so much, you want to write then.

Did you not find it difficult to start writing with such figures as Joyce and Beckett behind you?

Yes. Joyce is an absolute curse for an Irish writer. With Joyce's work it is very difficult to go beyond, particularly beyond the *Portrait*, which gives a kind of procedure to adopt and repeat endlessly, this autobiographical confession type of writing. Joyce is both a strength and an impediment. It is like being German and being behind Thomas Mann or Günter Grass. Every big writer burns all the surrounding countryside with his own way of looking at it. So it is difficult to get out from behind Joyce.

Beckett—there you have the opposite. Beckett says the artistic process is a contraction, not an expansion, speaking as a Protestant. Beckett's idea of improving a text is to take things out. Giacometti says 'The pen or the eraser, the pencil or the rubber, which is the more important?' You create something with a pencil, and you make space with a rubber. So, with Joyce, you have the possibility of endless permutations, varieties of the word, and with Beckett you have the opposite: how to contract. I suppose if you like one, you like the other. As opposites.

What about Flann O'Brien?

Myles? I'd cycle to the local lending libraries in Greystones and Delgany to borrow books for my mother, who was a great reader; and one of the books taken out was *At Swim-Two-Birds*. This would be in the late forties. It became a family secret reference work for my mother and two of my three brothers.

Some years back I did a radio piece about Flann O'Brien for the BBC and interviewed some of the brothers. I found that *At Swim-Two-Birds* was highly unpopular within the O'Brien family—it showed how poor they were. Well, a funny thing has happened to Flann O'Brien now that he is safely dead—his work has become almost too popular. I resent this because I regard him as a secret writer I discovered. Now everybody reads him. Sometimes with writers you like, you want nobody else to read them because they are your discovery. But now he's dead, so it can't harm him one way or the other.

Especially in your early writing, water figures prominently. I'm thinking of Killachter Meadow *for example. Was this conscious on your part and what did you mean it to signify?*

Do you believe in star signs? I'm Piscean. Pisceans can't escape water. I think you begin first of all by hating your destiny, so you hate your star sign, and you are afraid of water. I didn't like being washed, it was a terrible business when my mother began to wash me, until I discovered the sea. And the sea to me was the most extraordinary discovery. I was never told about the smell of the sea. Water is the most exciting thing I've ever encountered. Hitler felt the same way about fire, according to his arms minister, Albert Speer, the man who was in Spandau. He knew Hitler well and he said Hitler got very excited when he saw fire. It hadn't occurred to me that there is a lot of water in the works, that it's a very watery *oeuvre.* My favourite cities are cities with rivers and canals in them, Munich and Amsterdam, and Galway, and here in Kinsale with the Bandon and the sea. The more water, the better.

I was interested in the way in which you foreground writing and particularly your own life of writing, in Bornholm Night Ferry. *It's very autobiographical. Weren't you tempted to write a straightforward autobiography, and why did you eventually present it in a fictional framework?*

Everything is autobiographical. I don't believe in invented stories. Francis Stuart's novel *Black List, Section H* would be a better novel if he had gone on to straight autobiography instead of doing a fake autobiography, which weakened it. I can't invent anything. Something invented is weak; so you've got to use your own life and turn it round to make it into a story. Like the way parents used to bring up their children. They'd tell stories and could teach morality with the help of stories. I think something of that still goes on in writing. You are remembering what your parents did, and doing the same for an invisible family, your readership.

Maybe it's best not to have a lot of readers? Borges said that his first book sold 25 copies; he'd like to have met some of those 25 people. Not with 125, or 25,000, you can't meet all those. It would be nice to meet a few; I mean to write for a select few. And you write for yourself. Beckett says, 'Write for nothing and yourself. If you write to please others, you are barking up the wrong tree.'

Have you ever read Proust?

Yes, in English. Proust for me was a great discovery. I think you can read Proust at the wrong time because you've got to be in your mid-twenties to read him. To me Proust was a rare discovery. His mind is much more interesting than Joyce's. Proust's mind is fascinating. Between the two of them, for a drink or a meal, I'd prefer to meet Monsieur Proust.

Often sentences in your books sound like quotations that are difficult to trace. I'm thinking of sentences like 'No one walks with impunity under palms' in Images of Africa.

Yes, that's a quotation. I couldn't tell you where it is from. I think using quotations without attributing sources gives strength to a work of art, like signposts in a wilderness.

It is possible to lift quotations from different writers writing in different languages in different centuries, and put together a marvellous sentence. And this sentence is a complete crib. But nevertheless you are selecting them, one from Chateaubriand, another from von Hofmannsthal. If your memory is good enough, you can join them together to make a sentence. There's enough stuff written in order to put together a book just by picking up sentences. You would do it like music. I don't read a novel now for the sense or the plot, I read it for assonance and atmosphere and nuance. The plot is insignificant. It's more an aura, a legend; you are going back to a legend . . .

You seem to be fascinated with reworking your own earlier writing. I wonder whether you could say anything about that.

I think when you're writing well, somebody else is writing for you. Suddenly sentences seem to come out of the blue. Saul Bellow somewhere jokes about a Hidden Prompter. You wait for the Hidden Prompter to prompt. A lot of your own work is hidden prompting. So as a painter or a graphic artist would rework a line, I rework a sentence in order to get more juice out of it.

Reworking is actually a very painterly technique, isn't it?

There is nothing wrong with that. Though it can be very boring if you get too fond of your effects.

What is your attitude towards your own work now? Do you ever feel you want to change anything about it?

Some say what a pity that Keats died young or Shelley died young. But in fact everybody's life is already in the Great Book, and they die at exactly the right time. So the way I've written is exactly the way I would choose to write. Except, as you get older, fiction becomes less interesting. I don't read fiction now for pleasure. I read history, autobiography, or books on nature, like Hudson on the pampas, or White on Selborne. Books like David Thomson's *Woodbrook*. I read about the life of the ant, the life cycle of insects, the life of the swallow. All this is more interesting than fiction. I think as you get older, your taste narrows naturally. You read writers that matter to you, writers that are better versions of yourself. One writes, I suppose, to celebrate. That's the thing I have discovered; when you are young, you don't realise that writing is all celebration. Even the gloomiest writing is celebration. Even Beckett, who would deny it, is celebrating. Beckett's work is a kind of prayer, although he would hate hearing that. He would not admit it even to himself.

In your books there are several examples of the degrading effect of the modern industrial system on the individual's humanity, for example Eddy Brazill working in the cosmetics factory, Dan Ruttle slaving away in an ice-cream factory. . . . Do you think that our industrial system inevitably damages the individual?

This is an old Irish sad story. It's the jobs I had to take when I first went to London. I didn't want to work for a magazine, I didn't want to pollute the stream, so I thought I ought to know about how the underprivileged live, although I didn't really want to do it that way. These were the jobs I was just about qualified to do; and there I encountered the most miserable working-class on earth, the English working-class, who don't enjoy their life. Factory work is very dehumanizing. People who seem to be happy are Spanish agricultural workers. A neighbour of ours works seven days a week; I come back from a long walk in the mountains one Sunday evening, and I see a happy man. Show me a happy man who works in the big city, who is waiting for Monday to come round again. But here's a man who doesn't take holidays. He's in tune with nature, and nature is a great force that is disappearing from this world. The forests are going, the lakes are polluted. I suppose the world will have to end one day, with a bang or a whimper.

What does the title of the short story collection Felo de Se *mean?*

'Felo de se' again is a line lifted from *Murphy*. It means felony against the self—in the old days you couldn't be buried in consecrated ground if you committed suicide. And in *Murphy* there is a butler who commits suicide, and they ask about this, and someone says, 'Felo de se my arse.'

It's a legal term for a heinous crime. And I think it makes an appropriate title because I don't suppose I have ever been so miserable in all my life than when I was working in that damned cosmetics factory. But out of great misery comes great joy, because if you have it easy, you don't know how a lot of people live, and I think you miss a lot of life. I think Pinter, for instance, does not travel in the Tube now, and he is missing a lot of Pinterly life down there.

Killachter Meadow *starts with: The remains of Miss Emily Norton Kervick were committed to the grave one cold day in March of 1927. On that morning—the third. Isn't 3 March 1927 the day on which you were born?*

Yes, that's a family joke or my joke. You asked me why I use German locales instead of Irish locales. In this story, I changed my brothers into sisters and aged them (l think I must have been reading Beckett) and discovered that by describing awkward and finished lives, there's no end to what you can say about lives that are supposed to be finished. It's a more profitable line than happiness. You can't write about happiness really. If you're happy, you're happy, that's it. But if you're miserable, there's a great deal to be said about that. I suppose the writers I like, beginning with Schopenhauer, are all miserable sods. When they write, sparks fly off. They cry out to God, 'Why do this to us?' It's a useful anger. I think it was my wife's suggestion that I put the date of my birth in first. It was just an accident.

You once wrote in 'Meeting Mr Beckett' that you met him in Otto Beck's flat in Camberwell. Is he the character on whom Otto in Langrishe, Go Down *is based? Is he based on a real character?*

Yes, the real-life character was a German friend called Bernhardt Adamczewski, who went to South Africa to work in the Crown Mines. A bad accident happened there, and he took an action against the mining company and won it; then he had to get out as fast as he could. So he was going to write a definitive journal-novel, and he read me lumps of this, and this excited me intensely. He was writing in German exactly the huge novel that I never want to write. I don't want to be Thomas Mann or James Joyce. It's already been done. This German fellow also gave me stories. I had never found this excitement before. The excitement I used to get was from paintings. Most of my friends are painters. I would not mix much with writers. He was the first writer I'd known. Talking to him was as exciting as talking to a painter.

You once called Images of Africa *an account of 'things seen but not judged'. In its subtitle it is also called a diary, but the element of self-exploration is largely absent from it. Why did you call it a diary then? It is no longer called 'diary' in* Ronda Gorge & Other Precipices.

I think I wrote that originally as a radio play and put it aside. And Calder was doing the Signatures series and he could use it. It was the first undoctored script he ever published. I think with the first book I gave him there was no editorial supervision. And in this one I didn't change a word. In fact there are lumps that are agrammatical, the syntax is very wobbly; it's a radio play which got lost.

I've done radio work for the BBC. That's another kind of writing I find very interesting. You can't write as rudely and biliously as you might wish for radio; you've got to tone it down in order to make it acceptable. So you must find a muted way of writing lines, instead of getting fancier and fancier, which for me was a useful discipline. Limit your suggestibility, and just give a picture. In *Images of Africa* I wanted to write a political piece but omitting all references to things political. It's just an eye watching, and there is no judging at all. It's for the reader to say that the system is intolerable. But I don't say It—that Apartheid is iniquitous.

Were Balcony of Europe *and* Scenes from a Receding Past *conceived and written at roughly the same time and was there ever any idea of a different arrangement of the material?*

In fact it's all one book. I was writing in Spain, and one morning I made this great discovery that I was writing two books at the same time. I tried to go as far back as I could in *Scenes*, writing down the original impressions. Sometimes you get this distortion in an apple tree: there is another growth on it and out of the apple tree comes another tree. So here I found I was working on two books unknown to myself at the same time. But they were two quite different books. It's always hell for me, and for anybody else I dare say, to finish a book. Where is the next one? Here I had already 100 pages of a book I didn't know that I was writing.

In an extract from the novel that was to be Bornholm Night Ferry, *you had changed the names of real places to anagrams, but switched*

back to real place-names in the final version, with the exception of
Atepmoc for Cómpeta. Why was that?

I was going mad at that time. I found I was working in two
languages, neither of which I know a word of, German and
Danish, and was in fact turning to French. It's a sign of lunacy
when you start inventing words. I was coming up against a
stone wall. And now that Robin Robertson, the Secker editor,
has changed the names back to real names, suddenly the work
is no longer a bogus work, it's a real work. I was trying to do
something there that was not working, and then I had to drop
it.

So it was the editor's suggestion in the first place?

Yes. I thought, even if you use a real name and put it back to
front, it's still the real name, but in fact it isn't because you've
got to give some help to the reader. He can't read a work back
to front and the words back to front because it's nonsense. This
is maybe what happened to Joyce writing *Finnegans Wake*. He
thought he could do anything; he could fabricate a story that
would take the reader a whole lifetime to understand. This is
perhaps not possible; it's a kind of self-indulgence.

Wasn't Ronda Gorge & Other Precipices *initially scheduled to be
published in 1987 by Allison & Busby?*

Yes. That's maybe unfortunate for Allison & Busby, but very
fortunate for me because I left Calder. I was getting nowhere
with Calder. A friend of mine called Bill Swainson had left
Calder because he wasn't given enough freedom. So when he
went over to Allison & Busby, I wanted to leave Calder and
went to Allison & Busby myself. But presently, they went bust.
And I had two books ready. They were about to sign contracts

for these two books, and both would have gone straight into the hands of the receiver. And in fact they had gone as far as designing a jacket, an absolutely pathetic jacket in black and white. So I am very happy to have left Allison & Busby and gone to Secker & Warburg, who put some thought into the jacket and made it attractive, a book that people want to buy merely from the look of it.

What is the title of the short story collection that is going to be published soon?

Helsingør Station & Other Departures, *which is coming out in August.*

How many stories are in it?

Half a dozen. I was asked to produce twenty pages in a week, and I said, no, I couldn't do that. So I was given a fortnight, but not a day more. And I began working over in Kinsale in a way I have never worked before since I began writing. The Hidden Prompter was beginning to speak to me. I got a voice which was not male or female or living or dead. It said into my ear one morning 'Tiny Bodini has no peace because of the magnitude of his task'. I was getting up at five in the morning and working till about two the next morning. And instead of 20 pages, I gave him 160 pages. I think this is possibly the most interesting work I have done yet. It's the first time I've been able to live in a place and write about it without hiding and camouflaging, because I think I am happy in a certain way I was not happy before, here in Kinsale.

So none of these stories have been published before?

I think two of the stories have come from the first collection, *Felo de Se.* There are two long stories or novellas, one is of 110 pages and one is of 60 pages, and these are on love, a subject I am very interested in, love and battles, which are a kind of love. Isn't love a kind of battle? So in one I have the Battle of Hastings and an affair carried on in parts of North London, and in the other an untold love affair, with the Battle of Kinsale as the background.

I've found in Kinsale a kind of Mediterranean Ireland. In Spain I wasn't working as well as I could because I was hearing Spanish spoken. If I was going to write in Spanish, I would perhaps have written Spanish books. Since I can't speak Spanish, I was wasting my time listening to a foreign language. But here I have the feeling of Spain, and yet English is being spoken, all this English which is not quite English at all, but behind it is a hidden language, the old language, with a much larger vocabulary. I think Joyce's vocabulary is 127,000 words; but there were Gaelic-speakers in the West of Ireland for whom this would only be a beginning, as the late-lamented Myles the Mocker liked to proclaim. Not anymore; now they're all watching television.

Rückblick

The Irish Press, 2 April, 1968
Concluding the series 'Ireland is'

IRELAND IS . . . IS what? Is one expected to end the quotation, round off the refrain? An axiom lifted from *Finnegans Wake*, that useful compendium of old saws and half-truths, the mythic insight. Thus: 'Ireland sober is Ireland stiff.' Stiff with the cold?

I am familiar with a number of Irelands, and at least two Dublins, come upon at different times, and under different circumstances. A boat-train leaving Rosslare harbour, swans in the estuary and large white static horses (mirage of childhood) browsing in sloping fields by a well-proportioned gray granite residence fit for a country gentleman, English probably. That's one view.

After Euston Station in the 'black four o'clock in the afternoon of that Spring that refused to flower,' it's a relief. And then the reassuring vulgarity of the Sunday press, the half-crazy Gaeldom; we are back among our own. Eudora Welty from the Natchez Trace, travelling away from the wildly pretty colleens (they leave Euston, heavy-hearted, go by Yeats's old apartment at Woburn Buildings to their London bedsitters) to Fishguard, and to Cork by the *Innisfallen*, in 'The Bride of the Innisfallen.' Has any Irish writer bettered her account of a journey into Ireland? They all write about leaving it.

Frank O'Connor?

Even his name is false; and the one thing he is not is frank. His stories cloy on the palate.

A Dublin existed where Flann O'Brien sneered at Joyce (who was dead) for talking in Italian among his own family; and where Kavanagh sneered at Yeats (who was dead), presumably for not being more like Kavanagh. And now all four of them have passed away. And some of the painters (Neville Johnson and Patrick Swift) had not only left, but given up exhibiting. I knew that Dublin vaguely.

When I think of Dublin, I think of MacLiammoir, burdened with an excess of talents, come back to flatter the Irish in their local habitat, beat them at their own game. It's the national vice, swallowing indigestible quantities of flattery that would stick in anybody else's gorge. That peculiar buzz and drone that rises from the auditorium of the Gate when one of MacLiammoir's sallies has struck (or sunk) home. Spiced compliments fly like bon-bons across the footlights and explode among the expectant ladies and gentlemen with the force of hand grenades. Polyglot, talented in the manner of Cocteau, he serves them well. The long monologues of his later period replace the earlier lurid accounts of the Irish angst: The Mountains Look Different.

Dean Swift came and went, worried about preferment, lost his sanity. Joyce and Beckett left, Yeats stayed. Hard to think of Joyce as the Muse of Mullingar—those latterly discovered pages of *Stephen Hero*, archaeological findings—or Beckett writing in Dublin, out at Foxrock. Hard to think of Flann O'Brien, once the original impetus was lost, not impaired in some way by living day in, day out on the working site, a prey to sycophants, grinding out 'Cruiskeen Lawn'.

Would Camille Pissarro have been a better painter had he stayed in the West Indies and never gone to Paris? Would Kandinsky have been better advised to stay in Russia?

Stay or go; what gives sustenance? One doesn't know. Wild Geese fly. 'Wandering, a second nature of the Irish race,' Walafrid Strabo wrote from his garden at Reichenau, thinking of the Wandering Scholars.

One develops a reserve about the famous national charm, particularly when one lives far enough away from it. Flann O'Brien has surfaced as an international comic talent, late like Svevo, Joyce's Triestine pupil. Some of the grit comes back in the post-humorous work, back to source, twenty years on, like the remains of Casement, and the poet who defended him. The dispossesed Irish, still wandering.

A Letter from my Brother Colman

WE MUST PLAY a part. Our actions must mean something. But why engage them in one event rather than another or with one person rather than some other kind, if it's going to alter nothing? Difficulties here.

Perhaps writing is not so narrowly determinable, more open to alternative ways of showing the same thing? This serial way of having to put things one after the other is more difficult than manipulating the visual, where the relationships between the elements can be read not only backwards and forwards, but up, down and sideways; and things can be joined together from all sides. Also one can stand back and contemplate in peace what has been done, whereas in writing the connections have got to be maintained by an effort of holding them together in the head. The writer probably looks for a degree of finality not easily attainable in the old discipline, being mistrustful of having to deal with concepts as amorphous as 'character'.

There must be some procedure to be followed by which one discovers the literary element that is presumably common to different types of literature; the aim in dedication to which elements lifted out of reality are deprived of the infinite possibilities of meaning belonging to things in themselves and shown in relation to what is shared. One must have an aim, one would have thought. An aim, a plan, even an image. A couple of tramps waiting under a tree? It's a very old image, for a substantial metaphor to embrace all human life. An image: a stop the mind makes between uncertainties.

But a plan is only a means, a dry-looking thing, an aim between the proposal of which and its attainment there are many opportunities for the emergence of the accidental. In the exact exposition of a complex programme, the organisation of complex elements to their culmination in a single or at least more unified level, in the spectacle of the trajectory of a long shot which reaches the mark with some precision, one is intensely aware of the presence of the accidental (I mean emotions that have found their mark), by virtue of the rare occurrence of the avoidance of their being for once to have their way. In the accidental kept at bay over a sustained range can one fail to doubt the operation of a far greater benevolence of chance, a higher accident, than is displayed in the spectacle of the sum of accidents which is the customary aspect of unorganised phenomena? Is anything more inevitable or less interesting than chance?

Never mind if the result is not all at once perfect; at least you are given the valued intervention of chance its opportunity to put in an appearance. Waiting again. Like Hamlet, everybody was to wait several hundred years for final unarguable proof; the hope of science reducing things to unarguable matters of fact.

In the meantime all was in doubt: scepticism. In art: naturalism, the inability to go beyond the matter of fact, the given. A waiting upon events. An unwillingness to read the signs, to attempt to foresee; more waiting. What is it a sign of when you see a black cat? That depends on what happens after.

Waiting for Godot is different. As a play, it parts company with all that preceded it. The clever innovation here was to make boredom itself a theme: the non-happening happens. An Irish 'low-church Protestant high-brow'. writing in French, surviving in the Unoccupied Zone during the German National Socialist occupation of his adopted country, is put to his shifts.

If Mr Godot's coming is the important thing to which the waiting is an irrelevant interlude, these characters do not sit and do nothing at all; they use the time and the non-appearance for the quality it gives the interval; and they are not just making the best of a second-best but capitalise on it (while this eventuality does to some extent contribute to the conditions governing the behaviour of those who wait, it is not an exhibition in anticipation of which all other activity becomes devalued; it is rather a release of activity). The very irrelevance, insignificance of their behaviour in this non-productive interval is seen as an opportunity for an even greater activity than ordinary, for the very reason that it will have no consequence.

For it stimulates invention and gives a greater relish to their exchanges. They multiply and reverberate their 'Adieus!' now that they are not parting at all. The eloquence of Lucky, whose profound allusions can be justified only in so far as they are not obliged to make sense—how does this succeed in never quite allowing one to decide if it is wholly meaningless? Because one is never certain that the alternative to this interval of frank pretence is any more real.

If a realistic Godot came, the interval would be seen as real and just pretence; if he came and was fantastic. then they would not have been pretending and the waiting would have been consistent with the waited event, also fantastic, and all would be indeed meaningless. On the whole they seem to pretend that there is no reality beyond. Yet the evidence for it is hardly reassuring.

But if it is taken as real, it is pointless. And if it is fantasy, the ravings of lunatics, since the pretence is removed, then it gains in literal realism but becomes meaningless. We are offered two choices: take it as real either as frank pretence or lunatic behaviour; neither of which need have meaning, point. The second supposition leads nowhere; so one is left with the spectacle of meaningless behaviour justified. As long as Godot doesn't appear, it is quite plausible as a way to pass the time; (Beckett adds 'it would have passed anyway') irrelevant rather than meaningless. Meaningful becomes plausibly meaningless: a perfect means for the inducement of suspension of disbelief, since one expects no sense, on the understanding that on Godot's arrival a real play will begin. Example of the power of non-events to condition events, the power of the mere possibility of events. *Hamlet* back to front.

He could not even act on probability, wanting the confirmation of events, actual proof.

Here the appearance of an actual Godot would confirm the irrelevance of what had gone before. So long as he does not come, and as long as we also are kept in doubt as to the exact status of the play-acting, we see it as enhanced in value compared to how we would evaluate it if it was less ambiguously stated than it is. So doubt and ambiguity, too, add something to the actual or rather add the possibility of actuality to a situation which a real Godot or unambiguous (real) statement would make less real. The ability of these events to precede without the actual seems at one point to develop to the condition where there is a suggestion that its introduction would positively, and literally, be fatal. When one of the tramps suggests 'Let's hang ourselves!' there is a very strong suggestion that in their enthusiasm or madness they would, given a length of rope.

Philosophical, did I hear? Yes, reminiscent of the disputations of the Schoolmen about how many camels could pass through the eye of a needle; or was it how many angels could dance on the point of a pin? In any case the point was not to prove anything, but rather not to be caught in contradiction. They believed everything was possible; existence was not the test of the reality of things, but the demonstration of the impossibility of their existence was.

Beckett also proceeds by negation: one doesn't know that it means anything, but he is able to put it in such a way that it is not possible to say it means nothing either. This is obvious when one hears imitation Beckett, in which the phoney is painfully obvious. The tomfoolery of Arrabal.

You say Beckett points to doom? I wonder about that. To reverse what Connolly said of Scott Fitzgerald. who 'spoke of despair in language that sang of hope'; one could say that Beckett writes of hope in images of despair. Those people in barrels or buried up to their necks ought to be dead. Why aren't they?

But modern philosophy isn't pessimistic. Although it does not go as far as hope, it is positive. Beckett would appear to be pure Husserl when we find that he inaugurates a philosophy which is passionately interested in the tiniest detail of experience.

Husserl's early teacher Brentano was himself very much interested in the doctrines of certain mediaeval scholastics.

At back of it the idea that's worked out once and for all in a predetermined system to which we contribute nothing but to which we must comply.

Hemingway was different. He took up an extreme position. This compulsion is a horror of inaction, of impotent suspension between extremes, at the balanced position in the centre of a determined order of things. What he objects to is the inevitable unfolding of matters to a predetermined outcome. We must play a part. Our actions must matter: the monumental, deliberate descriptions of trivial activities, fishing, sailing or shooting and the exaggerated importance of doing everything the right way.

On the other hand the offhand way of putting what is really important: 'They shot the six cabinet ministers at half past six in the morning against the wall of a hospital. There were pools of water in the courtyard.' This is a levelling of extremes, an opposing of the natural relationship of extremes.

He is against nature and the acceptance of the balance that seems to prevail between the diversity of its extreme manifestations. He alters this balance in the direction of uniformity, the possibility of perceptible relationships between things, of understanding, deciding and acting.

The exaggerations of his life and work reflect an awareness of the difficulty of deciding about anything in the ideological circumstances of the times by the exercise of judgment alone.

The tough guy business was really in the interest of thought. The pursuit of danger gave a value to decisions when you found out surely enough about a mistake. He was not going to be caught like Hamlet in thought, when every possibility had its equal but opposite alternative and a balanced weight of values could never conclude. Everything about him was to be taken in terms of its opposite. Supreme irony.

The apparent simplicity of his work arises from the complexity of the material; the compulsion to action from awareness of the extremes to which it is necessary to go in order to give value to the act of decision in our time. He was tough because thought is tough. His anti-intellectual pose was against being associated with a devalued form of something valued. When asked by someone where he did his writing (since everywhere writers went had become spoiled by imitators), he replied with a statement which doesn't have to be turned back to front: 'In my head.'

In a way his work was the essence of deliberation, of choice. He liked to boast that he went so many rounds with Shakespeare; with Hemingway man controls his fate. His *amigo* Pound put it more grandly, from Castle Brunnenberg in a *Paris Review* interview: 'The first thing was this: you had six centuries that hadn't been packaged. It was a question of dealing with material that wasn't in the *Divina Commedia* . . . The problem was to build up a circle of reference taking the modern mind to be the mediaeval mind with wash after wash of classical culture poured over it since the Renaissance. That was the psyche, if you like. One had to deal with one's own subject.'

Technique was to be the test of sincerity. If a thing isn't worth getting the technique to say, it is of inferior value. The problem was to overcome the proneness to inaction arising with the Renaissance-Reformation world and its predestination, its acceptance. Sincerity in the old sense was impossible with the modern imagination. No one today reads an eleventh-century composition as men did in the eleventh century; or even as a scribe in the fourteenth century read it; changes in language and literary convention alone would make this difficult. Worse, we are heirs to a new world; our beliefs are different, our points of reference have been fixed anew, what we have lost and what we have gained are alike barriers to the possession of the past. Cioran contends that we are, unfortunately for us, a bunch of tattlers, chemically tied to words.

All successful 'thought', all language that grips, and the words whereby one then recognises the writer, are always the result of a compromise between a current of intelligence that emerges from him and an ignorance that befalls him, a surprise, a hindrance. The rightness of an expression always includes a remnant of hypothesis. Will Shakespeare knew a wench that married a man in an afternoon as she went to the garden for parsley to stuff a rabbit. He did. But now no more gardens. No more rabbits. No more serving wenches.

Sir Joshua Reynolds stood before a sitter as if standing before unexplored territory. Proust said that a book was a great cemetery. Kandinsky was in love with circles, and what he called the spiritual perfume of the triangle. Arthur Rubenstein, while playing Chopin, referred to a 'link'; you believe in it, 'a bit dryish, you know. But suddenly the piano begins to smell of perfume.'

A lady Professor of Finnish at the Sorbonne wrote to me:

'Yesterday I managed to write another funny poem. They are words in Finnish. I mostly make them to prove to Professor So-and-so that he is wrong when pretending that anything can be said in any language, that everything can be translated. So I try to say in Finnish things that can only be said in Finnish. And, in order to add to the secret, I try to make them with the techniques of old poetry, of professional mourners, women who used to cry at weddings and burials. Their rhythm lies in making as long lines as possible before the breath runs out. At the end of the line, as very little breath is left, their voices seemed to be really weeping, tired of sorrow.'

Walter Benjamin had a theory that every good translation of a text, adding to the ones we already have, brings us a little nearer to the ideal statements underlying the impurities of the original. Language too is strategy. Syntactical language, lexicology and semantics: the words before they enter in the strategical line of a phrase in order to attack.

In order for the mind to tap its full power, the concrete must serve as the mysterious. Our ideas are only the leftovers of a breath. Realism is not a matter of showing real things. but of showing how things really are. Reality is an illusion caused by mescalin deficiency.

Rambles with Johan Huizinga

A paper read at Ilkley Literature Festival in Yorkshire on 15 July 1982

There is no need to go out into the world. Everything is there without anything; the world is added. And always, whatever happens, there is everything to return to.

Dorothy Richardson: Deadlock (1921)

1.

For the Dutch historian Huizinga, just going for a walk was sufficient to throw him into a kind of trance. He did his thinking while walking. He likened the wigs of English judges in capital punishment days—the deathcap—to the dancing-masks of savages because they performed the like function: transformed the wearer into another being.

Ireland was, and perhaps still is, a curious place to walk in: you are walking into the past always. Even a dull flat country like County Kildare opens willy-nilly into the past. A curious past without Renaissance and Reformation, without a flag or government, without national identity, without street lighting, without an effective police force until Sir William Peel came along in 1822. The laws were not committed to writing until the seventh or eighth century. 'Thus separated from the rest of the known world, and in some way to be distinguished as another world,' wrote Henry II's historian Giraldus Cambrensis.

Why of course you recognise that old goatish smell. Huizinga wrote: 'There is not a more dangerous tendency in history than that of representing the past as if it were a rational whole, dictated by clearly defined interests.'

History: a servant sharpening knives. Pâté de foie gras stuffed with rat poison.

My constant companion, like a shadow in strong sunlight, has always been fear. Fear: the basis of all nastiness. In days gone by a man would sometimes let his horse choose the way. Not any more. Now no horse. No way. A good third of one's address book contains addresses of friends gone to another country, suicides, ex-friends, dead friends (the most reliable sort). A third of one's life is spent in sleep; two-thirds of the earth's surface lies under water, three-fourths of Connemara are less than one hundred feet above sea level.

Johan Huizinga considered his own work as a kind of poetry, a kind of dreaming. Historical understanding is like a vision.

I see the pallid mask of a scarecrow striding manfully downhill near the Dargle in County Wicklow. Pheasants are screeching in a pine wood, cattle are going home without a herdsman. A little boy lost or punished is weeping bitterly in the rain on the outskirts of Aughrim.

Albert Speer, Hitler's late Arms Minister, shut up in Spandau Prison for twenty years, the only Nazi in Nuremberg who confessed his guilt, locked away within a prison within a prison (West Berlin inside the DDR, within the Berlin Wall; Speer within Spandau Prison), discovers a felicitous thought in an American-English writer whom he had formerly despised. In his secret diary he quotes Henry James: 'Next to great joy, no state of mind is so frolicsome as great distress.' Amends it rather finely: 'There are situations in which fear and hope become one, mutually cancel each other out and are lost in the dark absence of being.'

The self-confessed guilty one walks across the Spandau exercise yard, where he had planted vegetables, a garden; he walks (in his mind) right out of Germany, out of Europe, across the frozen Bering Strait. He walks for twenty years, traverses the same distance as the perimeter of the Earth.

I was born fifty-four years ago in a big house called Springfield outside a village small and sad called Celbridge, in the ancient Barony of Salt, in the County Kildare, in the Province of Leinster, within the English Pale in Ireland. There was a Protestant graveyard at one end and a Catholic graveyard half a mile out on the Dublin road, for you can't be too careful with Catholic and Irish Protestants, particularly dead ones. You must separate them, otherwise they'll be at each other's throats.

High demesne walls abound there, as in County Kilkenny, another region settled by the English. Behind the lichenous granite walls and 'Protestant beech' hedges dwell the English-Irish, an enclave within an enclave, intent on cultivating and sticking to their old privileges; that is to say, cultivating superior English accents, and breeding pedigree pups.

The late arrivers wore tweed suits with double vents, deerstalker hats, jodhpurs. Large young College-educated men brayed, their young wives whinnied, whips were lifted, and off they went. Wasn't life the giddy whirl?

In *Holinshed's Chronicles* (Florio Society, London, 1586) it appears that the newly arrived English (1367) had no better name for the early settlers than 'Irish Dogg'—an insolence which the English of Ireland hurled back by calling them 'English hobbe' or churls. The Irish marked the coarser manners and cold reserve of the English by birth, by calling them 'Buddagh Sassanach', Saxon clowns. For they conceived it to be the mark of a gentleman to be free and affable with inferiors and equals; clowns are cold, they thought, but generally courteous.

My own good kind parents tended to look down on the natives, whom they found amusing enough in their way, as long as they knew their place. Meaning: lifelong God-given dependency before the kitchen range, if female; if male, at the pig-sty or the butchering-yard. Kildare is a place of follies. Castletown House, with its 365 windows, is now the property of the Irish Georgian Society; it was originally the country seat of the Speaker of the Irish House of Parliament. Satan himself is reputed to have dined there.

I knew my place. A thin-shanked pale Papist child, permanently unwell, difficult to feed, fearful of everything and most people, Priests and Guards particularly, hiding behind the old cook's skirt, or in the shrubbery, or behind the kitchen mangle where the cats shat (and there were many of them); or in the backyard in the cowshit and the hen droppings.

My progenitor was a puzzle to himself. Averse to abstract thought and any display of emotion, his life was one long war against boredom, always defeated in minor details. His life went by him like a shot. He had merely put in time. He did not believe in guilt, would not think of it, tried to cover it up; it did not exist. But if indeed it didn't exist, I the third son was often accused of it. 'He's getting red again! Look, he's got the guilty look!'

I felt myself to be permanently guilty and suffered agonies before Confession, the ordeal in the dark. With nuns and priests I lost my nerve altogether. They were unreal, scarcely human, intent on punishment.

The hardest thing for my father to believe in, to credit, was his own existence. For most of his life he had lived on inherited money—a copper mine in Arizona—and when that was gone lived on credit, and when that was gone, on hopes of winning the Irish Sweep. He frittered money away; it didn't interest him. He had never worked a day in his life, a stranger to honest toil.

In summer he made himself scarce in the long grass of the orchard, braced himself for the Irish sun, covered like a wrestler in cod-liver oil. We, his four sons, were up in trees or perched on walls, observing. To all callers he was not at home. We were instructed to say he was 'out' or 'not well' or (as a last extremity) 'gone away'. 'For good'. he wanted to add, but feared to go too far. Fox-like in his slyness, he waited, hid. He invented a stubborn ailment, 'The old appendix is at me again.' The long sunless winters 'took it out' of him; what winter could not remove was laziness, nothing could remove what was ingrained. He wanted to be left alone. He was my Da.

We bore no malice towards him, but we feared him. He had elements of the bully in his nature. His recourse with those he knew to be his superiors was affability, brazening it out, the merest bravado. He shrank as he aged. Finally he became pathetic.

He was the only son in a Longford family of fifteen sisters, which may have explained his furtiveness, evasiveness, fear of exposure. Not rowdy exactly or calm and assured exactly, but something hidden in between, a little craven. Fidgety, uxorious, a stater of platitudes, anti-Semite, a scuffler of gravel, a copious tea-drinker, a starer out of upstairs Windows, a great gossip, poking in his earhole with a safety match. His toilet was extravagant; that became his nature. He took hours preparing for town, a regular Pasha.

My three brothers and I, well-spaced-out walkers, none on speaking terms, arrived at Hazelhatch Station with a 'good' two hours to spare, following a two-mile walk. My father liked to impress the Station Master, the pair of them parading up and down the platform. The horse-faced lugubrious man watched my father, sucked Zubes, and my brothers and I watched them in sullen silence.

In the steam-driven trains of the Great Southern & Western Railway, the First Class carriages smelt of stale cigarette smoke, trapped air, upholstery, dust, hair oil. Framed sepia photographs like aquatints were set above the plushy seats. Hardy souls in loose bathing-drawers were wading in the sea at Lahinch and Parknasilla. Gents in baggy plus-fours struck poses on golf courses at Greystones and Bundoran. An advertisement for Fury's Coach Tours of Ireland was phrased with old-fashioned reserve: 'We Lead, Others May Follow.'

That was the high style then.

A monoplane flew low over Springfield, circled, came back low over the front meadow where the telegraph lines hung slack from a high beech. The daring pilot, a friend of my father's, waved before flying through the telegraph wires, cutting them as if with secateurs. The wings wobbled, the engine coughed, the pilot struggled with the controls. 'By Christ, he's down!' cried my father, delighted. But he made it over the plantation, heading for Baldonnel.

My father owned three gate lodges. One stood empty, one poor tenant paid no rent for years. Major Brooks hid in a bush when the tax inspector called, once in five years. My father hid himself in the orchard, ferocious-looking as a Pawnee Brave. The notion of paying taxes was repugnant to him. He was the absentee landlord permanently in residence.

A slow, bemused and sick goldfish rotates slowly in a tank of unchanged greenish water at the top of the stairs at Il Springhill Park, Killiney, a private nursing home for the dying.

A stale spent smell permeated the place reserved for them, presided over by a sour, ruddy-faced ex-nurse, Mrs Hill.

The old man's mind was elsewhere, his thoughts fitfully dwelling on the past. He had not much strength left in him, holding out his hands to the single red glow of the electric bar, his fingers opening and closing, a cat 'feeling the fires'.

Sometimes he wanted to be booked into a hotel (always extravagant) or into hospital, being uncomfortable under the strict regime of the ex-nurse—'that Presbyterian bitch'. He examined the contents of his pockets, abulge with letters, newspaper cuttings, a ticket stub for the Malta Sweep.

His liquids had been cut down; in the lavatory he flushed the toilet, knelt, drank from the flush. Dr Duff, the kidney expert, was in sporadic attendance. The old ones assembled in the living room downstairs, read magazines, dozed in their chairs. My old man sat forward at an angle of forty-five degrees from the chintz-covered armchair set before the glow of the electric bar, sunken into a past that no more belonged to him. Mrs Hill watched his every move.

She asks 'Have any, er, arrangements been made?' A formally tactful way of putting it, but I am shocked as if by an obscenity on her lips. The ex-nurse does not anticipate my old man living much longer. He will die here alone amid strangers.

With his close-clipped fingernails, Dr Duff taps the glass tank of unclear greenish water and the sick goldfish slowly turns over, giddily dying. 'Hmm,' Dr Duff says, and moves on.

A lawnmower was being pulled or pushed back and forth across thick scrub grass in the mist. I walked across Killiney Hill and through the neat suburban side roads of Killiney where flowering May shrubs hung over the footpaths, hawthorn and cherry. I brought a noggin of Jameson in my inside pocket; the old man swallowed and shuddered. That was more like it. The Druid's Chair pub, he informed me, stood where a Druids' headquarters had existed in former times.

With much squealing of brakes, the red single-decker No. 59 was going into a tight turn by the Sylvan Café where someone had painted NO five-foot high on a wall. A fog of freezing air was blown by the windows of Regan's airless pub where a tall Mayo man with incipient jigs was raising a double brandy, twisting his lips to receive it. Out of the fog came a pony and trap carrying tinkers with their pots and pans and red-headed children hanging on. They swept by, the father standing and hurling curses as the fast-trotting donkey, a blur of nomadic faces, vanished down the hill.

I walk in the park, look down into the seaweed beds. On the

slopes of Killiney Hill facing Regan's pub, a horse stands fetlock deep in the lush grass; on its back a jackdaw.

In a grim snug in Dalkey village a betting man encircles 'Royal Braide' in the afternoon list of runners at Leopardstown. My father holds a hot toddy between his hands and stares at me with unsteady watery blue eyes.

'This isn't right, Aidan. I never thought it'd come to this.' He can hardly walk, moving slow as a slug; the surgery has been too extreme. I feel my fingertips tingle. My old man had been a keen horseman in his day, a backer of horses, a dreamer of winners, a rider of women.

A mist rolled in from the bay, covering Dalkey Island in a trice. In the white clinging mist a blackbird sang sweetly. Above the low door of the sunken GENTS a notice read: MIND YOUR HEAD. My fingers still tingled. The face in the mirror told me: One day you too will be old and helpless. (the earth pulls towards it all falling bodies).

The Gnostics believed that the angels put to every dead person the same question: 'Where do you come from?' My father, evidently dying now, could not hold onto any subject; he was drifting, his thoughts wandering in vaguely concentric circles. Choice seemed both endless and tiresomely circumscribed. That was the way out. Muss es sein. Es muss sein.

At Il Springhill Park, a goldfish bowl with unclear water beginning to be toxic stands at the top of the stairs leading to my father's room. Near the bottom of the tank a sick goldfish is suspended upside down with its intestines hanging out.

The 27 May 1969 was a sunny, windy day; 'a perfect day for flying,' my wife said. Aer Lingus to Heathrow, change to Lufthansa, with stops at Bremen and Hanover, due

Tempelhof, West Berlin 20.00 hours.

A little time passes. We live on Beskidenstrasse in Nikolassee, near Slaughter Lake (Schlachtensee) and Krumme Lanke. French divers are crawling around the bed of the dark lake in search of parts of a Lancaster bomber shot down in the Kriegjahren. In the postbox at the gate I find a postcard from my brother. The message is brief: "Father died yesterday."

I buy a bottle of Jameson at the Self-Service, accept DM change from a woman with mildewed fingernails. 'Danke, danke.' 'Yesterday' was three days past; today perhaps my father is being buried in Dean's Grange cemetery in Dublin. I walk in Joachim Klepper Weg, break off some flowering shrubs, take them back to the house, which is lit up like a ship, arrange them in a jar, pour out two libations of Jameson whiskey. My small sons are all three having hysterics in a hot bath upstairs. You are soaping them, singing 'Frére Jacques' in German, and they are laughing their heads off.

Tracery of leaves, tracery of leaves. They look so defenceless, my three young sons in the bath, laughing at the absurdity of the Bruder Jacques. A page is turned, an old man sighs, leaves fall from the linden tree.

That which we are must cease to be so that we may come to pass in another being. Exist anew! *Earmoganten kitsch!*

What I mean to convey is: movements from the past as clear as sand in water, the strange phosphorous of the lost life nameless under the old misappellations. Why there are days when we scarcely know ourselves.

You can observe it any day on the streets of Dublin. Incredulous recognition of long-lost friends on all sides. Some of it of a theatricality which must be suspect, such as grasping the long-lost-one's shoulder and loudly expressing disbelief in his corporal presence, pumping his hand up and down the while. 'Is it yourself that's in it, Paddy? I don't believe it!'

Odd you may say, but so frequent an occurrence as to be an undoubted characteristic of the place. Watch for the phenomenon yourself in the perlieus of the Long Hall pub in South Great Georges Street. Our late father used to put them away there. Jamesons.

There are days when we do not belong to ourselves, assailed by mysterious sundowns, glorious endings of days. (The extraordinary clarity of the firmament above the little pier in Bealadangan. The small Starres do reele in the Skie.)

On 16 August of that year I am recalling, the voice of the dead Hound Dog was howling over the city, It was my youngest son's sixteenth birthday and the thirty-third anniversary of the destruction of Hiroshima, where 20,000 souls had perished instantly. At the corner of Harry Street and Grafton Street, near the defunct Grafton Picture House, the flower-sellers were offering bunches of siempre vives (Immortales), the little flowers of the Andes. The Sign of the Zodiac pub was renamed. In the old days the Guinness draymen would tether their great dray horses outside, come in for a pint, staring up at the heraldic beasts ramping in their stalls.

The transmission of ideas, records, order, social structure, belief, which comes to us through our literature, is not the same as transmission of those books when reduced to TV serials or single photo-plays. Some essential factor is lost; the element missing may be something grasped in the silent reading, the tone or the life departed that may still continue, resumes itself in us.

To learn is to submit to have something done to one.

But meanwhile the language of real life is disappearing. Soon it will be difficult to tell the difference between real life in a bar and a lager advertisement on ITV. Their discourse is already interchangeable, not too far removed from gibberish; a new-fashioned lingua from the ingenious advertising agencies. Heavily mannered cliché-speech again angles towards crescendo: the goal is the soft sell. Deep bathos. The DJs sound demented.

Reproductions of paintings harm the nature of the original: Modigliani's work cannot be seen for the first time as original, reproductions have rendered it passé. Monet and Cézanne suffer modifications of the same fate. Picasso naturellement.

To write is to attempt to assemble an astonishing coincidence of unlikely elements, so appropriate as to appear inevitable, to set up conflicts between so-called substances and so-called semblances. Character development and plot are only a distraction. Rather make concreteness rotate towards illusion; or vice versa. The image, the shadow, wildfowl screeching in a marsh, the ventriloquist's miming.

So, in effect, when you read you are dealing with a great many subtle unknowns—more perhaps than the spirit can bear.

Borges, the blind Argentinian seer and lover of the recondite, wrote:

In the creation of fiction, in war, in museums real or imaginary, in culture, in history perhaps, I have found again and again a fundamental riddle, subject to the whims of memory whether or not by chance—which does not recreate a life in its original sequence. Lit by an invisible sun, nebulae appear which seem to presage an unknown constellation.

Some of them belong to the realm of imagination, others to the memory of a past which appears in sudden flashes or must be patiently probed: for the most significant moments in my life do not live in me, they haunt me and flee from me alternatively. No matter.

Face to face with the unknown, some of our dreams are no less significant than our memories. And so I return here to certain scenes which I once transposed into fiction, often linked to memory by inexplicable bands, and they sometimes turn out, more disturbingly, to be linked to the future too.

History, as Marx pointed out, has an unsettling way of repeating itself, like trouble in our digestive system; appearing first as tragedy, then as farce.

I need hardly tell Ilkley that we are now well advanced into the second stage. The motorways have taken over the fields.

Tudor forests are replaced by factory complexes and high-rise flats and office-blocks. Nature has been routed, existing now merely as public parks, wild animal reserves for the curious: 'Scenery.' The great walkers are all dead.

We are offered an enfeebled substitute-life: 17.35 million stunned viewers watch *This Is Your Life*. A presenter, vaguely Irish in demeanour, who must appear to be agreeable at all times, has in him something of the monstrous. This exposure to so many unseen eyes must produce strange effects; he may suffer a psychic death. Lit by an invisible nebulae which seems to warn of unknown constellations, the brightly lit TV drawing room may be our mortuary parlour.

And consider 'replays' in sport: the artificial slowing up of actions already completed, the attempted freezing of time: Guy the Gorilla, alias the Somerset Giant, alias Ian Botham, thrice must repeat the stroke in slow motion, observed from three different camera angles. The general air of unreality in Real Life has been added to: afflicted with a sore big toe, the Mighty Allrounder clouts two hefty sixes over the sightscreen at Headingley. The young go about with miniature transistors plugged into their ears life a deaf-person's hearing aid. Dead to the real world and half-blind too, they do not notice the swallows come, do not notice them go.

That rough beast, League Cup Soccer, with attendant Yahoos stirred up by media hullabaloo, slouches out of winter into summer, as if the Christian Calendar no longer existed. Noise increases. Exasperation builds. Tempers shorten. The commentator also has a tendency to build towards crescendo.

Another passive 17:00 million viewers are back, staring at Coronation Street every Wednesday, come to join the 17.15 million strong who watched it on the previous Monday, 17 million of them for all I know duplicated.

Arabic is a language of the ear, spoken by illiterates. Its strength, its intense verbal life, derives from the alogical linkages of spoken language with its constantly refreshed concreteness. Television stales this freshness, long lost in much of spoken English.

Certain animals cannot breed in captivity. The will to live dies with them in the cage.

Their natural senses must suffer atrociously, deprived of the terrain that offers them life. Imagine living all your life in Goodge Street tube station, as in a time of war we hope never to be repeated.

History repeating itself as farce. Marie Antoinette and her Depressed Monarch working in the dairy at Versailles, pretending to be one with the French workers, pretending the French Revolution wasn't happening.

Nostradamus, sleeping in the sixteenthth century, saw the royal pair fleeing through a village he could name; foretold the French Revolution, perhaps in his dream saw Robespierre and the Guillotine. Foretold the Spanish Civil War, perhaps saw the bombs fall on Guernica; virtually named Baamondo and Hitler, whom who he called 'Hister'.

The ferrets were always loose in the burrow. The ogres do not die.

Ford, the American car-manufacturer, considered all history to be bunk. Self-made ignorant men tend to believe in an eternal present. The conveyor-belt must never stop moving: the profit system incarnate. A second before he died Ford knew perhaps, fearfully, that he had been wrong. The man who brought the motorcar into the world deserves the full treatment. What does the smooth De Lorean make of evolving history over there in Belfast?

To bring these revels to an end, Borges says somewhere that we change each moment in regard to a mirror, the moon, a book.

'It is well known that all the ogres live in Ceylon, and that all their beings are contained in a single lemon. A blind man slices the lemon and all the ogres die.'

James Joyce wrote to someone: 'Children might just as well play as not. The ogre will come in any case.'

Good night.

The Hero's Portion: Chaos or Anarchy in the Cultic Twoilet

Paper read at the National Poetry Centre, Earl's Court, London on 6 March 1980

'THE GREAT BODY of the people were of pastoral habits. A hearty, affectionate, loyal race of men fresh from nature's hand; uncommon masters of the art of overcoming difficulties by contrivances': thus Samuel Lewis Esquire in his monumental *Topographical Dictionary of Ireland* which appeared in three sumptuous volumes in 1837, published in Aldergate Street in this city. Royalty appears in an impressive subscription list. The Emperor of Austria, the King of Sweden, his late gracious Majesty Wm. the Fourth, Her Majesty the Dowager Queen Adelaide, and J. Abbot Esq., Governor of the Maryborough Lunatic Asylum in the Queen's County, Laois. Subscribing to this large work, dealing with the economy and general state of a country on its last legs were: a dead English King, a European Emperor who had never set foot in the place, the Governor of an Irish lunatic asylum, Ireland being then all one piece.

Now, as we have seen, the lunatics have made good their escape, got rid of the Governor and the asylum, and are at each other's throats to see who shall be Top Dog in a new united Ireland bursting with prosperity. By 'loyal', Lewis means, of course, loyal to the British throne.

But today for the first time since 1841, just before the Great Famine, when the uncommon masters of overcoming difficulties were reduced to eating not only their own dogs but their own dead, the Irish population register has shown an increase. The Irish are actually living in Ireland again. These statistics must be unique in the Western hemisphere. Loaded down with old grievances and burdened with ancestral wrongs, not all of them imaginary, the Irish race is about to enter the twentieth century just as the rest of Europe is preparing to leave it.

A word now on Catholic architecture, toilet facilities and Cultic monuments in general. It is tempting to think that no such thing as Catholic good taste exists, in view of the preponderance of Roman Catholic churches of unpainted cement or gray pebbledash, all as commonplace as old boots. The bigger they are, the uglier they tend to be, with large hoardings foreninst them showing a building fund several thousand punts in arrears. Their only well-designed parts, and this is surely by accident, are the fine wooden confessionals.

Into this Catholic category of richly unintended ugliness falls the so-called Garden of Remembrance, hard by the Rotunda Hospital in the capital: a low open-air mausoleum to commemorate our great Catholic dead, a brick-and-stone Alhambra guarded by ugly cast-iron gates, graceless as only a grandiose Catholic altar can be. The grim wall seems fit only for firing squads. And I seem to recall mighty bronze swans, or possibly geese, taking off over the Hugh Lane Gallery; the Children of Lir no doubt. It should be renamed the Garden of Resentment.

Speaking of monuments, a Dublin wit was once asked for his opinion of the bronze famine group in St Stephen's Green near the Garden of the Blind. Down the prick—saving your presences—of one of the famished ones, rainwater drips. Quick as a flash the answer Came: 'Urination once again'. Small wonder, then, that we Irish can never leave our great dead in peace, but must forever be making solemn promises to them, in English and Irish, Which can please neither party. Or, worse still, firing patriotic volleys over their heads. The Bodenstown crowd must be nervous wrecks by now.

I humbly suggest a moratorium on these activities: the Great Irish Dead should be given time to settle. 'I see a vast multitude,' Mr Beckett wrote sourly, 'in transports of joy.'

The dead are receding from us, no doubt to their intense relief; and that is only right and proper. Their true burial-place, their real memorial, lies in the hearts of the survivors . . . without resentments.

But to put aside the melancholy topic of the Dear Departed, I'd like to say something about the Irish Fairy. Every language, since the Tower of Babel was dismantled with a great yo-heave-ho of lapsus lingua, has had its secret, its undefinabie word. The Spanish have *duende*, and the Irish have Fairy. These undersized hysterical beings, said to have magical powers and to steal away newly dead Irish, their young sometimes cleverly substituted for newlyborn Irish in the cradle, had the secret once but they're not telling. Mr Joyce, who was sometimes worried by his chronic inability to think sufficiently deep Catholic thoughts ('We Irish think thus,' wrote the good Bishop of Cloyne; I disremember what it was he took out of his hat), unlike his rival, the Protestant Mr Yeats of Sligo, searching the deeps of his mind; he was perhaps hinting broadly at this septic-green Cultic possession when he made such a play of parallax and metempsychosis in the Blue Book of Eccles. The first, so the COD informs me, means: 'the apparent displacement of object; caused by actual change of point of observation.' And the second, metempsychosis: 'a supposed transition of the soul of the human being or animal at death into a new body of the same or different species.'

The imagination of a people long oppressed tends to produce, down the narrowing lanes of possibility, curious and hidden simulacra. shadowy likenesses, deceptive substitutes. In the case of the unfortunate Irish, from whom freebooters were forever for taking things and people away (even St Patrick himself, after fasting forty days and nights on a mountaintop in Connacht, where he had retired to commune with God, weeping until his chasuble was wet, like everything in that drenched province, thoughtfully removed the snakes; not all though: they are a tenacious breed and some Irish snakes still survive in high places); but in the of the Irish, as I say, always at odds with themselves and their own divided nature, the simulacra are those of power and control. The shadowy substances of what was theirs by right, taken away from them by force and given to others, who didn't always want it, even their language taken from them. The simulacra of the Irish, their *duende*, being sometimes slightingly referred to as the Fairies or Little People.

They arrived in a period of retarded or suspended development, like the diapause of insects, called by other names but always known for what they were by the poor people—Oakboys and Stealboys of the North, Whiteboys of Munster, elsewhere Peep o' Day Boys and Ribbonmen; but more usually they were known by their code name, the Fairies, the Good People, When the Irish found themselves in exile in their own country, speaking another language, With the lapwing and the leprechaun, they were the secret denizens of our great sunken silences, protectors of a previous broken-down life.

Less than ninety years before I was begotten in Celbridge, Co. Kildare, a mile from where Vanessa had lived and had some trouble with the sour Dean, the people of Kildare had drawn closer to the fairies in that they themselves were living underground on the bog, as you can read for yourself in Samuel Lewis. Up to the middle of the nineteenth century, the Bog People of Old Kildare were living like nomad tribes of northern Norway. In 1927, the year of my birth, nearly twenty-eight per cent of Dublin's population, thirteen miles away, lived in 5,000 tenements, into which squeezed 26,000 families. From the mid-1930s, when I first saw it, to the mid-1950s, when I left it, the city swarmed with tall Civic Guards armed with truncheons, and destitute itinerants were begging outside the Gresham and Shelbourne Hotels, the Royal Hibernian and Jammet's. Their children were dying in severe winters even into the 1960s.

The wages of farm labourers in County Kildare seldom exceeded fifteen shillings a week up to about 1940. The population of Celbridge was greater in 1837 than it would be ten years later when the last and worst famine came; and it would continue to fall until sometime in the 1960s, when life started again under the Guinness dynasty in Castletown.

When I was young and had no sense, my Da would regale me with tall stories of great eating matches; two champions, legendary trenchermen matched against each other, devouring young donkeys; contending for the hero's or champion's portion, as in the former days when the hindquarters of a Wicklow deer or Irish elk would be served up. The bravest hero took the thigh piece, and if another man claimed it, they stood in single combat to the death. Not Grimm-style stories about greedy giants, I see now, but oral folk tales reflecting fears passed down from father to son so that those terrible times of starvation would never be forgotten.

The poverty of a lower middle-class Dublin family such as the Joyces was all too typical at the turn of the century when Jim Jice (to rhyme with lice) came of age. The weariness of Stephen Dedalus is not all pose. Weariness, in any case, signifies insufficiency. 'Houses of decay, his mine and all . . . Dead breaths I living breathe, tread dead dust; devour a urinous offal from all dead.'

Urinous offal was common enough in the streets of Dublin. Ex-patriot Ulysses, come home with American gold, is recognised only by the dog Athos. Bloom associates copulating curs, seen below in Eccles Street, with the act of Rudy's own engendering. Circumstances just allow Virag's grandson to come into existence before he is imperiously swept out of it again; perhaps stolen by the fairies, who keep a close eye on the living to see that human misery is not too long perpetuated.

Stephen, the other half (the jaded half) of the split Irish mind, perceives his own forbears as 'a horde of jerkined dwarfs'. Would-be fairies perhaps, putative fairies. Mr Joyce, out of his own exasperation, out of the Irish past which he perceived as being rather grim, became a recorder of the endless moment.

'If we were all suddenly somebody else,' Bloom daydreams (as a child will say in play, 'Pretend I'm somebody else.') Or something else; maybe a cow, or a crow. 'There's no end to the earth because it's round,' Bloom thinks. His creator had occupied himself seventeen years writing a book to prove it. A document as extensive, perhaps more incomprehensible, than the *Codex* of the Venerable Bede of Jarrow; the parchment of which came from the hides of 1,555 calves.

The *Wake* all takes place in the sleeping round head of the pseudo-narrator and arch-progenitor HCE, almost but not quite the chemical formula for water, from the pen of the great Arien, labouring long in the only unconfined space he knew, the concavity of his own skull. The long history of a nation's woes were dreamed through in one man's troubled sleep. All human history had become an interminable Irish feud, a sort of nocturnal Donnybrook Fair. Could Irish conceit proceed further? Yeats's pseudo-characters Aherne and Robartes communicated their information through sleep, to Mr Yeats in his Tower, when putting together his, or their, version of *A Vision*.

The dying Mrs Gradgrind in *Hard Times* says: 'I think there's a pain somewhere in the room, but I couldn't particularly say that I've got it.'

The English primitive painter Beryl Cook, who illustrated *Ulysses*, detected authorial sinew in Mr Joyce's use of 'the words of the people', He broke down Dublin gutter phraseology to show the psychology that lay below: much beaten-down resentment. The Cultic Twoilet.

In the light, or rather obscurity, of these remarks, might not Bloom's dead son Rudy be regarded as a sort of urban Irish fairy? For your Irish fairy—small, mythical and sometimes mean—is formed, be it formed at all, of poor light, insufficient diet (they seem to live on mist near mountaintops, above the fabled milieu of 'great hatred, little room'), forced into being by the exigencies of a woeful climate and obliged to go on existing in vacuo, as the race to all intents and purposes fell asunder, or left for good and all. Which, some would say, is the history of Ireland from the time of Brian Boru to the ascent on to the throne of the second Elizabeth. Such internal pressure gave to the Irish a curious curved character, revealed as a blatant lack of tact, improvident ways, that tiresome vice known as irresponsibility, not to mention unpunctuality, a perpetual thirst that nothing could assuage, cyclical thought processes (difficult even for the thinker himself to follow), quite unlike the accepted English linear method; and the fixed notion that there is something inherently mean in action, as noted by the late Mr Cyril Connolly. With the no less fixed notion that the Irish are God's Own People.

A difficult bunch, in other words, to argue with.

You may recall the poker-playing Good Fairy in *At Swim-Two-Birds*. Like many an Irish gambler before him, he finds he cannot pay his way, hasn't even got a face to look properly embarrassed with much less a pocket to hold small change, in fact hasn't got a tosser. He has, in a truly Irish way, literally nothing. Nothing but opinions, generally poor. And having lost the hand and being required to pay up to the sinister devil Pooka MacPhellimey, promptly abuses the winner. A potted version, a cynic would say, of Irish English history over the past eight hundred years.

The malevolence of a master who cannot be crossed under any circumstances produced goblins; goblins are expelled by the exasperation and despair of the victim.

Hobgoblins are their suppressed rage.

Their modern equivalents (here I seem to see suns and astrological symbols painted on a caravan, and red-headed children in cast-off clothes, too big for them, are watching a bear dance to the beat of a tambourine) in my youth were called tinkers or gypsies and were thought to be untrustworthy near clotheslines and near children, the non-travelling children of others better off. But now they are known as travelling people, specialists in buying up deal cupboards and dressers for the suburban kitchens of modern Ireland; become suddenly all suburban like everywhere else. They have a secret sign-language of bent or broken twigs, a warning of dogs, kind or unkind householders. A sign-language in fine, recording human acquisitiveness and greed. A tramp told Lorna Reynolds: 'They're the mean shower of bastards up there. May the Devil piss on them. May he piss holy wather!'

Daniel Corkery in his book *The Hidden Ireland* refers to the practice in Donegal and Kerry, 'when everything else had failed', of bleeding the cattle which they had not the courage to steal, mixing sorrel through it and boiling the blood into a broth. So 'Kerry cows know Sunday' became a proverb; for it was to provide a Sunday dinner that they had to suffer. There is a choice Lebanese proverb: 'When the cow stumbles, the butchers run'; but that is a matter for the Lebanese. The Irish cow has been stumbling about now for a number of centuries and it's high time that it stopped doing so and started grazing like a decent normal cow, on its own pastures.

But to return to the fairies. They had their own secret language, a language fertilised above ground by the banishment and exile of a people to whom the land properly belonged; in other words, the lost hopes of the living.

Mr Joyce, who was himself split in so many ways, in an all-out attempt to chronicle a nation's woes, was part Dedalus, part Bloom (whose mother's maiden name is given as Higgins, who married the Hungarian Virag, who became or turned himself into the Irish Bloom, who soon turned himself into the Pseudo-Bloom 'Henry Flower', the wet dream in the brown mackintosh, debaucher of Martha Clifford; and himself cuckolded by half the able-bodied men of Dublin, if you could believe a fraction of what was said, and plenty was said, even the Lord Mayor implicated: Bloom, the non-travelling salesman, was the non-Christian offshoot of the Hungarian suicide Virag).

But to return to the past (the Irish have never left it): when Cromwell had finished his rather slapdash surgery on the race, the Irish found themselves to their surprise on sheepruns in Connacht. The fairies were left behind, sulking, to share the land with the conquerors, who could make very little of the natives and called them savages and cannibals.

Until such time as the rightful owners returned from their enforced sojourn in the west—locked away for centuries by geography and poverty—to find the big estates hidden behind high stone walls and Protestant beeches.

All subject peoples must feel their natures to be, however obscurely and however wrongly, biologically inferior. An 'inferiority' inducing doubts as to one's whereabouts and social position, and one's right to be there. In the adverse circumstances in which the average Irish all too often found themselves, all paddies might be patsies at heart. But they were not.

Herman Melville saw Ireland as England's 'close fish', swimming perilously close to the Great Whale's perpetually wide-open and ravenous jaws, which had previously swallowed up whole continents. Certainly to exist close to and be long dependent upon a great and cruel colonial power, cruel as all power must be, produces peculiar characteristics in the natures of its near dependants. It produces at one level a state of exquisite inertia—the celebrated Gaelic shiftlessness. Mr Joyce had of course a neat word for this too: 'Farsoonerite'. As he had a damning word for Neville Chamberlain's disastrous foreign policy of appeasement: 'Umbrology'.

The equally celebrated Irish melancholy can be seen, in this regard, as a projection of a psychic state: a state of fixed subjugation, learning the cursed word from the cursed mouth meant learning the curious submarine-rumbling lingo of the Great Whale. The Irish imagination was conferred upon us by centuries of occupation, walking the muddy roads about the grand walled demesnes.

'The last stages of an infirm life are filthy roads,' wrote an eighteenth-century English M'Lord, knowing himself to be secure in an aristocratic civilisation built up over two hundred years of plenty. Not so for the Irish.

At Puck Fair in Killorglin I fell into conversation with a Kerryman and was indiscreet enough to ask his trade. 'Ooooh,' he said, 'I couldn't tell you that. If I told you that, it would be a lie.'

The young Ezra Pound saw the older Yeats in 1908 as a 'great dim figure with its associations set in the past'; it was not the great dim figure who discovered fairies in such numbers around Kiltartan Cross, let it be said, but Lady Gregory. The Kiltartan fairies had been kept alive by an oral Irish tradition not in the earth itself, but in the depths of a banned language which Yeats himself didn't understand. Those Kiitartan fairies were all Gaelic-speaking teetotallers.

The works of Mr Yeats, Mr Joyce and the silent Master of the Boulevard St Jacques, who is regrettably not with us tonight, are works of calculated affrontery, creations of great arrogant minds.

The mumping physiognomy of those poor petitionary rogues Neary and Wylie, Watt and Murphy, Mercier and Camier, Vladimir and Estragon, can be seen as a great send-up;

they are all ex-TCD men come down in the world. Bite, agin-bite, bite! Sting, inwit, sting! Prototypical Irish generosity with its compulsive amiability, the cottage as an open house—a place for quarrels to be settled as loudly and publicly as possible—this pseudo-liberality could indicate something other than mere friendliness. A hundred-thousand welcomes, Cead mile failte, is surely a bit excessive? It could indicate fear and uncertainty. As can be detected, when viewed through narrowed eyes, in the works of Synge (behind the death wish), O'Casey, and the wish to please, so evident in O'Connor. As also in the works of Kavanagh and the Borstal Boy himself; the latter talent as flawed as Wilde's (who was as great an exhibitionist, and served time) but Oscar Wilde at least wrote his own plays. Behan was, one hopes, the Last Stage Irishman.

His funeral or wake in Dublin was stage-managed by his old Republican comrades-in arms, who were to claim him without more ado as another of their rough-and-ready martyrs—perhaps their first and only Irish Horst Wessel?—Although martyrdom came in his case in the form of over-indulgence in American patronage and excessive libations of John Barleycorn. Siobhan McKenna, rather carried away by emotion, jumped into his grave and hasn't come out since.

And did a wee birdie whisper to me that the library at Coole Park had art volumes of human nudes, male and female together and apart, which had been scrawled upon and defaced by moral IRA men in the cause of Irish freedom; and to such an extent that their embarrassed officer had to order them to burn the library in order to destroy the evidence of their scrawlings, and then burn down the house in order to bury it? The grand estate gates were later used as fencing posts to contain cattle.

The question might be put: on which side of that deep ditch was the Holy Irish Cow grazing when the house went up in flames? Time will tell. But it is a damnable thing to burn down a library, though libraries have gone up in flames from the time of Alexandria to Dr Goebbel's bonfires.

Without Lady Gregory, who knows, there might have been a lesser Yeats; one would be tempted to think so from a rereading of his *Letters* and her *Legends & Beliefs of the West Of Ireland.* All our hopes and fears are joined together in an inexplicable way; our weaknesses and our strengths. Since, without the probity of James Joyce and his low Catholic verbal excesses, who knows but there might have been a lesser Beckett?

On the plinth of the Freedom Angel in Munich, where I chanced to find myself in the Black September of '72 ('Mordfest' the Bavarian papers yelled) I read with a kind of creeping horror the aerosol squirt: LIEBE DEIN TOTEN. And KAOS ODER ANARKI. on Ben Bulben now you may read from afar: BRITS OUT. Into once-holy Ireland, legendary land of hyperbole, slouched the Slob Zeitgeist, that rough beast whose Irish hour has come around at last. All presently will be daubed over with the dark varnish of public moralising, as pernicious as the English elm disease which has now struck at Muckross Abbey. In Dublin they squirt: GO SLOW CORPO. In Belfast: NO GO PROVO.

Outside of politics and party bitchery you find thick tubular stuff like a Léger painting: EUROLEG, if you please. Whence came this concentration camp slang, this Auschwitz jargon?

But to return, finally, to the fairies. The bare-faced vulgarities of Eire Nua would be more than sufficient to drive them from the land. Even the cemeteries—a place of refuge where at a pinch a desperate fairy might hide away—are vulgar. Except Drumcliff. A proliferation of rank Protestant grass and weeds, combined with the presiding spirit of its most illustrious incumbent, about whom all Sligo fairies must feel protective, keeps it beautiful.

The fairies were expelled by the garden gnomes of an emergent middle class relentlessly undistinguished: wet ashes over live cinders. They who had no names for possessions, because they owned none, who could not be caught, much less captured, who could not even be seen being as it were the spirit of the land itself, emanations of a wounded racial psyche, have left Ireland with the eagles and the wolves. We are left with wall graffiti, in a place fit for the likes of those whose spirit, both sides bitterly agree, will not be broken, to set old Ireland free.

Hate, wrote Wilde in prison, is a form of atrophy that kills everything but itself.

Walkers in the Dream

ILKLEY MOOR IS haunted, ghosts abound there, walking about in broad daylight like you or I. How do I know? Well, I was up betimes yesterday morning and found myself walking on the moor by 7 a.m. I hadn't been walking for half an hour when I overtook a woman dressed in red who had appeared out of thin air and was walking there before me, not fifty paces separating us.

Presently she went out of sight down a dip in the road and when I came to where she had been, where I had last seen her, she had vanished from sight on the road stretching away towards Harry Ramsden's famous fish and chippery.

Years before that, in Andalucia, I liked going for long hikes into the foothills of the Sierra Almijara. With my two *amigos* Calnek and Callus, or sometimes just Calnek, I would set off at seven in the morning after black coffee and a shot of *anis*, to walk as far as we could, following aqueducts built by the clever Moriscos, walking into the hills beyond Nerja and Cómpeta, walking our feet off, boosted by Bustaid and joints, never finding the legendary fish trail to Granada, turning back in the cool of the evening with the goatherds and their flock skipping about. For us there was supper in Frigiliana with beer, and then the road downhill in the dark that took us to Nerja, to sit exhausted in the rough studio of Alan Tobias amid his smelly dogs.

Many years later Harry Calnek shot himself in a wood in British Columbia, unwilling to face death by cancer. He was my oldest and truest friend. Latterly we had a falling out, over nothing at all.

Lions Launch

Paper read at Collins Bookshop, Cork, at the
launch of *Lions of the Grunewald*,
16 November 1993

YOU HAVE TO try to keep your name before the public, Derek
Mahon used to advise; otherwise they tend to forget you. They
might begin to think you had given up writing or had passed
away. I may not have passed away yet but I have been twice
passed over in anthologies compiled by David Marcus, eminent
editor of *Tears of the Shamrock* on the vexed question of our long
struggle for true nationhood. 'Without an Irish context,' Marcus
pontificated, 'there cannot be any Irish writing.' A narrow view,
with which I beg to differ.

The fact that I have moved further and further away from
Irish subject-matter may have some bearing on my omission
from these anthologies. It would be unthinkable for him to
omit McGahern. In the *Picador Book of Contemporary Irish
Fiction* I am given three pages out of 508, with a delectable
crumpet in the shape of Irish colleen Marilyn Monroe offered
as an alternative inducement on the jacket, lightly dressed in a
halter, attempting to read *Ulysses* and having a hard time of it.
Whereas in the *Cork Anthology*, chosen by Seán Dunne and put
out by Cork University Press, my abilities are even further in
question, in that I am reduced to a meagre 2 1/2 pages in 427.
Does that make me an honorary Leesider? Certainly not. I'm a
Nought Point Four Corkman.

But at least I'm in the company of true dyed-in-the-wool Leesiders such as Father Prout, Frank O'Connor, Dan Corkery of UCC and that long stick of liquorice allsorts Sean O'Faoláin, who has posthumously been making a show of himself in our tabloid press, among the grunt and groan merchants who like to exhibit themselves there, naming no names but you know who I mean.

I am also in the company of the prolific William Trevor, long resident in Devon; and the peerless warbler of Inishannon who also shall be nameless. The song-thrush has a longish extract from her evergreen memoir that reads as sweetly as a devotional exercise to the Little Flower, compared to which my stuff must read like the Kama Sutra. But since a good or bad third of it is in defective German, you may safely leave it lying around. Irish subject-matter or no Irish subject-matter, one writes only out of impossible circumstances. Gore Vidal says nobody wants the novel any more. Paul Bowles, the American recluse hidden away in Tangier, living on slops, austere as a Trappist monk, told his publisher the other day: 'Books are finished. No one is going to read anything in fifty years.' He may be right. The true prophetic novels about the future, which we are already in, may not have been Omell's *1984* or *Animal Farm*, but Aldous Huxley's *Brave New World* and *Ape and Essence*, to which you might add Nabokov's *Bend Sinister*—prescriptive writing that show the systematic torture of children as part of a brainwashing process; the 'education' of a tyrannical order. In England two ten-year-olds kill a toddler for kicks and the Prosecution wants to know do the kids know right from wrong?

Certain things are of course unchangeable, immutable, such as the Elevation of the cross, water falling downhill, tidal equinoxes, and the regular appearance of the cork Examiner six days a week year in year out, like a wet wintry sun rising over *Cork* or the smile on the face of the Sphinx.

The Cork Examiner and *The Southern Star*, their banners

unfurled and wings unclipped by confining themselves
exclusively to local news, Gaelic sportsmanship on the muddy
GAA fields of Munster, dairy farming, hare-coursing, petty
crime, jobbery, partisan politics and other fraudulent practices
of one sort or another, with beauty contests and ploughing
matches thrown in for good measure, abide with us; and there
is no earthly reason why they shouldn't carry on forever. For the
news is always of that consoling variety that upsets nobody. It is
what the reader wants and is already well familiar with, reliable
as a good laxative.

G.K. Chesterton in Dublin

AROUND ABOUT THE time (and a jolly good time it was too) when *The Best Years of Our Lives* was running for months on end in the musty Old Metropole Cinema in O'Connell Street, I just happened to be seated in a barber's chair in an underground emporium in the vicinity of Clerys and what was formerly the Nelson Pillar, there where the trams started for Dalkey and Palmerston Park.

It was before unisex hair-styling had come into fashion and you could get a good clip for two bob old currency with a sixpenny tip thrown in. Maison Prost on Stephen's Green and Suffolk Street were the posh places.

My mother used to say that barbers were like slugs: they led such an unnatural life: The old one Who was clipping my hair would have been born around 1870, with bad halitosis and fallen arches, moving slowly, wearing the white smock that surgeons wear, and dentists too. No doubt he had behind him a long unhealthy underground life in electric light, with never enough exercise or fresh air, never a turn in the People's Gardens, putting in long hours for poor remuneration, in the days when trams ran and the elevated Bovril sign was spilling its stupendous neon lights all over College Green.

The old barber was wheezing into my ear about one of his clients who had come puffing down the narrow wooden steps off the street, a colossally fat man in an Inverness cape, with a cane and a wide-brimmed black hat, quizzing-glasses on a black cord. His great weight almost broke the chair. And whom do you suppose it was? The elephantine buttocks of the great essayist and debater who had disputed with Shaw and Belloc and unbelievers of every stripe who had and defended Roman Catholicism and written *The Man Who Was Thursday*, had masterfully occupied the very seat I was sitting on. How did you know it was Chesterton? I asked.

Susan Sontag in Sarajevo

Letter to *The Irish Times*, published 30 October 1993

Sir,

With respect, may I ask who has given Susan Sontag carte blanche to reinterpret that most austere of modern classics, *Waiting for Godot*, as she sees fit in Sarajevo, and moreover in a language she doesn't understand? Beckett had already refused permission for an all-female Dutch *Godot* and would surely have disapproved of this farrago.

Sontag's choice of a female Pozzo in a 'gender-free' (!) *Godot* with a strapping if undernourished adult male in lieu of the small boy as specified, augurs ill; but no iller than a *Godot* cut in half to accommodate the two tramps in triplicate. The wonder is that she left the moon alone. Beckett himself detested stage business and presumably had his own good reasons for limiting the cast to five. He would surely not have approved of these swinging changes—in order 'to update' his way of thinking, forsooth! Here a little womanly modesty would not have gone amiss.

(At the International Writers' Conference in Dublin a few years back, SS liked to assume her rightful place at the top table with Nobel Prizeman Brodsky and Nobel laureates-elect Walcott and Heaney, and was not to be restrained when it came to bounding onto the Kilmainham stage; these aspirations, alas, still seem to linger in her bosom, else why this pushful publicity?)

At the start of her Sarajevo campaign, one puzzled local pressman asked: 'who is this Susan Sondheim anyway?' I call upon Edward Beckett and Professor Knowlson to defend the copyright, which Beckett himself is in no position to do. Otherwise we may expect a musical *Godot*, an all-black one, *Godot* on ice, after Sontag by candlelight.

Yours, etc. Aidan Higgins, Kinsale, Co. Cork.

PS The mannerless male chauvinist pig W.B. Yeats wrote somewhere in his polemical works that when a woman (*per se*) gives all to an opinion, she must venerate it like some horrible stone doll. And, sure enough, regarding fondly her own truncated abortion, Susan's eyes 'Began to sting with tears.'

Some Thoughts from Herman Melville and Charles Olson

Whether it is the appropriation of space involved or the implied defiance of time or the encycladic assault on the heavens, MASONRY is especially associated with MYTH in man. The tale of the Great Tower is as ultimate a legend as the Flood, Eden, Adam . . . They must needs have been terrible inventors, those Egyptian wise men.

Herman Melville, *Journal*

Hemingway dismissed New York as 'the chicken-shit cement canyon town', preferring Paris and Venice.

[Melville] finds the source of the mosque dome in the tents of the nomadic tribes, the form of the minaret in the cypress tree. The colour of Asia is like those Asiatic lions one sees in menageries, lazy and torpid. Asia and Europe confronting each other at the Bosphorous are 'two women in a contest of beauty'.

Charles Olson, *Collected Prose*

Words, Words

'Words become fish, become fowl, become barnacle goose, become featherbed mountain.' James Joyce, *Ulysses*

Wasn't it Roman Taborski who referred to Konrad Korzeniowski, born in Russian Poland in 1857 and later to become famous as Joseph Conrad and influence William Faulkner, as 'a certain Pole with a wild look under the skin of his face'? He had passed his childhood in the shadow of revolution and later put on a brave show affecting to be a tweedy English country squire.

But Who (in Heaven's name) is this fellow Roman Taborski? I never even heard of him. Galsworthy remarked of Conrad 'the first mate is a Pole called Conrad and is a capital chap, though queer to look at.' He had a poor opinion of people, that was his Polish-English way, and probably had a poor opinion of Galsworthy himself.

Conrad's working method would have brought a dromedary camel to its knees, or tried the patience of a saintly saint:

I sit down for eight hours every day, and the sitting down is all. In the course of that working day I write three sentences which I erase before leaving the table . . . in the morning I get up with the horror of that powerlessness I must face through a day of vain efforts.

Thus in a letter to his publisher Garnett.

Words blow away like mist and like mist they serve only to obscure, they make vague the real shape of one's feelings.

he was to write elsewhere.

The thought might have occurred to him in Polish, come into his head in that language. He had fluent French and English but probably preferred to think in Polish, or could not prevent himself from thinking in that language, a habit or compulsion he must break himself of if he wished to write in English. The Polish thought would have to be converted into polished English, no pun intended, in one of those seemingly free-flowing and fancy-free sentences of his which in fact were hard-won and intricate, compressed, adjusted and readjusted until falling into a pattern that finally pleased him, met his requirements or had reached a point as near as he could get to what he wanted—like adjusting the sit of a velour hat on his head to complete the outfit selected for that particular day and given a final pat.

Unless, that is, he *thought* in English, bypassing Polish altogether. The thought may have occurred to him, come into his head in Polish but after his long sojourn in England, he himself speaking in English and hearing it spoken about him by lifelong English-speakers that language must have come easily enough to the Russian Pole Korzeniowski.

Period photographs show Joseph Conrad Esquire to be a distinctly natty dresser, unlike Wilde in his preposterous poses and get-ups, knee britches and flower in the buttonhole, wearing hats two sizes too small for his head.

Joyce on the other hand preferred to overdress, unlike his protégé Beckett who underdressed, dressed down; matching, so to speak, their totally different prose styles.

And Pound—what of him? For uncle Ez, who had spent a long time incarcerated in an American lunatic asylum, arriving at the Venice opera with cape and cane and dancing pumps, style was all.

On 20 February 1906 Conrad posted off the first thirteen pages of a short story called 'Verloc' to his agent. Written under a sunny wall near Montpelier, the subject matter being the Greenwich bomb outrage of twelve years previously. He later wrote a heartrending letter to agent Pinker, having added 30,000 words to the original short story that now had become the sinister short novel, *The Secret Agent*.

But, I ask you, kind reader, is it at all possible to lose one's own language, the mother-tongue? Perhaps so, as one acquires a friend only to lose that seemingly unbreakable bond; similarly with a language.

The German movie actress Hildegard Kneff, looking out the high window of her American hotel room, saw a bridge below and with some difficulty recalled the German word for bridge—Brucke. How could she ever have forgotten? She was losing her language, her Teutonic inheritance; the words were dying on her lips or had passed away. *Bruckebruckebrucke. Mordmordmord.*

How do you call a cat to come to you? It's impossible if the cat doesn't want to come to you.

Names, names. What's in a name? Depends on whom or what you refer to; plenty, sometimes.

Borges as a boy in Buenos Aires spent a great deal of time indoors. Little Jorge Luis and his sister Norah invented two imaginary companions, the Windmill and Quilos. 'When they finally) bored us, we told our mother they had died.'

Blindness began to come upon him in 1927, following no less than eight eye operations. In March of that year, if I may intrude here, I took the first breath of life and came bawling bloody blue murder into this accursed world.

One morning in June 1930 Borges and Adolfo Bioy

Cesares between them invented the imaginary third man, Honorio Bustos Domecq, who 'emerged and was to take over and rule with a rod of iron.' Between them they created the comic detective saga *Seis Problemas para Don Isidro Parodi* (*Six Problems for Don Isidro Parodi*).

To while away the time on a dull and steamy Argentinean day, Borges and a friend, it might have been Adolfo, decided to visit the local abattoir. There, sitting outside, they encountered an evil-looking oldster listening to the frantic bawling of the poor beasts within, awaiting their turn to be slaughtered. Borges asked *'Están matando?'* Are they killing? To which the old man responded with inexplicable relish and vehemence *'¡Sí, sí . . . están matando!'* Yes, yes. They're killing, they're killing!

My first wife, from the hot land of Apartheid, heard the older Borges give a reading in London and had him sign a Grove Press copy of *Ficciones*. It was a neat singular signature from a blind man who had taught himself Middle English—to baffle the Perön spies.

Joseph Conrad, born 1857 in Russian Poland, died in 1924 aged sixty-seven.

Jorge Luis Borges, born 1899 in Buenos Aires, died aged ninety-four in 1993.

And pray what became of the mysterious Roman Taborski? Did he ever die or just passed away (as the Irish do, or so averred the late philosopher [he had none] Arland Ussher) like the snows of yesteryear, or as the words that are blown away like mist?

Concluding

1.
What Is My Name?

"Pet names are a guard against loss, like primitive music."

Djuna Barnes
Nightwood

I AM FRANK in the morning and Adrian in the afternoon. Otherwise, I am Rory of the Hills, the archetypal homeless wanderer of Gaelic lore, to haughty Harold Pinter of Holland park in London, to Gerry Duke's ('the Dude') of Harold's Cross in Dublin, to Annie Proulx of Centennial in Wyoming, to Alice Munro of Clinton in Ontario, to Paul Durcan of Ringsend in Dublin, to Neil Murphy of the University of Singapore, to someone who teaches English in some Japanese University with my work on the syllabus, to Nuala Ni Dhomnhail of Dun Laoghaire, to Peter Denby-Smith of Snugglethorpe in North Yorkshire, to Janusz Sikorski of Bromley, to Rosita Sweetman of Hollywood in the wilds of Co. Wicklow. To my cousin Aideen (Mrs McKenna of Abbotsford, B.C.). I am Hippocampus Frazzlepat; to Martin Kluger of Eisenacher-straße in Berlin, I am Querido Amigo, to Mrs Sue King (née Pugh of Portsmouth) I am in the doghouse. To Nathalie Bennaquero and Christopher Hazool of High Wycombe. I am the Talkative Kinsaleite who walked them around Compass Hill. To Maureen Henzenfeld Bargas ('the Sparkled') of Montivideo and Berlin I am just

339

Higgins. To Patricia Anastasia Honchar whose Russian grandfather fell to his death from a loft in Titlis, I was her lost last
love (*mea culpa*). To Senora Elaine Kerrigan of Casa Mirabel
in Palma de Majorca I am Dear Aidan, to Anna Kokko-Zal-
caman of the Sorbonne I am the same, as with Toni Ungerer
of Coleen and to William Trevor of Crediton in Devon; to my
youngest son Elwin, who made me a Grandad four times over, I
am 'Pops'. To Mrs Fiona Adamczewski (née Doran) of Lewes in
East Sussex where Virginia Woolf drowned herself in the River
Ouse, I am Dearest Aidan. To our garbage collectors I am 'the
Bollocks' due to a tart letter I wrote to Peacock the Town Clerk
complaining of their driver smashing up our front step and referring to them as 'his henchmen', backing up a lie. To Eileen
O'Connell on Compass Hill I am the man with the stick and the
hat. To a walker around the hill I am 'Sir'. I believe his name is
Jim.

I saw what I took to be Frank Kienan approaching me one
morning, hailed me 'Frank!' as if identifying himself to me,
afflicted with poor eyesight. One of his eyes (the right) seemed
to weep for a single tear glistened on his cheek. We spoke of the
uncertain weather and how someone in his family was afflicted
with glaucoma. On parting, he again addressed me as Frank.
Freakish. Encountering my wife out shopping in the afternoon,
he said 'I met your man this morning. He was walking in the
wrong direction'. (i,e walking Compass Hill anti-clockwise.)

To Professor Gregory Schirmer, Head of the English Department at the University of Mississippi, I am Rory. His wife Jane
prefers not to call me anything, similarly with Mooney who
has moved from Roscommon to Spain, whereas his Dutch wife
Alexandra (née Wiegersma) calls me by my Christian name.

To the poet Derek Mahon prone to playing his cards close to
his chest, I am Diana Gishing (anagram of AH) retired school
mistress.

To Hannelore Schmidt of Berlin I was her dear "Schmutziq"
or even "Schmutzy", as terms of endearment (love, if it is
anything, is service, just that). Whereas to Hanne Vang of
Copenhagen (not to be confused with the poetess Nonna Jeiner
whose real name was Olsen) I am "skunk". To Erika Nosbusch-
Wittig of Schwabing in Munich I am Aidan, and also to
Stephanie von Meehen of the Netherlands. If my first wife had
a pet name for me I have forgotten it. To my da I was "A" when
in favour and "that pup" or "the brat" when out of favour.

To my mother I was her dotey.

* * *

Our street has been renamed thrice, Fisher Street became Higher
O'Connell Street became Higher Street. We are one of four
No. 2s. I hear that a bitter vendetta has been going on for years
between a married couple who live together in No. 2 at the
top of the Stony Steps. In an acrimonious divorce settlement,
as all such settlements must be, the wife got the house and the
husband moved into poorer quarters in another part of town,
near enough to be able to carry on a campaign of harassment
against the former wife calculated to make her life a misery.

He knocks thunderously on the door at four a.m, shouts
abuse and pushes offensive matter through the letterbox,
banging his fist on the window.

She seals up the letterbox, thus making postal deliveries
impossible, retires to bed as apprehensively as Gerry Fitt must
have retired with a gun under his pillow in the bad old days of
Sectarian Killing in Belfast. Awaits transfixed with fear for the
hammering on the door in the middle of the night, the abusive
shouting in the street.

One night when Zin was away I was woken in the dead of
the night by a giant fist hammering on my door, presumably
the drunken husband up to his tricks, but getting the wrong

No. 2. For some weeks thereafter I fearfully awaited his return, getting some idea of what the ex-wife must have put up with every blessed night, for she must have been terror-stricken, not knowing for certain when the ogre would return with perhaps more refinements of torture. Excrement on the doorstep, window smashed, vile graffiti.

I got to know second hand what must be commonplace in the North.

The fitful sleep of those who retire fearfully to bed every night in the embattled Province of ancestral wrongs and sectarian killings, Gerry Fitt must sleep a thin fretful sleep with that pistol secreted under his pillow.

Not too much sedation or sleeping pills or you may be shot in bed by an intruder with a balaclava coming upstairs with his shoes off, holding his breath and his murder weapon.

Alannah called me (a Piscean) 'Squid' when we played Scrabble. I call her (fond) Zinnia or Zin (tender), named after a flower and winning move in Scrabble. Put Z on a double and get a seven letter score and you win hands down. Now she calls me Moulton (fond), old Moult (fonder) and My Moulty (fondest), named after a character in a Wilde play, Oscar being very careful to allocate appropriate names for the servants. Didn't he once stop a print run because he had misnamed some character?

I am called 'The Shit' (pronounced 'sheet' as in bed-linen) by a fiercesome French lady whose mean husband I struck in the face thirty years ago. For he was a sham and a low sham at that and his lowness came out via the foodstuffs.

Delphiniums are slow to germinate. Similarly with grudges, but we have made it up since. I said to the postal delivery lady who knocked on our door delivering a package, 'You know my name but I don't know yours. I'm Aidan.'

'Well,' said she, looking me straight in the face 'I didn't think you were Alannah.' She speaks Greek, lived in Greece with a Greek man who gave her two children, two girls. She takes them to New Zealand in winter and they swim in the warm thermal springs.

I asked my dentist P.J. Power what name I should call him. 'You can call me any name you like,' he said. 'I've been called many things in my life.'

'Then may I call you P.J.?' I said.

'That would suit me fine' said he 'Now open wide and we'll see what we shall see.' It was in the morning he extracted four roots from my upper jaw.

The first time I attended the Cork Eye Clinic being treated for cataracts by the eye surgeon, Aidan Murray he asked me without any preliminaries 'Where did you get it?'

'From my mother, I suppose,' I said.

He was a man very sparing of speech, indeed he preferred to communicate by sign language. Twenty years before he was said to be the most eligible bachelor in Cork. He was still a handsome man, made rapid diagnosis, knew his job inside out and I had full confidence in him.

The cataract was operated on without any success and laser treatment followed with the same result. Macular degeneration closed the right eye for reading purposes, and then along came recurring iritis—a strange inflammation in which the eye attacks its own iris.

James Joyce was afflicted with this and lay in a darkened room bathing his afflicted eye. The modern treatment I received was to inject the eye itself and take a course of Maxidrex.

Mr Aidan Murray advised against Johns Hopkins in the USA but recommended Professor Susan Lightman in Moorfields Eye Hospital in London. Halogen light replaced the anglepoise. I retain one-third vision in the left eye and sufficient to work by, so why complain.

2.
Handy Andy

We encountered him on the train to Barcelona—the Talgo—on our way out of France—Port Vendres in the Pyrenées in our case, and somewhere deeper in the mountains for him whose name I forget. He had an eye injury from an accident with a van going on the wrong side of the road, or so he said. He regaled us with many a strange tale. He had trouble recalling our names and called us Jacob (pronounced Yacob) and Marlene.

Andy Hand, familiarly know as Handy Andy, as a lad had lost his right hand from the wrist down, and his right thumb, letting off fireworks, the missing hand replaced with a colossal crook. He ran a fish and chip shop in Kinsale, to where he was bound, a native of Hounslow West. He was barred from most of the hostelries in Kinsale where the villainous-looking crook was an object of common fear.

Then one fine day he did a runner and was never seen again.

3.
In the Psychiatric Ward

The staff had a masterly command of psychological jargon. Passing the front office one morning I hear one of them reprimand a patient: 'Two showers in one morning. That's paranoid!'

The notice read CLINICAL WASTE.

'What's this is your name again?'

In a set of white plastic mugs lined up on the windowsill overlooking the drenched car park I am identified as A. HIGGS. At least I think it must refer to me, not B. MUGGS.

David Lordan asked me, twice, whether I was a fisherman. No, I told him. You look like an artist, he said. I heard him tell one of the Filipino cleaning women that he was a stone mason; to Dr Margaret Madden he was a sculptor.

I asked him did he know the work of Scanlon who had erected a stone group of pyramids with stained glass windows let into them, in Sneem. No, he didn't.

'He is a sort of religious freak,' I said. 'A believer in an age of unbelief.'

'I too am a religious freak,' said Lordan.

'What form does your freakishness take?'

'I am the Holy Ghost.'

'That's freakish alright.'

Once the Holy Ghost gave me a curious handshake, a dry Masonic touch, the thumb used as the tongue in a French Kiss.

4.
Oddly Enough

A feature of the place was (a) no mirrors, (b) the night and day staff were male to a man, (c) the Head guru (Dr Hannah Hannigan) was certainly the female in charge.

Volunteers, acting as sort of street criers, walked into the wards at the appropriate times calling out 'Communion! Confession! Medication! Mass!' And most mellifluous of all

TEA-TIME!

TEA-TIME!

Small dumpy nuns in mufti distributed holy communion to the faithful. The sisters might have been offering Haagen Dazs.

Sometimes a priest came on his rounds, again in mufti, no sign of a Roman collar.

* * *

Somebody in the front office—perhaps Hannah herself—must have complained of David Lordan going about in dressing gown and pyjamas; because his apparel changed radically one day— black leather pants tightly fitted, studs, a decorative vest—the Rock Star incarnate.

* * *

One morning awaiting 'meds' (medications) distribution after breakfast I took a stroll with Lordan along a glassed-in corridor and he mentioned once again that he was the Holy Ghost, showing me some religious emblem about his neck that I couldn't see due to my poor eyesight. I looked into his eyes and saw nothing, saw that there was nobody at home, the house was empty.

'David Lordan thinks he is the Holy Ghost,' I told Dr Madden.

'David Lordan thinks he is many things,' she said.

He had walked about in night attire all day long, Lord Fop in carpet slippers, dressing gown and pyjamas. As likely as not silent with those who addressed him, disappearing down the back stairs to the smoking area below. Smoking was strictly forbidden in the ward, but I have heard the surreptitious scrape of a match at night, when all were asleep, and smelt the whiff of nicotine.

5.
Interview

Shortly after being voluntarily admitted by a Doctor Yap I was summoned downstairs to be interviewed by the head Guru Dr Hannah Hannigan where I failed to make a good impression.

We were not long into the interview when Dr Hannigan, a

forthright type, was good enough to inform me that I was the suicide type, to which I responded, 'You are a very stupid woman. There is no such type. Two of my best friends, threatened with cancer, topped themselves and neither were the suicide type. One overdosed in St Amour, the other shot himself with a point two-two rifle in a wood in British Columbia.'

'You might just as well say that Dr Madden here (she was taking notes assiduously to Dr Hannigan's right hand) is the suicide type.'

Dr Madden imparted a secret smile in my direction.

'We may come from the same part of the country, but that does not necessarily make us the same sort of person. No, we are all different,' I said.

'I belong to that curious category—the non-suicide type, given to making gestures with a blunt knife under an apple tree. Vague gestures.'

'We differ as much as different types of dogs, Greyhounds and Rotweilers, Alsations and Pekinese.'

'All dogs belong to the same species," said Dr Hannigan, 'all are canines.'

'I meant different types,' I said. 'savage or sweet-natured, big or small, amenable or saucy.'

Dr Madden wrote down 'saucy' and underlined it. Dr Hannigan began preparatory moves for ending the interview, putting away papers into her briefcase.

'We'll leave it there,' she said. 'Dr Madden and I shall be seeing you again. If I can be of help in any way let me know.'

* * *

'Black or bloody?" asked the nurse who was so concerned about my bowel movements.

'I can't tell until I see.'

'Let's have a look then.'

I stepped out of bed and threw back the sheet to reveal yellow diarrhoea from food poisoning. It was the colour of the daffodils in the vase by my bed, a present from a kind friend.

Once, leaving the bog, I fell out of my standing and came to lying face down on the corridor, to the amazement of two of the night staff.

Once leaving my bed, half asleep, I fell unconscious on the floor.

I had a period of falling unconscious and two days of the shits, from the food poisoning.

An attempt was made to deprive me of sugar with my porridge, given the mistaken notion that I was diabetic.

Breakfast over, the Filipino women set about cleaning up. A girl with big wobbly breasts in her loose nightgown sat opposite slurping milky tea like a calf at the milking pail.

The women scarcely spoke to each other breakfasting in silence and departing without a word, wrapped up in their troubles, whatever they might be.

You must never ask "When can I leave?" the doctors do not like this question, it is for them to decide when you should leave.

What are the saddest words in the language? Punishment, pleading, homelessness. Leaving aside all manner of illness and finally death.

Returning from lunch (spaghetti bolognaise) one day I spoke to a patient dressed to leave, sitting in the reception area. He told me that he had been in before. "I am a psychotic."

"And now you are cured?"

"I'm as right as rain."

* * *

After three weeks internment I myself was free to go. It was pouring rain in the car park as it had been when I arrived.

Postscriptum: The joy of returning home with Zinnia in the Peugot after the kindest possible treatment from Doctors Hannigan and Margaret Madden; others too, not forgetting the Filipino woman Zip, not forgotten. The rudeness or downright insult taken on the chin from a retort by an impatient patient who is not suicidally inclined but was at least unbalanced, temporarily at least, was forgiven by Dr Hannigan.

Goodbye to porridge and tea.

Pachanga!

6.
The Last Train Journey

Rory the Wanderer was obliged to visit the capital yesterday and returned today. From terminus to terminus there are a dozen pretty wayside stations, designed by an Englishman (proud in his chimney-pot hat, cigar in hand) and built by Irish labour, certainly the most attractive public works in the land, only flawed by the ugly lifts (elevators) later installed for the convenience of wheelchair-based travellers who couldn't manage to cross the arched footbridge.

So many miles of tracks, bisect five counties veering northward from

> Cork to
> Mallow
> Charleville[1]
> Limerick Junction[2]
> Thurles
> Templemore[3]

1 Turning northeast to
2 not in County Limerick, but in Tipperary, then comes
3 here we turn East

Ballybrophy[4]
Portlaoise[5]
Kildare
Newbridge
Dublin Heuston[6]

Three hours by train there, three hours to return. No piped Musak thank God. Sometimes there are delays, railmen in Day-Glo are always working somewhere on the line, standing in able-bodied poses as the train rushes by. In the train mobile phones are clamped to every ear, voices whispering, incoming calls buzzing.

The Irish are gregarious by nature. The women much given to chit-chat and men murmuring business matters into their mobiles with a freedom impossible in the Board Room.

We have left Mallow behind, the beet fields and the ghost of Elizabeth Bowen alighting with parcels from Brown Thomas and Switzers handed out to her by a train guard (porter), books and flowers, the jarvey dispatched from Bowens Court in good time to meet the train now hurrying forward to carry the loot.

Why is it that Limerick Junction always seems further away than it actually is? Further off when outward bound, even further away when homeward bound. It's not even in County Limerick, but in Tipperary. O'Grady says we all have our Limerick Junctions. Why can I never remember the name of the line of hills to the right that will remain within sight until we leave Thurles behind.[*]

Nowadays travellers rarely speak to fellow-travellers, is this

4 always coming as a surprise, always forgotten
5 Where diehard Provos are incarcerated in Portlaoise Gaol.
6 Formerly Kingsbridge Station
* The Galtees

reticence a courtesy for it might be considered rude to invade the privacy of total strangers, reading newspapers, rarely reading books, rarely off their mobile phones.

It wouldn't have happened in the old days, I can tell you. When I was young the First Class non-smoking carriages seemed to me as grand and as strange as the Trans Siberian Express. I did not speak but remained quiet as a mouse, unless I spoke to my father, who was incurably garrulous. My father spoke to strangers ("These are my two lads.") and they to him ("Grand lads, bound to grow up to be just like their father.") but to me all was strange even the smell from their clothes had a strange disturbing odour all its own. The scent of the women, the way they dressed for the journey, I felt a stranger to myself, travelling through a foreign land of strange customs.

The stations slid by with painful slowness. Again Ballybrophy appeared out of nowhere and vanished again, the people walking backwards along the platforms on either side, others hurrying across the arched railway bridge, alarmed cattle fleeing away in the fields beyond.

The guard spoke his spiel into the intercom for the last time as we drew away from Mallow. "Stand clear of the doors. The doors are about to close." And then we were away, next stop Cork and the end of the line. Thirty miles off and half an hour away, barring accidents, we will enter a mile-long tunnel where workmen were killed in its construction, to come out into daylight or what remains of it, alongside the platform, Ardan 2. And there Zin is, she was waiting, as the train draws to its final halt, she walks alongside. A gate yawns open, a door clicks shut, the journey is over. She is there waiting as the train draws to a final halt and the automatic doors sigh open all along the train, disgorging its load of Cork passengers anxious to be away, disperse themselves throughout the rain-sodden county. The Irish weather is like the Irish people, you canit trust it. In the

lifeless Lee the dead fish float belly-up. Dead fish float belly-up
in the turgid tide. But for Corkonians, ach, Cork is Elysium.
Ptoo! Ptoo!

A car ride of eighteen miles to the Curlew River and we are
home. Is it too late already or is there still time? In a forgetful
old age I confuse Saturdays with Sundays and vice versa. Have
I been around the hill today?

What day is tomorrow?

AIDAN HIGGINS, born in Celbridge, County Kildare, Ireland in 1927, wrote short stories, novels, travel pieces, radio plays, and a large body of criticism. A consummate stylist, his writing is lush and complex. His books include *Scenes from a Receding Past*, *Bornholm Night Ferry*, *Balcony of Europe*, and *Langrishe, Go Down*, which won the James Tait Black Memorial Prize in 1966 and was later made into a movie by Harold Pinter.

MICHAL AJVAZ, *The Golden Age.*
The Other City.

PIERRE ALBERT-BIROT, *Grabinoulor.*

YUZ ALESHKOVSKY, *Kangaroo.*

FELIPE ALFAU, *Chromos.*
Locos.

JOE AMATO, *Samuel Taylor's Last Night.*

IVAN ÂNGELO, *The Celebration.*
The Tower of Glass.

ANTÓNIO LOBO ANTUNES, *Knowledge of Hell.*
The Splendor of Portugal.

ALAIN ARIAS-MISSON, *Theatre of Incest.*

JOHN ASHBERY & JAMES SCHUYLER, *A Nest of Ninnies.*

ROBERT ASHLEY, *Perfect Lives.*

GABRIELA AVIGUR-ROTEM, *Heatwave and Crazy Birds.*

DJUNA BARNES, *Ladies Almanack.*
Ryder.

JOHN BARTH, *Letters.*
Sabbatical.

DONALD BARTHELME, *The King.*
Paradise.

SVETISLAV BASARA, *Chinese Letter.*

MIQUEL BAUÇÀ, *The Siege in the Room.*

RENÉ BELLETTO, *Dying.*

MAREK BIENCZYK, *Transparency.*

ANDREI BITOV, *Pushkin House.*

ANDREJ BLATNIK, *You Do Understand.*
Law of Desire.

LOUIS PAUL BOON, *Chapel Road.*
My Little War.
Summer in Termuren.

ROGER BOYLAN, *Killoyle.*

IGNÁCIO DE LOYOLA BRANDÃO, *Anonymous Celebrity.*
Zero.

BONNIE BREMSER, *Troia: Mexican Memoirs.*

CHRISTINE BROOKE-ROSE, *Amalgamemnon.*

BRIGID BROPHY, *In Transit.*
The Prancing Novelist.

GERALD L. BRUNS, *Modern Poetry and the Idea of Language.*

GABRIELLE BURTON, *Heartbreak Hotel.*

MICHEL BUTOR, *Degrees.*
Mobile.

G. CABRERA INFANTE, *Infante's Inferno.*
Three Trapped Tigers.

JULIETA CAMPOS, *The Fear of Losing Eurydice.*

ANNE CARSON, *Eros the Bittersweet.*

ORLY CASTEL-BLOOM, *Dolly City.*

LOUIS-FERDINAND CÉLINE, *North.*
Conversations with Professor Y.
London Bridge.

MARIE CHAIX, *The Laurels of Lake Constance.*

HUGO CHARTERIS, *The Tide Is Right.*

ERIC CHEVILLARD, *Demolishing Nisard.*
The Author and Me.

MARC CHOLODENKO, *Mordechai Schamz.*

JOSHUA COHEN, *Witz.*

EMILY HOLMES COLEMAN, *The Shutter of Snow.*

ERIC CHEVILLARD, *The Author and Me.*

ROBERT COOVER, *A Night at the Movies.*

STANLEY CRAWFORD, *Log of the S.S. The Mrs Unguentine.*
Some Instructions to My Wife.

RENÉ CREVEL, *Putting My Foot in It.*

RALPH CUSACK, *Cadenza.*

NICHOLAS DELBANCO, *Sherbrookes.*
The Count of Concord.

NIGEL DENNIS, *Cards of Identity.*

PETER DIMOCK, *A Short Rhetoric for Leaving the Family.*

ARIEL DORFMAN, *Konfidenz.*

COLEMAN DOWELL, *Island People.*
Too Much Flesh and Jabez.

ARKADII DRAGOMOSHCHENKO, *Dust.*

RIKKI DUCORNET, *Phosphor in Dreamland.*
The Complete Butcher's Tales.

RIKKI DUCORNET (cont.), *The Jade Cabinet.*
The Fountains of Neptune.

WILLIAM EASTLAKE, *The Bamboo Bed.*
Castle Keep.
Lyric of the Circle Heart.

JEAN ECHENOZ, *Chopin's Move.*

STANLEY ELKIN, *A Bad Man.*
Criers and Kibitzers, Kibitzers and Criers.
The Dick Gibson Show.
The Franchiser.
The Living End.
Mrs. Ted Bliss.

FRANÇOIS EMMANUEL, *Invitation to a Voyage.*

PAUL EMOND, *The Dance of a Sham.*

SALVADOR ESPRIU, *Ariadne in the Grotesque Labyrinth.*

LESLIE A. FIEDLER, *Love and Death in the American Novel.*

JUAN FILLOY, *Op Oloop.*

ANDY FITCH, *Pop Poetics.*

GUSTAVE FLAUBERT, *Bouvard and Pécuchet.*

KASS FLEISHER, *Talking out of School.*

JON FOSSE, *Aliss at the Fire.*
Melancholy.

FORD MADOX FORD, *The March of Literature.*

MAX FRISCH, *I'm Not Stiller.*
Man in the Holocene.

CARLOS FUENTES, *Christopher Unborn.*
Distant Relations.
Terra Nostra.
Where the Air Is Clear.

TAKEHIKO FUKUNAGA, *Flowers of Grass.*

WILLIAM GADDIS, JR., *The Recognitions.*

JANICE GALLOWAY, *Foreign Parts.*
The Trick Is to Keep Breathing.

WILLIAM H. GASS, *Life Sentences.*
The Tunnel.
The World Within the Word.
Willie Masters' Lonesome Wife.

GÉRARD GAVARRY, *Hoppla! 1 2 3.*

ETIENNE GILSON, *The Arts of the Beautiful.*
Forms and Substances in the Arts.

C. S. GISCOMBE, *Giscome Road.*
Here.

DOUGLAS GLOVER, *Bad News of the Heart.*

WITOLD GOMBROWICZ, *A Kind of Testament.*

PAULO EMÍLIO SALES GOMES, *P's Three Women.*

GEORGI GOSPODINOV, *Natural Novel.*

JUAN GOYTISOLO, *Count Julian.*
Juan the Landless.
Makbara.
Marks of Identity.

HENRY GREEN, *Blindness.*
Concluding.
Doting.
Nothing.

JACK GREEN, *Fire the Bastards!*

JIŘÍ GRUŠA, *The Questionnaire.*

MELA HARTWIG, *Am I a Redundant Human Being?*

JOHN HAWKES, *The Passion Artist.*
Whistlejacket.

ELIZABETH HEIGHWAY, ED., *Contemporary Georgian Fiction.*

AIDAN HIGGINS, *Balcony of Europe.*
Blind Man's Bluff.
Bornholm Night-Ferry.
Langrishe, Go Down.
Scenes from a Receding Past.

KEIZO HINO, *Isle of Dreams.*

KAZUSHI HOSAKA, *Plainsong.*

ALDOUS HUXLEY, *Antic Hay.*
Point Counter Point.
Those Barren Leaves.
Time Must Have a Stop.

NAOYUKI II, *The Shadow of a Blue Cat.*

DRAGO JANČAR, *The Tree with No Name.*

MIKHEIL JAVAKHISHVILI, *Kvachi.*

GERT JONKE, *The Distant Sound.*
Homage to Czerny.
The System of Vienna.

FOR A FULL LIST OF PUBLICATIONS, VISIT: www.dalkeyarchive.com

JACQUES JOUET, *Mountain R.*
Savage.
Upstaged.
MIEKO KANAI, *The Word Book.*
YORAM KANIUK, *Life on Sandpaper.*
ZURAB KARUMIDZE, *Dagny.*
JOHN KELLY, *From Out of the City.*
HUGH KENNER, *Flaubert, Joyce and Beckett: The Stoic Comedians.*
Joyce's Voices.
DANILO KIŠ, *The Attic.*
The Lute and the Scars.
Psalm 44.
A Tomb for Boris Davidovich.
ANITA KONKKA, *A Fool's Paradise.*
GEORGE KONRÁD, *The City Builder.*
TADEUSZ KONWICKI, *A Minor Apocalypse.*
The Polish Complex.
ANNA KORDZAIA-SAMADASHVILI, *Me, Margarita.*
MENIS KOUMANDAREAS, *Koula.*
ELAINE KRAF, *The Princess of 72nd Street.*
JIM KRUSOE, *Iceland.*
AYSE KULIN, *Farewell: A Mansion in Occupied Istanbul.*
EMILIO LASCANO TEGUI, *On Elegance While Sleeping.*
ERIC LAURRENT, *Do Not Touch.*
VIOLETTE LEDUC, *La Bâtarde.*
EDOUARD LEVÉ, *Autoportrait.*
Newspaper.
Suicide.
Works.
MARIO LEVI, *Istanbul Was a Fairy Tale.*
DEBORAH LEVY, *Billy and Girl.*
JOSÉ LEZAMA LIMA, *Paradiso.*
ROSA LIKSOM, *Dark Paradise.*
OSMAN LINS, *Avalovara.*
The Queen of the Prisons of Greece.
FLORIAN LIPUŠ, *The Errors of Young Tjaž.*
GORDON LISH, *Peru.*
ALF MACLOCHLAINN, *Out of Focus.*
Past Habitual.

The Corpus in the Library.
RON LOEWINSOHN, *Magnetic Field(s).*
YURI LOTMAN, *Non-Memoirs.*
D. KEITH MANO, *Take Five.*
MINA LOY, *Stories and Essays of Mina Loy.*
MICHELINE AHARONIAN MARCOM, *A Brief History of Yes.*
The Mirror in the Well.
BEN MARCUS, *The Age of Wire and String.*
WALLACE MARKFIELD, *Teitlebaum's Window.*
DAVID MARKSON, *Reader's Block.*
Wittgenstein's Mistress.
CAROLE MASO, *AVA.*
HISAKI MATSUURA, *Triangle.*
LADISLAV MATEJKA & KRYSTYNA POMORSKA, EDS., *Readings in Russian Poetics: Formalist & Structuralist Views.*
HARRY MATHEWS, *Cigarettes.*
The Conversions.
The Human Country.
The Journalist.
My Life in CIA.
Singular Pleasures.
The Sinking of the Odradek.
Stadium.
Tlooth.
HISAKI MATSUURA, *Triangle.*
DONAL MCLAUGHLIN, *beheading the virgin mary, and other stories.*
JOSEPH MCELROY, *Night Soul and Other Stories.*
ABDELWAHAB MEDDEB, *Talismano.*
GERHARD MEIER, *Isle of the Dead.*
HERMAN MELVILLE, *The Confidence-Man.*
AMANDA MICHALOPOULOU, *I'd Like.*
STEVEN MILLHAUSER, *The Barnum Museum.*
In the Penny Arcade.
RALPH J. MILLS, JR., *Essays on Poetry.*
MOMUS, *The Book of Jokes.*
CHRISTINE MONTALBETTI, *The Origin of Man.*
Western.

NICHOLAS MOSLEY, *Accident.*
Assassins.
Catastrophe Practice.
A Garden of Trees.
Hopeful Monsters.
Imago Bird.
Inventing God.
Look at the Dark.
Metamorphosis.
Natalie Natalia.
Serpent.

WARREN MOTTE, *Fables of the Novel:
French Fiction since 1990.*
*Fiction Now: The French Novel in the
21st Century.*
Mirror Gazing.
Oulipo: A Primer of Potential Literature.

GERALD MURNANE, *Barley Patch.*
Inland.

YVES NAVARRE, *Our Share of Time.*
Sweet Tooth.

DOROTHY NELSON, *In Night's City.*
Tar and Feathers.

ESHKOL NEVO, *Homesick.*

WILFRIDO D. NOLLEDO, *But for
the Lovers.*

BORIS A. NOVAK, *The Master of
Insomnia.*

FLANN O'BRIEN, *At Swim-Two-Birds.*
The Best of Myles.
The Dalkey Archive.
The Hard Life.
The Poor Mouth.
The Third Policeman.

CLAUDE OLLIER, *The Mise-en-Scène.*
Wert and the Life Without End.

PATRIK OUŘEDNÍK, *Europeana.*
The Opportune Moment, 1855.

BORIS PAHOR, *Necropolis.*

FERNANDO DEL PASO, *News from
the Empire.*
Palinuro of Mexico.

ROBERT PINGET, *The Inquisitory.*
Mahu or The Material.
Trio.

MANUEL PUIG, *Betrayed by Rita
Hayworth.*

The Buenos Aires Affair.
Heartbreak Tango.

RAYMOND QUENEAU, *The Last Days.*
Odile.
Pierrot Mon Ami.
Saint Glinglin.

ANN QUIN, *Berg.*
Passages.
Three.
Tripticks.

ISHMAEL REED, *The Free-Lance
Pallbearers.*
The Last Days of Louisiana Red.
Ishmael Reed: The Plays.
Juice!
The Terrible Threes.
The Terrible Twos.
Yellow Back Radio Broke-Down.

JASIA REICHARDT, *15 Journeys Warsaw
to London.*

JOÃO UBALDO RIBEIRO, *House of the
Fortunate Buddhas.*

JEAN RICARDOU, *Place Names.*

RAINER MARIA RILKE,
The Notebooks of Malte Laurids Brigge.

JULIÁN RÍOS, *The House of Ulysses.*
Larva: A Midsummer Night's Babel.
Poundemonium.

ALAIN ROBBE-GRILLET, *Project for a
Revolution in New York.*
A Sentimental Novel.

AUGUSTO ROA BASTOS, *I the Supreme.*

DANIËL ROBBERECHTS, *Arriving in
Avignon.*

JEAN ROLIN, *The Explosion of the
Radiator Hose.*

OLIVIER ROLIN, *Hotel Crystal.*

ALIX CLEO ROUBAUD, *Alix's Journal.*

JACQUES ROUBAUD, *The Form of
a City Changes Faster, Alas, Than the
Human Heart.*
The Great Fire of London.
Hortense in Exile.
Hortense Is Abducted.
*Mathematics: The Plurality of Worlds of
Lewis.*
Some Thing Black.

RAYMOND ROUSSEL, *Impressions of Africa.*

VEDRANA RUDAN, *Night.*

PABLO M. RUIZ, *Four Cold Chapters on the Possibility of Literature.*

GERMAN SADULAEV, *The Maya Pill.*

TOMAŽ ŠALAMUN, *Soy Realidad.*

LYDIE SALVAYRE, *The Company of Ghosts.*
The Lecture.
The Power of Flies.

LUIS RAFAEL SÁNCHEZ, *Macho Camacho's Beat.*

SEVERO SARDUY, *Cobra & Maitreya.*

NATHALIE SARRAUTE, *Do You Hear Them?*
Martereau.
The Planetarium.

STIG SÆTERBAKKEN, *Siamese.*
Self-Control.
Through the Night.

ARNO SCHMIDT, *Collected Novellas.*
Collected Stories.
Nobodaddy's Children.
Two Novels.

ASAF SCHURR, *Motti.*

GAIL SCOTT, *My Paris.*

DAMION SEARLS, *What We Were Doing and Where We Were Going.*

JUNE AKERS SEESE,
Is This What Other Women Feel Too?

BERNARD SHARE, *Inish.*
Transit.

VIKTOR SHKLOVSKY, *Bowstring.*
Literature and Cinematography.
Theory of Prose.
Third Factory.
Zoo, or Letters Not about Love.

PIERRE SINIAC, *The Collaborators.*

KJERSTI A. SKOMSVOLD,
The Faster I Walk, the Smaller I Am.

JOSEF ŠKVORECKÝ, *The Engineer of Human Souls.*

GILBERT SORRENTINO, *Aberration of Starlight.*
Blue Pastoral.
Crystal Vision.

Imaginative Qualities of Actual Things.
Mulligan Stew. Red the Fiend.
Steelwork.
Under the Shadow.

MARKO SOSIČ, *Ballerina, Ballerina.*

ANDRZEJ STASIUK, *Dukla.*
Fado.

GERTRUDE STEIN, *The Making of Americans.*
A Novel of Thank You.

LARS SVENDSEN, *A Philosophy of Evil.*

PIOTR SZEWC, *Annihilation.*

GONÇALO M. TAVARES, *A Man: Klaus Klump.*
Jerusalem.
Learning to Pray in the Age of Technique.

LUCIAN DAN TEODOROVICI,
Our Circus Presents...

NIKANOR TERATOLOGEN, *Assisted Living.*

STEFAN THEMERSON, *Hobson's Island.*
The Mystery of the Sardine.
Tom Harris.

TAEKO TOMIOKA, *Building Waves.*

JOHN TOOMEY, *Sleepwalker.*

DUMITRU TSEPENEAG, *Hotel Europa.*
The Necessary Marriage.
Pigeon Post.
Vain Art of the Fugue.

ESTHER TUSQUETS, *Stranded.*

DUBRAVKA UGRESIC, *Lend Me Your Character.*
Thank You for Not Reading.

TOR ULVEN, *Replacement.*

MATI UNT, *Brecht at Night.*
Diary of a Blood Donor.
Things in the Night.

ÁLVARO URIBE & OLIVIA SEARS, EDS.,
Best of Contemporary Mexican Fiction.

ELOY URROZ, *Friction.*
The Obstacles.

LUISA VALENZUELA, *Dark Desires and the Others.*
He Who Searches.

PAUL VERHAEGHEN, *Omega Minor.*

BORIS VIAN, *Heartsnatcher.*